Vagrant Summer

Written By:
David Seth McCrae

Title page art:
Matthew Cousin

Cover art:
Brielle May

Vagrant Summer
Book One of the Wanderlust Seasons Saga
1ˢᵗ Edition - Revision 11

ISBN – 978-0615451145

Cover art by Brielle May
Title page art by Thomas Matthew Cousin

Published by David S. McCrae (via Createspace.com)

Acknowledgements

God—for blessing me with the ability and creativity to produce Wanderlust Seasons; and the dedication to put it in print.

Much-deserved credit also goes to:

Sarah Cousin—for teaching me where all great stories begin. Eden would not be what it is now without your wisdom and insight.

Amy Lynn Brown—for everything you've done for me. Vagrant Summer would not be the story it is without your help.

Brittany Hadden—for seeing Vagrant Summer to a level of perfection with your knowledge, wisdom, and red pen!

Serdar Yegulalp—for introducing me to Lulu and helping me out with the publishing process.

Matt Cousin—for lending your artistic talents as well as the great question and answer feedback.

Brielle May—for taking the title of the first Dice fangirl, for your artistic contributions and the long brain-picking sessions.

Allen Osborn—for being a voice of logic and reason; keeping my eyes in perspective and my feet on the ground.

Keljar—for the consistency checks and epic proofing. Have fun in the Autumn.

Mom & Dad—for love and support.

Joe Ellis—for your careful eye and helpful suggestions.

Thank you, everyone for your support!

Contents

Prologue

Although a little worn out and slightly vexed by his tardiness, William had finally made it to his grassy hillside destination. Just as he had anticipated, about forty other people were in the vicinity as well, relaxed and carefree. Everyone was mingling and making small talk with each other as they awaited the main event.

William scanned the small crowd to soon find the familiar curly hair of his cousin, with whom he was in a race to arrive at his current location. The distracted young man was unaware of William's arrival as he glared up at the sky and waited.

William stepped slowly over to the man's side without even turning his head to look at him. "Well, can't win 'em all, right?"

His cousin didn't answer him.

William then spoke out, now turning his head to address him. "Theodore?"

Theodore's bloodshot brown eyes squinted into the distance. He deeply uttered, "There it is. See it?" He took his right hand out of the pocket of his khaki pants and pointed up to the sky.

William looked out to see a red flicker in the far distance. "Glad we got a front row seat, huh?"

A few more people began to crowd in with Theodore and William to get a better look at the miniscule red mark that interrupted an otherwise cerulean sky. All were silent for a moment. This was the show they had been waiting for.

Minutes had gone by without a sound other than wind and rustling grass. The red spot in the sky was slowly increasing in size. Soon enough, one couldn't cover the sight with a single fist.

William swallowed hard and asked Theodore, "Do you think everything will be all right in the end?"

Theodore hesitated. "What does my opinion matter now? In…" he paused to look at his watch, "…three minutes we won't be able to care anyway."

"Well," William declared, eyes fixed on the sky, "rocks that size would make you wonder…"

Theodore sighed. "Wonder, yes," he agreed, "but actually asking doesn't matter."

William didn't reply.

One desperate individual from the crowd drew a pistol from his coat and began to fire shots at the sky. A young couple shared an embrace, cuddled next to their newborn daughter. There was another man, lounging in the grass, smoking a cigarette. A young child was getting a better view from atop a nearby tree. The rest of them just stood in the grass; transfixed by the red mass in the sky.

"I'll ask you this, though…" Theodore said, "If you were in Eden right now, how would you feel?"

William inhaled deeply and turned his attention back to the skies. He could now see the craters, make out the garbled shape and feel his heart being torn in his chest. He closed his eyes and gripped his fist. But with one minute left, his mind snapped. He grunted and ran forward; his arms wide open. Without a word, he simply counted down the seconds in this mind. In those final seconds, he sobbed futilely, arms outstretched and ready to embrace the dawn of time.

Vagrant Summer

Episode 1: Final Thoughts of a Lonely Cause

Day 63

I

It had been a few months by that time—the time I was huddled next to a dying, makeshift campfire that I myself had built. The time I poked with stoic futility to keep what smoldering embers were left producing some sort of heat.

Within minutes, though, my campfire sounded its last crack and fizzled out. I sighed loud and lifted my head. Looking at the pile of blackened wood, I just nodded and gave an indifferent shrug. There were no worries, really. I was just going to stay cold and in the dark until the sun rose in a few hours.

Even though it was the middle of summer, the pre-dawn hours that morning were unseasonably brisk. So with the fire dead, my better option was to crawl back into my shelter and wrap myself up in my blanket. I wasn't freezing to death, so I took my time, casually chucking handfuls of dirt onto what was left of the charred firewood.

It was one of those mornings when I wished that my choice of clothing had been thought through better as well. My loose-fitting and many-pocketed trousers were enough to shield my legs from the chill. But my favorite, form-fitting black shirt had sleeves that only covered my shoulders. Making matters worse was the fact that my jacket was more like a complementing sleeveless vest. While I felt that the combination of dark tan and black looked pretty good on me, I literally shivered at the realization that making my outfit match didn't make it any warmer.

A gust of wind swept past my modest Gova Sector camp site. The whispers of leaves rattled the silence and echoed off of the tall trees that surrounded me. I looked up toward the treetops and quickly remembered why it had been so difficult for me to stay asleep. Camping in the Gova Sector alone for the past week was beginning to have a darker effect on my psyche. Though I had been alone since the beginning of the Revolution, the mere ambience of the Gova Sector at night was taking loneliness to a whole new level.

As I buried my fire pit, I was beginning to think about where I should go when I was to leave the Gova Sector. That was when I started talking to myself. "It's not too late to go back home, right? I'm not exactly part of this whole thing. Just trying to get away for a little while…"

I then remembered exactly what it was I was staying away from. As far as I was concerned, there was nothing at home worth turning around for. My parents were abusive, making the household a perpetually hostile ground for me and my siblings. Not that I really cared much for my brother and sisters either. The love lost between me and the rest of my family created an ever-present downward spiral that I could no longer bear.

No reason. No reason at all to go back to that. The intensity I felt at the mere thought of it caused me to stand to my feet for the first time in hours. I tensed up and kicked some more dirt onto the dead embers. "No reason," I said aloud.

I brushed the dirt from my pants and crawled back into my shelter, feeling kind of odd. Just the thought of even going back home sent my brain scrambling to think of something else. The tempestuous train of thought was interrupted by a familiar abdominal rumbling.

It was time to eat something.

Since I wasn't really inclined to build another fire, I broke into the granola I had brought with me. Eating some of that would tide me over until the sun came up. Then, I'd try to build another fire to cook some oatmeal.

Through occasional shivers, I rustled around my backpack to gather the breakfast supplies. Realizing the convenient size of camping gear always put a smile on my face. Fitting a pot, pan, plate and eating utensils for one person to take up as little space as possible was indeed a godsend for somebody trying to survive on his own. The malleable shaping of a bag of oats was just as convenient.

After having everything ready, it was time to simply wait for sunrise. I was replacing items displaced in my searching when I picked up my coin purse. I stopped for a moment and looked it over. This was the money for absolute dire emergencies; most namely, to purchase food.

This money, 182 Arna in coins, atop the supplies I brought with me, was to last me quite a while. As dismal as I make it sound, it wasn't as bad as most would make it out to be. All it was really going to take was self-control and knowledge of my priorities. Needless to say, I had plenty of both. I put the money away, quickly curled back up under my blanket and dozed off to my thoughts.

Everything seemed to be how I wanted it, though. Despite the fact it was a bit lonely sometimes, I was glad to finally have calm and quiet times all to myself. I didn't have to worry about being bothered by anybody for anything. There was nothing but peaceful, relaxing, carefree time that I could use how I saw fit. The thing that made it feel even better was that I was venturing the great outdoors while I was at it. It was the inherent masculine drive for adventure that really made the experience feel a whole lot more refreshing.

II

I woke back up with a stretch and a shiver. It was still cool out, but the sun was rising. I gathered my breakfast supplies and began to inch my way out of my shelter when I heard the ever-familiar rumble of thunder. "Damn it!" I mumbled, reaching into my bag.

I pulled out my small transistor radio headset and tuned in to the Second Channel Airwave Broadcast for a weather report. From the sound of it, I was going to be stuck until the afternoon. The last thing I wanted to be doing was hiking in the rain. I put the radio away, and in doing so my cooking kit caught my eye. It seemed oatmeal was out of the question too. I settled for more granola.

As I waited out the rain, that peeping voice of reason kept pecking away at the weaker side of my brain. It kept trying to tell me it still wasn't too late to turn back. While under other circumstances I'd have listened to it, my searing hatred for my family was well overpowering it. I was going to stick to my agenda on this, no matter how long it was to take.

After thinking further into it, I was wondering if I could really consider myself to be among the Causes. Although I left my home at the same time as the thousands of us had planned, my motives weren't as close to the others' who had also run off. Then again, we were talking thousands. I'm sure personal reasons weren't discounted from the historic walkout that began the Revolution.

I began to reminisce about where I was four months ago before that present time…

It was the last time I accessed the discussion forum for the Interactive Network's Tome Grid. Many had been discussing the frightening accuracy of one of the latest releases: *One Summer.*

Written by a man named Devon, *One Summer* was a method of shedding light on the way the land of Eden was being run. He cited examples of his claims from our recorded history as well as our present day. But what made his work so special was that his arguments about Eden's controlled structure were not in a list; but were expressed throughout the events of a love story with big adventure and lovable characters.

Regardless of the format though, his ideas got through to thousands upon thousands of people.

For as long as anybody could remember, any major decision that governed Eden's infrastructure was carried out by a lone body of people known as the Fifteen. Everything from the train systems to the media and everything in between was regulated by these people. Even though the commoners had no say in the way Eden worked, they always accepted it for what it was. The Fifteen may have held all of the authority, but they used it to keep the structure of Eden in a perfect and regulated balance.

However, after reading through *One Summer*, people from all over saw the land of Eden in a whole different light. We felt like servants to the Fifteen after understanding the author's viewpoint on the tight stranglehold of their methods. As such, we saw that the best course of action to escape a life of servitude to the Fifteen's system was to free ourselves from the normality of our society.

This particular mindset began to slowly seep through the population of Eden. As it did, it became easier to see that the younger generation was more adamant about doing something about it. Many of the adults didn't see as much of a need for change in Eden as people my age did.

It soon became troublesome for parents to keep their kids from talking about the book. Since *One Summer* questioned why jobs were assigned to individuals based on their Interactive Study Grade, teens across the landscape, too, failed to see the point in it. Many began to shun the Fifteen's way of doing things; insisting on the freedom to choose what they desire.

That was only the beginning of the overall impact *One Summer* left on the people of Eden. Thinking deeper into the book's meaning, people all over Eden were throwing out questions left and right:

Why are there only three channels on the radio? Why not more? Why do they all have to be controlled by one person?

Why can't the Fifteen create a carriage powered by something other than a horse? They have the power and the resources to! Better yet, why not have a vessel that can fly like a bird?

Why are businesses only allowed to bring in a certain amount of Arna a month? Sure, the amount we are allowed to keep is quite enough for us to live. Why can't we keep the rest of it though?

Why can't an average citizen take the place of a member of the Fifteen who has passed on? Where do the new members come from?

These were just a few examples of the lengthy list of inquiries spouted by the citizens of Eden.

As more and more people read *One Summer* and word of its message spread, it finally caught the attention of Eliza. She is the member of the Fifteen who is in charge of monitoring the content on the Interactive Network.

Not too long after she discovered it, the book was deleted.

With *One Summer* no longer on the Tome Grid, the discussion forum for the popular work had also vanished. With it, any and every topic concerning questions to the Fifteen's system were gone.

It was obvious that the Fifteen were angered by *One Summer* and the effects it had on the citizenry. However, many wondered if wiping out the book was a good idea for Eliza. Because what resulted from her actions was one common thought among all those who read and understood it: "The author was on to something and the Fifteen did not like it."

Outraged by their sudden inability to discuss the subjects further, two people secretly created a new discussion forum. Soon after its completion, INMails went out to a few people, who were asked to forward it to their friends. The message was simple, especially to those who knew what it meant:

Dear Reader,

Discuss the book! Be a Cause!

The phrase "be a Cause" was a link to the new discussion forum.

Word of the new forum spread quickly and discreetly. Soon, the number of members spiked and the questions surrounding the methods of the Fifteen resumed circulation. Members of this new forum became known, only amongst each other, as "Causes".

Many measures were taken to keep the forum hidden from the eyes of the Fifteen. First, the book's title, *One Summer*, could *never* be posted since a future IN search would lead anybody straight to the forum. Second, since "cause" is such a common word, singling the forum out in an IN search would be near-impossible. Lastly, the existence of the forum was to never be discussed in public.

It was on this very forum that a single user put forth the idea to emulate the actions of the characters in the book. He was known as "Hatcher".

His proposal was to have a considerable mass of people walk out from their work or schooling all at the same time. While it seemed possible, many didn't see it as much of a plan at first.

Soon, however, other users began tweaking the suggestion until it eventually formed into a thorough and impressive blueprint. Hatcher became the mastermind and the small group of users who modified his initial suggestion became known as "The Producers".

Hatcher and the Producers began to organize a list of rules that the Causes would abide by during the days that would follow the Great Walk. Their planning soon became a simple list, easy for every Cause to understand:

Rule one: Although this is an attempt at a revolution, this is a peaceful protest. No acts of violence or destruction.

Rule two: Keep to yourself or in groups with only other Causes. Do your best not to contribute to the system.

Rule three: You are welcome to forfeit your role in the Revolution at any time. Your support is still appreciated.

Rule four: Maintain peace amongst each other and the citizenry. We are out to change Eden, not to destroy it.

Rule five: Please respect the wishes of Hatcher and the Producers. The best way we can succeed in this change is to show maturity, understanding and order.

Those were the rules that every Cause agreed to. Upon posting those rules, the date of the Great Walk was set and Causes across the land began to prepare.

The last stage of preparations involved finding a way for the Causes to stay in contact with each other. One of the creators of the new forum decided to take it upon herself to organize a special faction of people known as "Contacts". She was known as "Black".

Being a Contact was one way to assist in the Revolution without directly involving oneself. This role was assigned to those who didn't quite feel easy about walking out of their current life situation. This way, they could still live comfortably while still participating.

Black made it clear that being a Contact was different from being a Cause. For one thing, they could not directly involve themselves in the affairs of the Causes. Also, since being a Contact was more of a *job*, it was up to the Causes to offer them gratuities for their services.

The other aspect of it being a job was the fact that being a Contact would actually replace whatever job the individual previously had. This way, they could still hold true to the Producers' rules by not contributing to the Fifteen's system during the Revolution.

Black laid out simple rules for the Contacts to abide by in addition to the Producers' existing set of rules.

Rule one: We are here to help Causes, not *be* Causes. Keep your names to yourself.

Rule two: Your laptop is your life, guard it as such.

Rule three: Contacts must make themselves distinguishable to Causes without being conspicuous to the average citizen. Thus, Contacts must wear mostly white when they are out on the job.

After the rules were in place, Black allowed members of the forum to sign up to be a Contact. Within a day or two, about 700 Contacts put their usernames on the list.

With everything in place, the plan was ready to be executed. Causes and Contacts alike readied themselves for the start of the Revolution.

Finally, the Great Walk occurred. At that time, roughly 13,000 adolescents ran away from their homes and their responsibilities all at the same time.

The most important factor for the Causes was the fact that Eden's population only hovers between 170,000 and 190,000 people. With 13,000 of them suddenly no longer contributing to the balance of Eden, the very structure of our land became compromised. The Great Walk grabbed the attention of the Fifteen almost as quickly as it took the Causes to pull it off.

This was an attempt at turning Eden around, a revolution that would change the way society would treat us. Most importantly, it would show the Fifteen that it was time for a full-on change. For the past few hundred years previous, the Fifteen had found countless ways to help those in power stay there, while at the same time blocking out the average man from having any political influence. This left them to shape Eden as they saw fit with no care for the opinions of the commoners.

Yes, it was time for a change.

III

After the rain died down, I struck camp and continued onward. Onward, of course, was going any random given direction. One would say I was lost, but my personal favorite euphemism was that I was simply "being aimless".

If there was anything I would be looking for at the time, it was a Contact. It had been a whole week since I last posted with one, as well as check any new findings by my fellow Causes. It would be a courtesy for me to post and tell everyone I was still alive.

As I put my thoughts into sentences for my next post, the unmistakable sound of a charging train filtered through my ears, causing me to stop where I was. I sighed with relief, then quickly focused my hearing. Though the sound of the train seemed to echo from all directions at once, I managed to pin the sound down as coming from my 3 o'clock. I turned to the right and made haste.

It took about a half an hour to reach the Southern Gova Train Station.

I highly doubted the presence of a Contact since the Gova Sector was not a very popular location. Regardless, the station would at least be a good place to refill my water bag and leave the Gova Sector altogether.

After filling up, I stepped onto the platform for the westbound line. Out of the corner of my eye, I saw a young man sitting on a bench and looking through his bag. Just by looking at him, I felt it safe to assume he was also a Cause.

For anybody participating in the Revolution, there was a certain "look" that we could identify each other by. This particular person had just that. He was obviously in his later teens which put him in the appropriate age range.

However, there was more to it than just looking and being young. As far as the true look went, the clothes made the Cause. Several extra pockets sewn into one's pants were a telltale sign of the need for storage space beyond a backpack.

Excessive use of protective accessories was an indicator as well. Even I was sporting cloth coverings on my elbows and thin, fingerless, leather gloves on my hands.

Lastly and most obviously, the possession of a large backpack or duffel bag was the crowning feature to the whole "Cause Look". Every Cause was living out of a bag of items as they took part in the Revolution. Causes and backpacks practically went hand in hand.

As I approached the young man on the bench, I became more and more assured that he was on the side of the Revolution. The black bandana over his hair, the extra pockets in his jeans and the water bag hanging off of his belt were enough to convince me.

The youth was oblivious to me as he removed his plain red shirt in a fashion that boasted his masculine physique. He then reached into his bag, pulled an olive green shirt from it and put it on.

I took a seat on the bench and waited for him to finish. After straightening his clothes and closing his bag, he took notice of me. The two of us nodded to each other.

He took a look at my belongings, looked me in the eye and said, "The book?" He came off as very joyful.

I addressed him with a smile. "The book." As I assumed, this young man was indeed a Cause. Using the phrase "the book" was a way to make sure we were talking to another Cause. The phrase was like a secret code to open communications between one another.

"Are you a Contact?" he asked me.

"I was just about to ask you the same thing," I smiled. "Seeing as neither of us is dressed in white, I guess we're out of luck."

"Looks like it." He removed his shirt again and turned it around after noticing that he had put it on backwards by accident.

I figured since I wouldn't find a Contact until I set foot into another Sector, I'd ask him about the state of affairs. "Is there any trouble out there in civilization? Are the police stepping up patrols?"

"Nah," he shrugged, "Everyone still appears to be indifferent. I think people aren't threatened by us since everything has remained non-violent."

"Well, that's how it has been since the beginning."

"Watch out, though; it has been two months since the Great Walk. Police may look to get tired of us soon enough," he warned, giving me a glare of caution through his sharp brown eyes.

I combined two of our topics to present another thought. "Speaking of two months and Contacts, I'm surprised that the Fifteen haven't found the Contact forum yet."

His eyes widened and his face grew excited. "I was thinking the same thing. It's so funny that a name as simple as 'Cause' hasn't been found out yet."

"Well, the Causes are doing a good job of keeping the name to themselves. Could you imagine what would happen if the Fifteen found out the name 'Cause'?"

He answered with a regretful tone. "The first thing they would do is find the Contact forum. It would give them a considerable advantage against us."

I exhaled, considering the thought. "Let's pray that everything just stays the way it is until the Fifteen hear our demands."

"Do you think they'll listen?"

I thought about my answer carefully. "I think that is the question on every Cause's mind. The Fifteen appear to be having trouble keeping Eden in balance. They may comply with us if things get bad enough."

He nodded in agreement. "Until then, we just stand our ground and stick to the Producers' agenda. It's not like any of the Causes out there are suffering."

"That's pretty much the plan," I declared. After a brief pause, I asked him, "When was the last time you saw a Contact?"

"Just yesterday as a matter of fact," he boasted, resting his right ankle up onto his left knee. "Actually, there's an interesting piece of information you'll want to know."

"What's that?" I asked.

"Some guy dressed in blue has been running around playing hero."

I was intrigued. "A guy in blue?"

"Yeah," he chuckled, looking to the sky. "He's got all the ladies looking to meet him and a few daring rescues under his belt. People have already started posting about it."

"I guess it's something I'll have to check out for myself, huh?"

He nodded. "You're better off, yeah." He took a beat before realizing we had not introduced ourselves. "Oh, I'm Jonathan. My name is 'Skipstone' on the forums."

I introduced myself, "I'm Dartmouth. 'Brigg' is my user name."

"Ah, so you're Brigg, eh?" His reaction had me figuring he knew of my exploits on the forums. "What brought you here to the Gova Sector?"

"What else other than camping out?"

His lip curled as he saw through my explanation. "More like 'hiding out', right?"

"Yeah, that too!" Before I got a chance to continue though, the train pulled in and was ready to take passengers. "Are you getting on?" I asked Skipstone.

"Oh, no. I got off of the last train that came through. I was just resting here a bit more before I go 'camping' myself."

I stood, prepared to board. "In that case, I'll catch you some other time."

"Drop me a message next time you see a Contact!"

"You too. Take it easy and travel safe." With that, I proceeded to board the train. Since trains exiting the Gova Sector were free of charge, all I had to do was hop on and find a seat.

I caught eye of an empty booth at the end of the car and casually made my way over, catching glimpses of a few fellow Causes who gave me a brief glance as well. When I made it over to the seat, I noticed a little girl sitting across from it. Although she looked much younger than me, she appeared to be a Cause.

This sparked my curiosity. A girl who appeared no older than twelve was taking a stand in the Revolution by herself. Thinking it over a second time, something didn't exactly add up. I took the empty seat, choosing to find out what the girl's story was.

There was something about her clothes as well. She was wearing a short denim skirt, a plain white shirt, a pink visor and white sneakers with a pink stripe down the sides. The ensemble looked like that of Lauren, the female love interest from the book. I kept to myself the fact that a girl of her age and build wouldn't be able to emulate a look as buxom as that of the character though.

Before I opened my mouth to speak, the look on her face was

the last thing to catch my eye. I realized that in the time I had been sitting across from her, her facial expression remained unchanged. It was a cold and stoic stare with empty, lifeless eyes. She looked very troubled. Her sullen expression was stopping me from saying anything until the train began to move.

I had a difficult time thinking of how to break the ice until I decided to go with the foolproof introduction. "The book?"

The little miss blinked and twitched a bit, as if my question yanked her out of a hypnotic trance. She looked up to me and promptly turned her gaze aside with a nod.

"That didn't accomplish much," I thought to myself. "Are you all right?" I asked her.

She repeated her last motions. This time, though, she didn't nod.

There was a long and awkward pause. "I see you're dressed like Lauren from the book." I was trying to get some kind of reaction from this girl that wasn't just a look or nod, but she didn't respond at all that time.

Now, it was beginning to worry me. A girl this young wasn't safe if she failed to be attentive to her surroundings. Anyone could just snatch her up and she'd never be heard from again. Things weren't exactly piecing together. I at least wanted to know what she was doing all by herself, especially since her appearance was that of a Cause.

Getting creative, I sat back in my seat and with the straightest face asked her, "What do you do when you're riding your oven down the street and all the wheels fall off your fireplace and you don't have enough scrambled eggs to paint the front porch?"

The girl's eyes narrowed and her eyebrows slowly rose. She then cracked a smile, looked at me, and began laughing.

"That's better!" I said with a wide grin. I was glad to get her talking.

She apologized, stifling the rest of her giggles. The young girl looked over me and my possessions. "The book, right?"

"That's what I asked you! Yes, the book." I was glad to finally get an adequate response. I asked her, "So what was with the long face?"

She seemed very timid answering. "Well…I just have a lot to think about."

"Well," I said, reclining across my seat, "don't go thinking so much that you can't see what's going on around you. A cute little girl like you is liable to be taken advantage of. It's especially a problem if you run into some of the...less reputable Causes."

She smiled sweetly. It seemed that I was not the first person to call her a "cute little girl". That idea seemed a little more like fact as she gave me an unexpected response. "How do I know you're not one of them?"

"Me?" I had to think for a moment. That wasn't exactly a question I was prepared to answer. "Actually, the reason I wanted to talk to you was because I was wondering what you're doing here all by yourself."

She folded her arms in objection. "I don't even know your name!"

"Likewise." I leaned forward and extended my hand. "My name is Dartmouth."

"I'm Mika." We shook hands. Mika had a weak and shy handshake.

Her name was like none I had ever heard before. "Mika, eh? That's a rather unique name."

She grinned. "Yeah, I get that a lot. But like anyone else, I wasn't the one who chose it!"

I broke eye contact with her and looked out the window. I enjoyed the sight of the scenery whizzing by us as I continued to ask Mika for information. "So Mika, as I was asking, you're a Cause as well, right?"

"Well, sorta..."

"How 'sorta'?"

She was straightforward. "Actually, I'm searching for my father..."

Hearing a girl that young coming out with news like that was like having pins driven into my heart. It provided adequate insight as to why she was by herself. "Your father?"

"Yes," she nodded. "I haven't seen him for several months. I just recently returned home looking for him; but he wasn't there. All that was left was a note. It didn't mention where he was going or what he was doing. It only mentioned that he left with no intention of returning." She fought a sob.

Briefly oblivious to the idea of being sensitive, I asked the next question. "So how does that fit you in with the rest of the Causes? You've obviously read the book."

She sniffled and continued. "I'm just using the Revolution as a front so I can ask for help from Causes. But it hasn't done me very well since every time it seems somebody wants to help me...well, you know..."

"What?"

"Less reputable Causes."

I nodded. "I see; you *do* know what I'm talking about."

"Every group that tried to help me always had one boy who would always try to get me alone and stuff. Then the other people of the group would tell me that I'd be better off looking for somebody else to help me." She let out a frustrated sigh.

I decided to play the older brother for a moment and dropped some advice to her. "Well, as long as you know what to watch out for, you'll be just fine. It's better to distance yourself from those types before they think they can take advantage of you."

Mika just smiled, sweeping her blonde locks away from her deep blue eyes. She readjusted her visor and reclined in her seat as I was. She seemed like a very casual young girl. In all honesty, if she had been a few years older, I'd have asked to help her out with hopes that would benefit my own biological urges. Nevertheless, I was very sympathetic to her position and could understand why she was acting as a Cause.

Mika sought help and I felt I could be there to provide it. This time, somebody with better intentions was on her side.

I sat up straight in my seat and met her eyes with mine. "Mika, if you're still interested in having help finding your father, I'd be glad to join you."

"Really?" she peeped. "Do you really mean it?"

I leaned forward and lowered my voice. Mika leaned in as well, all ears. "Look, I completely understand if you decline. The other young men out here are being their own, feral selves. It wouldn't surprise me at all if you thought I was one of them as well. That being said, all I can really do is *tell* you that I'll help you find your father in hopes that you'll trust me." I took a beat. "I'm just asking because I don't think it's a good idea to leave you to go about this by yourself."

She gave me an understanding nod, pleased with my words.

"You'll help me out?"

"I'll do my best," I assured her. "What do you say to going into town at the next stop and asking around? Do you have anything on hand that could help us to look for him?"

Mika reached into the front pocket of her backpack and pulled out a piece of canvas. She looked at it herself before handing it over to me. "This is him, my father."

I took a good look at the piece of canvas to see an obviously hand-drawn, black and white picture of a very stern-looking man. It was very well drawn, with a definable level of detail. This was definitely a worthwhile piece of help for the search. I couldn't help but ask her, "Did you draw this yourself?"

Mika smirked and bounced in place as if the illustration was a source of pride. "Yes. What do you think?"

Impressed, I chuckled. "I think you're pretty good at drawing people. I also think this will help us out quite a bit." I took a deeper look. Though the picture had been drawn with a lot of care, there were distinct erasure marks around the ears and the eyes. It seemed she had striven for perfection out of love for him. "You and your father must have been pretty close when he was around, right?"

"What makes you say that? I'm his daughter. Of course we were close."

I apologized. "I'm sorry. It's just that family togetherness has been a foreign concept to me over the past several years."

"Your family fights a lot…?"

I spared her the harshest of the details. "So to speak. We certainly never get along."

"That's why you're out here—to get away from them for a little while?" she asked.

"Actually…" I froze for a moment before deciding to show her the one thing I would usually keep hidden. I rolled up the left leg of my pants and adjusted my seating to show her the huge scar on the back of my leg. "When you've got things like this to remind you just how violent your parents can be, you're better off being anywhere but where it happened."

Mika gasped at the sight of the marking that ran from the back of my knee to my ankle. "That looks horrible. How did something like that happen?"

I caved in and chose to tell her the story. "Well, it was two years ago. I was fifteen at the time…"

IV

"I see," Mika stated with deep sympathy. "That sounds terrible."

"That's only the half of it, but it appears you've heard enough." I had just spent about a half an hour sharing with her several stories of the harsh conditions I lived in back at home. "So you see," I continued, "I'm in on the Revolution simply because I had to get away from all of that. The best part is that if I can find a place to settle in all this, I'll never have to go back!"

Mika hastily interjected. "You're just going to abandon your family like that?"

Remembering the abuse and hostility I lived in back at home was the only thought that helped create my reply to her question. "Correction: I already have…"

Mika looked out of the window and away from me for a moment. "That's really sad. Won't you get lonely?"

I huffed, feeling very sure of my methods and motives. "I won't need to worry about that. I've been mostly on my own for the past sixty-something days anyway. It's actually pretty refreshing to not have to deal with other people."

Mika kept from eye contact as she continued contesting my position. "My father always told me that even people that want to be alone still need somebody. If everyone just kept to themselves, where would we be today?" Mika was silent, thinking about what I had said. "You know what?"

"What?" I asked.

She turned quickly back to look at me, deliberately letting her hair whip around her head. "You can come with me to help find my father. This way you won't be lonely and I'll have help. It's a win-win situation." Her reasoning was rather sweet, albeit a little naive.

It seemed like we now had coexisting motives. While I felt she needed somebody with her to protect her, she felt I needed somebody to keep me company. With that in perspective, how could I decline?

"Sure thing!" I agreed with a nod.

She let out a sweet giggle. "I knew you'd see it my way."

With that agreement, Mika and I became a team. It was the first time since the beginning of the Revolution that I found the need to travel with somebody. It wasn't just for me though. I truly felt that this girl needed protection.

Finally, I was no longer alone in my travels. Sure, there were some concerns on my mind about the need to care for another person. However, I knew that any doubts I had would be put out once I got used to having company.

Episode 2: The Ordeal of Pata

Day 63 (Continued)

I

The train's next stop was the most densely populated sector in all of Eden—the Pata Sector. Causes would make their way to Pata since the many inns there were practically safe havens from the many who opposed the Revolution, as well as police.

Winding up in the crowded Pata Sector was beneficial to our search efforts. It would be easier to find a Contact as well as information concerning Mika's father. It felt almost natural for me to help in Mika's search since it gave me something exciting and purposeful to do.

We arrived in the Pata Sector's easternmost station, aptly named Station East. Looking to the sky and seeing how late the hours were becoming, I asked Mika if it was all right to hold off searching until the next day. She seemed understanding of the decision and chose to follow along.

I recommended that Mika hold onto my hand as we navigated through the bustling Station East. It was best to keep her close and move quickly since station security was on a vigilant patrol.

Just as we exited the station, I promptly froze in place as a hand swiftly clutched my shoulder. I darted my head to the left to see a rather feminine-looking hand with the wrist bandaged halfway to the elbow. Before I acted rashly though, I heard a woman's voice ask me, "The book?"

I released my breath in great relief as I turned to see who had stopped me. "Yes, the book," I replied.

A slender young woman who stood about ten or twelve centimeters shorter than me was the perpetrator of the sudden halt. A red shirt with short white sleeves draped just onto the beltline of her knee-length denim shorts. Her feet were comfortably set in sturdy red walking sneakers with contrasting white stripes and propped-up heels. The girl appeared to have been injured seeing as her left wrist was bandaged up, as well as her right ankle, which had dressings halfway to the knee. They appeared as the only physical blemishes the alluring redhead had on her trim, athletic body.

The woman looked at Mika with a raised eyebrow. "She's with the Causes?"

I corrected her. "She's with me—that's all that matters. Now if you'll excuse us…" I turned away and made an attempt to continue along, barely giving the woman a second look or any more of my attention for that matter. I was still rather startled by the way she had approached us.

"I don't think so!" the woman persisted as she grabbed Mika's other hand.

I felt the tug. "Hey, what's the big idea!?" I contested, stopping once again.

"The big idea is…" she scowled, stepping up to me, "I'm not letting you take that little girl with you. I know what you're thinking!"

I rolled my eyes and exclaimed, "Oh, come on! You're not serious!"

In the back of my mind, I knew something like this was bound to happen eventually. What surprised me about it was how soon it had actually occurred.

There were huge arguments on the forums about things like this before the Revolution began. Basically, while the girls wanted to take their stand in the Revolution as well, they feared how the men would treat them. It mostly derives from what I was telling Mika about "less reputable Causes".

"I *am* serious," the irate young woman grumbled. "I saw you get on that train alone. Now I see you with that little girl in tow. Where are you headed now; the nearest inn?"

Her assumptions forced a little more furor into my tone with her. "Are you insisting that I'm looking to...?"

I stopped for a moment.

Quite a few ideas hit me all at once. The combination of memories from my time on the forums generated a topic-changing question: "You're 'Kay', aren't you?"

She blinked, staring at me with mild disbelief through her limpid green eyes. It was as if my guessing her identity pulled the next sentence out of her mouth and sucked it down the small storm drain at her feet. "E-excuse me?"

"You're Kay, from the forums." I felt I was now in control of the conversation. I jogged her memory by reciting one of our heated run-ins. "If I'm not mistaken, you're the one who said I was 'full of it' when I said, 'It all depends on the man's intentions in the upcoming days. Any man who's in on this just to run around and be lawless doesn't deserve to be among us'." Kay's face briefly twitched as I continued. "Also, if I'm not mistaken, you countered by saying..."

"Okay, Okay!" she interrupted, "I get the idea." She paused for a moment, exhaling with a slight grunt as she placed her loaded, black duffel bag to her side. She regained her composure and guessed my identity. "You must be Brigg. Nobody else would remember *that* level of detail about what I post."

"Well, my real name is Dartmouth. Brigg is just my username on the forums." I pointed to Mika. "This little one here is Mika." I extended my hand to Kay.

She introduced herself formally as she firmly accepted my handshake. "I'm Susan. Call me 'Kay'." After a brief pause, she asked, "So, where are you two going anyway?"

Mika answered her, "Well, we *were* going to look for a place to stay for the night...like you said."

"...If that's all right with you, of course!" I facetiously added.

"Actually," she pondered a moment, "I read last time I saw a

Contact that there was a really nice inn around here owned by and old man named Roy. It's cheap, he helps Causes, *and* there's another Contact stationed there."

"Is that so?" It sounded a little too good, but it wasn't a time to be skeptical or picky. Also, since the news was posted via Contact, then it was at least worth our time to look into it.

Mika seemed taken by the sound of that package. She took my hand again and readied herself to go. "Thanks!" she said to Kay as she walked with me. "See you around."

"Uh, hold up!" she called to us. "I'm going with you!" She slung her black bag back over her shoulder and ran to catch up with us.

Her insisting to come along had me stop short after only a few paces. "What's this all of a sudden?" I asked, turning back to her. "What do you have to be following us around for?"

"Well," she quickly replied, shrugging slightly, "if we're all going to go to Roy's anyway, what's the point in having us split up? Also, I at least have a rough idea of where the place is. I can help lead you there."

I growled low to myself and shook my head as I saw right through her explanation. "Can't you just be honest and say, 'I still don't trust you alone with that little girl'?"

"I figured you understood that without me having to say it," she smiled smugly.

"Whatever," I scoffed.

Mika tugged on my hand. "Don't worry about her. Let's go."

I grunted in discontent as I gave Kay a silent signal to lead the way. "Ladies first…"

She haughtily stepped ahead of us. Reluctantly, we followed her.

II

I couldn't help but mock Kay's previous claim; lacing my voice with a high, sneering, sarcastic tone. "*I at least have a rough idea of where the place is. I can help lead you there.*"

We had been searching for Roy's for over an hour, growing slightly more annoyed with each passing minute. We had that continuously growing sensation that this all could have been avoided if Kay had just minded her own business.

On the other side of the coin though, I should have been more persistent in pushing her away from us. I addressed Kay with slight anger. "Honestly, I have no idea why I let you sweep me into this."

"Oh, come on," she defended. "Would you have even heard of Roy's if I hadn't said anything?"

"Probably," I answered in a shout. "I may have even found it quicker."

Mika yawned, equally irritated by Kay's behavior. "I knew we should have just left her back at the station."

I sought to differ. "That wouldn't happen. She would have followed us anyway. To her credit though, she does have a point that we'd be stuck for a safe place to stay the night if she hadn't told us about Roy's."

Audibly mentioning the inn caught the attention of the young man walking in front of us. He stopped to address me, turning so quickly that his lengthy black hair fell over his right shoulder. "The book?" he asked.

Slightly startled by the sudden change of pace, I answered the gruff-looking youth. "The book."

A baggy pair of dark green pants and a simple gray shirt made up the young stranger's outfit. His backpack was quite unique, though. All of his personal belongings were stowed in a large, brown cloth ring which hung off of his left shoulder and came across his body to rest on the right side of his waist.

He took a look at the girls and began to stroke his thin goatee. His lazy brown eyes casually exchanged gazes between himself and the three of us as he filled us in on his reason for stopping. "You mentioned Roy's, right?"

I nodded. "That's right."

An inviting grin came to his mouth. "I'm going back there right now. I'll be getting a room there for the night. Are you lost looking for it?"

I glared at Kay. "Very much so."

The stranger looked to the both of us and was able to conclude that Kay was the one responsible for our position. "I see…"

Feeling spiteful, I added, "This woman doesn't know where

she's going."

He laughed. "Well, who is this woman and who are you?"

I introduced myself. "My name is Dartmouth; Brigg from the forums."

His face lit up. "You're Brigg?"

I pointed to myself. "Yes, that's me."

It appeared that he was excited to meet me in person. "Bro, it's me, Doctrine!"

This was a delightful surprise. I was face to face with a good friend of mine from the forums. "Doctrine?"

"Well, my real name is Sydney. You can call me either or." Doctrine shook my hand as he looked over Kay and Mika again. He slyly grinned to me. "Very nice there, Brigg. You seemed like the type that would be sporting that type of luggage."

"Excuse me?" Kay protested.

"Uh," I corrected, pointing to her, "this one isn't really with me. She's just following me around. This is our good friend Kay!" I made sure to emphasize sarcasm on "good friend".

He slapped his forehead. "Oh, God! How'd you wind up with *her* following you?"

Mika yawned wide. I saw that as more of a signal than anything else. The young miss implored, "Can we just go now and talk later? It's getting late."

"Fair enough," he agreed. "Follow me. I'll take you to Roy's"

III

It was another five blocks to walk. We were fortunate to have somebody with us who actually knew what he was doing.

We arrived at Roy's inn in what seemed like no time. The place was a two-story brick structure that muttered "squalor" over "hospitable". It wasn't exactly what you'd look at for a comfortable night's rest. The dark, narrow alleyways to both sides of the building didn't help much either.

Doctrine began to explain in a toned-down voice just loud enough for us to hear over the buzz of the crowded street. "What we have here is a guy looking to capitalize on the Revolution. He recently opened this inn and his business hasn't been the best. This is the Pata Sector, though, not exactly a high-end neighborhood."

"Obviously," I added, looking over the exterior again. Mika drew a bit closer to me as Kay took her other hand.

"Trust me; it looks better on the inside. The rooms are cheap, too. It's only 15 Arna for one night."

I sighed as my expectations fell past my comfort zone. "As long as we aren't at risk of being turned in to the authorities, I guess this beats anything else."

We entered the inn and first took note that Doctrine was surely not specific about how much better it looked on the inside. The lobby was dimly lit and the furniture looked a little too close together. It was as if we walked into a stuffy antique shop rather than an inn. I could see, though, how one would get the "simple and cozy" impression of the place.

An older man with graying hair stepped up to the counter and greeted Doctrine. "You're back."

We let Doctrine do the talking. "Hey Roy, I hope you still have vacancy because I brought some friends back."

"Uh…" Kay began to speak. I lightly elbowed her, having the feeling she'd question the way Doctrine phrased our addition to Roy's guest list. Kay whispered to me, "We barely know this guy."

I needed to calm her down before she could say anything that would stifle our luck. "Hey, don't complain. It's a cheap room. I don't know about you, but I feel like getting a shower some time soon."

In response to my scolding, Kay smelled her clothes. She quickly ran out of things to say.

I saw Doctrine hand over 25 Arna to Roy. He was then given a room key and pointed to the stairs.

After Roy went back to his office, I said to Doctrine, "I thought you said rooms were only fifteen Arna."

In a laid-back yet proud tone, he replied, "True. But why have one person pay fifteen when four people can pay six apiece?"

Kay didn't stay silent as long as I wished she had. "So you're saying you used us for your little discount?"

"You sure do complain a lot!" I said to her. "I'll pay a measly six Arna over fifteen any day. And if you think a little more about it, Doctrine is even covering the last Arna, paying seven."

"It's just my way of saying 'thanks'," Doctrine chuckled.

Mika let out another yawn as Doctrine opened to door to the room. No sooner was the door open did Mika make her way toward the only bed. "Thank you very much, Mister Doctrine," she mumbled, placing her backpack at the foot of the bed. She flopped on and made herself comfortable under the light brown blanket and decorative throw.

Kay, Doctrine and I placed our things down and began to situate the room. While we were smiling at how cute Mika was in taking to the bed, we realized that there was only enough room on it to fit two people. It would be easier on the second person with Mika's petite frame occupying the other side.

The rest of the room wasn't exactly very spacious, but it had enough room to fit all of us and our property. There would also be enough room for two to sleep on the floor once we got situated. At least it had a nice, clean bathroom with a working shower. The room itself looked like the lobby below—antique and dimly lit. It seemed a lot less stuffy and a little more welcoming though.

As I took a seat in the leather chair in the corner, Kay threw a set of blankets in my lap. "I found these stashed in the closet."

I unfolded the thick, tan comforter as I caught what Kay was saying to me. "Um…"

"Um, nothing!" she sneered. "You're sleeping on the floor."

"Okay!" I stood from the chair, letting the blankets fall onto the floor. I raised my voice slightly. "Now you're starting to get on my nerves!"

"I'm just calling it like I see it," she snipped back.

"What are you going to do for Doctrine?" I challenged. "Are you going to kick him to the floor after he went through the courtesy to lead us here?"

She tersely responded, pointing to each subject she stated, "Girl…boy…bed…no!"

"Who do you think you are?" I argued, stepping forward. "Is this how you've been spending your time as a Cause? Have you just been following other Causes around and telling them what to do?"

She paused and turned her shoulder to me. "Actually, yes."

I threw my hands into the air and turned my back to her. "No wonder you were by yourself when you came up to me!"

Kay began to speak up as well. "What's that supposed to mean?"

Doctrine stepped out of the bathroom. "Children, children!" he interrupted. We stopped for a moment so he could have his say. "Damn, if I had known it was going to be like this, I'd have just paid the whole 15 Arna and stayed alone."

I held up my hands in defense. "Hey, I told you she wasn't with me when we met."

"While you do have a point there, I'd like to get a good night's rest regardless." Doctrine turned to Kay. "It's your turn to use the bathroom. Brigg and I will discuss this."

Kay huffed and stormed hastily into the bathroom.

Doctrine turned to me and looked me in the eye. "Honestly, if it will avoid further outbursts like that, I'll take the floor. I don't mind." He stroked his goatee again as he recalled the question he had previously asked me. "Now that I remember, I asked you how you got paired up with that woman in the first place."

"That's right; I never answered you on that." I felt free to go on a red anger tangent speckled with harsh, black, opinionated commentary. While I managed to fit all of the facts in, I was indeed inclined to vent my frustrations of Kay's mere presence.

"Whoa…" Doctrine remarked, "…and that all happened today?"

"Yeah, all of that happened in the span of the last twelve hours. I picked up Mika, and Kay has been following me ever since." I turned to Mika, expecting her to say something. But she was already fast asleep under the covers of the bed. All I got from her was a solid, slumbering expression.

Just then, there was a knock on the door. Doctrine walked over and took a look through the peephole. "The book?" he called to the visitor.

"Contact," a female voice answered.

"That's right," Doctrine said as he opened the door, "I had Roy tell the Contact that we were here."

My heart lifted a bit. I was relieved to finally be able to post on the bulletin board.

The Contact let herself in. She was a fair looking woman, clad in mostly white as most Contacts were. She swiped her long red hair away from her face and introduced herself. "Yes, I will be your Contact this evening."

Doctrine called on me. "When was the last time you posted?"

"About a week ago," I answered.

He walked over to his bag of items, pointing to me as he passed me. "In that case, you're going first. Some people are probably worried about you."

I replied with the obvious explanation. "Well, I *was* camping out in the Gova Sector all week. It's not exactly easy to find Contacts out there."

The Contact appeared to have a fixation for organization as she began situating herself at the small, wooden table in front of the leather chair. Instead of simply pushing the lamp and clock aside, she picked them up and placed them back on the table in a way that seemed to make that simple space in the corner of the room look like a comfortable workstation. By the time she was ready to have us make our posts, she had made that chair the most inviting spot in the room.

The endearing stranger relinquished the seat in front of the computer and instructed me to take my time posting on the forum. She was in no hurry.

I first took a moment to send a private message to Skipstone, whom I had met earlier that day. After that, I checked for any new topics of discussion.

That was when the topic Skipstone told me about caught my eye. It was called "Blue-clad Glory Seeker?" I couldn't help but check it out.

"What do you have there, Brigg?" Doctrine asked me.

After reading a few of the posts made by other Causes, I replied openly, "A Cause I met in the Gova Sector told me about this. According to the topic here, there's some guy who dresses all in blue. He has been going around and helping Causes at what appears to be completely at random."

He sounded surprised. "You don't say. I knew I should have read that when I first saw the topic."

Kay came out of the bathroom as I continued reading posts. I resumed speaking. "When a group of Causes asked who he was, all he said was 'Blue' and ran off."

Seeming to be impressed, Doctrine chuckled. "It sounds like someone wants to be the mystery hero during the Revolution."

Kay interrupted with a high mark in her voice, indicating that she may have had something relevant to say about the man. "You're talking about that guy in blue."

We turned to her, noting she was wearing nothing but a long towel and the bandages over her left wrist and right ankle. My curiosity of what she might have known stilled any incoming comments, keeping me on the subject. "Do you know something about this guy?"

"I don't *know* anything about him. However, I saw him once. He foiled a thief who had swiped another Cause's backpack. That's all I can really say about it."

I turned back to the screen. "I guess we'll keep an eye on that topic. For now, I just need to make my post in 'I'm Still Alive'." That topic was reserved specifically for people who were absent from the forums for a period of more than three days. It was a method of reassuring every Cause of each others' health and safety.

Kay seemed displeased with the lack of news I could provide to the community. "You've been gone from the forums for a week and there's nothing to report other than that? There has got to be *something* interesting that you could…tell…the…" Kay slowed her speech to a stop. She realized that if she had finished that sentence, I would have gladly obliged her by posting the day's happenings. Instead, she grabbed her things and went back into the bathroom; saying nothing else.

I thought for a moment as I was making my post. Once I was done with it, I clicked on "New Topic". With a sinister grin on my face, I began to type.

The Contact knew what I was up to. "No malicious topics!" she reminded me.

"Oh yeah," I sighed, turning to face Doctrine. I stood from the chair and presented it to him. "You're up."

He paused for a moment, pointing behind him with his thumb at Mika. "What about her? Should we wake her up so she can post too?"

I stopped to think before answering. Remembering that Mika was never a Cause to begin with, answering Doctrine's question in front of a Contact was going to take some care. Even though Contacts were not directly affiliated with the Causes, I was still uncertain of how one would react to knowing that we were breaking the Producers' Second Rule.

The forum for Contact posting was specifically reserved for those who were registered at the time the Revolution began. Since Mika was never registered with the forum, she couldn't post. As such, she would be quickly identified as not being a Cause. What made the matter worse was her age. If this Contact were to find out twelve-year-old Mika was not with the Causes, there was no telling what kind of trouble it would create.

After a rather suspicious pause of thought, I answered Doctrine. "Remember? Mika told us that she posted yesterday. She said she'd be fine earlier."

"She said that?" Doctrine replied. "I don't remember."

I had to try again. He obviously wasn't catching on. "Oh, that's right. She told me that just before you ran into us on the street. It's alright. Mika will be fine."

I wasn't sure if he understood the truth or just accepted my story for what it was. Either way, he let it go and approached me to take over the chair.

I made no obvious signs of relief, but inside, I quivered at this new realization. While I committed to helping Mika search for her father, it was going to make things difficult if certain people discovered her position in relation to the Revolution.

To ward off any outward indication that something could be wrong, I put those thoughts in the back of my mind to stay focused on the activity in the room.

Kay emerged from the bathroom in sky blue cotton pajamas. "Yeah, Brigg. No malicious topics." She turned to the Contact expecting a supporting comment.

Instead, the Contact stood vigilant, monitoring Doctrine's posts.

Kay folded her arms and raised an eyebrow at the focused young woman. "You Contacts don't say much do you?"

I reminded Kay, "They're not supposed to. You forget that they are not like Causes. Associating with us too much would likely get them more directly involved."

"Brigg is right," the Contact agreed.

"Think about this, too," Doctrine added. "When has a Contact ever given you his or her name?"

Kay and I both had to consider that. The man had a point.

"Hopefully never," the Contact said with a witty lilt. "We're here to help you, not *be* you. Black made rules for us, too."

While taking her reminder of Black into consideration, I stepped over and sat at the foot of the bed.

Kay glared at me, her mistrust of my motives still prominent.

With seething disinterest in her inaudible assumptions, I rolled my eyes and moved over to the corner opposite of Mika. I left plenty of room for Kay to sit between me and the sleeping girl. All I thought of in doing that was preemptively shutting her up

At that point, all we could hear was clicking and typing as Doctrine continued to make posts on the bulletin board. It was as if he had not seen a Contact in weeks. Either that or he had a lot to report that he hadn't told us yet.

Just as he was wrapping up his posts, he announced, "Hey guys, we've got a newsflash here. It's straight from Aeon!"

This was good news. One of the Producers was making an announcement for all Causes to see and discuss.

Kay and I stood and made our way over to the screen. The two of us began to read the post word for word as we loomed over Doctrine's shoulders.

He began to speak as Kay and I were still reading. "It looks like eight of the nine Producers have finally congregated at their meeting place."

I nodded as I skimmed over the rest of the post. "Sure took them long enough!"

This was a key piece of news that every Cause was to know. The Producers, the very people who planned out the Revolution, were finally gathering at a special meeting place they had recently designated. However, there was still one who was not with them.

We read through the list: Bogen, Lily, Aeon, Ki, Rosa, Moll, Matthias and Cecilia.

There was a noticeable problem with the list of attendees. "The only one still missing…is Hatcher…" Kay muttered.

After a brief pause, Doctrine added, "That's actually a very big deal that *he* be the one missing."

Unsolicited, I began reciting a quick history lesson for us. "Hatcher is the originator of the entire plan. He's the first one to ever make mention of emulating the actions in the book. That's why he changed his user name to 'Hatcher' in the first place."

Kay interpreted the metaphor. "As if his plan hatched from an egg so to speak…"

Doctrine kept his eyes on the screen as he nonchalantly dignified Kay's comment. "Yeah, something like that."

I stood back straight and folded my arms. "Why would the creator of the entire plan be the last one to show up?"

He sat back in the chair with a slight grunt. "I don't know. Distance?"

"That would make sense," Kay shrugged. "Eden *is* a lot of land to cover."

"When was the last time Hatcher even made a post?" I curiously asked.

Doctrine sat forward again to engage the laptop. "Let's check."

Kay came at me with an unexpected iota of praise. "Good idea, Brigg."

"Thanks," I stoically accepted.

A moment later, Doctrine had an answer. However, instead of simply speaking it, he opted to mumble it with a slight sense of dread. "Five weeks ago…"

There was a brief, uncertain silence.

He followed with additional facts, spoken with a reprise of similar anxiety. "Making matters worse is what he posted…"

I dared to ask. "Which is…?"

Doctrine quoted in a deep, different voice as if he assumed it was how Hatcher sounded in person. "Don't confront the Fifteen without me. The success of the Revolution rides on my presence at the time of the confrontation."

Kay raised her voice in mild anger. "So you're saying that the Causes are stuck until Hatcher meets with the rest of the Producers?"

"Essentially…yes," Doctrine sighed.

I turned to once again gaze at Mika, who was still soundly asleep. I felt sort of jealous that the little miss would have a lot less to worry about than the Causes would. On the bright side, though, Mika's mission gave me something productive to pass the time that would be spent waiting for Hatcher to arrive.

As I turned back to the others, Doctrine addressed Kay. "Is

there anything you need to post?"

She thought a moment, making her way over to the bed. "Nah, I've got nothing relevant. If you wouldn't mind just editing your post to tell everyone I'm fine as well, I'd appreciate it."

As irritating as Kay had been that evening, Doctrine saw no harm in such a small favor. "Sure thing," he said, clicking on a function to edit his post.

Soon after that, we dismissed the Contact with our sincerest thanks. Doctrine, Kay and I chipped in two Arna apiece to give her a generous tip for her time and service.

Kay quickly commandeered the other half of the bed next to Mika. Seeing that, Doctrine and I assumed our sleeping arrangements. I let Kay's continued wariness of my presence slide for the night in lieu of simply being too tired to care anymore.

I took the tan comforter, my pillow from my bag and a spot on the floor between the door, the bed and the bathroom. If anyone started moving around in the morning, it'd be sure to wake me up.

There was a different feeling in my heart as I laid to rest that night. I knew that there would be a lot more to look forward to the next day. I closed my eyes with one last thought: "What is going to happen tomorrow?"

Day 64

I

I was awoken that morning when Mika tripped and fell on top of me. Fortunately, the girl was light enough to keep injury at bay.

"Good morning, Mika!" I laughed. "Nice to see you too!"

Mika rolled to the left with a stammering apology peeping from her mouth. She stopped and sat, curling into a sitting ball with her arms around her legs. "Good morning, Dartmouth!"

Her salutation seemed a little too formal for the casual atmosphere between us. "Oh, feel free to call me 'Brigg'," I insisted.

Finding no harm in one or the other, she responded, "Sure thing…Brigg." Mika then stood up, grabbed her things and proceeded to the bathroom.

The sun was just beginning to peek through the window as the first beams of the morning light spread themselves across Kay's face. She squinted and grumbled, rolling away from them to face toward me. I quietly sighed and shook my head. I found it a shame that the soft, feminine features of Kay's natural beauty would go back into hiding once she was wide awake with her attitude on full display.

Doctrine seemed to have slept well also. His mouth was agape and his body was sprawled across the floor with a blanket rumpled over him. I chuckled at how humorous it looked.

Content, albeit groggy, I sat up and simply waited for my body to conjure the energy to stand. As I did so, I heard the shower turn on and a slight rustling of clothing coming from behind the bathroom door.

It was at that time I remembered what the agenda was for the time being. We were going to head out to search for Mika's father. I was thinking "we" at the time because I knew Kay was going to follow us once we left Roy's anyway. I groaned low at the thought and hoped Doctrine would follow along as well to help maintain order.

One more detail brought concern to my mind. With no idea where to start and only a hand-drawn picture to go on, I felt that the search for Mika's father was going to require some patience and care.

Naturally, the best thing to do in that situation was to ask other Causes first. The Pata Sector was crawling with Causes in its crowded city streets. It wasn't going to be hard to pick one out and ask them. This was, however, an operation to be proceeded into with caution. There was no telling where and when police would be around.

While considering the subject of police, a thought of Hatcher crossed my mind. I couldn't help but wonder if Hatcher had, just maybe, been captured. To top things off, the rest of the Producers would probably only wait around so long for him.

The key thing that all Causes knew at that time was that the Fifteen had made no direct attempt to confront us since a lone incident in the very beginning. It was the police in each individual sector that had been carrying out captures of Causes.

As the threat of sector police kept Causes on their toes, many were negatively anticipating for when the Fifteen would finally make another move of their own. Everybody knew that the power and influence of the Fifteen was still far greater than that of the Causes.

Regardless, morale remained high. Hopefully, Hatcher would show up before anything catastrophic happened.

II

After everybody was awake and showered, we prepared to embark. Before beginning the search, though, our first destination was the lobby for a free breakfast.

We marched down the staircase to find four other people, two boys and two girls, just outside of Roy's office. A dainty redhead in a yellow shirt had her ear to the door, gently knocking on it.

The other young woman, a tall beauty in a long, dark blue skirt and shawl, crossed in front of the two males and took a seat on a nearby chair. "It's been ten minutes now!"

At first look of the two young men, I immediately became curious of the strange white rectangles that were sewn into the backs of their matching black shirts. As I whispered my thoughts on it to the others, the one on the right openly stated, "If he wants us to just go away, he could at least poke his head out of the door and say it."

I walked up and tapped one of the men on the shoulder. "The book?"

He was a bit alarmed at first as he swiftly turned his head to answer, "The book."

The other boy turned to us as well. I glanced to him before addressing both of them with my next question. "All of you?"

He nodded. "Yeah, all of us."

I brought my voice back to speaking volume and addressed the girl at the office door. "What's the problem?"

"You see," she said, "Roy locked himself in his office and won't come out. Not only do we have to return our keys—but the free breakfast hasn't been set up yet."

The young man on my right took his room key out of the right-front pocket of his brown cargo pants and held it up next to his face. "Obviously, talking to Roy is more about the breakfast than it is the keys," he smiled.

Doctrine stepped past us to approach the girl in the yellow shirt. "How do you know Roy is even in there?" he asked her.

She backed up a few steps from him and pointed to the bottom of the door. "If you peek under the door, you can see his feet."

Doctrine did as instructed, getting on his hands and knees to take a look. "Yeah, I see them," he called out.

The male on my left joined the girl in blue by sitting in the chair across from hers. As he flopped down, he grunted impatiently. "We've done everything short of breaking down the door."

"That won't be necessary," Kay smiled, stepping up with her bag open. The gleam in her eye and the confident push in her voice put all of the attention in the room to her.

The young lady in blue didn't seem convinced. "What are *you* going to do?"

Kay produced two small hairpins from her bag. "I'm going to pick the lock."

Doctrine backed away from the door and gestured in a way that presented the task at hand to Kay.

"Just give me a minute," she boldly boasted; kneeling in front of the doorknob.

As Kay attended to that, all of us took the time to introduce ourselves. The girl in the yellow shirt was named Chloe; the woman in blue called herself "Twilight Maiden"—which was obviously her forum name; the young man in the brown pants called himself "Bark"; and the other youth, who was wearing denim pants, called himself "Pitch".

I chose to ask Bark and Pitch about the white rectangles on the backs of their shirts. Even though I was the only one who asked, the two of them directed the answer to everybody in the lobby.

The rectangles that were sewn into the shirts were made of loop-end velcro. After mentioning that, Pitch reached into his small green duffel bag and brought out another rectangular piece of cloth. "Art shirts!" he triumphantly exclaimed.

Bark muttered in response, "It was my idea. He's better at making clothes than I am."

Playfully ignoring Bark's self-praise, Pitch handed me the cloth. "See, that cloth is art canvas with hook-end velcro sewn into it. Now, you can illustrate on it and stick it to the back of the shirt for everyone to see!"

Bark added another important detail. "When you have to wash the shirt, you just peel the art off of it so it doesn't get ruined."

All of us reacted, very impressed by the creativity their shirts involved. Chloe was the first to ask them, "Are you selling those?"

Reflecting the true teamwork between them, Pitch answered, "We will, once the Revolution is over." He then shuffled quickly through his bag again and pulled out another art canvas backing.

Bark was smiling. "Oh, you guys are going to love this."

Before we let them continue, we checked on Kay. She was still working on the door, grunting and mumbling to herself.

I shrugged and turned back to the two excited young tailors.

Pitch unrolled his piece of canvas to show all of us a design he had created himself. It was a picture of an analog alarm clock with fifteen hours on it instead of twelve. A small toolbox overflowing with tools was illustrated next to it. At the bottom, below the symbolic artwork, "Time for a change!" was written.

Doctrine folded his arms in front of himself, nodding slowly. "We're fixing the Fifteen's clock. I like it!"

Pitch proudly presented his future plans. "When the Revolution ends, we're going to market this particular backing to the Causes who participated. I don't know what we'll charge though."

I couldn't wipe the smile from my face. "That is awesome. You two will do well selling these."

"You see," Bark replied, "this is why we're in on the Revolution. We don't want to be *assigned* our occupations. We want to stay a team and market these shirts."

"That's a good, strong, solid reason," Twilight Maiden commented.

"Thanks!"

She stood up and walked to us. "I only say that because that's not a far cry from my reason. I also want to market clothes."

Mika responded to Maiden with a sense of anticipation in her voice. "I would love to see more of the clothes that you made. If they look as pretty as what you have on right now, I would be at your store all the time!"

Twilight Maiden's face grew bright with the first smile anybody had seen on her that morning. "Why, thank you!" she beamed. "That is so sweet of you to say."

Mika addressed the seamstress as well as the two tailors. "Are the three of you together in a group?"

"No, she's not with us," Bark replied.

Mika followed up with a bold claim that served to put everyone in a good mood. "She should be."

Kay, not quite feeling the same way, called to the little miss from the office door. "Mika, what are you doing?"

The joyous expression on Maiden's face suddenly fell off at the sound of Kay's unnecessary question. "We were all about to ask you the same thing!" she snapped back.

Everyone in the lobby took notice that Kay had failed to open the office door. I chose to take her error and rub it in. "You're now two for two on failure to deliver after opening your big mouth, Kay!"

Chloe cut off her side conversation with Doctrine to add her share of words. "Does this girl really know what she's doing?"

Doctrine took his cloth ring backpack and opened one of the pockets. As he rummaged through it, he growled, "I knew she wouldn't get us in there."

"Give me a break!" she defended. "At least I'm trying something!"

Doctrine, now annoyed at her tone, pulled a large knife out of his bag and walked over to Kay with a menacing posture. He stood to her side and pushed the blade of the knife to block her view. He ordered her with a deep, grinding tone, "Move!"

Kay froze as she stared into her own eyes through the reflection of the blade. Seconds later, she slowly backed away.

Doctrine inserted the blade of the knife between the door and doorway. After jostling it and jiggling the doorknob for a few seconds, the door popped open.

Everyone began to slowly file into the room while Doctrine leered at Kay with a silent, scolding stare. Mika and I walked past them slowly, waiting for him to say something.

Chloe was the first to speak on the state of things. "I don't like the looks of this."

"That makes two of us," Pitch agreed.

The four of us turned our focus to the alert from inside Roy's office. Mika and I continued ahead, leaving Doctrine and Kay to themselves. It seemed he wanted to have a word with her in private.

I stepped into the office with Mika close behind. "What's up? What happened?"

Bark and Twilight Maiden were examining objects that were strewn about Roy's office. Roy was slumped forward with his head on the desk. He looked to be sleeping, as the expression on his face was rather relaxed.

Pitch surprised the room by stating what should have been obvious from the start. "This guy's dead."

Mika gasped and hid behind me.

In a soft, calm tone, I gave her some instructions. "Mika, go to the lobby with Doctrine and Kay. We'll take care of this."

"Okay," she nervously nodded.

"Actually," I thought again, "send them in here too. Also, lock the front door to the building and make sure nobody sees you do it." After ordering her, I took a deep breath in an attempt to calm myself.

Mika nodded, quickly scampering out of the office. Doctrine and Kay came in shortly after.

Kay walked up to the desk and carefully scrutinized the layout of objects on it. A moment later, she interrupted what little chatter there was by saying, "Bad Jayda…"

All of us turned to Kay, who had picked up a small bag from off of the desk. Inside the bag were small gray beads the size of peas. "Let me see that bag," Doctrine curiously requested.

Silent, she threw the bag to him.

He examined it, shaking it a bit before throwing it back to her. "Bad Jayda, you say?"

"Yes," Kay answered seriously. "This Jayda is way too aged to be safely taken." She dropped the bag back onto the desk.

Pitch shared his knowledge with the room. "Jayda is safe to get high off of only until its color starts turning to more of an olive green—or at least, that's what I've heard…"

"So he was getting high off of that," Chloe reiterated, pointing to the bag.

Slowly, I began to remember hearing of the Jayda plant before. People get hallucinogenic highs when the tiny bulbs from the plant are suckled on. Some people even use the leaves from the plant in baking and cooking for a bit of a trip to go with their dinner. Apparently, there was a lot to learn concerning the plant. I had had no previous knowledge it could have been lethal.

Kay explained a view. "I can understand that there are a lot of people who use Jayda. They prefer to use it when the bulbs are still ripe and flavorful. Once it starts changing color, though, the taste becomes bitter, slowly losing its sweetness. From there, the only people willing to take it are those who simply want to experience the euphoria."

Hearing Kay's words, I became hungry for more information from her. "You seem to know quite a bit about Jayda."

I suddenly felt that I had said something wrong as Kay became defensive. "Yeah, and my reasons for knowing are none of your damn business!" She paused, further examining Roy. "All you need to know is that this man is dead and it's that over-aged Jayda that did it to him."

Bark countered. "Shouldn't he have known that Jayda that color would kill him?"

Twilight Maiden shrugged. "Maybe he just didn't know."

Doctrine stepped in. "Look, it doesn't matter why he took it…" He turned his head to look at the body. "…anymore at least."

With a bit more volume, Kay replied, "How can you say something like that so casually?"

"Come on, let's be realistic here!" He shouted back. "We have a dead body that we have to figure out how to deal with. I don't know about you all, but I don't feel like getting shipped home—or to the Labor Fields, for that matter—because of this."

Everyone saw the point Doctrine had and most of us agreed with him. Kay however, had a look on her face that told me she still had something to say.

"So what do we do about it?" I asked, fearing an unsavory answer.

Appearing reluctant, Bark and Pitch hung their heads and left the room. I was guessing that the two of them were simply going to leave. Chloe and Twilight Maiden made their way toward the door as well. "It was nice meeting you," Chloe said quietly.

Doctrine, Kay and I were left alone with Roy's body. I had the horrible feeling that we were going to have to follow suit on leaving the body behind.

Mika stepped back into the room, trying to keep her sight away from the desk. "Are they going to get help?"

Doctrine hung his head. "No."

Mika's eyes widened. "Why not?"

He walked over to her and kneeled down, placing a hand on her shoulder. He looked into her eyes to emphasize the seriousness of the situation. "There's something you need to understand, Mika—we cannot afford to be accused of this."

"He's right," Kay sniffled. "It's hard to just leave him like this, but he's right."

I was slightly shocked and a little bit torn. I felt that wasn't fair to leave Roy's body behind like that. It was almost like disrespecting the dead. I was hoping for an alternative; but I knew one wouldn't come.

Doctrine stood back up and turned to the rest of us. "Leave the doors open. Make sure it will be easy for anyone to just walk right in and find him. As for us, we're escaping out the back."

"We're just going to leave him?" Kay objected. "Shouldn't we at least contact Morie to come collect the body?"

I was interested to hear Kay mention one of the members of the Fifteen: Morie. She is the member who is responsible for the collection and disposal of the dead. Kay had a point that a situation like this warranted summoning her.

Doctrine proceeded to the back exit, preparing to leave us behind if he felt he had to. "If getting Morie over here is your idea of a good plan, you can stay behind all you want. I'm out of here!"

I stepped close to Kay and made an attempt to hurry her along. "This isn't exactly easy for me either. Doctrine does have a point though. You know that if you call on Morie, you have to wait for her to arrive on the scene before you leave."

Kay sighed and nodded as an understanding Mika left to follow Doctrine. It seemed that Kay had a lot more to say about this and was keeping it to herself. She was looking over Roy's body one last time; shaking her head in fiery discontent. "Let's…just go," she muttered.

To somewhat make her feel at ease, I reminded her about how hard it felt for me to leave a body behind like that.

Inside, I began to get the feeling that there were some aspects of the Revolution that were only going to last for so long. If other Causes had to make choices the likes of what we had just done, it would be easy for personal beliefs to overtax the rules that were put in place by the Producers. Finding Roy dead like that was automatically a lose-lose situation for all of us. That was well indicated when the other Causes left us in haste.

Hopefully, Kay would realize that leaving was our best option. I knew I did.

III

It took Kay and me a couple of minutes to catch up to Doctrine and Mika. Once we were regrouped, we took our time and paced ourselves to a stroll. Everyone was quiet, though, still trying to absorb what had just happened.

Suddenly, Kay spoke up, "Today is Sunday, isn't it?"

I answered her before I knew for sure. "I believe it is."

She clapped once with a relieved grin. "Good! I want to go to the nearest chapel."

I gestured, knowing what she was getting at. She wanted to go to a chapel so she could pray and ask God for forgiveness. It sounded like a good idea since I also felt rather tainted by our actions.

Doctrine was the only one to push off the idea. I had to ask him, "What's the deal, Doctrine?"

He sounded rather annoyed. "Let me level with you. I'm more inclined to get out of the Pata Sector altogether. I've spent way too much time here and what just went on at the inn was the last straw."

"So, I take it you're not coming with us," Kay declared, stopping to turn to him.

He repeated his position with a strong pulse of conviction. "No, I'm not. I'm not really a chapel person either. I'll pray wherever I want. I don't need a chapel to do it in."

"Come on, it's Sunday!" Kay insisted while grabbing his hand. "Just come with us to the chapel. After that, you can do whatever you want. It's not like we're asking for your firstborn child."

Kay's reasoning got Doctrine to calm down a bit. Regardless, he stood by his motives and refused attendance. "I'd much rather just get out of here before the next train departs." He gingerly retracted his hand from out of Kay's grasp.

Mika asked him, "You're really leaving, just like that?" She sounded disappointed; as if she had been expecting him to stay.

He smiled to her the way a big brother would. "Don't take it personally, Mika. If there is any one person in your group that bothers me…"

"Say no more," I interrupted him.

Kay caught on and objected. "Hey!"

Mika presented her hand to Doctrine. "It was nice meeting you, Mr. Doctrine! Thanks for helping us out."

He shook her hand and ruffled her hair a bit. "You take care, too, Mika. Despite what the two of them think of each other, you've got good help there. They'll find your father in no time."

Mika smiled back to him the way a little sister would. "Thanks!"

Doctrine turned and addressed me again. "I've got to hand it to you though; you guys are a lot better than some of the other Causes I've been meeting lately. Sometimes I just want to choke some of these guys."

"I know what you mean!" Kay chimed in as she glared in my direction.

"Yeah," he smirked, "you came close." He took a beat as Kay's brow furrowed. "Kidding, kidding!"

"Violence is forbidden for Causes anyway, remember?" I stuck my tongue out.

My addition actually elicited a chuckle from him. "Whatever, you goof."

I saw no possibility of him changing his mind. I accepted it for what it was and bid him farewell. "Travel safe, alright?"

He replied in kind. "You be safe too. Just be careful in your search."

With that, Doctrine left us. It was a bit hard to see him go; especially since we always got along so well on the forums. I was hoping I would see him again.

As I watched him disappear into the street, Mika tugged my shirt. "Are we still going to the chapel?"

"Yes," I answered, looking to her. "Let's get going."

IV

Remembering our escapades from the previous night, we managed to backtrack to a nearby chapel without much trouble.

People in Eden gather at chapels on Sunday to pray to God and ask forgiveness for their sins. Mika, Kay, and I felt it was wrong to leave Roy's body behind at the inn, so saying a prayer at the chapel seemed appropriate for us.

The other good thing about chapels is that they are sanctuaries from the outside. We'd temporarily be free from the view of the public eye. We had to take into account that even though many of Eden's citizens were indifferent to the actions of the Causes, there were still quite a few who strictly opposed us. Seeking solace in the chapel was a good way to keep away from those types, if only for a few moments.

The three of us entered into a moderately spacious and modestly decorated room. An elaborate carpet sprawled up the center of an otherwise hardwood floor. The fluid repeating patterns of beige, maroon, and mauve led directly from the entrance to the altar on the other end of the chapel. To each of the path's sides were four rows of stained-wood pews, followed by two rows of kneeling stands. Stained-glass windows bearing images of God's attendants, the Angels, illuminated the room with help from the Sunday morning sun. The only thing interrupting the scene of serenity was the sight of the chapel attendant lighting chandelier candles as he squirmed to keep his balance on a rather aged ladder.

The three of us proceeded at our leisure toward the altar. My head turned repeatedly as I soaked up the calming, righteous atmosphere the chapel was giving off. My appreciation for the interior grandeur of the building was summarized by a simple whisper. "Wow."

Kay was impressed too. "For being in the Pata Sector, this chapel looks really nice."

"You said it," Mika quickly agreed.

Once at the altar, we prepared to perform a Repentance Rite to have our sins forgiven.

The Repentance Rite is an ancient method of prayer that is specifically used to ask God's forgiveness for sins beyond your average white lies or harsh behavior. It is performed at the individual's discretion upon larger trespasses such as breaching one of God's Ten Commandments or other mortal sins and immoralities. It went without saying that using a Repentance Rite for leaving Roy's body behind may have been a little much. As I said, though, they are performed at the individual's discretion. Having known some people who used the Rite for everything made me feel a bit more at ease about it.

We kneeled at the altar and readied ourselves to perform the Rite. The altar consists of ten candles in a semicircle with a kneeling stand in front of each. At the center of the altar is a black candle that represents all of the sins of the people of Eden. When performing the Rite, you choose a kneeling stand to pray at and use the black candle in the middle of the altar to light the candle in front of the stand. This is supposed to represent placing your portion of Eden's sins between you and God, presenting them to Him and asking His forgiveness for them. After your prayer, you snuff the candle, which represents your sins being forgiven and essentially erased from His judgment.

Kay, Mika, and I took our time and performed the Rite; asking God to forgive what we felt was a great transgression. To me, this felt a bit more reassuring. While it wasn't going to bring Roy back to life, it helped me feel less guilty about not doing anything about it. After all, we were all innocent in relation to the incident in the first place.

Upon snuffing the candle and standing to my feet, I sighed, rather relieved. I looked to Kay and Mika and they looked to me with sheepish smiles. Without saying a word, we knew we had done the right thing by at least coming to the chapel that morning.

Just as we stepped off the altar, a voice spoke to us from halfway down the chapel. "You guys too, huh?"

We all looked forward to see the four Causes we met at the inn that morning: Chloe, Bark, Pitch, and Twilight Maiden. They had come to the chapel as well. "Hello again!" I casually greeted.

Bark dropped a question to the three of us. "Feel better?"

I answered in a plosive exhalation, "Oh, you have no idea."

Chloe sighed. "That's good to hear. We're here to do the Rite also."

I took two steps toward the closest pew and sat on the armrest. "I figured we weren't alone on thoughts of wrongdoing."

Pitch looked us over again. "Not all four of you felt the same, apparently. Where's the other guy that was with you?"

"Actually," Kay cut in, "Doctrine split from us soon after we left the inn."

"He didn't want to come here?"

"Apparently not," I regretfully replied.

Mika spoke up, changing the subject. "The four of you are a group now?"

Twilight Maiden dignified the little girl's question with a mature, sisterly countenance. "Yes we are, Mika. It's all thanks to what you said to us back at the inn."

"Yeah," Bark agreed. "It made perfect sense to have two tailors, a seamstress, and an artist on the same team. We can learn a lot from each other as we wait for Hatcher to unite with the other Producers."

His words caught my attention to the subject. "Ah, so you all heard about that?"

Chloe clarified the chronology of how the news traveled. "I was actually the only one of the four of us who knew as of this morning. The Contact told me that the newsflash was posted while the previous group was making their posts. I suppose you three were part of the group she mentioned."

I nodded. "Yeah, that was us."

Kay, Chloe, and Twilight Maiden swept themselves into a conversation about the Producers and Hatcher. As I sat back and listened intently, I saw Pitch out of the corner of my eye. He leaned in to whisper to Mika.

I tried to focus my hearing to eavesdrop since the look on Mika's face slowly grew more cheerful. She covered her mouth and giggled. "You're welcome."

After Pitch stepped away from Mika, I gestured for her to come to me. I spoke quietly so as not to speak louder than the more important conversation in the room. "What did he just say to you?"

Mika turned from me and looked over to Pitch. To me, it seemed as if she was asking his permission to answer my question without actually saying anything to him. I glanced over to Pitch just as he gestured to Mika with a shrug and a brush of the hand.

The little miss smiled wide and turned to address me again. She cupped her hand over my ear and whispered. "He said, 'Thanks for telling the pretty girls to travel with us'."

"That's really cute," I whispered back. "What's even funnier is that it wasn't even your intention for that to happen."

"I know. It surprised me."

Unexpectedly, I had a thought completely unrelated to anything being spoken of in the chapel. Regardless of its lack of relevance, it was still more important to us than anything that was going on or being said.

I made a request at a normal speaking volume. "Now that I think about it, Mika, can you hand me that picture? We can at least ask these guys if they have seen your father."

Kay, having overheard me, turned her head to us. "That's right!"

Mika took the piece of canvas from her bag and stepped over to hand it to Twilight Maiden. The other three peered over her shoulder as I asked them, "Have you seen this man before?"

They examined the drawing closely, occasionally looking to each other with shaking heads and puzzled looks. At their own individual times, they gave a negative reply.

After a moment, Bark asked Mika, "Did you draw this?"

Mika sheepishly bobbed her head. "Yes. That man is my father."

Mumbling among the four of them ensued. It seemed that they were really looking to find a way to help Mika.

Pitch was the first to say anything concerning the picture. "These erase marks around his face don't really help much…"

Chloe apologized. "I don't think we'll be able to help you."

"That's all right…" Mika groaned, taking the picture back.

Bark extended his hand one last time. "I'd hate to cut this short. If you'll excuse us though, we have a Repentance Rite to perform. We want to get out of this sector as quickly as we can after what happened back at Roy's inn."

Pitch patted Mika on the top of her head. "Good luck in your search!"

"Alright," she peeped, grinning to him.

Kay, Mika and I took turns shaking their hands and declaring a pleasure in meeting them all. While I was a bit upset at having no real lead in our search, I took into account that they were the first people we had asked. Hopefully, there would be more Causes who would have more information for us to work with.

We left the chapel, head-on into our search.

V

Several hours of searching efforts passed rather quickly. The activity occupied us until well into the evening.

Without actually keeping count, we safely assumed to have had tracked down around thirty-five other Causes. Despite the number of people we asked, every one of them delivered the same negative response to the picture with a sincere apology to go with it.

Though a fruitless day for our purpose, it was a good time to grow accustomed to traveling in a group. It seemed important to try to bond since one person among our ranks was still somewhat unwanted.

Once the sun fully set, we felt it was time to begin looking for another inn to stay at. I regretted not having asked any Causes where they were taking up shelter that day. I suppose that is a testament to the priority of Mika's mission to me.

It soon got to a point where we were all getting tired. Thus, any inn would do, whether or not it was one that was assisting Causes. In that case, though, we would consider ourselves lucky to encounter a Contact as well.

A ways into our search for a good place to rest, Kay pointed to somebody who appeared to be a Cause. He was walking into a nearby inn with a content, relaxed expression emanating from his drowsy-looking eyes. Though the unusually high collar of his sleeveless green shirt covered his mouth, we could feel his merriment without having to see a smile. "Somebody's looking forward to a good night's rest," Mika said with a snicker.

"Yes, we are!" I exhaled.

Kay commented with a humorous observation. "He doesn't need to sleep. That bed-head he's sporting makes it look like he just woke up. He should be wearing a hat to cover that mess, not a visor."

I rolled my eyes with a chuckle as we proceeded with an increased pace toward the billowing white awning that sheltered the front of the building. Just as we stepped onto the property, the same young man came running out of the entrance, dashing in our direction. A worried and frantic look overtook his previously cheerful disposition.

We could hear a man shouting from inside the inn. "Go back home if you want to sleep somewhere!"

The youth began to look behind himself as he continued running. He clearly did not realize that he was going to run into us.

I pushed myself a bit forward and braced myself for an impact, lining my hands up to catch his shoulders as he ran at full speed into me. As his body met my hands, Kay assisted in holding him still so neither of us was to fall over.

As the young man continued his hurried actions, I asked him, "The book?"

He calmed himself a bit, but still seemed inclined to get as far away from the inn as possible. "Yes, the book," he replied, still walking away.

I cut to the chase. "I'm to understand they don't want us in there."

He stopped, adjusted his glasses, turned to me and said, "All of the inns are being like this."

"All of them?" Kay asked, leaning her head forward.

He signaled to us to keep moving. "Yes, all of them are. This is as opposed to yesterday, when a good amount of inns were accepting Causes."

"What happened?" I wondered.

"Well," he paused and sighed, "rumor has it that a group of Causes poisoned an innkeeper with bad Jayda bulbs."

I could feel the wave of shock sweep over the three of us. I tried to remain calm as if none of us knew anything specific. "Really?"

"Yes, come," he instructed, swooping his arm in a leading manner. "I know a cafe we can sit at. I'll tell you the story."

Even though we had a rough idea of what really happened, we couldn't blurt it out and risk looking suspicious. Any given Cause would be jumping at the chance to have the real story. We chose to play it safe and began to follow him to the cafe.

As he led us along, I initiated the usual string of introductions. "By the way, I'm Dartmouth. Brigg is my username."

"I'm Susan; Kay is mine."

"I'm Mika."

The young stranger stopped in his tracks; following a short

beat with an unexpectedly haughty scoff. "So you're Brigg, huh; paired up with Kay, of all people…"

I just sighed at the now-familiar irony. "Yeah, we've been getting that a lot today."

Still facing forward, he threw his hands up in a wide, exaggerated shrug. "Perhaps you'll recognize *my* name." He stopped and turned to meet my eyes with a cold gaze. "Call me 'Dice'."

The name hit me like a sack of five-Arna coins. I didn't have to say a word back to him since the two of us were acquainted enough from our interactions on the forums.

At that moment, I was truly engrossed in the misfortune of encountering yet another Cause I did not get along with on the forums. In this young man's case, most of the time I would deliberately bump heads with him and at times insult his reasoning. The two of us were the true opposite of friendly.

Kay knew of the shoddy relationship between the two of us as well. "See, this is why you don't insult people on the forums!" she scolded.

"You're one to talk!" Dice and I replied simultaneously. We then looked to each other, slightly surprised at our mutual ire.

I could tell that Dice was a lot less inclined to fill us in on what he knew. Although we were there when the incident occurred, there may have been some inkling of information that we hadn't heard. I was going to try and gain his trust for the time being. However, if he wasn't going to cooperate, I wasn't going to sweat it.

After a long and awkward pause, Mika felt the need to ask, "So, what *do* you know?"

He turned to get a good look at Mika, lifting his brow with a slightly intrigued countenance. He then reached into the lower left pocket of his black cargo shorts.

Upon pulling his hand out, he produced three black dice with white dots. "I don't call myself 'Dice' for nothing," he vainly remarked.

"What the heck is he doing?" I thought to myself. "Is this for real?"

He rattled the dice a bit before throwing them to the side of the building next to us. "Odd," he called, guessing the outcome.

Mika tapped me on the shoulder and whispered in my ear. "Weird…"

"You're telling me."

We followed and examined the dice. The results were one, four and five.

Dice huffed, nodding his head. Seeming bothered by it, he picked up his dice and put them back in his pocket. "They came up even, so I'll be good for now. Let's just go." He sounded mildly annoyed at his self-inflicted defeat.

VI

It was a short two blocks to a welcoming table at Vivian's Outdoor Café. We took our seats, Kay to my left and Mika to my right. Dice sat at the opposite end of the table from me. His interest still appeared to be fixated on Mika.

After placing an order for beverages, Dice got down to business. "As I was saying, police found an innkeeper dead in his office around noontime. The news was on transistor broadcast within the hour. Since then, it has been quite the news item of the day."

Kay reacted. "Transistor broadcast?" She then turned to me. "I guess that's why all of the other inn owners know of it."

"Yes, that is true. To make matters worse for us though," Dice continued, "guess who made the broadcast…"

We had a feeling that Dice was going to name somebody of significance—a member of the Fifteen. With a news item like this, transistor broadcasts could be interrupted on all three channels by the man he was about to name.

"Humph," he grunted, "Figured you'd know it was Naro. I'll give you the benefit of the doubt and assume that you just forgot his name for a brief moment." The way he phrased it sounded like a shot at my intelligence—which I'm never fond of.

"I know who Naro is!" I growled.

"Don't let him get to you, Brigg. We don't want to make a scene," Mika advised, coaxing me to calm down. As she finished her sentence, our beverages arrived.

Kay waited for the waitress to leave before grabbing the conversation's reins. "So you're saying that the Fifteen are using this incident to put some heat on us?"

"Well," he said, exhaling, "I heard a repeat of the broadcast on Channel Two. Naro directly blamed a group of unidentified 'Revolutionaries'." He made quotation marks with his fingers. "What I'm getting at here is that this could be an incident completely unrelated to the Causes as a whole…"

Mika chimed in, appearing to finish what Dice was saying, "…but they're using it to make people hate Causes and be afraid…"

Dice slapped his hand on the table, glaring at Mika with extreme vexation. He condemned her with cold anger. "*Never* finish my sentences."

With an expression of deep apology, Mika fearfully folded her hands in her lap. It appeared she was not willing to say much more after being intimidated by Dice's grating words and piercing gaze. Her face glowed with the slight red of embarrassment.

I stepped in to defend her. "That wasn't necessary!"

Mika shook her head and addressed me. "Don't worry, I'll just keep quiet."

It began to feel like I was on the forums again. The goal of defending new faces from Dice's harsh communication skills was surfacing for me once again. "No, you have a right to speak up when you please. You don't need to be afraid of him."

Kay interrupted the tangent. "Can we stay on topic here?"

Dice chuckled, tilting his head forward to his straw. "For once, I actually agree with you, Kay." He sipped his drink.

I folded my arms in front of me and sat back in my chair with the same indignant posture I would model for my siblings. "You can keep talking. I'm listening."

"Good. It's hard to absorb information when you're flapping your jaw anyway."

I chose to appear unaffected by his increasingly irritating behavior. At the same time though, I was beginning to wonder why I was even subjecting myself to this treatment. A lot of me just wanted to reach across the table and punch his lights out. Only for the sake of obtaining the unknown details did I decide to give him one more chance for the duration of the conversation.

"Actually…" he trailed off, pulling his dice out of his pocket.

I sighed with a grunt, "This again…"

He began to shake the dice as a glazed expression of thought came to his eyes. "Eight or less to continue," he predicted, throwing the three dice onto the table.

The results were five, four and two.

"You failed again," I announced.

He raised his voice in a vicious sneer as he picked up his dice. "Why don't you try listening next time? In case you didn't understand, this conversation is over." He stood up and dropped two Arna on the table for his drink.

His wager repeated in my head, helping me notice that he was right. That fact alone brought me into a fit of anger. "What? You're just leaving like that?"

Kay sat forward in her chair. "You can't do that!" she protested.

"Apparently I can." he jeered.

I argued his change of face as well. "The odds of rolling eight or less on three dice are uneven anyway!"

Dice had his explanation at the ready. "I suppose that should tell you how much I was inclined to continue." He picked up his backpack and began to walk away.

As our attention was fixed on him, we didn't take notice to who was standing in his way as he turned. Before Dice even took five steps away from us, he was stopped short by a Pata Police Guard Officer.

Upon realizing who had approached us, it felt like time had stopped. I checked our surroundings to notice two more Pata Officers to our left. We were surrounded.

My heart sank into my stomach to meet what little of my beverage I had imbibed. As the first officer backed Dice back into his chair, I could picture the four of us being taken away in restraints.

A worse thought coursed through my brain. I wondered what would happen to Mika if the police found out she was not with the Causes in the first place.

My first instinct was to shout for everyone to split up and run. However, seeing as how slowly and casually the officers approached us, I figured it best to hesitate and listen before acting.

The officer that stopped Dice addressed the four of us as a group. "We are under the impression that the four of you are

Revolutionaries. Am I right?"

It took a moment for me to remember that the general public still referred to the Causes as "Revolutionaries". This was a vital detail to commit to memory while the encounter with the police unfolded. It would be an unspeakable blunder to inadvertently reveal the name "Cause" to the police.

Kay, Mika, and even Dice looked at me as if they wanted me to suddenly be the group representative. I felt slightly uplifted to see the panicked expression on Dice's face once again. I knew that before I could bust his chops about it though, it would be best to just answer the officer's questions.

My thoughts were well with me to the point where the officer lost patience and asked me directly, "Are you the leader of this group, young man?"

I took a deep breath and exhaled to calm myself. "Yes," I answered with a quiver.

I looked to the other three, trying to muster a confident façade. I signaled with my hands for everyone to stay put for the time being. Our group had to come off as orderly and mature as possible. Maybe, just maybe, we would have a chance to escape if the time seemed appropriate.

The officer looked to his partners and nodded. He came back to us saying, "I'm Officer Ryan of the Pata Sector Police Force. Before we continue, I'd just like to fill you in on what's going on."

I asked him, "Is this about the mysterious poisoning of that innkeeper?"

"Yes, it is," he replied, seeming startled that I knew. "Seeing as you seem to know about it, we'd like to ask for your cooperation. We've been instructed by Vade to round up Revolutionaries and bring them to the Gateway Inn for questioning."

The name of another member of the Fifteen had presented itself. "Vade…" I nervously repeated.

Ryan made an attempt to calm us. "Since you are Revolutionaries, we're aware that her name is probably the last one you want to hear."

Dice cracked another comment. "We're not particularly fond of the term 'Labor Fields' either!"

Ryan laughed at Dice's wit before concluding the announcement of his mission. "Trust me, we are only trying to get to the bottom of this. Once we find the murderer among your allies, you are free to go. We're not here for anything else but the culprit."

I inquired for more details. "Why do you specifically need to find Revolutionaries?"

"Were you listening to anything I said?" Dice bitterly interrupted. "I told you: Naro placed the blame on us. Thus, the police are going to seek _us_ out for questioning."

"The young man is right," Ryan agreed. "The fact that it was likely to have been done by a Revolutionary is the only reason we're bringing you in. You'll be assigned a room for the night and will be questioned. Once we're done with you, you'll be free to go in the morning."

"So," Kay mumbled, "you just need us to cooperate and answer questions?"

Ryan nodded. "Correct, miss."

"Well, guys," I announced, "these _are_ police and they are asking for help. They're also giving us a pardon in exchange for cooperating. We can't lose here."

Dice rolled his eyes. "Say it out loud, why don't you!"

"Well," the officer spoke, "that is the reaction we've been getting all night from the ones we already have at the Gateway."

There was justified hesitation in our decision to assist the police. It appeared that Naro's influence on the public had quickly taken effect toward the Causes. We were being rounded up like Terra Sector livestock and confined to the Gateway Inn.

Not a single thing about this situation seemed proper. To me, personally, this was obviously some sort of trap set up by Vade. It would not have surprised me if other members of the Fifteen were in on the setup too.

Our arrival at the Gateway Inn was greeted with nervous smiles and desperate gazes from other Causes involved in the police search. It seemed that they also sensed the bearings of a trap. Now knowing that it wasn't just me feeling uneasy made the sensation that much worse.

Including the four of us, the police had managed to wrangle in a sizeable audience of Causes—although comparing that to the 13,000 of us made me wonder if this was the amount that somebody like Naro or Vade would have had in mind.

To me, there were a lot of questions about this. The less I knew, the harder it was going to be to improvise. Ultimately, I only made myself frustrated and frightened. Not only that, I had brought two of my fellow Causes with me, along with a young girl who had nothing to do with the Causes in the first place. Thus, guilt was slowly seeping into the emotional mix.

Kay whispered to me, breaking my concentration. "Remember, we use our real names here. Got that, Dartmouth?"

"Sure thing, Susan," I whispered back.

Since we knew Mika wasn't using an alias, the two of us turned to Dice. He gave us a cold, uninterested gaze as he declared his name, "Charles." He then turned away from us and began to separate from the group.

"Where are you going?" I asked.

"I'm going to go eavesdrop on the officers to see what they know about this whole thing. I'll keep my ears open for any other names of the Fifteen."

"You think this is a trap too?" Mika asked him.

He turned back to look her in the eye. He pushed his glasses up the bridge of his nose as he sharply spoke. "You would have to be stupid to not think this is a trap."

Kay placed a comment into the conversation. "The names 'Haz' and 'Dallas' come to mind in a situation like this."

Dice agreed. "Haz, Dallas, Vade—it doesn't matter. Any one of them can slap you in the Labor Fields so quickly your head would spin. However, it wouldn't surprise me if Naro showed up. He seems to be the one who started this whole thing with his broadcast."

"We should leave here the moment the police are finished with us," I announced.

"Definitely," Dice agreed. "I'm going to see what I can find out."

"Go for it." We dismissed him.

An officer took position in front of the crowded foyer and began announcing the layout of the questioning procedure. They were going to have three Causes to a room. Once settled in, the police would fingerprint and question the Causes in each room as a group as well as individually.

This was obviously going to complicate things since we had a group of four. Topping it off was the fact that three of the four of us knew what really went on concerning the murder of the innkeeper. I was going to make the executive decision to separate Dice from Mika, Kay, and myself.

Before I could begin explaining my plan, the police began creating the groups of three for us. It was obvious that they were deliberately choosing Causes at random and pairing them all up. Anybody who was traveling in a party appeared to go into a low-key panic.

Kay nudged my shoulder. "What do we do?" she asked with urgency.

I made a split-second decision that would keep us out of trouble in case we were to get separated. "Just tell them the truth."

She quickly shook her head with a sense of disbelief. "What?"

I turned to Mika. "You got that?"

Mika reluctantly complied.

I looked at Kay, having quickly thought of a reason for my recommendation to tell the truth. "Your fingerprints are on the evidence, Kay."

Surely, she remembered also. Her eyes widened upon her realization. Kay had to tell the truth to justify her fingerprints being on the key piece of evidence.

"You," an officer called, addressing Mika, "little girl!"

Mika looked at him and pointed to herself. "Me?"

"Yes, come over here."

Mika nervously looked at us for a moment before bidding us good night.

Kay and I fearfully watched Mika make her way over to the officer. However, I breathed a sigh of relief when I noticed that she had been selected to be paired with Dice and another girl.

I exhaled and relaxed. "I guess they thought Dice wasn't with us since he was across the room."

"It would appear so," Kay replied.

Within moments, the two were out of sight. "I guess this leaves you and me with someone else here." I was confident that the situation would remain in our favor.

Kay groaned as she looked over the crowd in the lobby. "I wouldn't be too sure. The police are splitting up all of the groups."

Before I realized that was the case, a tall, bulky officer called to me. "You, sir!"

A second later, a female officer called to Kay. "You ma'am!" Suddenly pulsing with fear, the two of us stepped away from each other and over to the officers.

I hesitated for a moment, looking only once to see Kay's desperate, frightened eyes gazing back at into mine before the two of us slipped out of each other's sight.

VII

The policeman gave a stern order to me as he led me up to room 3-12. "Wait here. We'll return later when we're ready to question you." I quivered as I watched the officer close the door behind him as he left.

After that, I just continued to stare at the door, concerned about the others. It worried me even more that I still didn't trust Kay to tell the truth to the police.

I then began wondering why I was concerned with Kay—or Dice for that matter. The two of them had done nothing for me but add grief and hostility to my otherwise enjoyable travels. If I was truly anxious about anyone, it was Mika. If she were to be captured and sent home, who would be there to greet her? Her father was still missing and I wasn't sure if her mother, whom she never mentioned, would be there either.

As the other two Causes made small talk with each other, I was considering my options. I was still under the suspicion that this was all a setup staged by Vade and Naro. It would only be a matter of time before a form of retreat would be necessary.

Even though it would serve to complicate escape, I knew in my heart that I wasn't leaving without Mika. Getting her roped into this crisis was my responsibility, and I refused to let her wind up in anyone else's hands before reuniting her with her father.

Suddenly, the other young man in the room broke my train of thought. "Thinking about Kay and Mika, right?"

I could only exhale in frustration.

It took me a few seconds to realize exactly what had just been said to me. I began to turn around, asking, "How did you know about…?" Finally getting a glance at the gentleman, I realized that

I had just been roomed together with Doctrine. It was a much-needed pleasant surprise. "Sydney! How are you still in the Pata Sector?"

He approached me, extending his hand for a shake. "I got sidetracked on my way out. Before I knew it, hours had passed on me. I went to get onto the train and sure enough, the police were right there. They told me what was going on and I agreed to cooperate."

I folded my arms and gave him a wry grin. "This is coming from the same guy that said, 'We can't afford to be accused of this'."

He protested my remark. "Lay off! I know just about as much about this as you do."

"Pretty much..." He had a point.

The girl who was paired with us in the room interjected. "Wait a minute! Are you two saying that you know something about the innkeeper's murder?"

I tried to change the subject as I uneasily greeted her. "Hi there! Sorry about that. You know, with all of this going on, it's easy to forget such mannerisms as introductions and all."

Doctrine chuckled. "Nice recovery there, Dartmouth."

"So it's Dartmouth and Sydney, eh? I'm Zoe." She lowered to a whisper, "'Month of May' is my name on the forums. Mostly everyone shortens it to 'May'."

We quickly exchanged our forum monikers. I didn't know of her, but she knew of me. I reiterate, for somebody as outspoken on the forums as I was, that still remained no surprise to me.

After the introductions, her topics of priority went right back on track. We began to explain to her what we knew about the whole situation. Most importantly, we let her know that we had nothing to do with the plot. We just so happened to be at that particular inn when the whole thing went down.

The conversation teetered into discussing recent goings-on. The three of us eventually touched base with the subject of Hatcher. Zoe shared all of the information she was able to discern from her Contact visit from earlier that day. As of that time, there was still no sign of him. The Producers declared they could only wait for him for so long. Regardless though, many Causes still felt confident Hatcher would show up.

Our talking was cut short by a knock at our door. It was now time for the police to focus their interrogation on our group.

They asked to see Zoe first. She cooperated and followed the officer. After they were out of sight, I said to Doctrine, "Looks like we're next, huh?"

He just nodded, not saying anything.

Suddenly, the air in the room felt heavy. Doctrine's mix of slight actions and awkward silence caused my heart to shudder in my chest. Something had quickly begun to feel off-kilter.

I thought a moment as I tried to relax myself by sitting on the bed. "What do you plan on saying to them?" I asked Doctrine.

He didn't look at me as he gave his answer in a dark and serious tone. "Do you plan on telling them the truth?"

My eyes involuntarily darted to the right as I spit out a quick reply. "Yes."

He laughed. "That's just like you."

"What do you mean?" From the sound of his voice, it almost felt like he was going to march up to the police and accuse me.

He breathed a few deep breaths. "Look, Dartmouth...Brigg...buddy..." He turned and rigidly ambled over to me; putting his hands on my shoulders.

The silence that ensued was long and disturbing. I stammered a bit before telling him, "If you're going to say something, you'd better say it now before the police come back."

His hands gripped my shoulders a bit more firmly as they began to shake. "I don't know how I'm supposed to say this...but..."

"But...?"

His hands released their grip, now simply resting on my shoulders. He then succinctly muttered, "You need to run."

I had to hear it again to believe it. "What did you say?"

"You," he then added, "and anybody you have with you, need to run."

I got a chill. "I...don't get it."

Doctrine explained in an ominous manner. "It should have been obvious from the start that this whole thing was a trap. We were all able to see that Naro is capitalizing on a tragedy to put us all in a bad light. That being said, I know something the other Causes at this inn do not."

I feared to ask. "What's that?"

"While everyone here *thinks* the Fifteen will show up tonight…" he took a deep breath before continuing, "…I *know* they'll be here, horse coaches and all."

I shook my head, unable to believe what I was hearing. "You're not making any sense. How do you '*know*'?"

"I…" He couldn't answer.

I thrust myself away from him, letting his hands drop to his side. I then placed mine to his shoulders and gave him a shake. "Tell me how you know!"

Doctrine seemed stiff and slightly panicked. "I…I…heard the officers talking. Vade, Haz, Naro, Biktor and a small troupe of police will be here with a caravan of horse-coaches to arrest us all and take us away. They plan to strike while we're asleep in the free rooms here they used as bait."

Either Doctrine wasn't telling me everything he knew, or he really was as on edge as he seemed. Most baffling for me was why he hadn't informed everybody of the details he knew of concerning the trap. Mildly frantic, I asked him, "Why are you telling just me? Why didn't you tell everyone this?"

Doctrine swatted my hands off of him and took a couple of paces away from me. "Haven't you heard enough to believe me? Just do as I say and get out of here."

I felt he didn't understand my question. "Yes, I heard that part! I'll ask you again: Why only me?"

Before he could answer, the officer returned with Zoe. Without hesitation, he asked Sydney to be next.

Looking back to me as he followed the policeman, Sydney hung his head and shook it slowly. Just before the door shut, he poked his head back in one last time. The last words he spoke before he left rang in my head for several moments after he was out of the room: "In case there are any regrets."

Zoe looked at me with puzzlement spoken loudly in her expression. "What is that supposed to mean?"

I could only shake my head. "I honestly don't know."

I took the next few minutes to explain to Zoe the information relayed to me by Doctrine. It had turned out that Zoe, too, had plans to escape before the Fifteen were to get too close to the Gateway. She was planning on skipping out soon seeing as her role in the interrogation was done. "Hopefully, I'll be able to get out of here without being seen. Either that, or I'll tell them I'm going out for a bite to eat."

Her suggestion lightened the mood a little. "That actually sounds like it could work. Go out for dinner and just don't come back."

"That's the idea," she smiled.

I was suddenly struck with the feeling of doing my part in the investigation. In all of the commotion with Sydney, I had almost forgotten why we were there in the first place. I expressed my thoughts on the matter to Zoe. "Actually, would it bother you to wait until Sydney comes back? I'd also like to tell the police what I know. Once I come back from my questioning, we'll all go for it."

"Well, didn't he mention you having two other people?" she wondered.

That really got me to think. Before I did anything, it was imperative that I find Mika. Considering the way Dice and Kay had been behaving, I felt it worth my while to try and lose them. However, with Dice having been assigned to the same room as Mika, leaving him behind would be difficult if for some reason he felt the need to tag along. The memory of his brow rising at the sight of her replayed in my head for a brief moment, fueling the idea that he may want to know more about her or why she was with me.

"You're right," I confirmed before changing my attitude. "If anything, I need to find one of them and ditch the other two."

Zoe gasped, finding my remark surprising and unfair. She began to scold me as she sat down next to me on the bed. "Now why would you want to do that?"

My brow fell flat as my eyes cast an apathetic glance into hers. "Are the names 'Kay' and 'Dice' familiar to you?"

She pondered it for a few brief seconds before her look of thought was replaced with one of confusion. "What are you doing traveling with _them_?"

I threw my hands up in an exaggerated shrug. "I've been getting that all day!"

Zoe stood and took one, long, striding step toward her backpack as she reached her arm out to grab it. She sat back down and placed her bag between us. Her questions continued. "Who is it you want to keep with you? I heard Sydney say the name, but it seems to have slipped my mind."

"Let's just say it's someone who I can actually get along with." I decided to spare her the finer details of Mika since I still wasn't sure how knowledge of her situation should have been handled.

The two of us continued with tales of our personal exploits. She was impressed by the fact that I had spent an entire week in the Gova Sector. The curious young woman had been wondering if hiding out there was worth the risk of being distanced from society. I assured her that as long as she didn't wander too far from the train as I had, she would manage just fine.

We carried on about nothing in particular as we waited for Doctrine to come back to the room.

Fifteen minutes passed.

Ten more minutes passed.

After ten more, we began to worry.

Our fear was met with a reason when thundering footsteps began sounding up and down the hallway. It quickly got our attention, springing us to our feet and thrusting us into a scramble. Before I had my bearings together, the shrill voice of a panicked Cause rang throughout the building. *"THE FIFTEEN ARE HERE! EVERYBODY RUN!"*

Zoe and I quickly realized that we should have made a break for it when we had the chance. I felt guilty for keeping Zoe in the room, essentially preventing her from escaping the trap before it sprung. "Damn it, I should have let you go it alone instead of waiting."

She was halfway to the door, speaking to me as she exited. "Well, if I'm quick enough, I can get away. In that case, it won't be a big deal. See you around…maybe."

Out of the open door, I saw several Causes running for the nearest exit. That was the true indicator that it was not a joke or a false alarm. The Fifteen had arrived.

I stuck my head out into the hallway before stepping out into it. Within seconds, I caught sight of Mika running in the opposite direction. Cupping my hands over my mouth, I called to her as loud as I could. *"Mika!"*

Mika managed to hear me over the commotion. She turned to me and began to run. "Brigg! They're here!"

I reached out to her and took her by the hand. "Where were you going?" I asked her as we began to follow the others to the emergency exit.

The little miss was in a big hurry; pulling my arm as an insistence to follow her. "I was going back for Dice."

I had no interest in retrieving that stuck-up jerk. I tried to lead Mika toward the exit. "Don't worry about him. He can take care of himself."

The determined little girl objected, "That's not what *he* was telling me!"

Hearing her say that prompted me to stop tugging for a moment and look to her. "What is that supposed to mean?"

Mika used the same logic she presented to me the previous day. "I think Dice needs to have someone to travel with too!"

I met her argument with a sound solution. "If that's the case, then he can find company with somebody else!"."

Looking into Mika's suddenly sullen eyes, it was obvious that my reply was not what she had had in mind. "Okay," she reluctantly whimpered.

I led her by the hand and began to speed up our pace as a few more Causes passed us. Stopping in the hall had cost us precious seconds—seconds that spelled the difference between escape and capture.

Suddenly, a large crowd started to spew back from the exit to the stairs. A deep, grainy voice called out, "They're guarding the emergency exit! We've lost a few!"

An uproar ensued. "We're stuck!"

"What are we going to do!?"

"See? I told you this was a trap!"

Mika's grip on my hand loosened. It was plain to see that she had easily lost hope.

The clamoring crowd of Causes now cluttering the hallway had become frenzied. A voice from the end of the hall interrupted the havoc. "We've got two of them coming up the stairs. We have to turn back around."

I saw this as a chance to speak up. "Two of what?"

The youth's voice rang back as the group began to double back down the hall. "I don't know what they are, but they're definitely *not* Pata Police—WHOA!" With an echoing burst, the door at the end of the hallway slammed shut. "They're here! Someone help me hold this shut!"

"Not Pata Sector police?" That fact stood out as a confusing detail.

"What are we going to do?" Mika asked, tugging on my hand.

I decided to save figuring out the police issue until after we eluded the Fifteen. With Mika's question fresh in my head, I loudly declared the one option that seemed to be our only chance. "Window exits!"

An unsure young lady called back to me. "There are no window exits!"

Another girl added an unfortunate fact. "We're on the third floor, too!"

As more banging and shouting from the exit filled the hallway with tension and fear, the notion to lead the panicked mass to safety suddenly overtook me. I contested their uncertainties with a rigid posture and certain conviction in my attitude. "I don't think there are any other choices right now! You can all either follow me or be captured!"

With that being my choice of the last word, I ran into the nearest room; having several other Causes follow me. Many of the others dispersed into other nearby rooms. As for the two brave souls who guarded the door to buy us that half a minute of time, they were last seen being pulled to the other end by what one could only assume were special police working for the Fifteen.

I let as many into the room as I could before I felt the need to begin the escape. I locked both locks on the door to stall for as much time as we could get.

Just as I finished fastening the door, a hand gripped my shoulder from behind. It was a familiar left hand, bandaged halfway to the elbow. Kay's growling tone of voice rang in my ears. "Brigg, just *where* did you think *you* were going without me!? Were you planning on ditching me?"

I grunted deep in sheer disbelief, swearing that I thought I lost her. Mika spoke up. "Kay! Just leave him alone!"

A few seconds passed as I was thinking of how to outwardly react to this. Sure enough though, the other Causes in the room began murmuring to each other.

"Brigg with Kay?"

"They always argue so much."

"Last pair *I'd* expect."

"They're probably 'reconciling their differences', if you know what I mean."

I called them all to attention to cease the chatter. "All right, that's enough! Yes, it's very funny. Hahaha, let's all laugh it up!" I turned to Kay. "Escaping now, explaining later. I'm only letting you follow along because we *all...*" I pointed to the group, "...don't have time to argue about this."

There was a clatter in the hallway as Kay confirmed my stance with an unexpected understanding.

I hastily reached into my bag. "Who else has rope?"

A few raised their hands and began to shuffle through their bags as well.

"Pull it out and tie some knots in it!" I commanded. I took my length of rope and tied it to the base of the bed. I called to the rest of them. "When you escape from here, the only things you need to do are run fast, run far, and run like you stole something!"

They all agreed.

Within moments, we had constructed a length of rope with which we could safely drop into the alley below. One by one, the Causes began to file out of the window.

Kay asked Mika, "Are you going to be all right going down that rope by yourself?"

Before Mika could answer, there was a loud bang just outside the room. The door shook violently and the room itself rattled with the blow.

The tallest, strongest-looking young man in the room ran to the door and began to hold it back. "Everyone, *get going!*"

The other Causes were now going faster and faster. Unfortunately, too many people overloaded the rope. The bottom leg of the bed broke under the weight, sending the Causes on it tumbling to the alley below.

"Oh my God!" Kay exclaimed, looking out of the window. "Is everyone all right?"

We were running out of time. I pushed Kay out of the way and onto the bed. "Throw that rope back up here!" I ordered.

It was taking the Causes in the alley below a moment to get themselves together. From what I could discern, though, everyone seemed to be fine.

One of them pitched the leg of the bed back up to me, but I missed catching it. After two more tries, I got hold of it and began to tie the rope to another leg of the bed.

The locks on the door were beginning to rattle. "Hurry up!" the burly Cause shouted.

"Kay, go!" I barked.

She started to give me her brand of attitude. "You know I'm going to wai—"

I cut her off. "Yes, yes, I know! Wait for us, then! Just go, now! That door is not going to last!"

Mika jumped and shouted at the sound of another impact on the door. She threw herself into me and clutched the side of my shirt. I felt her shaking as she wept fearfully.

I leaned in to console her. "Mika, don't be scared. Just think of your father and how you'll be able to see him again if you escape from here."

A tear rolled down her cheek as she looked up to me. "Thanks."

Kay was now out of sight. The only people left in the room were Mika, the young man holding the door, and myself. I asked him, "Are you going to be all right?"

He grunted, holding back another blow to the door. "Well, this is probably the end of the Revolution for me. Don't worry about it though. It's going to end for all of us eventually, right?"

"Right." I agreed as I patted Mika on the head. "Mika, it's your turn. Go ahead and wait for me with Kay."

She nodded, sniffling one last time before taking herself slowly out the window.

I turned back to the strong youth one last time. "What's your forum name? I'll want to thank you personally on the forums next time I see a Contact."

"Pibs," he said with a grin. "Thanks a lot, Brigg."

"No; thank *you*. I'll make sure you get the credit you deserve for this."

With the next hit to the door, the doorknob shot off and hit the floor. "You have to go, now!" Pibs said.

I backpedaled upon seeing the doorknob at my feet. I swiftly turned toward the window and made my escape, leaving Pibs behind to complete his sacrifice for the near-twenty he helped make it out of the Gateway.

During my descent into the alley, I looked to my right to see another group of Causes escaping using the same method we did. Getting a closer look at the bottom of their rope, I could see the unmistakable high collar of Dice's green shirt. He seemed to be preoccupied with himself and not taking notice of me. I felt that it was time to just let him bother somebody else.

I then looked to my left and noticed that Kay was leading Mika down the alley by the hand. My first thought was that Kay was trying to be the one to ditch me instead.

"Oh, that stupid bitch!" I said aloud. Looking down, I saw that I was low enough on the rope to simply let go and drop.

Upon hitting the ground, I stumbled; accidentally tripping somebody. "Hey, watch where you're going!"

"Sorry!"

"Wait…Brigg?" The voice—it was Dice. "Brigg, Kay is taking Mika away!"

I stood straight and looked down the alleyway. "Yes! I know! Follow them!" I couldn't let Kay get away.

Dice just stood there, took his dice out of his pocket and started to roll them.

I shouted, "Does it look like we have time for that!?" I grabbed him by the front of his shirt and thrust him in the direction Kay was running. I dashed out ahead of him, re-establishing my intention of losing him in the confusion.

VIII

Pure anger fueled the speed of my running. My one chance to get that woman off of my tail had suddenly turned into a race to catch up with her. Though she was actually trying to get away from me, I wasn't going to let her take Mika with her. Fortunately, I had caught sight of Mika in just enough time to see which way Kay was leading her. They turned right through another alleyway.

I made the turn and saw Mika again. The way her legs were moving made it look like Kay was dragging her. It only served to further enrage me. I continued pursuit as Kay took Mika for a left turn.

Shortly after they were out of sight around the corner, I heard Mika give out a cry of pain. I gave a quick thought to the worst.

Before my negative thoughts got out of control, though, I turned the corner and saw the two of them. They had stopped. Mika was collapsed on the ground, holding her left ankle as Kay kneeled down to help her.

We were well into the last straw with this. Without hesitation, I began walking over to Kay; fully conscious of the seething scowl that occupied my appearance. She scrambled to her feet and began to turn away; knowing full well that I wasn't going to let this slide.

Without really thinking about it, I grabbed the woman by the shirt and pinned her back up against the outside of the nearest building. The top of her ponytail was the only thing to cushion her head as it bounced off of the brick structure.

"Why did you do that!?" I shouted.

Her eyes widened—she was indeed frightened. Kay gripped my arm with her desperate, shaking hands.

"Answer me!" I demanded, pushing and shaking my fist into her collarbones.

Mika called out. "Brigg, please; don't hurt her! She only wanted to protect me!"

"Yeah, and look what happened!" Still gripping Kay's shirt, I pulled her away from the wall to give her a good look at the injured girl. "Is this your idea of protection!?"

Dice showed up, took one look at Mika and immediately began attending to her. Mika was happy to see him, telling him about how she had gone back to look for him earlier. Watching the two of them getting along had a calming effect on me.

Before I let the calm sink in though, I pulled Kay close to me and said, "The next time you pull a stunt like that, you had best be thinking about protecting *yourself* before anyone else! Understand?"

Her quivering bottom lip and the tear rolling down her left cheek accentuated her fear as she meekly nodded. My message was loud and clear to her.

I let her go. A brief, awkward silence was about us; the kind where everyone seems afraid to be the next one to speak.

"I don't think she expected you to throw her to the wall there," Dice muttered.

"That was scary, Brigg. You didn't have to do that," Mika scolded.

I countered, "*She* didn't have to drag you like that. You twisted your ankle."

Dice agreed with me—the first time I could recall him doing so. "He does have a point there, Mika,"

It seemed that Mika and Dice being separated from us earlier that evening had proven beneficial. Dice wasn't acting as disagreeable as he was before that incident. Perhaps it would not have been a bad idea to invite him to follow us. After all, we still were not far from the Gateway Inn and still at risk of being found by the Fifteen.

Despite the history between myself and Dice, I saw the need to ask a favor of him. "Dice, can you carry her?"

"Can you carry her things?" he grinned. "Does this mean you're inviting me along with you?" he asked.

"Well, you and Mika seem to be getting along and…"

He interrupted me, "That doesn't mean I think any more of you."

"Another boy…" Kay murmured.

I turned around to her, raising my voice again to keep her on edge. "You have said quite enough tonight!"

Dice stood, lifting Mika onto his back. "Is, uh, *that* coming with us?" He was referring to Kay.

I picked up Mika's bag and slung it over my shoulder. Tagging along with Dice's remark, I said, "Only if *it* wants to."

"Come on, guys," Mika groaned, finding our pronouns unfit.

I addressed Kay. "Do you understand? If you're going to follow us, that is all you're going to do; follow. I'm leading here, so you had best know your place." I nodded to Dice. "We're going now."

We kept to the back alleyways of the Pata Sector. Though I didn't really know the layout of the city, the motive to stay concealed behind buildings and structures kept us busy with improvisational navigation.

We had to stop and rest frequently. Dice and I even switched off carrying Mika and her things from time to time. Kay continued to follow us too; but wisely kept her distance, as well as her mouth shut.

An hour had passed since the raid on the Gateway Inn. Doing nothing but trekking away from the inn's location since then put us pretty far away from danger. We finally felt it safe to stop.

The ground in that well-shrouded alley was a very firm soil. I asked Dice to get my blanket from my bag and place it onto the ground along a wall.

After he set it up, I placed Mika down onto it. She was very tired and was struggling to stay awake.

"We'll have to stop here for the night." I looked over at Kay, expecting her to object.

Dice was looking around. "This will have to do since no inn is going to take us."

"No other choice…" Kay mumbled, hanging her head down low.

Seeing Kay like that made me feel a tiny bit sorry for what had done earlier. As much as I didn't want to, I was going to have to be the first to show signs of apology. It was the only way I could get everybody working together. I called to her, "Kay."

She slowly looked up to me. "Hmm?"

I pointed to the vacant space on the blanket next to Mika. "You're here for tonight. It's the least I can do."

"I…don't understand," she peeped.

I stepped over to her as Dice checked Mika's ankle. "I should not have put my hands on you earlier. Though it's no excuse for it, I'm not sure what came over me."

"I thought…" she didn't finish the sentence; appearing confused.

"Look. If what happened back there showed me anything, it's that we both want the same thing. The two of us want this little girl back to her father safely."

"…Three of us!" Dice corrected.

I was intrigued by that. "You too?"

"Yeah," he sighed, "Mika took the liberty of telling me all about her situation earlier. She has just as much of her own business to take care of as we do as Causes. I can kinda relate to her too, you know?"

"How so?" Kay wondered.

He briefly chuckled as if he had inadvertently opened a subject he wanted to avoid. "Don't worry about that. That's for me to deal with."

I finished with Kay. "I know it's going to take some time for you to trust me. You must have some big issue against men…"

"That's not your business!" she interrupted, finally speaking up.

I reached to put my hand on her shoulder, but she twisted away.

I backed off. Without another word in that conversation, I concluded by presenting her once again with the other half of the blanket. She walked over and silently laid herself down.

Dice had a blanket in his bag as well. He set his blanket down next to mine and laid down onto it, his head close to Mika's.

Given the circumstances, Dice and I had to forgo any inhibitions we had against each other. I got comfortable next to him; my head near Kay's. Not another word was spoken for the remainder of that night.

Though I was exhausted, questions plagued my thoughts as I slipped quickly to sleep. I was wondering why the Pata Police were not there when the raid occurred. I was also wondering if that Zoe girl made it out alright. Yet, there was one question I remember most distinctly:

Where was Doctrine…and why was he right?

Day 65

I

Sustaining comfort in that dark alley eventually proved impossible. I awoke for the fourth time that night with numbness in my left arm. Frustrated, I exhaled with a grunt that seamlessly swept into a wide yawn. My eyes opened, letting in what faint light the stars in the sky provided. It was still not enough, though; I could barely see a thing.

As I continued laying there, the pale gray luminescence slowly but surely overtook the pitch-darkness. Gradually, my eyes began to adapt to the poor visibility brought on by the dead of night. By the time I found it in my interest to sit up, I felt I could use my eyes with confidence. Every movement I made from that point forward was carefully dictated only by what I was able to see.

I stood to my feet and looked down at the rest of my group. Dice was laying flat on his stomach, sleeping silently. Mika was snuggled under Kay's arm; resting her head on her shoulder. Kay had her arm around Mika as well. It looked as if the two of them were keeping each other warm. A brief, noisy gust of wind burst past us almost as if to tell me that that was the case.

Mika shifted in her sleep.

My eyes soon became focused on Kay. My harsh handling of her began replaying in my mind. I clutched my hands together as I reminisced about pinning Kay up against the building. I remembered myself saying, "Why did you do that!?" I could distinctly recall the look on her face. My best assumption from back there was that she was afraid of what I was going to do to her at the time.

As I tried to focus, a memory caught me off guard. I could remember the times where it was the front of *my* shirt being grabbed, *my* back to a wall. The familiarity of it was all too real to me. I gave it a last moment of thought before my father's voice emerged from my memory and shot through the silence. "Why did you do that!?"

I simply shuddered, as I do often when remembering things like that. My teeth clenched as I scrambled to think of something else. However, my mind was set back; once again reminding me that my real purpose out there was to escape the very things that fogged my memories with fear and anger.

I finally realized that through my actions that previous night, I was not doing a very good job of distancing myself from the violent natures I sought so desperately to leave behind. I knew I was going to have to watch myself in the coming days. Keeping any fit of anger in check was not going to be an easy task considering the people who I allowed to accompany me. But for my sake, and Mika's to an extent, I had to put myself up to that challenge.

I dropped to my knees; slowly lowering myself next to Dice on the blanket. I laid flat onto my stomach and, yet again, tried to get comfortable. My eyes shut and a loud breath pushed itself from my lungs. Just before slipping back into slumber, I quietly muttered to myself, "Why *did* you do that?"

II

It was going into the early hours of the afternoon and Kay and I had barely said a word to each other. Mika wasn't having any complications with her ankle. So for the most part, I dropped my grudge over Kay's recent actions. Most of anything said among any of us was by me, instructing everyone where to go to keep us on as low a profile as possible.

Sticking to the alleyways of the Pata Sector was proving to be more difficult as the day rolled on. As more people began to crowd the streets for Pata's everyday bustle, more and more people were beginning to notice us. It went without saying that four people trekking through alleys with backpacks of personal belongings looked rather suspicious. Knowing that only furthered our inclinations to look before we turned any corners. Considering the events of the night before, all of us were very tense, fearfully anticipating that the Fifteen were still on our trail.

Dice was the first to crack. Once we were in an area with enough cover, he asked for us all to stop. "Hey guys, what do you say we sit still for a little while?"

Without the specifics mentioned as to why he chose to stop us, Kay simply asked him, "You think so too, huh?"

Dice nodded. "Yeah, it's getting a little too crowded out there."

Despite my desire to keep moving, even I was in agreement. I asked openly, "So what do we want to do from here?"

Without hesitation, Dice replied, "We should wait here until evening; or at least until things calm down out there."

Mika seemed to be the only one who had something negative to say about it. "Is it a good idea to stay in one place, though?"

Kay began making indifferent gestures, almost seeming as if she were afraid to speak.

Her mousiness caused a spark in me. It wasn't the time to be keeping ideas and suggestions to ourselves. On that thought, I said to the others, "We are a group here whether we like it or not. If you feel you have to say something, go ahead and say it. In a situation such as this, we can't afford to be silent to one another."

Dice saw where I was going with that little speech and added his own words to the mix. "Communication is going to be a vital role in keeping us all together and out of the hands of the Fifteen."

I looked to Mika and saw a face rife with worry. "Is something wrong, Mika?"

She didn't give me an answer right away. She hemmed and hawed, unable to find the right way of expressing her thought.

It wasn't until I shot her a coaxing look that she told me what was really on her mind. "What is this going to do to looking for my father?"

I let out a sheepish groan. It wasn't that I forgot about the search, just that staying in the Revolution was our top priority. Now that we were seeing opposition, it was all the more reason to keep the purpose of the Causes in the forefront of our minds.

It took a moment for me to verbally answer Mika's question. I presented a sensible slice of logic to the anxious youngster. "If we get captured by the Fifteen, the search is over...for all of us. We have to get out of this and into the clear before we can go back out there to look for him. You understand, right?"

She actually smiled at my choice of words. Mika obviously realized that we couldn't help her find her father if we were not there to support her.

Dice added, "So, we can all agree that eluding the Fifteen and *their* police is the first thing we have to take care of."

There was a sense of silent understanding as I pulled my blanket back out of my bag, set it on the ground, and took a seat on it. That was my way of indicating to the others to kick back and relax. Dice's previous suggestion to wait until later that evening was a bit easier to adhere to after putting more thought into it.

I took the time out to explain to the others exactly what went on at the Gateway Inn. Mika and Kay were especially intrigued by the details of Doctrine's presence at the time. By the end of that discussion, the two of them were asking as to why Doctrine seemed to know about the trap. Although he told me at the time that he simply overheard it from some of the officers, I found it strange that the Pata Police were not there when the raid occurred.

I began to wonder if somebody tipped him off and he came to the rescue, only to get caught up in the investigation himself. But if that would be true, why didn't he tell me about the raid until Zoe left the room? There were many possibilities, but none of them added up properly.

It was at that point we decided it would be in our best interest to keep our eyes open for a Contact. Surely if there was something Doctrine failed to tell me, he may have posted it on the forum. It was highly possible that news of the raid had reached the forums by that time. All we needed to do was add what we knew about the incident to any related information posted by other Causes.

Hopefully then, the answers we were looking for would surface.

Waiting around for the right time was almost as stressful as it was boring. However, it gave us time to reconcile, as well as further share our opinions on what appeared to be the Fifteen's eventual decision to act against us. It brought to light our concern for the Producers' position and the ever-present question of Hatcher's situation.

I didn't want to be one to lose hope easily. But the fact that nobody had heard from Hatcher in five weeks made it seem much less possible he would show up. Surely he would be met with strong disapproval if he waited until the last possible second to show up. It wasn't the right time to be waiting around for him, though. We all felt it would only be a matter of time before the Fifteen went on a full-on crackdown on Causes.

Kay and Dice didn't beat around the bush when it came to expressing their concerns for the Causes as a whole. Mika seemed the most occupied, though. If the Revolution were to end so abruptly, there was no telling where she was going to end up. Even worse, there was no telling if she'd ever see her father again.

III

The cover of darkness we waited for was finally upon us. All one could hear were the light gusts of wind that softly howled through the Pata Sector's torch-lit streets.

It was time to move out. However, even with the dark of the night in full effect, there was no telling when or if a hostile entity would emerge. It went without saying that we'd have to watch our backs. We were still not sure if the Fifteen's officers were any different from ordinary police.

We finally stepped out of the alleyways, boldly setting foot into the open street. Upon looking around the vicinity on that firm dirt road, wide grins spread across our faces despite the tension.

Apparently we were not the only ones who had been waiting for night to fall. From out of the shadows, more Causes swept into the dimly lit street. Each one was carefully making their way toward a safer area. The familiar sight of Causes scampering down the street in low profile lifted our confidence. It easily reminded us of the day the Revolution began.

We stuck to the side of the street as we quickly paced in the direction the rest of the Causes were headed.

Dice made mention that Station East was back in the other direction. I told him that that was exactly the point. Expecting to get out of the Pata Sector by train would be way too obvious. Vade's Officers were probably guarding the stations, ready to take in any unsuspecting Causes.

It appeared that there was an unspoken consensus to get out of the Pata Sector on foot. The sector had become hostile ground after the events of the previous night. Getting out of there altogether in the quietest fashion seemed like the safest option.

Now came the time to make a very important decision: what sector we would escape towards. We had some decent options since the three closest sector borders were those of the Gova, Terra, and Fanda Sectors.

I was far from willing to return to the Gova Sector after having had spent the previous week there. Therefore, Gova was ruled out.

The Terra Sector seemed like a welcoming option. Since it was mostly farmland and greenhouses, the population was all farmers, livestock herders, and botanists. The lay of the land was also very wide open with most of the population spread out in small farm houses. It was definitely a viable option to hide out and lay low for a while.

Lastly, the Fanda Sector presented a much better opportunity to find Mika's father before she got dragged further into danger. Fanda is a sector that is more about business and entertainment than homes and neighborhoods. It is home to the acting stages, one of Eden's two Game Coliseums, and Eden's Grand Station. At times, it can be just as crowded as the Pata Sector since people from all over Eden go there to unwind and have fun.

As the four of us continued following the other Causes, Dice, Kay, and I weighed the options carefully. Mika, on the other hand, was focused solely on finding her father. Thus, she was voting for Fanda all the way.

I found myself siding with Mika as well. My reasons were no different than they were the day I met her. Helping Mika was my main concern, so wherever she wanted to search, I would be there to help.

Kay, however, felt it safer to distance ourselves from as many people as possible. But as Mika and I both knew, Kay's judgment and credibility had a 0-2 record with us. Also, her impulsive actions in trying to escape with Mika were still fresh in all of our minds. I took no hesitation in mentioning that aloud.

Kay let out a frustrated sigh. "What? Does my opinion not matter here?"

It started to feel like the same argument over again. "I didn't say that."

She took a stride to me. "Then why did you even bring that up?"

I growled with a necessary disinterest in conflict. "I only said it because it's true!"

She huffed. "Didn't you say a while ago that everybody's input is important?"

Dice shot me a crooked smile—an expression that clearly stated his pleasure in seeing my own words turned against me. It appeared that he was game to team up with Kay to antagonize me.

I answered Kay in an attempt to bring a preemptive halt to possible confrontation. "Yes, I said that. Your opinion is important."

"Well then, what's the problem?"

I thought of a quick, clever answer that I hadn't quite thought of before. "The problem is that if we distance ourselves, we also single ourselves out. If we're found out there in Terra, we have nowhere to run. Whoever finds us will be exclusively focused on our party. That's different from last night since there were so many other Causes there to be taken besides us."

Dice sounded impressed. "I'm surprised, Brigg. That is a very good point."

"You, of all people, actually agree with me?" It was the last thing I had expected to hear from him.

He shot me down. "I didn't say I agreed; I only said it made a good argument." He then said, "What I'm now wondering is who would be out there to find us. Surely Vade would stick to residential and business areas to find Causes. Also, in case you forgot, Naro's Radio Tower is in Fanda as well."

It was true. I clearly forgot that fact. I brushed it off though.

"Regardless, I still think it is best we try to blend in with other people. Mika wants to go to Fanda. I want to go to Fanda. So we're going to Fanda whether you like it or not."

Dice reached his left hand into his pocket. He then hesitated for a bit; waiting for Kay to say something.

Kay took some time to think of a response as Dice continued to contest my logic. "I can't help but have the sinking sensation that you're going to get us all captured."

I twisted the subject in another direction. "I figured you'd want to stay with Mika as well, right?"

He took a deep breath as his gaze turned to the ground. "Honestly," he exhaled, "if that constitutes dealing with *you* day in and day out, I think I'd be better off going with Kay to Terra."

Mika stopped walking upon hearing Dice's words. "I thought you said you'd help!"

Dice appeared to coldly dismiss whatever previous conversation he had with her. "Look kiddo, I told you why I'm out here doing this in the first place. I can't take care of my business if I'm toiling in the Labor Fields."

"Fine then, Dice!" I shrugged, annoyed by his arrogance. "Do whatever you want, I don't care."

He held his arm out, pointing his whole hand to me. "You heard the man, kiddo. I'm out of here." Dice began to cross the street to take an upcoming left turn that would take him toward the Terra Sector. On his way across, he called out, "Come on, Kay. We don't need this guy!"

Kay followed him for only a few steps before calling to him. "In case you forgot, Dice, I'm not leaving Mika alone with him. I don't want to go to Fanda, but I'm more concerned about Mika's safety."

I called to him as well. "Looks like you're on your own."

Dice stopped halfway across the street and turned back to us. With surprise laced in his voice, he asked, "Are you serious, Kay?"

"Of course I am."

Other Causes passing by watched as our group appeared to fall apart in the middle of the street. Their whispers crept through the sounds of their hurried footsteps as if every one of them had something to say about the scene we were creating. The fact that we were speaking louder than any Cause on that road was more than enough to have anybody focus their attention to us.

Dice continued to stand in the middle of the street, appearing to be affected by his new situation. He was all up for leaving us behind if Kay had gone with him. But with Kay's position set in stone, he actually seemed hesitant to go through with it. He reached into his left pocket as he took a few steps toward us. He stopped a few meters in front of us, letting out a disgruntled sigh as he pulled his dice out. His hand dropped to his side with each die gripped between each finger as he pondered a wager.

We waited for him.

Kay took a step toward him as if she was about to say something. I held my hand out and gestured for her to save it until the dice rolled.

A young man sped between us, briefly turning around with a warning to hurry up.

Dice looked to Mika with apologetic concern. Whatever he and Mika talked about back at the Gateway Inn, it certainly was giving him food for thought concerning his roll.

After a few more seconds, he finally announced, "All dice: odd." He turned his palm forward; and with a flick of the wrist, sent his dice tumbling to the ground between us. I heard Mika peep a brief, sad groan as the results presented themselves. The dice came up one, five and four.

Mika whimpered in disappointment.

Smirking, I began to help Dice pick them up. "Looks like you're going to Ter…"

He quickly interjected, grumbling, "…Fanda with you guys."

Befuddled, I tilted my head up and handed him his third die. "But you said…"

He interrupted again, "Did I say what I'd *do* if they all came up odd?"

Mika cheered. She seemed glad to have Dice as one of us.

Without saying much else, we followed the road that would lead us to the Fanda Sector. I took the period of silence to think about what I should do about Kay and Dice.

It seemed to me that as soon as I would manage to get along with one of them, the other would turn around and start acting like a jerk. There was no chance in shaking off Kay easily, and Dice appeared to have a number of issues beyond his purposes for participating in the Revolution.

For Mika's sake, though, I felt it best to keep them both close at hand in case things got too hairy for only two people to handle. If worse came to worse, I was willing to send either of them off to take a hit for the team. After what had been going on during the past two nights, I truly began to feel that their capture was not of my concern.

The awkward silence between the four of us was interrupted when Kay stopped for just a second and turned around. "What's up?" I asked her.

She cupped her hands around her ears. "Listen. Do you hear that?"

It was faint, but it was obvious as to what the noise was. In the far distance, echoing through the streets, we could hear commotion and shouting. A loud thump resonated, stopping some of the other Causes to pause in either fear; curiosity or both. After a moment, I overheard one bystander say, "That's gotta be Vade!"

The entire ruckus was coming from the direction of the path to the Terra Sector. Knowing this made me feel a bit triumphant.

However, celebrating my logical victory would have to wait. Mika was trying to hurry all of us along. "Come on, guys. We have to get far away from that."

I chuckled reassuringly, trying to bury the recent argument. "Now it's about where we're *not* going, right?"

Kay smiled and nodded as Dice simply rolled his eyes. Normally, I would have challenged him again. Instead, I turned toward the Fanda Sector and took off running. Without a second thought, the others followed as well.

IV

The next two days of the Revolution seemed to go by slower as we continued avoiding Vade by day, and skulking through the shadows at night. Tensions continued to run high as news continued to spread about the Fifteen's actions.

Naro even went to the trouble of making a transistor broadcast to boast the supposed futility of our attempts to escape.

Another member of the Fifteen also stepped in to make

matters worse for the Causes. Cenia, the head of community relations and social moderator, placed a curfew on the citizens of the Pata Sector.

Now, *any* person seen on the streets after the torches were lit would be approached by the Fifteen's special police. If it was a Cause, they were taken away. Anybody else would be given a warning and sent back to their home.

Since it was so easy to distinguish a Cause from an ordinary person, this made the chances of being captured much higher. In many cases, it was Cenia's curfew that made the Pata Sector that much more difficult to get out of.

During this time the Causes got a good chance to see their new enemy: the Fifteen's Special Police Force. Those lucky enough to have seen a Contact during that time quickly took to nicknaming them the "Gray Police" when the news was spread.

Instead of the traditional neutral blue worn by most police in Eden, the Gray Police uniforms were a distinct dark gray with what appeared to be an armored cap. Their belts toted two rods as their weapons. One was the traditional night stick. The other, however, was a frightening-looking metal stick with a dark rubber grip on one end and three pointy claws on the other. One could obviously see which end was used to attack.

Many Causes found themselves unsure as to what this sudden spurt of captures actually meant. Some felt that the Fifteen were trying to restore some of the balance that was lost when the 13,000 Causes shirked their duty to society simultaneously. Others felt that the more uncouth youths out there were painting a bad picture of the Causes as a whole, like the few bad apples that spoil the bunch.

Whatever the case was, morale remained mostly unshaken. The Causes were making progress. If the Fifteen were going through that much trouble to bring us to a halt, there had to be something more to the captures than what was seen to the naked eye.

Day 68

I

Stressed and exhausted, it felt as if the moonlight of the midnight hour was demanding I go to sleep. I had to stay awake though. Kay and I were the ones keeping watch as Dice and Mika slept on his blanket.

We found ourselves once again hiding in the shadows of the Pata Sector's alleyways. This time, though, we were hiding behind a conveniently tall stack of crates. It was a welcome change to a bare and open alley where we could easily be seen. Kay and I were pacing left and right, passing off what was left of my bag of granola to each other.

We had taken to the idea of sleeping in shifts. Of course, it was a wonderful idea if you were the one on the blanket. Keeping one's eyes open on pure adrenaline was even more straining given the circumstances by which it was required. It had to be done though. There was no telling when, or if, we would be seen.

Gray Police officers were a common sight now. With the curfew in place, all it would take was for us to be seen and that would be it for us.

I was too tired to assure myself of a chance of getting away. Moving from one place to the next was a great risk every time. With all things considered, the four of us had done a fine job in staying out of the clutches of Vade and her officers.

I quickly peeked out of the alley, focusing my gaze through a small crack between two crates.

Our next objective was only a few hundred meters away. It was a bridge. The border to the Fanda Sector was only a few kilometers past the other end of that bridge. The main problem was that three Gray Police officers were on the lookout for anybody violating the curfew.

"How does it look out there?" Kay asked me in a shuddering whisper.

I told her the situation, adding that I felt it wasn't going to change any time soon.

Kay rose to her feet, mustering the courage to step further out into the alley and look into the street. She was able to see much more than I could have out of the tiny crevice I had been hiding behind.

After a minute or two, she reported as well. "It looks like we're not the only ones waiting to get across that bridge."

"No?"

"Yeah, we've got a few groups waiting behind some of these other buildings as well."

I rested my eyes, leaning my head into my lap. "Think we're going to move soon?"

She sat back down next to a soundly sleeping Mika, leaning back against the crates. "Not sure." She suddenly buried her head in her hands and grunted. "Ugh, how can something be so exciting and so *boring* at the same time?"

I felt the pain of her lamenting. "I don't know. Something better happen quickly before any more Gray Police officers come to stand guard."

An hour passed…very, very slowly.

The sound of running wiped away the boredom as quickly as it did the silence. Hearing those hurried footsteps making way down the middle of the open street prompted me to spring to my feet. Kay and I began to gather our possessions together while waking up Mika and Dice. Within seconds after that, I stepped from behind the crates to get a clear view of the street and the bridge.

I wasn't the only one curious about the source of the sounds. Just as Kay said, several other heads poked out of other hiding spaces throughout the vicinity. Kay, Dice and Mika soon joined me to catch a glimpse of the sudden commotion as well.

Three figures stood in plain view of the officers guarding the bridge. A discussion between them began, but we were too far away to hear anything. As the guards took careful steps toward them, it seemed as if these three other people were taunting them away from their positions. It was obvious that these Causes were running a distraction to help those in hiding cross over to the other side.

"They're insane!" Dice whispered.

We saw two of the Gray Police order the third to continue standing guard. That third guard took both of his weapons off of his belt and began to wield them with a defensive yet menacing posture. He seemed almost like a spider, sitting perfectly still until its prey was to fly unexpectedly into its web. Sure enough, anybody trying to cross the bridge would find themselves on the receiving end of a brutal attack.

The three youths began to take steps back as well. It appeared that in an attempt to distract all three of them, the officers didn't seem to feel so outnumbered at three to two. The officers drew their rods, one of them saying the first thing to become coherent to me: "We're taking you three in!"

In a split second, one of the men on our side pointed behind the officer and shouted, "*Now!*"

The two officers looked behind themselves to see nothing but the bridge they stepped away from. With their guard down, the three brave distracters jumped the Gray Police, grabbing their weapons and trying to wrest them from their grip. One of the three, a young woman, shouted into the open night, "Everyone, make a run for it!"

We were briefly frozen with awe and fear. Kay began to push us forward, snapping us out of it. "Let's go, this is our chance."

I shook the rest of the cobwebs out. "Yes, just steer clear of them all."

Causes began filing out of the alleys and into the street, all looking to stampede the bridge. A number of Causes, including us, slowed down a bit as they approached the confrontations. Many were still afraid of the weapons the Gray Police carried.

The lone third guard began to scamper in place, overwhelmed by the amount of people that suddenly showed up.

In the entire ruckus, one last figure showed up on the bridge. In a flash, he effortlessly yanked the last guard's rod from his hands and began to swing it at him. With the last guard distracted, every Cause in the street ran full speed to get across the bridge before the advantage changed.

The last Gray Police officer on the bridge took his nightstick and readied himself to engage the mysterious youth. The four of us kept as far away from the scuffle as possible as we blew past it.

Once we were almost to the other side, Kay stopped for a second, forcing the rest of us to follow suit. She looked back to the last man to appear that night and simply called to him. "Blue, is that you?"

Without even turning around to look at her, he called back, "Not a time to distract me, just go! Make sure everyone knows that good ol' Blue took care of you all."

I reached and grabbed Kay by her right wrist. "You heard the man! Let's get going!"

The four of us sped off into the night.

It seemed that Blue, the fabled glory-seeker, wasn't working solo in his efforts to help the Causes. However, Blue's actions, as well as those of his entourage, were in direct contradiction to the rules set by the Producers.

The events of that night presented the question as to whether or not Blue was actually a Cause, or if he was just helping in his own fashion to make a name for himself as the rumors surrounding him suggested.

Whatever the case, his actions led us all to safety for the time being. The whole ordeal that spanned those past few days had been exhausting and frustrating. Thankfully, that chapter of the Revolution was over for us. Finally, we were able to stand down, relax and take our time.

Our next stop was the Fanda Sector. Now that we were out of hostile territory, the search for Mika's father would continue once we recuperated from the Ordeal of Pata.

Episode 3: Choosing Sides

The situation in the Pata Sector grew increasingly worse. With Naro, Vade, and Cenia in command of the Gray Police, more and more Causes were winding up in the hands of the Fifteen. Any Cause who made it out of the Pata Sector was considered lucky.

Vade continued to keep the pressure on. Soon she announced that a fourth member of the Fifteen—Riley—would be doing his part in cutting off the Causes.

Riley is the man in charge of the train systems that run all throughout Eden. Thus, as a way to contribute to Vade's plan, Riley cut off train services in the partitioned section of Pata. People could enter, but leaving was out of the question.

The Causes in the Pata Sector were now forced to fend for themselves. However, the rest of our forces spread throughout Eden extended moral support to them. Though it wouldn't prevent them from being captured, the principle of the gesture was still felt.

The Fifteen truly had the advantage over the Causes at that time. That was when something highly unexpected occurred.

With the countless words of encouragement from our side to our peers, who would have thought that soon after the Ordeal of Pata, two Causes would stand out to bring true physical opposition to the Fifteen?

We didn't see it coming...until...

Day 69

I

It was a humid and overcast morning with the heat of summer making the outdoors all the more miserable. Luckily for us, we were seated comfortably in a small restaurant in the eastern section of the Fanda Sector. We took our time for the weather to break as we ate breakfast in the pleasant and colorful atmosphere that the quaint street-side eatery provided.

Dice's observant eyes were what brought us to enter that restaurant in the first place. As we were passing by it while looking for other Causes, Dice had spotted a Contact sitting by his lonesome through the window.

Having not seen a Contact in several days, we decided to hold off our search for an hour or so to make our posts. Mika didn't mind since she was well aware of everything we had to say.

My first order of business was to honor my word to Pibs. I began a new topic with an opening post that detailed his heroic actions back at the Gateway. I also added that anybody who escaped because of Pibs's stall tactic should reply to thank him as well.

Kay, Dice and I took turns passing the Contact's laptop

computer between us. There was as much to be said about the Ordeal of Pata as there was to learn. The thread on the Contact Forum took just two days to reach nearly 70 pages of posts.

The most important information was a particular observation made by two members who shared one forum name: "Al & Jal". They compared the Ordeal of Pata to a similar series of actions carried out by the Fifteen at the start of the Revolution. The only difference was the location of the attack.

Specifically, on the night of the Great Walk, a section of the Lucra Sector was partitioned off and heavily patrolled. Anyone who was found roaming the streets at the time of the Great Walk was tracked down and captured. Within the first two hours of the Revolution, 300 Causes were already in custody. What had happened in the Pata Sector was the exact same type of attack: partition, patrol and capture.

"It sounds like Al and Jal know what they're talking about…" Dice mumbled, concentrating on his typing.

"…Maybe a little too much?" I asked.

"No," Kay huffed, protesting my tone. "I've heard too many promising things about Al. Whoever Jal is, I'm sure he or she is helping him put all this information together."

Kay's words sparked another question from me. "Speaking of hearing promising things, what was with you and Blue yesterday?"

"What do you mean?"

I tried to find the right words to say in order to keep the conversation civil. "Well, you just seemed to stop and call to him as if you two knew each other."

Kay justified her actions. "Oh, I was just making sure it was really him. You remember the post you read about him right?"

"Well, yes."

"It was just like the thread said. Guy dressed in blue sweeps in to save the day…"

I saw her point, gesturing to move on to the next subject matter.

Mika took her fork from halfway to her mouth and placed it on her plate to speak quickly. "If it was just Blue, then who were those other guys?"

Dice spoke, having just made his post. "They were random volunteers."

We all looked at him. Kay asked for all of us, "How do you know that?"

He told us what he read. "Blue actually posted in this thread. He says right here: 'I walked around through the groups that were waiting to cross the bridge and asked them to help. It took me an hour and a half to find 3 people with enough guts to step out there with me'." He stopped talking and continued examining the other posts.

"Did Blue mention any names?"

He recited the list Blue had posted. "Memento, Al and Tricky were his helpers. The only female in the mix was Memento."

I gave it a moment of thought. "So, Al was there too, eh?" It appeared to be a reasonable explanation for Al's other post.

Dice gave another newsflash, reading the screen with his finger. "After this wave of useless 'thank you' posts here, Blue goes on to say that it was actually thanks to Al that they all made it out of there."

Something didn't make sense to me. "Who is to say that the four of them would stay together after one incident?"

Kay cut in. "I don't think that would be the case. Anything we've heard of about Blue up to this point made it sound like he preferred to work alone."

We all looked to Dice, anticipating a response to that as well. "I've got nothing," he sighed. "After Blue mentioned Al's role in the ordeal, he has made no other posts since then." We waited a moment. "However, there's an indication that Blue and Al spent some time hanging out yesterday."

"How is that?"

Augmenting the first few words, he made his observation. "It looks like Al & Jal made a late-night post yesterday. At the start of that post they say that Blue *'just* left to do his own thing'."

Mika chimed in with a thought that stopped the conversation flat. "Kind of makes you wonder where Jal was the other night…"

That got all of us thinking as we turned to look to the precocious preteen. Two people sharing the same forum name would surely stay together. Even the name sounded like that of a young couple. While contemplating the possibilities, I chuckled pleasantly. "You sure are observant for a kid, Mika."

"I'm just saying what I'm thinking."

Kay had something to say too. "In case you forgot your own words, any input is important."

Kay's remark elicited a reaction from Mika and Dice. I rolled with the punch though. "Glad to see my words have impact."

"...Especially when they're sent back at you," Dice grinned.

It was a cheap shot, but I had to let it roll off. In a public setting, we had to keep arguments and scenes to a minimum. I just continued eating; still trying to remember why I let Dice tag along in the first place.

I observed him as he tapped away, concentrating on his thoughts and keyboard strokes. After a few minutes, he exhaled with audible discontent. He rolled his eyes and leaned his head into his hands, shaking it in a manner of disapproval.

"What's wrong?" Mika asked.

Dice kept his volume low as he made the announcement. "New hot topic: 'Getting back at Naro'; posted by none other than the heroes of the moment, Al & Jal."

His words roused all of us.

Dice moved the laptop to the center of the table to where all of us could get a clear view of the topic. Besides the Contact, the rest of us crowded around the screen to read the first post.

Posted by: Al & Jal
Topic: Getting Back at Naro

After that whole thing that happened in the Pata Sector, we can see that the Fifteen aren't going to stop until we Causes walk away. Something's up, and it's costing our side innocent people. The two of us are pretty sure nobody murdered anyone and that's all just an excuse.

So here's what we're thinking. The heat on us all started when Naro accused Causes of the murder of that inn owner. But to spread the word quickly, he made the accusation over transistor broadcast.

Now, of course we'd all like to just get up and take out Naro. But if Naro is out of the picture, another member of the Fifteen will probably just take his place. As long as they can make broadcasts, they can keep putting the pressure on us! So here's our idea:

We need to take out the Radio Tower in the Fanda Sector. Without transistor broadcasts, the Fifteen won't be able to throw as much heat on us as they have been. *We're calling as many Causes together as we can to ransack or destroy the tower. All we're wondering is how many people we can get and when the best time to do it is…*

Anybody have any suggestions?

> *Al & Jal*

"What is that!? They can't be serious!" Kay exclaimed.

Dice turned the laptop to face him again. After scanning the topic for a few moments, he said, "Well, if 400 plus replies to this topic—"

Mika interrupted, "400 plus!?"

I stood from my seat and stepped behind Dice to read over his shoulder as Kay and Mika continued to watch us with curiosity in their eyes. Upon the first few glances, my brow lifted. After reading a few of the posts, it began to look like a plot was really forming.

"May I?" I asked Dice, looking to usurp control of the laptop.

"By all means…" he sighed, shifting his chair to the side.

I ran a search for all posts made by Al & Jal. All the while, I was trying to think of a way I could respond to this topic. Something in my heart didn't sit right with this. Sure, Al & Jal made a few good points, but attacking the Radio Tower didn't feel like the right answer. On that last thought, I found the post I was looking for:

> *Posted by: Al & Jal*
> *Topic: Getting Back at Naro*

> *It's settled then! This Sunday during the broadcast of "This Week in Eden" is when we'll take care of this once and for all. That way, Naro will be right there to see just how big a mistake it was to make us the bad guys.*

> *Al & Jal*

Dice chuckled with intrigue, "Well, this is certainly an interesting development."

"When do they plan on doing it?" Mika anxiously wondered.

Worried, I exhaled through my nose before answering. "It's happening Sunday."

Kay's eyes widened. Her voice sounded surprised at how soon the announced siege would occur. "That's the day after tomorrow."

I nodded, "Something about this seems wrong to you too, huh?"

Her reply was not quite what I had in mind. "Actually, I was thinking that we should probably hustle up if we want to join in too. We are pretty far off from the Radio Tower, after all, right?"

Mika spoke up. "Wait a second...something's wrong."

"What?"

She dropped an unexpectedly logical argument for a girl her age. "Won't that just make them madder at us?"

"Who cares if it makes them angry?" Kay jeered, brushing off Mika's question. "Look kid, they can get angry all they want. But if they can't make transistor broadcasts, then they have no way of slinging mud at us in front of the general public."

I was quick to interject. "Wouldn't they take more drastic measures, though?"

"Like what?"

"Well, if they'd go out of their way to close off a large area of one sector like they did the other day, who's to say they won't...I don't know...close *all* sector borders..."

"...Or maybe even shut down all the trains," Mika added.

I nodded in approval of her input.

Kay took a moment to respond. "Transistor broadcasts will be one less thing to worry about."

I glared into her eyes with a slight motion of my head. "I don't think you're seeing the big picture here..."

Dice laughed heartily, leaning on the back two legs of his chair. "Ah, I feel like we're on the forums all over again."

He captured everybody's attention with his display of seemingly-all-knowing arrogance. His attitude towards the situation didn't feel constructive to finding a better solution. "What do you think about this, Dice?" I asked.

"Me? I honestly don't care either way. But I will tell you this: If you intend on throwing yourself into the fray to try and stop this, you've got over 400 Causes to convince." He leaned forward in his chair and cockily gave me a pat on the back. "You have two days. Get crackin', big shot!"

The others continued eating as I took the next few minutes to put my thoughts into words. Within moments, I began typing my post of protest:

> *Posted by: Brigg*
> *Topic: Getting Back at Naro*
>
> *Am I the only one in this thread who thinks this is a bad idea? I don't know about you all, but I've been noticing the continuing trend of the Fifteen using drastic methods to stop the Revolution. Yes, I'm aware that there have only been two major capture attempts…but still.*
>
> *What I'm getting at is this: if we all storm the Radio Tower, who is to say what the Fifteen will do in response? Really think about that for a moment.*
>
> *My group and I have been talking about this. The Fifteen have the power to close off sectors and shut down the trains. They could even have the citizens of Eden hunt us down for rewards or something.*
>
> *So please, for the sake of every Causes neck, I must discourage this attack on the Radio Tower. Just continue going about your business.*
>
> *Brigg*

My hands were shaking. I was nervous as to how the other Causes on the forum would respond. "The thread is still busy, so I'll check it again in a few minutes."

Mika mumbled with a mouthful of egg. "Think they'll listen?"

I could only shake my head and hope.

Kay made her opinion known. "Dice does have a point. Getting over four hundred people to change their minds in such a short time sounds like a pretty tall order."

Kay and Dice did a good job of making the task sound completely hopeless. The more they spoke, the greater the feeling of imminent failure became. Sure, ignoring it and letting it happen anyway was an option to take into consideration. But deep down, I knew the consequences would far outweigh whatever message

Al & Jal were hoping to send by ransacking the Radio Tower.

As expected, when I refreshed the forum looking for replies to my post, I was bombarded by negative responses. In some cases, questions of my allegiance came forth from some of the more outspoken Causes. It was a thoroughly disheartening sight.

"The look on your face says it all, Brigg." Dice remarked; his voice emanating a mild sympathy.

I rubbed my face with my hands and mumbled, "This is definitely serious business."

Kay took the liberty of reminding me, "Yeah, well, the Interactive Network is serious business right now!" She huffed, setting her empty plate to the side.

It was at that point I realized that by participating in the Revolution, I was committing myself to a lot more than what I bargained for.

Apparently, I had associated myself with a bunch of over-zealous youths who sought to uncover the truths about Eden at any cost. It didn't surprise me now that those costs included self-sacrifice, because that was definitely what that massive group of Causes was headed into.

I knew in my gut that these machinations would not achieve any beneficial results for the Causes. It would only serve to anger the Fifteen and lay the foundation for them to act more severely toward our side.

Something had to be done. On that forum, though, it became painfully obvious that words alone were not going to do it. We had to take action.

However, with no time to plan properly, I stood up from my seat and said the first thing that came to mind. "We have to go there…"

"I see," Kay smiled, pleased. "So you see that this is how it is going to be?"

Dice readied himself for a roll, kneading his painted wooden cubes in his left hand. "I know what he's going to say…" he groaned.

I took a deep breath before finishing my statement. "…We had better get there in time if we intend to warn Naro about what is going to happen."

"WHAT!?" Kay shouted.

"Interesting…" Dice slowly muttered, casting his dice to the table.

Even Mika seemed a little shocked at my idea. "Are we really going to do that?"

The first valid explanation popped into my head. "It's the only way we can buy the Causes more time until Hatcher shows up."

Kay recoiled. "Hatcher, you say? Why didn't you mention him sooner?"

"In all honesty…" I took a beat, breaking eye contact with her, "I just thought about him."

"Even more interesting…" Dice whispered under his breath. He picked up his dice again and rattled them some more.

Kay rolled her eyes and addressed Mika and myself. "Well, while his dice decide whether or not he should follow with us, I'd like to take this time to ask if you are out of your freaking mind. Well?"

I gestured in a way that demanded an answer to my next question. "What other options are there?"

"We could just ignore it, you know…"

"…And let the consequences of *their* actions come to us?"

She stopped, waiting for me to explain.

I stated a startling point of view. "If the Causes raid the Radio Tower and the Fifteen retaliate, it's safe to say that *all* Causes, whether they were involved in the raid or not, will be sought after."

Kay took a moment to consider it. "All of them?" Her tone had changed.

"Yes, all of them. Including…" I let Kay piece together the end of the sentence for herself as I slowly turned to look to Mika.

Mika looked briefly puzzled, staring right back at me. Kay, too, looked to the sweet youngster, whose mind was in a fleeting moment of disarray.

Reluctantly, Mika pointed to herself and stated the obvious question with a distinct quiver in her voice. "…Me?"

"Why is that?" Kay wondered. "What would the Fifteen want with Mika?"

I turned the floor over to Mika to answer Kay's question. "Mika, would you be so kind as to state for us, once again, why you are here with us in the first place?"

"Well…" She shyly lowered herself back into her chair. It was apparent that my assumptions concerning the Fifteen had Mika in a fit of nerves. "I said before that I'm only hanging around with the Causes so they can help me find my father."

Kay objected. "Wh-what does that have to do with anything?"

"That's exactly my point!" I countered with conviction. "Mika has never once expressed interest in the motives behind the Revolution."

"Wow," Dice interrupted. "Once again, I find myself understanding what Brigg is talking about. Mika has nothing to do with the Revolution. But the Fifteen won't care about that if they retaliate. All they will care about is revenge. Unfortunately, Mika will be completely innocent, being found guilty only by association."

"Thank you!" I sighed. "I'm glad somebody understands me here."

"That's right," he nodded, zipping his collar up the rest of the way to cover his mouth. "Now that you've brought up enough points to make it obvious you are not going to change your mind, this is where we part."

My face scrunched up as Dice's declaration caught me off guard. "Are you serious!? After all that…"

"All that mutual back-scratching…" he cut me off. "Sure, it was nice hanging out and all, but I am not going to rush head-on into that level of trouble." He picked his dice up off of the table and tipped the Contact. "Maybe I'll run into you again. But until that day comes…just try to stay the way you are. That goes for all three of you."

He had one foot out the front door of the restaurant by the time I thought to ask him. "What do you mean by that?"

Dice didn't answer me and just kept on walking. He was soon out of sight.

One thing became certain to me: Dice was no ordinary youth. There was a lot he never really bothered to say about himself. To top it off, his method of "decision-making" was unlike anything I had ever seen in my life. He was truly a strange young man, capable of keeping everyone guessing.

I couldn't help but ponder what was really going through Dice's head when he left us so suddenly. The way the whole scene unfolded made me feel a little bit awkward. It truly gave me the impression that Dice had only been out for himself the entire time he was traveling with us.

Personally, it didn't matter to me at the time as to whether or not we'd see him again. I just wished he had left us saying more than he did. There was that feeling of something missing in his sudden change of direction. Kay, Mika and I felt that hole he left; and all we could do about it was let it creep around in the back of our minds until the day we'd meet again.

II

My heart was set, Mika was willing to cooperate, and Kay was still focused on following the two of us around to keep an eye on me. Looking back on it, it was indeed an odd mix of motives to form a group.

Nevertheless, my point concerning Mika's peril had quite an impact. The young miss convinced herself to help me stop the raid on the Radio Tower instead of simply waiting for the worst to happen.

Kay, on the other hand, was more interested in not leaving Mika alone with me for even a second. Of course, since her other option was to be abandoned by us anyway, she felt it necessary to do what she could to help out with our new mission.

Although Kay had done a fine job of making things more difficult, it seemed that I was becoming more tolerant of her the more she followed me. It was as simple as accepting the fact that she was only being herself: an overly cautious woman who was quick to suspect wrong-doing.

I wanted to spend time over those next couple of days to try and make Kay feel a little more like part of the group. It would have been a welcome change from confronting each other at the drop of a coin. A change in my own attitude felt like a good start.

Despite the need for unity among us, Kay still maintained a low approval rating with Mika and me. It was still going to take her quite a bit of redeeming behavior to get on our good side.

All throughout our hasty journey to the heart of the Fanda Sector, we heard many Causes make mention of the raid that would take place that Sunday. However, not once did I hear anything about any nay-sayers on the topic. It seemed to me that my words not only fell onto criticism, but were soon washed away from the news altogether. The more I heard about it, the more difficult the task of stopping the raid seemed.

I warned Mika and Kay that it would not be a good idea to tell anybody of our intention to warn Naro. There was no telling of the consequences if news of our mission was revealed to the rest of the Causes. We decided to keep low and act as if we were going to mind our own business throughout the ordeal. Hopefully, if I ever found the need to introduce myself, nobody would remember the post I had made in Al & Jal's thread.

The three of us had a lot of ground to cover in order to make it to the Radio Tower. However, it was by no means impossible. Something would have had to severely sidetrack us in order for us to fail in making it there in time. But with no Gray Police in sight, we were clear to take the most direct route there.

The only thing holding us up was our decision to fulfill Mika's wishes. We would spend some time showing off Mika's picture and asking about her father. I felt that Kay and I owed it to her since we had not really been spending a lot of time helping her to begin with. Mika was delighted that we finally had the opportunity to take time-outs here and there to help her as I had intended to from the start.

The last thing on my mind, though certainly not the least important, was how we were going to go about warning Naro of the incoming throngs. Everything, ranging from how we would approach and enter the Radio Tower to the very words we would say to Naro, had to be carefully planned. It all had to come off flawlessly in order to make it look like a warning instead of a threat.

We knew for a fact that it was not going to be easy. The risk involved was almost unspeakable. The concept of facing one of the most recently hostile enemies of the Causes did seem rather self-destructive. Regardless, we felt it had to be done.

This was for the well-being of the entire population of Causes. It was also for the Producers, who still patiently awaited the arrival of Hatcher. Most of all, it was for Mika, along with anyone else who was merely mingling with the Causes for reasons unrelated to the Revolution.

Day 70 – Evening

I

Gathered around a small table in a stuffy chapel basement; Kay, Mika and I focused on a blank cloth parchment. The suspense brought on by our plans to speak with Naro only served to add a heavier feeling to the atmosphere.

I prepared a black marking stylus, taking the tip to the cloth's corner and scribbling on it. There was an odd sense of relaxation in the smooth, sliding sound of every back-and-forth stroke. Although the canvas was otherwise blank, our hopes were high to have it marked with the bearings of our plan for the next day.

Within moments of testing the stylus, I reached over to the upper left corner of the cloth and wrote "12 Noon", saying it softly as I marked it.

"Naro's broadcast goes on the air at Noon, tomorrow," Kay reiterated in a nervous exhalation.

I'll never know why, but the next image that that passed through my mind was that of me getting tackled by a Gray Police officer. It caused me to wince and lightly shake.

Trying to maintain a façade of bravery, I brought my fists to my face. The back end of the stylus rested gently on the middle of my forehead as it seemed to disappear from sight down the bridge of my nose. "What time do you think it would be best to approach the Radio Tower?" I asked openly.

Kay loudly replied, "'Half past *never*' sounds like a promising prospect!"

Her unexpected comment put the first smile on my face since the start of that day. My hands dropped quickly, falling to dangle between my knees. I smirked and shook my head to let her know that her comment was acknowledged, yet unlikely.

More importantly, Mika found it amusing as well. However, her eyes looked hopeful that Kay's reply would be taken into consideration. It was apparent that she was the most anxious out of the three of us to find a way to back out.

Replying to Kay's answer, I asked her with a stare, "Seriously, Kay?"

"Yes," she groaned. Kay threw her hands into her lap and leaned far back into her wooden chair. She let her head and neck hang off of the back to give her a view of the ceiling.

I turned back to Mika to witness the full extent of her fear. Her head was hung and her hands were folded and fidgety. "It doesn't make sense," she mumbled quietly.

"What?" I wondered.

"You've been saying you wanna keep me out of trouble. But we're going to the Radio Tower tomorrow and..." She stopped and sighed loud, giving off the feeling that her words and thoughts were tangled together.

Kay took the floor. "I'm still not sure how we let you talk us into this."

I felt no inclination to dig for answers to that. With haste, I said, "I'm not sure either." Then, to change the subject back, I took the stylus to the parchment again and wrote "11:00 am".

Mika objected. "That only gives us an hour to do something!"

Kay scoffed and shook her head. "Knowing Brigg, that's exactly the point!"

"You're a step ahead of me, you two," I said with a grin. "We want to warn Naro with enough time to act..."

Kay stopped me briefly. "What are you saying?"

Mika was equally put off by my words. "You want them to send the Gray Police after the Causes?"

"No, no, no!" I interjected; gesturing defensively. "If we warn

Naro too early, he'll have a troupe of Grays on the mob. However, if we wait too long to warn him, we may not have enough time to create a solid retaliation."

As I reached to mark that on the parchment, Kay stamped her foot in protest. "What kind of plan could we possibly come up with in an hour?"

I stopped and looked her square in the eye; responding with the utmost honesty. "I have no idea!"

Kay threw her hands up and rolled her eyes. "That's just great!' She stood and began to pace about the room. "You mean to tell me that the only thing we can actually plan is approaching Naro, and that everything else will have to be improvised…" Kay paused to raise her voice. "…That is, IF he doesn't have us arrested on the spot."

Her comment on imprisonment felt like a knife in my heart. Once again, I tried to remain calm. "That's pretty much it." At that moment, I was fully aware of how unsure of myself I sounded. I gritted my teeth and shook my head as I became overcome with second thoughts.

With my eyes droopy with fatigue, I reviewed the parchment. "12 Noon" and "11:00 am" remained the only things written. In retrospect, it was a waste of canvas since what we had planned was not that hard to remember.

"I'm going out to get some air!" Kay huffed as she took hold of the railing on the staircase. "Don't do anything I'd have to kill you for doing."

I knew full well what she meant, but saw no need to tease her about it. Mika and I simply watched her make her way up the creaky staircase toward the chapel's upper level. Mika felt the need to say one last thing to her. "Don't be too long, Kay!"

Hearing Mika, Kay stopped just before the top of the steps. All we could see of her was her feet. She said nothing as she appeared to turn around and take one step down. Then, she stopped again, turned back, and left the basement.

To avoid a scene, Mika and I chose to keep to our opposite ends of the table. Surely if Kay saw the two of us any closer than that when she got back, I'd never hear the end of it.

"Brigg, she needs to start trusting you more," Mika sullenly remarked.

I exhaled as my eyes stayed fixed on the top of the stairs. "Tell me about it!"

Mika reached over and turned the parchment so my writing appeared right-side up to her. She looked it over with an unsure expression dominating her face. Unexpectedly, the young miss opted to completely change the topic. "Kay told me that it's hard to know who to trust."

I was a bit stunned at her choice of subject. I replied in a way that kept me from vilifying Kay. "In many ways, she's right."

"Really?" She seemed confused by my agreement.

"Now that I think about it…" I said as I put a question together in my head.

"Yeah?"

"Now that we're alone, there's a question I've been meaning to ask you, Mika."

An innocent look of curiosity suddenly overtook her doubtful disposition. "What's that?" she asked intently.

"Think back to when we first met…"

"Alright."

I came out with it. "On the train that day, did you think, even for a second, that you couldn't trust me?"

She sat back in her chair with her arms folded and her head tucked down to her chest. After thinking a moment, she answered. "Yes. It was when you first sat down and tried to get my attention."

I pointed at her. "That right there is what Kay was talking about. I had to gain your trust, show you I wasn't a bad guy. Am I right?"

"Yeah," she hummed before turning the question in another direction. "So why doesn't Kay trust you? You've shown her that you're not a bad guy."

Lowering my tone, I looked back to the stairs and said, "Kay thinks my kindness is all an act. She thinks I'm looking to get you alone and take advantage of you."

As I spoke my mind, Mika tried to get my attention. "Um…"

I was still focused on ranting about Kay. "That woman has some problem with men or something. Kay was thinking the same thing about Dice, furious that the two of you were paired up at that hotel…"

Mika spoke louder. "Brigg…"

I acknowledged her. "What's up?"

"I just realized something." Mika rotated her head to look around the basement. "I just noticed that Kay left us alone."

"Yeah, I kind of noticed it too a few minutes ago when she went out for air." I chuckled. Focused on that, I failed to realize why she brought it up specifically.

"Don't you get it?" she pressed.

The way she said it got me to think about the detail a little harder. "Kay left us…"

"…Alone."

It finally hit me. The mere fact that Kay left us to ourselves bore the slight sensation of unity between the three of us. It appeared that by leaving the basement, Kay had developed some inkling of trust that my intentions with Mika were good.

"I'm not out of the woods yet with her, though," I grumbled.

"It's a start," Mika shrugged.

I gestured toward her. "As long as you still trust me to help find your father, that's all that really matters to me."

Mika smiled, breaking eye contact with me. "You really mean that?"

"Definitely!" I assured her. "Once again, I'm really sorry we have to make this little detour."

She quickly shook her head. "Don't sweat it. It's like you said: if the…um…" She seemed to forget how I worded my motives for stopping the raid.

I laughed as I repeated my words. "If the Radio Tower goes down tomorrow, the Fifteen will target every Cause. Even though you are not one of us, they'll still come after you regardless."

"Right. It makes perfect sense."

I rephrased it. "I'm mainly doing this for our long-term protection. This will stall both sides and give us time to find your father."

Mika had a request. "Can we say we're doing this for Dice too; wherever he is?"

"Sure," I said, seeing no harm in that. Feeling nosey, I asked her, "What exactly did the two of you talk about anyway?"

Her eyes got wide. "Me and Dice?"

"Yeah."

She was succinct with her answer. "He told me not to tell you."

I sounded off with a laugh of accepted defeat, "That's just like him."

It felt relaxing to be able to talk to Mika without any interruptions. The two of us kept swapping random questions and answers about ourselves and others. At one point, we had almost completely forgotten about our plans for the next day. It was like nothing else mattered to us other than the words we exchanged.

I took the opportunity to ask her about her clothes; once again pointing out that she was dressed like Lauren from the book.

Mika was shy to answer to my inquiries at first. She was under the impression that I would laugh if she told me the real reason she was dressed like that.

Of course, I promised I wouldn't.

Mika's face was turning red as she began to speak softly. "I like the character so much; I want to grow up to be just like her. I figured this was a start."

I began to think back to reading *One Summer*. The character Lauren was a smart yet carefree teenager who had an equal amount of respect for herself and others. As the author, Devon, described her, she was a "sharp and quick-witted young woman whose beauty was the envy of boys and girls alike."

"I see," I nodded.

Mika clarified her motives. "I want to grow up smart and pretty. It's sort of the other reason I like having Kay around."

I recoiled. "Say what?"

"I figured that would surprise you," she giggled. "I want Kay to teach me how to be a woman. She looks like she can show me the right ways of things."

For some reason, I suddenly felt uncomfortable. I felt like we were on the doorstep of that special talk that parents have with their maturing children. I cut the subject short, somewhat regretting asking the question in the first place. "Maybe when Kay gets back, I'll excuse myself and you two can talk."

"That would be nice." She grinned nervously as she tugged her skirt down a bit.

On cue, Kay returned to the basement. She spoke on her way down the stairs. "I've come to the conclusion that you are insane."

"Maybe just a little bit!" I wittily responded as I stood from my seat.

Kay squinted at me as I patted Mika on the head passing her. "Where are you going?"

"Air sounds good to me too."

"Go for it!" she invited. "There's plenty out there for everyone."

I promptly exited the basement; leaving Mika to talk with Kay about things I assumed I did not want to hear.

As I stepped outside, the cool air of the late hours hit me like a soothing caress. The feel of it caused me to close my eyes and indulge in the sensation.

Upon opening my eyes, the first thing to grab my attention was the Radio Tower. The target was only one kilometer down the street. It reminded me of how fortunate we were to find a place to spend the night that was so close to our destination.

I stood erect and stared at the tower for several minutes. As my thoughts cycled, I felt my heart react in numerous ways. Many of these reactions were shudders, chills and that sudden heavy feeling you get when you are afraid.

In the end, though, I breathed in deep and blew it all out through my nose. In my mind, I saw us succeeding tomorrow. That was all I needed to bring my spirits back up.

One last chill shot down my spine as the thought of the Gray Police pushed my focus aside. It was a testament to how incredibly risky the operation was. I couldn't help but think of how low I would feel if I were to lead us all to our capture.

I shook the thought out. There was no more room for uncertainty. Our hearts and minds had to be in the mission to the fullest.

Confidently, I raised my finger and pointed to the tower in the distance. I spoke quietly. "I can't believe I'm going to save your ass tomorrow. Please, hear us out and let us work together to stop this."

Even though I knew nobody heard me, it felt better to get that out. If anything, it served to solidify my confidence in my motives. I'm sure if the tower were a sentient being, it would have thanked me for my comments.

With my hope restored, I returned to the girls and reviewed

the plan. We were to enter the Radio Tower at 11:00 a.m. sharp. This way, Naro would not have enough time to retaliate drastically against the Causes. However, from there, it would have to be played by ear based on Naro's reactions to our news and advice.

With only slight hesitation, we settled for that to be our plan to stop the raid. Soon after, we executed the first part of our plot: A good night's rest.

Day 71

I

The three of us woke up at about 9:30—just the right time we needed to. This gave us plenty of time to gather the courage to make our final preparations for approaching Naro.

We had only two hours to act. The Causes were going to start gathering and marching toward the tower at 11:00. "This Week in Eden" was to go on the air at noon. That was when the Causes were planning to flood into the tower and take it out.

Having planned that one-hour window the previous night, timing was everything. We wanted to warn Naro, but not with too much time left to act. The last thing we needed was giving Naro enough time to summon a whole force of Gray Police.

It was about time to finally execute our plan. "How do you two feel?" I asked calmly.

"I'm nervous," Mika quickly answered.

Kay looked down to her. "You're lucky. You're just nervous. I feel like I'm going to throw up."

I took a deep breath and let it out very slowly. "What are you two so nervous about? This was my idea in the first place. If anything happens to us, it's entirely my fault."

Kay sarcastically shouted back, "Oh, thanks! I feel *so* much better now!"

The two of them got silent on me. I was actually afraid to say anything else beyond a signal to move forward. There wasn't much left to discuss anyway. All we knew was our goal and our means of achieving it. Everything else, the outcome included, was not for us to decide. Our own words and actions were the only things we were in control of. Our true fate was in the hands of the enemy.

II

By the time 11 o'clock rolled around, the three of us were making our final approach to the entrance of the Radio Tower. I took a moment to notice just how misleading the name "Radio Tower" actually was. The building itself was only two stories tall and constructed of strong, gray-colored stone. The actual tower was the large, metal structure protruding from the top of that building.

The three of us were about a hundred meters away from the tower when we noticed an older man approaching the building from around the corner. It appeared that this man was being escorted to the tower by one Fanda Sector policeman and one Gray Police officer. With such an entourage and the fact that he was carrying a cast-iron case, I found it safe to assume that he was Naro.

Sharing my assumption, Mika spoke. "Is that Naro? He doesn't look very...Fifteen-ish." She almost sounded disappointed.

I couldn't help but agree with her. "I was thinking the same thing..."

I jogged a bit closer to get a better look as he entered the tower. His beige short pants and long-sleeved collared shirt didn't really emanate an essence of authority. The only thing making him look remotely important was the iron case he carried on his right side. Those who had seen Naro in the past could verify that he always had that case near his person at all times.

I turned back to the girls. "I'm certain that is him. I guess we'll find out soon, right?"

Kay exhaled rather audibly as she stopped walking for a

moment. Without directly answering my question, she said, "I always pictured the Fifteen as the type who would intimidate people by making themselves look much more powerful than that."

Mika and I agreed.

This development lifted some of the stress we were feeling. However, we knew for a fact that the Fifteen were an unpredictable party and that Naro could just as easily toss us to the Labor Fields just in time to go on the air for his broadcast.

Just for a brief moment, I was questioning my sanity one last time before taking the next few steps forward. I could feel my stomach doing somersaults in combination with Mika's hand shaking in mine.

Kay was very fearful as well, "I repeat, I can't believe you talked me into this, Brigg."

In a sudden burst of confidence, I broke free of the quiver in my soul, taking the lead with a solid stride. "Let's just get this done. We all know the worst that can happen. If anything goes wrong, I'm sure there's a way we can prove that we came to help."

Kay didn't seem so convinced. "How can you be so sure?"

"Hopefully they'll give us a chance to explain the whole situation. If we have enough room to speak, we'll be in good shape."

Mika sided with Kay seemingly out of last-second desperation to back out. "What if they don't do that for us?"

I didn't want to answer that question. I just threw my hands up in an unknowing gesture and opened the front door to the Radio Tower. After all the hesitation, it was finally time for our chance to change what could have very well been the end of the Revolution for every Cause.

We stepped into an empty lobby. Flat, firm, tan carpet covered the floor to all four corners. The large window above the door gave light to the barren, rectangular foyer. A lone metal folding chair with a green pillow on the seat was the only piece of furniture in the room. It was up against the wall opposite the front door with two other doors to each side of it. The door on the right was locked with a large gate covering it from top to bottom.

After the front door closed behind us, we were able to notice another eerie property of the creepy, vacant foyer. There was no sound. It was as if we had all gone deaf.

Kay was the first to take hurried steps toward the more inviting of the two doors on the opposite end of the room. I, however, decided to examine the other door. Indeed, it was tightly secured with no chance of budging without a key. I ran one of the bars between my fingers before stepping away to rejoin the girls, who were patiently waiting for me.

Just as Kay reached for the handle, the door flew open. To our equal surprise and horror, the tall, menacing figure of a Gray Police officer stood before us.

Mika shrieked in a way I hadn't heard her before. In trying to back away, she stumbled to the floor.

Kay backed up several steps, pulling my hand to follow her. "I knew this was a bad idea," she rapidly declared.

The officer spoke before we had a chance to move any great distance. "What are you doing here?"

I thought quickly. If we ran, we'd be chased. Since the officer didn't make any sudden moves, I saw to simply answer his question. "W-we're here to see Naro."

Kay released my hand and calmed down a bit. Mika scrambled to her feet and hid behind us. We prepared ourselves for anything that the officer could do.

It took us a moment to get our bearings straight as the Gray Police officer stepped from the doorway and looked us over. "Are you Revolutionaries?" he asked.

"The million Arna question," I thought to myself. It was the one thing I was hoping we wouldn't be asked. The consequences of answering that question truthfully would set the pace for the upcoming hour. I swallowed hard and reluctantly nodded.

The officer walked around us in a circle with his massive hands stroking the gruff stubble on his chiseled chin. We kept our eyes on him as he continued to scrutinize us with a scornful, paralyzing glare. Once he was in a position between us and the door, he withdrew his nightstick from his holster and held it to his side. "Naro was expecting this."

The three of us cowered back much further than before. "He was?" I asked. "Does that mean he knows about what's going to happen?"

The officer raised a bushy eyebrow, apparently intrigued by

my question. "What do you mean? What's going to happen?"

Stammering at first, Kay chimed in. "W-w-wait; we asked you first. Why was Naro expecting us?"

The officer stepped to us. "Not so much expecting you specifically, but Naro anticipated that Revolutionaries would show up one day and try to get on the air during his broadcast." He put his nightstick away. "I'm going to ask you to state your purpose here."

It seemed to me that things were starting to calm down; but we had to remain on our guard. The truth got us on the good side of the intimidating officer; so I found no harm in telling the man what was going on. "You see, we're not really looking to wind up on the air…"

Kay cut me off, "We really just need to talk to Naro before he goes on."

"Concerning…?" the officer pressed.

I chose to let loose and spit it out. "This goes back to you asking us about what was going to happen. We came here to warn Naro that as soon as he goes on the air, this Radio Tower is going to find itself under siege by a mob of Revolutionaries."

His face crunched. "A mob!?"

His authoritative roar instantly shot fear into all three of us. I felt Mika jump and clench the back of my vest.

I continued to explain through the tension. "Yeah, a mob! We tried to talk them down, but they wouldn't listen!"

The officer suddenly seemed very unsettled. "And you're telling me you came here to give us a heads up about it?"

We gestured positively, preparing ourselves for the results of our delivery of the big news. Sure enough, the Gray Police officer ordered us, "Wait right here." He scurried through the door and up a flight of stairs.

Shaken, we waited. The air in that silent foyer became a lot less stuffy as our hearts lifted. It was at that point I was finally convinced we had done the right thing.

Now the only thing we needed to do was figure out a way to keep the Radio Tower safe. I was sure that if we pulled together with Naro and the Gray Police everything would turn out for the better in the long run.

III

The officer retrieved us from the lobby and led us to an office on the second floor. Inside, Naro was preparing the last of the news items for "This Week in Eden". We were told to enter without knocking since we were expected guests.

There was little hesitation at this point. Everything seemed to loosen up and our confidence had a sturdy foundation. Together, Kay and I pushed open the large double-doors to take us into Naro's office. Mika cautiously crept in behind us through the dead center of the entrance. I heard Kay inhale deeply as her pace slowed. I kept to her pace while Mika decided to stop completely. By the time the doors closed behind us, we felt like we had entered an entirely different building.

Naro's office stretched very far back, the room itself exuding an ambience of power and mystery. Farther back it seemed as if the place stretched even farther out to each side. Seven desks, each resting on its own individual decorative rug, were placed in a triangle on the far end of the office with enough space between them for one to slip through. The desk along the back wall took up an entire side of the triangle while the other six made up the other two sides. A thick, red carpet stretched from those desks all the way back to the door where we entered, making a path that interrupted the dark blue carpeting underneath. To our right, we saw a comfortable-looking red sofa and loveseat facing each other with a simple table between them. The one thing that really grabbed our attention was the series of painted canvases along the walls. Each one depicted landscapes of Eden's eleven sectors. The 11th painting, which was twice the size of the other ten, was a landscape of the Fanda Sector.

"It doesn't even feel like we're at the Radio Tower anymore…" Kay whispered.

"I know. This is the biggest room I have ever seen."

"Intimidated?"

"Yeah, a little," I agreed.

Mika whimpered, stunned by the sight and size of the office. She jogged to catch up with the two of us and took our hands into hers. We slowly proceeded to the desks.

The silence that enveloped us as we continued toward the

back of the office was interrupted by the sound of a shifting chair and a drawer shutting. A figure, Naro specifically, emerged from his unintentionally hidden position and greeted us on sight. "Welcome, Revolutionaries!" he bellowed mightily.

I locked up. Naro's voice was strong and well projected. The way they were spoken, those two words sounded like he said so much more. It was almost as if his foremost priority was boasting his authority with an attempt to send us cowering into a corner.

It certainly wasn't the time for fear, though. This was the man we had to warn of the upcoming raid.

Kay nodded almost as if she was bowing to him. "Hello," she said meekly.

Mika discreetly leaned in to me. "You were right; it was him in front of the tower."

Naro continued to speak in his authoritative tone. "Please step forward here to my desk. I've been expecting you."

I tried to act casual to ease my nerves as well as those of the girls. "Yeah, the officer told us about that."

We soon found ourselves positioned in the middle of the desk area. To our right, two women— whom we didn't notice on the way in—were each occupying two of the other desks. They were typing away at computers, seeming very engrossed in their duties. They knew we were there, but saw no need to address us.

Naro let us observe for a few more moments as he put the finishing touches on his news list for the show. Once he was finished, he got right down to business with us. "Now then, let's cut right to the demands here. What is it you want to say during the show?"

Throwing off his need to push the conversation along quickly, I stopped it short by replying, "Well, nothing actually…"

My answer elicited a dark chuckle from Naro. "Surely you can't be serious."

"No, I'm quite serious," I briskly defended. "We had no intention of coming here to interrupt your show."

Naro lurched up from his chair and erectly ambled his way around the desk. The three of us began to backpedal, keeping our eyes fixed on him. "This…" he began, easing up on his booming tone, "…is not going as we had predicted."

"Predicted?" I repeated.

He slid his rectangle-frame glasses down away from his narrow, gray eyes and proceeded to wipe them with a white cloth he produced from his pocket. "Yes. We even had ten of our Gray Patrol on standby…"

Those words he spoke presented the perfect chance to throw him for a loop as well as warn him of the danger. I interrupted him by laughing pompously. The fact that Kay and Mika reacted as well supported my move.

"What's so funny!?" Naro shouted, seeming offended.

I shook my head confidently as my stare caught Naro square in the eye. "You're going to need more than ten of them."

"A lot more than ten," Kay added.

One of the two women sounded slightly panicked as she spoke without turning to us. "What are they talking about?"

I dropped the ambiguous act and approached the next part of the conversation with the utmost seriousness. "Look, this is the situation…"

Over the next few minutes we explained the plot of the siege to them, as well as stated our true intentions for being at the Radio Tower. They didn't buy into it at first. Only after several minutes of supported explanations did they choose to believe us.

Naro looked a little pale and seemed a bit on edge. "That many of them…?"

I felt completely in control. My heart raced as a sensation of invincibility coursed through me. "Yes, that many! You did a good job of angering a large number of us Causes. The mob I mentioned are indeed the hundreds of Causes who are taking it too far. We came to warn you…"

I was cut short by the jarring sensation of a flat hand being brought swiftly across the back of my head. "You idiot!" Kay shouted.

The sudden jolt startled me. I shouted back at Kay, completely sidetracking the conversation, "What was that for!?"

Kay's eyes were wide and full of distress. "Do you realize what you just said?"

I tried to repeat myself, unable to immediately pinpoint my alleged error. "I said that he did a good job of angering the Causes, and we came…here…"

Kay, with her voice still raised, condescendingly held her hand to her ear. "One more time…"

I slowed down my speech and examined my words as I spoke them. "He angered…the Caus…"

That was it.

In my episode of overconfidence, I had inadvertently revealed the secret name that the Revolutionaries had given themselves. Worse, I revealed it directly in front of Naro.

Naro began to laugh. He was on to my slip-up and had already begun to ponder the possibilities open to him with this critical piece of information. "All this time…" Once again, Naro's tone and demeanor changed back to that which was present when he welcomed us.

My heart quaked and my head dropped down to meet the top of my chest. Mika tried to comfort me by giving my hand a gentle squeeze. It wasn't doing any good, but I smirked simply to reassure her.

There was no comforting myself, though. Both Kay and I knew the seriousness of this blunder. All I could do was prepare myself for the consequences.

"Eliza!" Naro called.

One of the women at the desks responded, poking her head out from behind her computer monitor. She was a fair looking, middle-aged brunette. As she stood, her garb caught my attention: an all-encompassing, dark gray cloak with solid, decorative shoulder pads. A wide, rising collar spread elegantly behind her head. "What is it, Naro?" she asked intently.

Kay cut in, pacing around angrily. "…*Two* members of the Fifteen! You just revealed our name to *two* members of the Fifteen!"

"Three, actually," the second woman added, keeping her eyes fixed on her work. "I'm Sandra, nice to meet you. I appreciate your actions here today."

Kay walked away from me and over to the sofa. She took another shot at me on her way there. "I need to sit down and wait for the Gray Police to come arrest us!"

Naro had waited patiently for the tangent to end before he addressed Eliza again. "Yes, Eliza. Please, run a search for any sites related to 'Causes', 'Revolution', and the 'Radio Tower'. That should take us to what we've been looking for. Also, see if you can get a hold of Biktor and ask him why his little friend didn't tell us about this."

Elated by Naro's command, she looked at me as she responded, "I'm on it!"

Ignoring the ridicule emanating from Eliza's eyes, I addressed a part of Naro's string of orders. "His little friend?" I wondered.

Naro quickly covered his words. "Nothing you need to worry about now, young man." He then approached me up close. Although he was a few centimeters shorter, he still stood strong and dignified in front of me. "You, boy, have saved us a lot of trouble."

My head was still hanging low with my thoughts racing. I was at a loss for ideas and all I could think about is how that mistake didn't have to happen. Now, the Fifteen were practically at the forum's doorstep and it was entirely my fault.

I could hear Naro talking to me, but his words were going in one ear and out the other. It was difficult for me to understand anything beyond my sudden feeling of worthlessness.

Within moments, though, my trance was broken by a loud bang and a strong, mature voice. "Hold it!"

I could hear Kay responding to the sudden commotion as Mika and I quickly turned around. "Who is this now?"

At that moment, I looked up to see the perpetrator of the interruption. A tall, youthful man with a slender build, shaggy blonde hair, and a purposeful stride was making his way up the red carpet.

It was obvious at first glance that this young man was definitely a Cause. His dark brown pants seemed to hold many items in the six zippered pockets sewn into them. His belt held two small pouches to each side which jingled with the sound of Arna coins as they bobbed about his waist. A simple, dressy-looking blue shirt waved around, not tucked in. Over that shirt, he wore a dark red robe with black trim in quite an odd, yet efficient fashion. The back of the robe was actually folded up to his shoulders and held in place by a second belt that hugged his chest. It seemed that the way he wore that robe gave him even more storage for his personal items.

"And just who do you think you are barging into my office like this!?" Naro roared.

"Last time I checked, my name is Bogen. And on behalf of…" He stopped short in his introduction and took a look around. After a moment to think about it, he addressed me. "Brigg, I presume."

A sudden wave of shock swept over me. One of the Producers, Bogen, had arrived on the scene. It appeared that he was there for the same reasons we were. I pointed to him as Mika stepped aside to join Kay over on the couch. "How do you know who I am?"

As Bogen stepped past me to talk with Naro, he placed his hand on my shoulder and moved in close to my ear. If he had gotten any closer, the tuft of blonde goatee in the middle of his chin would have been tickling the side of my cheek. "You're not the only one who objected to the upcoming raid. But I certainly didn't expect you to actually show up here."

Still stunned, I assumed, "Which is why you entered the office the way you did…"

"So, if I understand correctly," Naro interrupted, "you're all here to stop your own kind from destroying your own enemy."

"It doesn't make much sense to me either," Kay replied from across the room. "Personally, I wanted to let it happen at first!"

Eliza called to Naro. "I found it, Naro. They have an entire forum on the Interactive Network. The whole 'Cause' business is what kept it hidden for so long. It seems they are led by a group called 'The Producers'."

"What!?" Bogen hollered, turning to me with disbelief. "How did they…?"

Before he finished his sentence, I raised my hand, guilty as charged.

Bogen was livid. "You told them!?"

I shrugged my shoulders as defensively as I could. "It was an accident."

Bogen gestured to stay on the topic of the raid. "We'll talk about this later. There isn't much time left before the rest of the Rev…" he stopped speaking, shooting me a frustrated look to further accentuate his furor at my mishap, and corrected his statement. "There's not much time left before the other *Causes* get here."

I knew I was going to have a lot of explaining to do. If one

Producer knew about it, sure enough, when Bogen returned to the rest of them, they would all know it too. There was no telling what would happen to me from there.

Naro called everyone to his attention after hearing a brief report from Eliza. "I can't believe I'm doing this, but I will be willing to bargain with you if you can stop your Causes from succeeding."

Bogen stepped forward. "I am one of the leaders of the Revolution for the side of the Causes. I have more than enough influence to take care of this myself."

I huffed. "So you are basically saying we came here for nothing?"

"On the contrary, Brigg!" Bogen said, turning to me. "The more Causes we have on this side, the better. I'm sure a lot of people have read your post based on how many negative replies it got. I felt your point deep down, though. I, too, agree that this raid is not the right answer." He patted me on the shoulder. "Mistake or not, you're still on my side in this as long as you still want to stop it." He extended his hand to mine, and we shook hands. His grip was tight and sure.

Kay and Mika came walking back to join in the talks again. "We're running out of time here..." Mika reminded us.

Bogen bent down to meet her face to face. It was quite a ways considering Bogen was significantly taller than all of us. "You're right, little girl."

She giggled, shyly turning sideways and folding her hands in front of her. "I'm Mika!"

Bogen pleasantly chortled and ruffled her hair. He then kissed her on the forehead.

Kay gave him a protective shove. "Get your hands off of her!"

Bogen caught his balance as he responded with grit in his voice. "And you are...?"

"Kay."

"Kay, you say?" He started turning back and forth alternating gazes to the two of us. "Wait a second. Brigg is with Kay?" He laughed out loud. "I thought you two..."

Naro displayed sudden fury. "Can we get on with this? My tower is going to be under siege within the next few minutes!"

Once again, Naro's shouting sent all of us into a shiver.

Seeming almost shattered with nerves, Bogen took the conversation while Kay, Mika and I gathered our things. "Right...bargain. I heard you say bargain. What kind of bargain were we talking?"

"What do you want from me in exchange for your help?" Naro offered.

"Well," Bogen exhaled, calming down, "There is quite a list of things that the Causes are looking to ask for from the Fifteen as a whole."

Naro scoffed. "Like what?"

Bogen lazily shrugged, "The answer to that will come in due time, Naro." He followed up with a deep breath and a solid demand. "What we really want right now is for you to call off the Gray Police from the Pata Sector and restore the train service. If you promise to do that, we will promise to do our best to stop the raid."

Naro looked to Eliza and Sandra, appearing to seek their opinion on the matter.

"I don't see a problem with that deal," Eliza said as Sandra agreed with a brief nod.

Naro blew a long breath before continuing. "...For how long?"

Bogen was on top of keeping his haggling in our favor. "You and I will discuss that after we stop the raid. There's a special announcement I've come to give you on behalf of the Producers. We don't have the time to go over all of the details though. Trust me, it won't obligate you to do anything more than I've already asked."

Naro thought a moment before taking a key out of his pocket. "Sandra!" he called.

Sandra stood. She was wearing a robe similar to the one Eliza had on. Though they dressed the same, the noticeable difference between the two was that Sandra looked ten years younger and had a lighter shade of red for her hair. The docile, charming woman prepared for Naro's instructions.

Naro threw the key to her. "I need the yellow case from the gated storage room."

Sandra nearly missed catching the key as she confirmed her order. "Sure thing."

Naro turned back to us. "All right, I'll leave it be for now. However, if you fail to stop the raid, our Gray Units will stay as is."

Something struck my mind. I blurted out, trying to contribute. "Also…"

Bogen seemed annoyed. "What was that for? You're killing my whole vibe here."

"We still need an apology."

Naro laughed heartily. "An apology for what?"

Trying to tie up all the loose ends, I said, "An apology for accusing Causes of the murder of that innkeeper in the Pata Sector."

"You know what, he's right!" Bogen agreed, snapping his fingers.

Naro regretfully shook his head. "I'm afraid I can't do that."

"Why not?"

"You see," he explained, "one of your Causes was indeed the murderer that night. My fellow leaders Biktor and Haz have already caught up with the perpetrator."

"Is that so?" Bogen nodded. "Well, at least whoever it was is no longer associated with us. They sure caused us a lot of unnecessary trouble."

Kay let out a notable sigh. She also seemed relieved that there was no longer a murderer running free with the Causes.

"It seems we have reached our agreement then," Naro concluded. "As long as you keep this tower safe, I will call off the Gray Police and resume the train service in the Pata Sector."

"It is agreed," Bogen announced.

Naro shook each of our hands to seal the deal. "Yes, agreed."

Just as we looked to the clock to see that only seven minutes remained, Sandra returned with the yellow case that Naro had sent her for. Naro ordered her over. "Ah, good! Sandra, bring it here." He then turned to us. "Give us a few moments will you?"

Bogen pulled Kay, Mika and me aside. "I just wanted to thank you all for being here. It made things a lot easier." He then addressed me specifically with a tone of regret. "However Brigg, by your slip up, they found the forums."

"What is going to happen to me?"

He lightly squeezed my shoulder and got close to whisper. "I don't know. In any other case, I'd have you seen as a traitor to the Causes. However, this is a delicate situation that obviously required some sacrifices. We're at a disadvantage right now against the Fifteen since they know some of our secrets."

"Are you implying to let the raid happen anyway?" Kay interrupted.

"Not at all. The Causes will just have to find better leverage. According to Hatcher's last post, he has the trump card for our side."

"But that was over five weeks ago…"

Naro interrupted us. He was done talking to Sandra and we were almost out of time. "Young people, I have something very important that will help you."

The four of us drew closer to him as he took the yellow case from Sandra and prepared to present us with its contents. Kay spoke the first thing on her mind. "You're giving us a tool to help us do this because if you go out there, there's no telling what that mob of Causes would do to you, right?"

"You are a bright young woman," he complimented. "That is absolutely right."

I inhaled deeply as my nerves calmed. I was beginning to feel a lot more relaxed with this sudden feeling of unity with the enemy. As odd as it sounds, I was glad that the Fifteen had become accepting of us because of our decision to act against our own.

Naro opened the case to reveal a strange device I had never seen before. It was like a small gray box with a handle sticking out of the bottom of it and a wide red cone popping out from the side. It looked as if the tip of the cone had been driven into the box. There was a small button on the handle. The device was surrounded by a protective material to keep it from damage while in its case.

As we stood there bedazzled by the mysterious tool, Naro began to explain what it was. "This is a voice amplifier. Feel free to take it by the handle."

I was the closest to it, so I reached in and grabbed it. It was a little weighty, but easy to wield with one hand. Looking closer, I saw a circular screen on the back of the box part. "How does it work? What does it do?"

Naro replied with his wisdom. "Well, as its name implies, it amplifies your voice. You can use this so you can speak louder than the entire gang of Causes headed our way. The fact that you'll even have a device like this should stop their advance."

"They'll have no choice but to listen to us then," Mika added.

As I continued to rotate it about in my hand to examine it from every angle, I asked Naro, "What do I do to use this?"

With a laugh at my quizzical curiosity, he taught me. "You simply press the button on the handle and speak into the screen."

As instructed, I pushed the button on the handle and spoke: "*LIKE THIS?*" I asked.

Everyone in the room jumped and covered their ears at the sudden burst of noise. "Yes, like that," Naro replied, slightly amused.

Bogen made an observation. "It's no big surprise that the head of entertainment, *communications,* and media is in possession of such a unique device."

Kay wondered, "Why would you give us control of something like this? Surely you had it hidden away for a good reason."

Naro found it appropriate to not answer her question just yet. The time was 11:57 am. Naro was to go on the air and we were going to stop the raid. "I will explain everything later. Let's get through this and we'll have a chat after my show."

Bogen took the voice amplifier and the lead. "He's right. Let's get out there and stop this madness." The four of us, now led by Bogen, rushed back to the entrance of the Radio Tower.

Naro bid us good luck.

IV

We burst through the front door of the tower to see the legion of Causes drawing close. Mika immediately backed away behind the rest of us, suddenly overtaken by the sheer size of the assembly. The rest of us gaped in amazement at the result of Al & Jal's planning.

Apparently Al & Jal had a more powerful influence than we had anticipated. The sight of the crowd put us under the impression that this was just the start of a full-on rebellion rather than a simple protest.

Since the congregation made their way up the middle of many

of the Fanda Sector's streets, the average citizens had all cowered indoors. It was quickly realized that even if we stopped this mass from taking over the tower, they had already dealt damage to the title "Cause". It felt like the non-violent creed that the Producers had put in place was coming to a crashing halt.

Bogen's brow furrowed. The front line of the whole rabble slowed down at the sight of us standing at the Radio Tower entrance. He found that brief hesitation as his chance to speak up and stop their advance. "I refuse to let this happen while I'm in charge here!"

His words reached me through my overwhelmed state. "Th-they're all yours."

Bogen nodded to us then turned to address the crowd. He lifted the voice amplifier to his mouth, pushed the button and belted out as loud as he could, "MY FELLOW CAUSES...STOP!"

The mob's marching slowed a little more, but they still seemed determined to complete their mission.

"They aren't listening!" Mika cried out.

Bogen let Mika's comment in one ear and out the other as he lifted the amplifier to his lips again. "AS A MEMBER OF THE PRODUCERS, I, BOGEN, ORDER YOU ALL TO STOP THIS!"

That was it. With the right words spoken, the flock of Causes began to react. Soon, the front line came to a stop, turning around to stop the rest of the crowd. The chain reaction took several moments to bring the Causes to a complete and attentive halt.

There was clamoring and excessive chatter from the once-hostile mass. We allowed them a few minutes to talk amongst themselves as we finally caught our breath. The sounds of speech were littered with instances of not only Bogen's name, but my forum name as well.

Kay spoke quietly to me. "It seems that word of your post got out as well."

Rickety, I nodded, still shaken by how close we were to failure.

Kay continued her comment. "Now, if this gang doesn't run us over anyway, we'll consider ourselves very lucky."

I shared my own perspective of luck with her. "We were already lucky to have Bogen show up like that. They probably would not have listened to us otherwise."

Bogen continued speaking to the horde, leaving a dramatic pause between each sentence. "CAUSES, THIS PLOT WAS BROUGHT TO MY ATTENTION BY OUR CONTACT, BLACK. I READ EVERY LAST POST IN THAT THREAD UP TO A FEW DAYS AGO. IT WAS THAT DAY THAT I NOTICED THINGS HAVE GONE TOO FAR. WE SHOULD NOT BE RESORTING TO ACTS OF DESTRUCTION LIKE THE ONE THAT WAS PLANNED FOR TODAY."

The audience reacted. Many of them could be heard referencing Naro's hostile messages toward our side.

"PLEASE ALLOW ME TO FINISH!" Bogen ordered, slowly bringing the bickering to a stop.

"Definitely lucky, like you said…" Kay whispered. "They're listening. There is some order to this."

Bogen resumed his speech. "I DON'T KNOW IF AL & JAL ARE HERE. FRANKLY, I DON'T CARE IF THEY ARE OR NOT. BUT IF THE TWO OF THEM CAN HEAR ME, I JUST WANT TO LET THEM KNOW THAT I WILL NOT ACCEPT BEHAVIOR LIKE THAT AMONG OUR KIND HERE. MYSELF AND THE REST OF THE PRODUCERS WORKED LONG AND HARD ON ASSEMBLING THE RULES THAT THE CAUSES SHOULD ABIDE BY DURING THE REVOLUTION. WHAT AL & JAL SUGGESTED WAS GOING COMPLETELY AGAINST EVERYTHING THAT WE WORKED SO HARD TO PUT TOGETHER."

We could see the Causes nodding, understanding what Bogen was saying. Light murmuring resonated through the mass.

I stepped forward, trying to take the voice amplifier from Bogen so I could say something. He jerked his hand away and gave me a smile. "Don't worry. You'll have your chance to speak."

Kay muttered something I couldn't quite hear. When I turned to ask what she had said, she refused to repeat it. She and Mika began femininely snickering to each other while Bogen was piecing together this next statement.

I let it go and walked past the two girls, re-entering the Radio Tower lobby. I quickly grabbed the lone chair and brought it back outside; offering it to Bogen to stand on so the crowd could see him a little bit better.

Bogen took position on the chair and released another newsflash into the ears of the Causes. "AS OF RIGHT NOW, THE PRODUCERS ARE STILL WAITING FOR HATCHER TO ARRIVE. ONCE HE DOES, WE WILL MEET AND DISCUSS OUR DEMANDS AS PLANNED. UNTIL THEN, I HAVE SPOKEN TO NARO. HE IS WILLING TO CALL OFF THE GRAY POLICE AND RESUME ALL TRAIN SERVICE UNDER THE STIPULATION THAT THE RADIO TOWER REMAIN UNDAMAGED."

The multitude threw itself into a mild uproar at this news. It was apparent that many of these Causes were looking for some more action to pass the time and cripple the Fifteen. They actually pressed forward a few steps, forcing Bogen to shout into the voice amplifier until they came back to order.

After that, Bogen handed the amplifier to me. "It's my turn?" I thought aloud.

Nervous, I took the amplifier into my hand. I usurped Bogen's position on the chair and suddenly froze. Looking out at that mob was like coming face to face with everybody who shunned me on the forums. The thought of every set of eyes piercing me like a thousand sewing needles sent a quiver down my spine.

I tried to shake it off, breathing deeply. I swallowed hard and gave my speech to the awaiting audience. "FOR THOSE OF YOU WHO MAY NOT HAVE GUESSED IT BY NOW, I'M BRIGG. AS OF A FEW DAYS AGO, I APPEARED TO BE THE ONLY ONE WHO ACTUALLY OPPOSED THIS ACTION. UP UNTIL TEN MINUTES AGO, I THOUGHT I WAS ALONE…"

"Uh…Hello!" Kay called out.

I recoiled at realizing that mild slip-up. I rolled with it and continued. "…I THOUGHT *WE* WERE ALONE IN THIS. I WASN'T SURE IF WE WERE DOING THE RIGHT THING BY COMING HERE TO WARN THEM OF YOU ALL COMING. WHEN BOGEN ARRIVED, HOWEVER, THAT TOLD ME SOMETHING. IT TOLD ME THAT THIS SIEGE WAS A BAD IDEA FROM THE START. EVERYTHING ABOUT IT WAS WRONG AND AL & JAL SHOULD BE ASHAMED OF THEMSELVES..."

"Where are you going with this?" Bogen impatiently asked.

I spoke to him quickly, without the amplifier, "Give me a break, I'm nervous."

"He *is* the only person who posted against this after all," Mika assisted.

I grabbed the first thing out of my brain to squelch the situation and projected it through the amplifier. "ANYWAY, I THINK IT WOULD BE BEST IF WE JUST CONTINUE TO GO ABOUT OUR BUSINESS AND WAIT FOR HATCHER TO ARRIVE. WE'VE DONE A GOOD JOB OF STICKING TO THE ITINERARY OF THE PRODUCERS. LET'S JUST TRY TO KEEP IT UP. I'M CONFIDENT THAT ALL OF OUR QUESTIONS WILL BE ANSWERED IN DUE TIME ONCE THE FIFTEEN HEAR WHAT WE WANT."

The Causes cried out various responses while some in the back of the crowd seemed to listen and leave. A jumble of the people dispersed and left. Nevertheless, many didn't seem so convinced. Their main argument was the fact that Hatcher had not been heard from in quite some time. Without solid proof that Hatcher would show up soon, any attempt to diffuse that argument would fail.

It seemed that Bogen thought of a quick enough response to the audience's newfound lack of confidence. He hurriedly whisked the voice amplifier back into his possession and took my spot on the chair. "I DIDN'T WANT TO HAVE TO RESORT TO THIS; BUT I'M LEFT WITH LITTLE CHOICE." His dramatic tone hushed the crowd once again. They were ready to hear anything he would dish out to them.

Kay read my mind and shared a mutual feeling. "I don't like the sound of this."

Bogen reluctantly continued. "IF IT JUST SO HAPPENS THAT SOMETHING HAS GONE WRONG WITH HATCHER, THEN THE PRODUCERS ARE GOING TO HAVE TO PROCEED WITHOUT HIM."

There was an awed and delicate silence. Everybody in attendance now knew that Bogen was serious business! For the first time since the legion arrived, there was finally absolute silence among every one of them who had stayed that long to listen. Bogen's words even had Kay and Mika very intrigued.

Boldly, Kay was the first to speak up. "I thought Hatcher said that…"

Bogen cut her off with the amplifier still active. "I AM AWARE OF HATCHER'S ANNOUNCEMENT OF CRUCIAL INFORMATION AND HIS REQUEST FOR US TO WAIT. THAT IS WHY WE WILL GIVE HIM ONE MORE WEEK TO SHOW HIMSELF OR POST ON THE FORUMS. IF WE DO NOT HEAR FROM HIM BY THAT TIME, THE PRODUCERS AND I ARE GOING TO PROCEED IN OUR TALKS WITH THE FIFTEEN WITHOUT HIM."

The announcement itself exuded an unsettling air. This came from the same mouth that moments ago criticized actions that went against the Producers' rules. "We're going to defy Hatcher!?" Kay exclaimed.

Bogen defended himself and his decision. "Hey, I'm just as much a Producer as Hatcher. I should be able to override his word at a time like this."

The horde began to talk amongst themselves as Kay, Mika and I began to question Bogen's actions. "What do you mean 'time like this'?" Kay pressed. "We stopped the raid, didn't we?"

Without missing a beat, he put a bigger picture into view. "Who's to say this won't happen again, huh? Who's to say Al & Jal may not plot another get-together like this?"

I added to Bogen's side. "We don't know what every individual Cause is thinking. Maybe this raid attempt would give other Causes the idea to try this elsewhere."

Bogen interrupted me, still directing his argument to Kay. "I'm certain that the rest of the Producers are not up for cleaning up any huge messes the likes of which we could have seen here today."

Kay sounded uncertain, yet willing to accept Bogen's announcement. "I hope you know what you're doing."

Without another word to her, Bogen turned back to the crowd of Causes and readied his voice one last time. "PLEASE CONTINUE TO GO ABOUT YOUR BUSINESS. WE WILL SEE TO IT THAT NARO CARRIES OUT HIS PART IN OUR NEGOTIATIONS. OTHER THAN THAT, THERE IS NOTHING ELSE FOR CAUSES HERE TODAY. PLEASE RETURN TO WHATEVER IT WAS YOU WERE DOING BEFORE THIS."

Grumbles and mixed reactions could be heard from the multitude of Causes as they began to spread out and leave.

Our mission of stopping the siege on the Radio Tower was a success. That feeling of great accomplishment washed over me as I sat in the chair to catch my breath. Mika approached me and placed her hand on my shoulder. "We did good, huh?"

Bogen answered for me. "We're not done yet. We need to wrap things up here with Naro. Then, I have to get back together with the rest of the Producers and tell them what happened here."

I stood, grabbed the chair and began to lead everyone back into the Radio Tower. Just as I reached for the door, there was a loud bang. We all looked around to see that a small object had been thrown in our direction from what was left of the grouping of Causes.

Mika picked it up off of the ground and gasped in surprise. We gazed at the object: an unmistakable black die with white dots.

Mika giggled as she grabbed the voice amplifier and turned toward the streets. "IT CAME UP AS A FIVE, DICE!"

We heard his voice over the rest of them. "Damn it!"

I couldn't help but smile as well. I took the amplifier from Mika and called out to him. "GET YOUR BUTT BACK OVER HERE WHERE YOU BELONG!"

It seemed to me that Dice's decision to leave us may have been thrown to the wayside by a later roll of his dice. Either that or he chose to participate in the raid by rolling. Either way, his decision-making method found its way to bring him back to us. He was still the disagreeable, cynical, sarcastic stick-in-the-mud we always knew. But in a way, it felt good to have him back.

V

It took us most of the afternoon to bring the whole episode to a close. Most of it was spent in Naro's office, being specific about the terms of our negotiations. Naro assigned Eliza to send a message out to all of the Gray Police and order them to return to the Exta Sector and the Labor Fields. This would keep them out of the public eye and out of the Causes' hair.

The resuming of train service was a problem though. After the trains were ordered to stop, the crews began maintenance on them or simply went home. It was going to take some time to bring the trains back to running order with full crews.

Naro assured us that he wouldn't drag in carrying out his end of the negotiations. He had Eliza send a message to Riley to get the trains back up as soon as possible.

We had questions for Naro as well. The biggest ones on our mind concerned the strange voice amplifier he provided for us. Nobody in Eden had ever seen such a device. It put us under the impression that there were many more creations for communications and that Naro knew every one of them.

Naturally, Naro wasn't going to discuss the amplifier, its inventor, or its origins. All he told us was that it seemed like the most appropriate tool to use to stop the siege and if the circumstances had not been so extreme, he would have never shown it to us in the first place.

It was at that time we saw a side of Naro that was a lot more into his authoritative role than the Naro we saw at first. He told us the Radio Tower was his home. His life and its mission all rested within the tower's walls. Communications, media, entertainment, and everything we heard from the radio were the focus of Naro's existence. By the time he got done explaining to us how important that tower was to him, we felt as if he would drop dead on sight if anything were to happen to it.

There was something about that conversation that told me there was more to being a member of the Fifteen than any of us could ever understand. To hear Naro being overly passionate about his role as a key person in Eden's very structure left a chill behind at the thought of the mysteries that surrounded it.

The whole discussion almost tempted me to throw some questions at Eliza and Sandra. However, it was best to keep from trying to find out too much at one time. We already had Naro pour himself out to us. We weren't about to try to bite off more than we could chew.

Bogen also took time to explain to the three of them that the Producers were prepared to discuss bringing an end to the Revolution. This, of course, meant that our demands for the truths about Eden would have to be met. Bogen left that detail out though. He only wanted to persuade them with the aspect of putting Eden's state of turmoil to a close.

Naro, Eliza and Sandra responded rather cooperatively. They viewed the outcome of the raid as a ray of hope for the Causes and the Fifteen. They told us that this was our opportunity to work together and restore peace to Eden once again.

Bogen had them fooled though. By omitting our specific demands from the conversation for the time being, he lured them into a sense that we were ready to surrender. The sly man's tongue was very slick and his words were carefully chosen.

By the time the negotiations were over, Bogen had their attention. They were willing to listen to anything we had to say if it meant the end of the Revolution. They chose a meeting place not too far from the location where the Producers originally gathered. Once there, the terms would be discussed.

Mika, Kay, Dice, and I kept our mouths shut most of the time. When prompted to speak, we simply agreed. I had said enough that day to mess things up, but it seemed to me that by the next week, it would not have mattered anyway.

It was going into the evening by the time we said goodbye to the three members. Bogen set out to rejoin the rest of the Producers to wait for Hatcher. He kept to his word and was going to announce to the public that Hatcher had one week to arrive at the meeting location.

Everything looked to be in place. But whatever key piece of information Hatcher had would then be factored out of our leverage against the Fifteen. All we could do is hope that Hatcher's presence at the meeting would not be as important as he declared it would.

Finally, with the raid prevented and peace restored for the time being, we could continue with what brought the four of us together in the first place:

We had a week to search for Mika's father.

Episode 4: Hatcher's Response

Six days passed and there was still no sign of Hatcher. By this time, the forum found itself flooded with countless opinions concerning where he was and what he was doing.

Al & Jal still remained the most outspoken duo among the entire population of Causes. Unfortunately, instead of adding input to the subject of our missing leader, they chose to set their sights directly on me and my party. With their influence established, they continued questioning our allegiance throughout the waiting period.

Nevertheless, with Naro's end of the bargain upheld, many Causes found it difficult to judge us too harshly.

Still, my slip in revealing the name 'Cause' to the Fifteen was brought to light. It was the biggest factor in the negative judgment my party and I had been receiving.

On the topic of the day of the raid, though, it was known that Al & Jal *were* in attendance. The reason they did not step forward when we were holding the mob off was a mystery.

Fortunately for us, their lack of action turned some criticism toward them. If they were so adamant about the siege of the Radio Tower, why did they let us win so easily?

The forum was now a colorful tapestry of mixed reactions from those on the Revolution's side. The Producers themselves even expressed a disinterest in my words and actions with Naro. But with the Fifteen meeting with the Producers the next day, they decided not to label me or my group as anything unsavory. Surely, Bogen must have convinced them to spare our name.

Bogen didn't stick around with us long enough to help figure that one out. This put me in a position to draw conclusions with my party with no insight from those we considered as a higher authority.

We tried not to dwell on too many questions though. Our top priority was finding Mika's father before the Revolution proceeded further.

We were delighted to have Dice back as part of our team. Despite his naturally disagreeable nature, he needed no effort to show us just how knowledgeable he was.

I knew that when I had first met him in person, I was foolish not to realize just how vastly intelligent the surly youth was. Upon comparison, we found that his Interactive Study Grade was noticeably higher than mine or Kay's. This was a fact that he knew we'd commit to memory for the events in which he would offer his own brand of advice.

Dice also explained in better detail why he left us in the first place. He was merely looking out for his own skin. At the same time, he did it to see from a distance that I wasn't just blowing hot air when I chose to step forward and stop the raid.

His words, not mine.

What he didn't expect to do was find himself roped into the mob by nothing else but a roll of his dice. To my credit, though, he told me that he factored the possibility of meeting up with us again into his odds for that fated roll.

Kay appeared to have warmed up to me just a little bit. However, she was still a far cry off from fully trusting me or Dice alone with Mika. Once again, I tried questioning her about that topic. But as before, it was met with the same speech about how Mika and I paired up on the train so suddenly two weeks back.

I was still finding it difficult to accept her attitude toward me. Though we wouldn't say it, Dice, Mika, and I were secretly hoping that she would eventually change her mind.

Our times of traversing Eden's landscapes felt to be growing short. The end of Bogen's deadline was at hand.

Day 77

I

The search for Mika's father took us further westward through the Fanda Sector. But it was on this day that we found ourselves at the border of the next sector, Binda.

Binda is a large, residential sector dotted with small business districts. Its landscape and layout are similar to two of its neighboring sectors; Archa to the northeast and Doma to the south. Binda also shares its northern border with the Exta Sector, where all of Eden's products are assembled and shipped from. Being so close to both Exta and Fanda make the sector the most beneficial to live in; and the most populated one in Eden.

We were given information from a lone Cause concerning our search for Mika's father. He happened to see a man who looked like the one in Mika's drawing. He was assisting a business in the sector's lower eastern side. Though it seemed a bit unlikely that her father would be in such a plain-sight place, any lead was better than coming up dry.

Mika was very excited at how close we seemed to be. It was the best clue we had received since we started the search. The jumpy young girl's attitude shifted from timid yet cheerful to excitable and talkative. She was no longer keeping herself in the distant meekness that she had portrayed through our previous situations. Mika finally felt like she belonged with us rather than just following a group of protectors. This was her time to shine and we were there to smile with her.

Dice spoke grandiosely upon our crossing the sector's border. "Welcome to my place. I hope you enjoy your stay."

"You're from Binda?" Mika asked.

"Yes. My home is quite a ways west from here, though," he added. Quickly, he jumped in with one last thought. "Before you get any ideas, no, we are not going to pay my house a visit."

Mika smiled, pushing the sharp tone of his comment aside. "Fair enough."

Dice turned the subject on the rest of us, asking where we all came from. Within our answers, Kay and I discovered that we were both from the Doma Sector and Mika was from Archa. Dice chuckled at the coincidence in the findings. "Well, at least the two of you have *something* in common, right?"

Mika sweetly giggled, stepping behind Kay and pushing her toward me. "Now, if the two of them could just get along we could have something going on here."

"Mika!" Kay gasped as she bumped up against me. "Don't give him ideas!"

I was completely lost for words. It was not because I couldn't think of any, I was just afraid to reply to that. Even though my hands went into the air when she drew close, Kay gently pushed me away by my shoulder.

Dice shot a comment to us. "That will only be what the two of you make of it."

"Trust me," I replied, "I don't plan on making anything of it." I began to walk a little faster with my hands still raised.

"You wouldn't want me anyway," Kay abruptly stated.

As Dice hurried to catch up with Mika, I stopped to engage Kay again. "And why is that!?" My arms returned to a relaxed state as I turned, waiting for her to respond.

As soon as my eyes met hers, I locked up. The expression on her face made me feel like I had said something wrong. Her eyes were open wide and her pupils were like specks, as if she had thought of a thousand answers at once. It sent a chill into my heart.

I nudged her shoulder. "Kay?"

She gasped and shook briefly, blinked a few times, then looked at me. She opened her mouth a little then softly bit her bottom lip. "…Never mind."

It felt strange. One of us definitely said something we shouldn't have. "What…?"

"I said never mind!" she snapped. It took her a moment to calm herself, but without another word, she ran to catch up with Mika and Dice.

I followed, still feeling off-key.

Our first order of business was to locate the Delta Business District—the exact point where the borders of Doma, Binda, and Fanda connect.

In the center of the district, there is a decorative landmark that actually outlines the borders. Citizens of the area oftentimes find themselves playing around like children, acting like it's a big deal to go from sector to sector in an instant—or to stand in two sectors at the same time. It was that very landmark that would be the starting point for our searching that day.

II

Once we arrived in the Delta Business District, Mika took the picture of her father back out and handed it to me. She felt it was necessary for us to refresh our memories as to what he looked like.

Everything seemed to be going smoothly except for the fact that something still bothered me about Mika's illustration. The heavy erasure marks around the man's eyes left a lot of room for a potential error if it were to be left up to Kay, Dice, or myself to spot him. Only Mika would be the one to be one-hundred percent certain that any one man would be her father.

Dice was the most wary of this detail. He went so far as to verbally question the accuracy of the drawing. Mika defended herself, feeling she made no mistake in doing the best she could.

Kay sided with her as well, stating that certain people can have trouble drawing certain body parts. I could relate to that argument as well since I was not that good at drawing at all.

Dice knew he was being a little harsh, but played it off as just being "realistic". He declared that our chances of finding him were lower than they could be since the illustration was not completely accurate. Regardless, we kept our eyes open for Mika's father as we made our way to the Delta Landmark.

Each business we passed on our way to the landmark was met with our eyes peering through the windows and scanning any outdoor kiosks. Every café, inn, and shop was invaded by our four-person search party as we methodically picked the path to the Delta apart. This was one lead that we were not going to take lightly. By the afternoon, we felt the whole business district knew this fact.

At one point, the proprietor of a fabric shop reinforced our previous lead. His information led us to believe that Mika's father was assisting businesses at random to earn Arna and food. Mika agreed that it may have very well been true given the circumstances that were present before he went missing.

However, the fabric store owner told us that the man was last seen in the Doma area of the district. This was good news since we were headed in the direction of the borders at the Delta.

All the way there, Mika was bubbling in a way I had never seen her before. Her excessive energy was keeping all of us positive and motivated.

Gathering leads had us so anxious and occupied that before we knew it, the Delta Landmark was within sight.

There we were, standing on the Delta. The monument in the center was a stone statue of a guardian angel. Underneath the statue is where the lines of stone that marked the sector's borders extended from. Each line stretched all the way to the edge of a circle marked on the ground in the same gray stone that the lines were made of. The circle was 75 meters in diameter. Any ground within the circle that was not a border line was covered in brick, embedded into the ground that surrounded the statue. Beneath the angel statue, the name "Delta" was engraved in the base. Along the edges of the monument were benches and decorative foliage that gave the entire area a much more welcoming look.

The four of us took a break on one of the benches. It felt good to have gotten so much done before evening. Now, with the Doma Sector in sight, it was time for a seat and a snack. I took my bag of granola out and began to pass it around.

"I'm beat!" Mika announced.

Dice slyly commented. "It must be from all of your bouncing around all day!"

She bobbed up and down in place with a titter in her voice. "Why, whatever could you mean?" she asked sarcastically.

He rolled his eyes. "My point exactly."

Out of the corner of my eye, I could see a girl on another bench watching us. I briefly looked at her and continued my attention to my group. "Well, we're finally onto some information that is actually taking us somewhere. There's a very good chance that we are within arms reach of her father."

Dice grinned and nodded. "I admit, I guess I'd be excited too if I was her."

The young woman on the other bench was starting to distract me. She kept looking at us, then looking into her things in an off-rhythmic pattern.

I decided to bring it to everyone's attention. "I'm sorry to kill the mood here, but we have somebody watching us. She's on that bench over there."

All of us looked to the girl over on the other bench. The next time she looked at us, her eyes were met with all eight of ours. She shuffled her belongings around and put them all away. Within moments, she stood to her feet, turned to us and began walking in our direction. She was wearing black pants, black shoes, a white blouse and a dark gray cape with a short, standing collar.

"What's with her?" Dice wondered.

"I don't know, but we should be prepared for..." I stopped in mid-sentence. My memory gave itself a kick-start as the woman's gentle face became much clearer as she drew closer. Though her clothes were different, her face was unmistakable. "Zoe? Month of May, is that you!?"

"Zoe? Month of May?" Kay asked.

"Yes, it's her, from the forums!" I stood from the bench, ready to greet her. "We met back during the ordeal in the Pata Sector, when we escaped Naro's trap and Vade's police at the hotel. She was in my room when all of us got separated."

"I see," Kay nodded.

Zoe stood erect, giving off a very mature air. "Brigg, it's nice to see you again."

"Likewise!" I smiled, stepping to her to give her a friendly hug. "I'm honestly glad to see you again. I thought that maybe Vade captured you back in the Pata Sector."

Zoe daintily scoffed. "Don't worry about it. It's in the past."

Kay greeted her, then asked, "Did you come over here just to say 'hello'?"

"Actually," she replied before a pause, "I came over here to see you."

Kay's brow rose. "Me?"

"What's that about?" Dice whispered to me. "Those two never met, right?"

Zoe approached Mika, who was seated next to Kay on the bench. "May I, little girl?"

Mika relinquished her seat to Zoe, who cut right to the chase. "I noticed from a distance that you are injured." Zoe was, of course, referring to Kay's bandages.

Kay seemed a bit nervous as she broke her eye contact with Zoe and looked to her left hand. "Oh, these?" She wiggled her fingers to display full functionality. "It's nothing."

Zoe opened her bag to display what appeared to be a million-use first aid kit. "Whatever hurts, I'm sure there is something in here that can help ease the pain."

Kay replied in steadfast defense. "There is no pain here for you to relieve."

I wanted to step in before a scene could be made and try to get the stubborn girl to cooperate with Zoe. "Please, Kay, she's only trying to help."

She continued to stand her ground. "I don't need any help here. I can take care of my own wounds."

Zoe persisted again to help her. "If I could just see the injury, I can recommend a treatment."

Dice took a shot at calming the projected storm. "She's right, you know. You should know what treatment options…"

"That's enough!" Kay belted out.

Her outburst silenced all of us.

Remaining stoic, Zoe took her refusal graciously. She stood from the bench and accepted Kay's position on the matter.

She brought her open bag over to me. Out of it, she handed me three vials and explained them one by one. "This green one is an antibiotic gel for cuts to prevent infection. This greenish-yellow one is a salve for burns and rashes. Lastly, this red one slowly develops scar tissue into regular skin."

"Is that so?" I was intrigued by the effects of the red gel she presented. I leaned in close to her. "Can I get two or three of those? I've got this big scar on the back of my leg that I'm kind of embarrassed about."

"Oh, certainly!" She smiled, presenting me with two more red gel vials.

Mika ventured to ask her, "What else do you have in there?"

"Why, I have all sorts of medicines and...oh yeah." she stopped, remembering something. Zoe dug through her bag and pulled out a roll of dressing. "...Bandages." She turned to Kay and handed them to her. "The least I can do for you is give you fresh dressings for your wounds. The ones you have look a little old."

Kay looked at her for a moment then reached her hand out. "Thank you." She sounded ashamed of her previous rudeness.

Zoe took her hand into both of Kay's, delivering the bandage with a friendly, caring grip. "I'm just glad I was able to help you in some way."

"This is a big help," I assured her, examining the red gel.

As Zoe left us to continue her own business, I offered her to join us. She declined, declaring that there were many other Causes like us who needed help. She assured us that her newfound role as a medic for the Causes was a very rewarding position for her. However, she could only benefit from it if her efforts were widespread among those who are in immediate need. We respected her position and allowed her to continue on her way.

Dice had to ask, "That was kind of out of the blue, wouldn't you say?"

"Very out of the blue," I replied. "I honestly didn't think I'd see her again."

Mika smiled as she continued to watch Zoe walk away. "She was really nice. You should ask her to be your girlfriend next time you see her!"

Once again, Mika had found a way to harp on the fact I didn't have a girlfriend. I tried to cut her naïveté short. "D-don't be ridiculous."

"I'm not!" she responded with a pout. "She's kind and knows about medicine and…"

"And that's the problem," Dice cut in.

Once again, a quick, sharp comment from the young realist had our undivided attention. We all looked at him, expecting a thorough explanation.

"Why is that a problem?" I asked him.

Dice kept his eyes focused on Zoe, who was soon about to disappear from our sight. "Where would a Cause get a vast array of medical supplies like that?"

I gave the obvious answer simply to keep Dice talking. "A hospital, of course."

"It's not that simple, Brigg," he continued, shaking his head in disapproval. "I managed to catch the comment where you *thought* she got captured back in Pata."

"Yes…"

He turned to face me, catching me square in the eye. "Those captured wound up in the hands of the Fifteen, correct?"

"Right…"

Dice thought carefully about his choice of words. "Call me crazy, but I think that she really *was* captured back at the hotel."

We all reacted in our own way. Dice really put himself out there to help us see a different logic on this one.

He compared Zoe's situation to our encounter with Naro. We helped Naro, and he presented us with an unknown piece of technology. Dice's conclusion was that somehow, Zoe was given her medic duties by Sandra herself in exchange for something unknown to our guessing.

This was an unfortunate realization since we had already met Sandra in person. But since we really didn't speak with her too much about medicine, we weren't able to see a link between her and Zoe.

One thing quickly became clear to us: we needed to make sure that the gels and salves provided by Zoe were really what she said they were. Since this medicine was probably provided by Sandra, we had every right not to trust it first-hand. The only thing we knew we could trust were the bandages that were given to Kay. I decided to wait before applying the red gel to my scar. Until I was sure the gel was safe, it wasn't going anywhere outside of its small, glass container.

That being decided, we prepared to continue our journey into the Doma Sector.

As we embarked, Dice addressed Kay. "So Kay, what is the big deal with…"

I sensed Dice's curiosity in Kay's bandages. To keep the peace, I jabbed Dice in the ribs with my elbow.

"Ow! What was that for!?"

"Your own good," I muttered.

III

We targeted a line of shops that was within view of the Delta Landmark. It wasn't long before we were presented with the best news yet. A glass sculptor identified the man in Mika's picture. He didn't catch the man's name, but he directed us to where he last saw him. The sculptor told us that he was assisting a café three streets away.

Mika took off running, almost leaving the rest of us behind.

Excited by this lead, all four of us started running through the streets. I could hear Mika chattering through her panting, "We found my daddy, we found my daddy…"

Dice got close to me as we ran, "It's going to suck to see her have to leave us."

I nodded in total agreement. "There's a bright side to it though…"

"What would that be?"

A snide tone crept into my words. "Kay has no reason to follow me now."

Dice breathily laughed as he sarcastically announced, "The ulterior motive finally presents itself!"

I laughed with him. "I know, right? Don't get me wrong though. This was more about helping Mika than anything else. The way the Revolution is turning, I don't think she's safe with anyone but her father."

Dice humbly replied, "I couldn't have said that better myself, and I don't say that to very many people."

We rounded the last corner to the third street. Upon first glance, we saw Mika, who had stopped short in her tracks. Her attention was fixed on the café in the distance and the two male waiters who were attending to the tables. I took Mika's picture out of my pocket and alternated between looking at it and examining the faces of the waiters. We were still too far away to make a positive match.

"Mika, what's wrong?" Kay asked, placing her hand on Mika's shoulder.

"I…" she hesitated.

Dice was adjusting his glasses, joining me in the visual comparison. "I'm seeing a resemblance to the one on the left."

Mika spoke up. "I think we just need to get closer."

Kay stopped her. "Hold on a second. Are you alright?"

Mika shrugged. "Yeah, I'm okay. I just can't believe it's almost over for us."

I patted her on the head. "Hey, we can stick around for a little while. We still have time before the Producers do their thing."

She happily beamed toward me.

We walked the rest of the way to the café. By the time we got there, the two waiters had gone back in to retrieve orders.

We waited outside for them to return, taking a seat at one of the tables next to the door. Mika turned her chair to face the door so she would be able to greet her father on sight. She fidgeted anxiously, wobbling back and forth while peering through the doorway.

I rested my head in my hands, eagerly anticipating the reunion.

"I bet you feel satisfied," Kay said as she leaned far back into her chair.

"Well, for a number of reasons…"

Dice interrupted me. "He's wondering if you'll leave him alone now."

Kay laughed. "Of course! As long as he's not aiming to pick up any more young girls, I have no problem leaving him. What about you, Dice?"

Dice took a moment to think. He then reached into his pocket and presented his dice to us. "You know how I respond to those kinds of questions."

"Yes, yes. We get the idea."

I looked back to Mika, who had stopped her bouncing. "Mika?"

A tear rolled down her cheek. Kay smiled and got her attention. "You're that happy to see him?"

Mika sniffled and began to cry. She then uttered the three words that would crush all of our hearts: "That isn't him."

The young girl's bottom lip quaked, her eyes flooded and her face was soon buried in her hands. The very sight of it quickly sank all of our good spirits.

My head shook, desperately trying to hold back tears of my own. It killed me to see Mika in such a state. Kay, on the other hand, while shedding a tear of her own, took an almost motherly approach to Mika's dismay. She opened her arms and invited her to come close. Mika soon found herself wrapped in Kay's embrace.

The waiter approached us. It was true that he bore close resemblance to the man in Mika's picture. He had the same narrow chin and dark, crew-cut hair. However, it was obvious that the erase marks in the picture around the ears and eyes were the deciding factor in directing us to the wrong man.

The busy gentleman immediately noticed Mika's distress. "Is that girl alright?"

Mika continued crying into Kay's chest as the rest of us tried to find a way to answer the man's question. We dismissed him, insisting we had the situation under control.

Dice, Kay, and I remained silent, simply waiting for Mika to finish letting it all out.

This incident really opened my eyes though. It made me realize that finding Mika's father would be a much more difficult task than we thought. Who was to say that a future lead would take us right back to the same guy?

With only the hand-drawn picture as our best clue, this event made the entire search seem impossible to succeed.

IV

All of us noticed Mika's attitude changing back to the timid girl we knew her as at first. Having her biggest dream ripped from her hands was a heavy blow to her delicate heart. She hadn't said much to us and was actually keeping herself more shut in than I had ever seen her.

That night, we found shelter at a three-room inn near the Delta landmark. In order to keep things calm for Mika, I was willing to submit to any sleeping arrangements that would be suggested by Kay or Dice. Luckily, with two beds in the room, a comfy chair, and plenty of space, everyone was capable of getting a good night's rest.

Mika bathed alone as Kay, Dice, and I quietly discussed where to go from there. Dice recommended that it would be best to take our minds off of Mika's father for a little while. According to him, the events of that evening called for a change of direction. Maybe finding a way to distract Mika from the sudden heartbreak was a sound solution to bringing her spirits back up.

I took this time to declare the need to focus more on the events of the Revolution.

Tomorrow, a very important meeting between the Fifteen and the Producers was to take place. I announced it best for us to stay around the Delta throughout the next day. The events of the meeting were going to be announced live over the radio as it would be the week's edition of "This Week in Eden". It was in many Causes' best interests to be listening in as the meeting was taking place.

We hoped that Mika would understand that it was our priority as Causes to stay updated with the events that would transpire when the two parties were to meet. We knew she had been through a lot, so we were not willing to pressure her into doing anything she didn't want to. If she was still willing to participate with us, we would support her decision with open arms. After all, she never referred to herself as a Cause in the first place, but someone who merely mingled among them. We concluded that whatever Mika decided to do from that point was fine with us.

Dice excused himself from the room. He was going to run out to grab some snacks and bring them back. He was also looking for some time alone to himself to gather his thoughts and ideas. His tone sounded like he was coming up with another plan.

Before he stepped out, he hesitated, turning around in the doorway. "You two want anything while I'm out?"

I was indifferent. "Not really…"

Kay, however, had a sweet tooth. "If you happen to pass by a bakery, see if you can grab some cupcakes or something."

Amused by Kay's unlikely craving, Dice closed the door and left.

I took the opportunity to empty my backpack onto one of the beds to reorganize it. It was then I realized that all of my granola was gone. "I should have asked him to fill this…" I thought aloud, expecting Kay to respond.

Kay was distracted in her own bag as well. I watched her sift through her things as she remained oblivious to my observing her. I ignored any intentions of grabbing her attention and finished emptying my backpack.

After looking at my items for a few moments, I figured that it was going to take me some time to get it all re-packed properly. With the work ahead of me, I chose to go into the task without the possibility of being interrupted. "I think I'll use the bathroom now before I get too involved with this."

Kay heard me loud and clear that time. Unfortunately, that was when everything seemed to shift back to square one. Since Mika was still occupying the shower, Kay protested the call of nature with a steadfast conviction. "Absolutely not! You're going to wait!"

Her accusing tone hit just the right spot on me, irritating me slightly. Trying to remain calm and collected, I shifted the focus and presented the restroom to her to apply her new bandages.

Surprisingly, she refused.

"Cut me a break here!" I insisted. "It's not like Mika has anything you don't."

Once again, she was ready to butt heads with me. "That's a perfect mental image for you now, isn't it?"

I gestured in denial, trying to wrestle with her words. Alas, I admit, the image of Kay bathing Mika in the tub flashed in my mind for a brief moment. I shook it out and retaliated. "I'm not that kind of guy!"

Kay got up close to me. "Then what kind of guy are you exactly? What kind of guy talks to little girls he never met before then invites them to travel with him? What kind of guy smooth-talks his way out of ever looking to be in the wrong?"

I understood her first question; but as far as her second one went, I had no idea what she was talking about. I tried to answer her.

Before I could utter a word though, she was back at my throat. "What kind of guy goes completely out of his way to throw one woman aside just to be around another?"

"The only reason I tried to 'throw you aside' is because I never asked you to come with me in the first place. Now we're back to this argument!" Something occurred to me as I was venting at her. "And is there a reason you had to wait for Dice to leave to start saying all of this?"

"Don't try to change the subject!" she charged. "I just want to know why you chose to help Mika when you obviously don't seem to want anybody else around."

"You have me all wrong there!" I shouted. "I only want people around who are not going to antagonize me or give me a hard time." I paused to let her absorb that comment. Lastly, I answered her initial question in an all-out fury. "Do you want to know what kind of guy I am? Well, I'm a very annoyed guy. I'm a guy who is tired of being followed around by you. I'm a guy who really wishes that we found Mika's father tonight. I'm a guy who is tired of your crap and I'm a guy who just wants you to go away!"

Kay smirked smugly, knowing she had me on edge. "…The kind of guy who wants no interference when he's ready to take advantage."

The combination of her tone, the ugly look on her face, and the fact that she was unrelentingly slandering me to my face were all I needed to lose control of my better judgment. I quickly drew my hand up and swiped it across her face, hard and fast. The sound echoed throughout the room as Kay helplessly stumbled to her side and onto the floor. My hidden rage had overtaken me again and I felt that it wasn't going to stop until I got my point across.

I grabbed her by the front of her shirt and pulled her to her feet. Just as I had done in the past in the dark alleys of the Pata Sector, I dragged her by her shirt and thrust her up against the wall.

She shrieked upon impact.

I pointed to the window next to us. "You say one more word and I swear I will throw you out this window," I lowly growled.

"But…"

I threw the window open with my one free hand. Kay began scrambling at my arm's length. She was resisting with every gram of strength she had in her.

To stop her, I pulled my clenched fist up to her neck and began applying pressure. "Now you listen to me and you listen good…"

Kay began to gasp for air. I let up a little bit before pressing my fist again. She nodded, indicating cooperation.

"You know," I began, glaring into her widened eyes, "Mika is alone in the bathtub right now. She is in a very vulnerable position. I could just as easily choke you to death, drop you out this window, lock Dice out, and have my way with her all night long if I wanted to. Do you see what I am trying to say here?"

She nodded again, clawing at my wrist. Her face was changing color and her eyes began to flow.

I continued to try and set my record straight. "I'm going to ask you a simple question. Why don't I do everything I just mentioned and have a romping good time with that naked little girl in there?" I let up on her throat to allow her to answer.

She spent a moment catching her breath. Watching her struggle to breathe actually got me to calm myself down.

I slowly gathered the idea that I had gone a step too far. To partially make up for it, I answered my question for her. "…Because it is wrong."

Kay collapsed to her knees, unwilling to look at me. Once she had the strength to look up at me, she took it upon herself to stand. Still short of breath, Kay muttered the only phrase that could summarize all of her thoughts: "You…no-good…backslider!"

I shrugged it off. "I'm only trying to get my point—"

Unexpectedly, perhaps since I was caught up in what I was trying to say, Kay quickly balled her fist and plastered it across the left side of my head. I felt my neck pop and saw my vision blur as I staggered back in a daze. The remorseful part of me felt that it was deserved while the part of me that was just choking her wanted nothing more than to really throw her out the window.

Kay advanced on me, preparing to swing again. I thought quick not to do anything rash and decided to guard myself until she chose to stop.

The furious young woman only got in a few more swings until we were finally interrupted by the scolding voice of a towel-clad Mika. "What are you two doing!?"

Kay and I froze in place and were promptly rendered speechless. For the first time, we were actually witnessing Mika infuriated.

The scowling little ball of fire turned to me, making her initial question rhetorical. "I heard what you said, Brigg. How can you even say those terrible things?"

I was still at a loss for words when I tried to answer. "It was an example…"

Mika cut me off. "Kay, why do you keep pestering him?"

Kay focused an outburst on her. "For your information, your 'protector' here almost choked the life out of me! I know he is capable of so much more and is just waiting for me to step away!"

I scolded Kay. "I don't see why you have to yell at her. She did nothing wrong. And, for the last time, I am not trying to…"

Mika lifted her voice to a loud shout. "Both of you stop this right now!"

The way Mika hollered out her command was unlike anything I had ever heard come out of a twelve-year-old. I took the following seconds of silence to feel the side of my face, which hurt to touch.

Mika approached Kay and looked over the red hand mark I had left behind. "It's okay," Kay said softly, looking at me. "I sort of pushed him too far."

Still exuding anger, Mika replied, "Well, stop doing that! I'm tired of seeing the two of you fighting because of me."

Those words reverberated in my head for a few minutes, showing me something that I had not thought of before. I never realized that Mika felt to be the one responsible for the shoddy relationship between myself and Kay.

Then, it hit me. It was my violent outburst back in the Pata Sector that had Mika feel at fault for all of our quarrels. She wasn't really seeing the bigger picture between us. I had to correct this.

For once, it appeared that Kay was on the same page as I was. Kay stroked Mika's hair, trying to calm her down. "We're not fighting because of you."

"Yes," I agreed, "it's not your fault. Remember, we didn't get along well even before we met in real life."

Mika objected. "But you were both doing so well. I thought that you two would have made up by now." She turned to Kay. "All I ever see you do is accuse him. What did he do wrong?"

I felt that this was turning to my favor until Kay mentioned the other time I put my hands on her.

Mika chided me, telling me to take a good look at the mark I left on her. Mika then told Kay that she was no better. It turned out that Kay wound up bruising my face with her first punch. That being realized, Mika made one last call for us to get along. She insisted that Kay start trusting me, and ordered me to keep my temper under control.

Before the end of the whole episode, Dice returned. Once he opened the door, it took him a good minute or two to draw his own conclusion as to what happened while he was out. "It would appear that the young miss has finished her bath just in time to stop you two from killing each other."

I stood to greet him. "Close enough…" I offered my hand to Kay once again to help her to her feet.

Dice snickered. "So, did Mika make you two kiss and make up?"

"Maybe in your dreams," Kay jeered, accepting my hand.

Mika stood up as well and began to walk toward Dice as she started explaining what was going on. To our surprise, Mika hadn't even walked four steps before finding her briefing cut short.

Unwittingly, Kay had her foot holding Mika's towel to the floor. As the little one walked toward Dice, her towel was pulled off.

Dice and I thought fast and averted our eyes in the nick of time. The girls scrambled to get Mika covered back up quickly as I enjoyed the view out the window.

"I saw nothing, I swear!" I called out, still facing the other direction.

Dice responded with a manner of regret in his voice. "Speak for yourself…"

We all reacted. Poor Mika groaned in definable embarrassment.

Dice then dropped the other half of his statement. "…Just

kidding."

Mika's whimpers were quickly replaced by her seemingly signature giggles. Within moments, the humor of the whole thing became contagious. Even Kay—who would have gouged our eyes out at any other time—was red with laughter. Dice's joke had hit just the right spot that it needed to break the tension that had developed within the room.

The rest of the night went by smoothly, with a hint of awkwardness. Kay and I were still calming down from our altercation. Despite that, though, we fully participated in mapping out our actions for the upcoming days.

Surely, what we were to plan would depend on the results of the Producers' meeting. We decided that until we knew what happened at the meeting, we would stay put in the Delta Business District. We made our only mission for tomorrow to sit back, relax and tune in for "This Week in Eden".

The meeting was to take place tomorrow. The excitement among the Causes was felt all throughout Eden that night. It was finally time for the Producers to come forward and lay down the Causes' demands on the bargaining table.

There was that itching feeling in the back of my head about Hatcher though. There was still no sign of him, not even a forum post. I continued to hope that Hatcher's information would prove irrelevant in the end. The only other thing I could hope for was for him to arrive at the last minute.

Day 78

I

I opened my eyes during the early morning hours to realize that it had happened again. It seemed to me that every time Kay pushed me to the point of violence, my inability to sleep soundly granted me the time to lay back and regret it.

Standing slowly out of my bed, I crept over to the window and began to peer out of it, but I wasn't really able to see through to the other side. The window appeared to enter into a dark, midnight void with my lone reflection standing within it.

That being enough to focus on, I took a good look at myself and said, "You have to stop doing that, you know?"

Far deep inside of me, I felt that instinctive rage that I believed was inherited by my father. Slowly but surely, I could see myself turning into a man much like him if I couldn't take it upon myself to change the way I react to certain pressure. I knew that if I didn't do something about it soon, any trust I had gained from my party up to that point would quickly fade away.

I continued to talk to myself. "Stop letting her get to you."

"Sound advice!"

The sudden sound of another person's voice gave me a start. I turned to see Dice. He was grinning crookedly, as if it was his intention to scare me.

Dice took his left hand and swept it through the scraggly, black mop on his head. He was not wearing his glasses or his visor, let alone a shirt. His body stood pale and slender with barely a sense of masculinity to it. Still, he carried himself with the high-minded haughtiness I learned to know him for.

I spoke quietly to him with a lift of my shoulders. "I know it's sound advice. I'm just having a hard time putting it to use."

"Tell me something I don't know," he huffed in a whisper. "I give you credit for being quick to admit that you can't handle that woman."

I argued with his comment almost immediately. "It's not that I can't handle her. The trouble is the fact that she still sees no reason to trust either you or me."

He pulled his dice from his pocket and kneaded them in his left hand. "I know she doesn't trust me. But you know what I do about it?"

I narrowed my eyes and ventured a Dice-style guess. "…Not care?"

"Precisely," he replied. "If she's just going to continue being a gigantic bitch, then I'm not really looking to gain her trust in the first place."

His reasoning confused me. "If you don't like her that much, why did you even bother coming back to us?"

"I already told you, I rolled…"

Sensing falsehoods, I interrupted him. "Don't give me that. I refuse to believe that you came back purely on a roll."

"Since when did I tell you to believe me?" he cryptically inquired.

I gave his question serious thought, desperately trying to find one instance that would answer it.

Before too long, Dice answered for me. "I tell you what I tell you because it is fact. Anything I don't tell you, you don't need to know in the first place. That combined, I have absolutely no reason to lie to you."

I tried to argue back at him with something solid. "Isn't omitting information a form of lying, though?"

"It isn't lying," he sneered, "it's just a form of not telling the truth."

It looked like the one tiny hole in his argument. "So what did you omit?" I asked.

Dice had his answer as if it were planned out from the beginning. "This is where you lose, Brigg." He flashed his dice, holding them between the fingers of his left hand.

"Are you serious," I scoffed.

"Since I'm feeling generous," he chuckled, "I'll tell you that information...*if* I just so happen to roll a number divisible by three."

I rolled my eyes. "Fine."

The dice were cast onto the floor. All three of them came up ones.

I smiled wide. "Ha, three. You lose!"

"Don't be stupid!" he growled back. "Three is a prime number, not divisible by anything!"

His harsh words and the somewhat hidden accuracy of his statement were like a punch in the gut. I had gotten carried away and lifted high, but he was on top of my almost-victory and was there to bring me back to reality.

"Just remember," he said, picking his dice up, "I will always tell you everything I feel you need to know. If I don't do it immediately, I will do it eventually. Take heart in the fact that even though I'm not particularly fond of you, you do have my trust and I would never lie to you."

I wasn't sure what to say in response besides, "Thank you."

He patted me on the shoulder. "Just ignore her bitching. She'll get over her man problem sooner or later."

I simply nodded, catching my reflection in the window one last time. "Let's get back to bed."

"Yeah," he agreed. "This time, stay in it, okay?"

II

The morning was beautiful and the Delta found itself buzzing with excitement that day. From end to end and all around the statue, Causes gathered in a public mass. However, this was not a scene of protest or an act of destruction being planned. It was the anticipation of the meeting between the Producers and the Fifteen that drew the assembly together.

Police were on the scene as well. As they observed the activity in the Delta, it didn't take them long to notice that all who gathered were just talking, laughing, swapping stories, and even picnicking. They stood guard and provided crowd control, even finding themselves conversing with us as well.

This gathering was planned up upon the announcement that Naro was replacing the week's edition of "This Week in Eden" with a live broadcast of the meeting. The fact of the matter was that there was no news more important than that which could end the Revolution and restore order to Eden.

A few hundred Causes were in attendance and anxiously awaiting noontime. At that time, everyone would turn on their transistors and crank the volume all the way up. The meeting would be heard throughout the Delta, leaving nobody in the dark about it.

The four of us spent the time up until noon socializing with the masses. My name had become quite famous, and many Causes were very pleased to meet me.

Kay and Dice had become quite popular as well since they were in my company. Many Causes still found it amusing and ironic that I was traveling with the two of them. We all got a good laugh out of it.

Mika, however, was still a mystery to many. Since she was not originally a Cause, she was not a member of the forum. We took this time to introduce her and her situation to the community. Many were receptive to Mika and offered to stay in contact if they were to come across her father.

It was a very uplifting morning. Spirits were high and anticipation resonated throughout the Delta. Soon, the ending stages of the Revolution would be within reach. The end of the Revolution would bear the truths about Eden that we were certain the Fifteen were keeping hidden. This would be the day that all would know the truth.

The days of the Fifteen's absolute control would soon be over and a new era of Eden would begin.

III

Noon struck. The Causes all sat about the vicinity of the Delta Landmark, fidgeting with excitement. One after the other, transistor radios were presented by individuals and propped up high. Switches were flicked on and volumes were increased until the sounds from them reverberated through the streets as we all planned they would.

The time had finally come when the first words of the broadcast came forth from every speaker. "Good afternoon, Eden. I'm Naro and this is a historic edition of 'This Week in Eden'."

The Causes cheered, but remained mindful that silence among them was priority. None of us could afford to miss a word of the meeting with the Fifteen.

Naro made his full introduction to the show. "With us here today are eight youths from all around Eden who claim to be the leaders of this rebellion Eden has been dealing with. We'll start with you, Bogen, and work our way down the table."

Bogen began to speak, trying to start off by being funny. "...And what a table we have here, folks!" He chuckled half-heartedly and continued. "Yes, my name is Bogen and for all of the Causes listening in who would know what this means: He did not arrive."

There was muttering and mumbling among the assembly. Everyone knew well that Bogen was indicating that Hatcher never showed up. In the time it took the Causes to calm down, the rest of the Producers had finished introducing themselves.

The next part of the broadcast was actually quite a treat for those who didn't know all of the names of the Fifteen. Each member was passed the microphone in order to state his or her name to the audience.

They started with the men: Naro, Haz, Dallas, Biktor, Syre, Riley and Joseph.

Then the women announced their attendance: Eliza, Sandra, Estyr, Morie, Cenia, Vade and Rayna.

It didn't take long for the Causes to realize that only fourteen members of the Fifteen were present. Naro stated that the last member, Aegis, could not make it to the meeting.

After the formalities, the Producers and the Fifteen officially started the long-awaited event.

Joseph of the Fifteen was the first person to speak. "We want to make Eden aware of the different kinds of damage your actions have inflicted since the start of this whole mess." Joseph passed the microphone to the other members, who began listing the problems they had been having with keeping Eden in order.

"Police resources are stretched to their limit; especially our Gray Unit."

"Research on Interactive Studies has halted. We can't issue occupations to anyone participating in this rebellion of yours."

"Vacant housing plots are going into disrepair. Young people like you all should be preparing to move into them."

"Injuries among your numbers are staggering. I cannot keep up with medical procedures." This was obviously Sandra speaking.

Lastly, Naro shared a complaint of his own. "I keep on having to interrupt people's entertainment programming with news of your shenanigans. The citizens are growing weary of it all."

The microphone was handed back to Joseph. "That is only a fraction of the problems we are facing in order to keep Eden in the peaceful and balanced state we once had it in. I want every one of you revolutionaries out there listening to understand the trouble we are having and end this nonsense."

One of the other Producers huffed loud enough to be heard through the mike.

Joseph addressed him, "Do you have something to say, young man?"

The sound of the microphone being passed was now familiar by that time. "Yes, I do," the Producer replied, sounding very confident. "You want us to just understand you and give up when you haven't taken the time or effort to understand us?"

A female Producer chimed in. "Matthias! Remember, an attitude won't get us anywhere with the Fifteen."

"Come on, Ki. You know I'm right."

"Yes, but you could have said it a little more professionally!"

The Causes in the Delta were amused. We all knew that what the two were saying was right, though. Matthias' point was that the Fifteen made no effort to understand our position. Eden's leaders only saw us as a menace and wanted nothing more than to put an end to our protest.

Bogen had called the two to order and taken mike from them. "What Matthias is saying is actually a reflection of the way all of us in the Revolution feel. We feel that our wants, needs, and feelings are being tossed aside for the sake of keeping this balance you speak of."

Applause rang through the streets. Bogen had hit the right spot with those few sentences.

"You've got us all wrong!" the voice of a Fifteen member roared.

Bogen acknowledged him. "Um, 'Haz', was it? Do you have something to say as well?"

Haz was given the floor. "You say that your *needs* are neglected? What you fail to understand is that you need to forgo wants and feelings to achieve what you *really* need in this lifetime." His voice had heart and sincerity pouring out of every word.

There was silence in the streets and in the meeting as well. Everyone was trying to comprehend what Haz was trying to say. The next one to speak was Matthias again. "What makes you think you know what we need?"

"I've got this one…" Joseph announced darkly.

"All yours," Haz confirmed, passing the mike back.

Joseph began to utter what was to be the most harrowing statement that could be spoken by a man of power. "It isn't so much that we know each individual person needs. It is that we know exactly what all of Eden *doesn't* need." He took a beat, giving everyone a moment to understand and absorb his answer.

"Interesting choice of words," Dice remarked on the side.

Joseph followed up by saying, "We know for a fact that Eden does not need your Revolution. Now, stop it. Return to your homes and help the communities of Eden clean up the mess you've all made."

There was a brief moment of thought. Every Cause from far and wide knew that it was finally the time we had been awaiting. This would be the moment that the Producers announced our true demands to the Fifteen. It was time for the truth to be revealed to all of Eden. Sure enough, we could hear the Producers conferring in the background of the broadcast.

The Causes in the Delta were expressing mixed emotions. Some were grinning in anticipation. Others seemed to be concentrating, staring into nothing while awaiting the next statement. Every emotion in between could be felt as the chatter across the airwaves slowly came to a stop.

Loud announcements for silence filled the Delta as every Cause eagerly awaited the Producers' response.

Bogen was handed the microphone. "We will not back down until we are satisfied!"

"How do you intend we do that?" Joseph asked off-mike.

"We the Producers, and every Cause out there scattered across the landscape, demand that you answer our questions."

"What are those?" Joseph asked.

Bogen took a deep breath and spoke. "Why, for the last 600 years, have the leaders of Eden kept things in this constrictive grip that you call 'balance'? What purpose is it serving? What is it preventing that Eden 'doesn't need'?" His voice was gradually getting louder and more dramatic. "Why must Eden subject itself to your view of the way things should be?" Bogen finished up with two, final, bursting questions. He went all out and quoted two questions from the last paragraph of the book. "Why are we kept from making our own life decisions and forced to have them made for us? Do you realize that those decisions we're kept from making could be the ones that move Eden forward to a new age of prosperity?"

The positive reaction from the throngs at the Delta was almost deafening. Even the police officers watching over us were impressed. Citizens along the streets and in the nearby shops were applauding as well. It seemed that since our demands were now out in the open, people finally understood the position of the Causes. They even appeared curious as to how the Fifteen would respond.

Once the multitude calmed, the familiar sound of off-mike huddling could be heard. The Fifteen were talking amongst themselves.

Suddenly, Joseph spoke again. "The answers to these questions will satisfy the Revolutionaries?"

A female Producer answered, "With action, of course, but yes."

Several of the Fifteen's members reacted. "Action?"

Bogen answered their curiosity. "You know, change, perhaps?"

"Change…"

The Fifteen continued their private discussion. Within a

minute, the mumbling stopped short. Joseph spoke to the Producers as a whole. "This is something that our side must decide on elsewhere. If you will excuse us, we will return as soon as we have chosen what to do."

"Take all the time you need."

The romp of footsteps slowly filtered into the sound of a shutting door.

Within an instant of the door closing, Bogen took the mike and made an announcement to the Causes. "We, the Producers, would like to thank you all for being a part of the Revolution. While the Fifteen discuss their response, I just want to say that I am truly pleased that the Causes held strong. Brigg, if you're listening—and I know you are—thanks for helping the Causes down this path."

Calls and hoots were directed at me by those who knew I was in the Delta. Mika hugged me while Dice patted me on the shoulder.

Kay made no physical contact, but gave me a very special look. Her eyes resonated with pure respect and her smirk displayed approval. She could not deny my place among the Causes whether she trusted me or not.

I smiled back and nodded only once, just enough to oblige her gesture.

Minutes felt like hours as the Causes in the streets and the Producers at the meeting continued to wait for the return of the Fifteen. To keep the show going, Bogen and the others continued to ham it up on the radio as they waited. During that, Bogen took the liberty of making a bold statement that didn't sit easy with me. "Hatcher, if you're out there, we managed just fine without you."

Many of us soon wished Bogen could have anticipated the level of irony in that very remark. For as soon as he finished saying that, the Fifteen returned from their deliberation.

Unfortunately, they were not filing back into the meeting in the professional manner that we had anticipated. No. Loud bursts rang across the airwaves as if the doors to the meeting room had been kicked open. "Nobody move!" a voice shouted.

"What's going on?" I asked, addressing the Causes as a whole.

One of the Producers shouted loud and clear. "Gray Police!"

Screams and shouting were heard over the radio mixed in with sounds of chairs knocking around, scampering, tumbling, and banging. The only thing certain was that chaos had erupted at the scene of the meeting.

The negative sensations found their way into the Delta. Causes began to panic as they awaited any coherent sentences to be spoken from the meeting.

My mind was focused solely on the sounds emitted from the broadcast. Once the noise cleared up, a few discernable sentences rang clear throughout the landmark.

"One of them got away."

"How?"

"He was too quick."

In the background, somebody hollered loud and clear before her voice seemed to fade into nothingness. "Causes! Stay strong! They are hiding something! They have our answers!"

Naro's familiar shout boomed, "Lock them away until the Causes stand down!"

"No!" I shouted desperately. "This can't be happening!"

"This is terrible," Mika agreed.

A voice rang out over the crowd. "The Producers have been captured!"

"Didn't you hear? One got away!" a girl called back.

"Actually," I mumbled, low enough to where only the others could hear me, "…the fact that even one got away could be very important."

"You think it could be Bogen?" Dice guessed.

It took me a mere second to think about that. "That's very likely."

The sudden sound of a hand bumping the microphone brought the Causes in the Delta to full attention. The sounds of shuffling, shouting and havoc had subsided. The radios were almost silent where only a light muttering peeped over the airwaves. After a moment, the deep, angry voice of a woman spoke the final words of the broadcast of the meeting:

"Causes, this game is over. Return to your homes and we will set your Producers free. Be mindful that as of right now, you have no leaders. You are merely nuisances with futile questions. This is your only warning. I swear that as the head of justice in Eden, I will make it my duty to put an end to this by any means necessary."

"On behalf of the Fifteen, this is Vade, signing off this edition of 'This Week in Eden'. Good day."

The broadcast was cut.

IV

A heavy and disrupted air circulated throughout the Delta as the transistor radios were shut off and put away. Fear began to set in and some Causes had already begun to think the worst.

The Producers had been arrested by the Fifteen and there was nothing anybody could do about it. With the closing of that broadcast came the dawn of the darkest day of the Revolution for the Causes.

The mass in the Delta slowly gathered the strength to converse with their peers and partners. Many were questioning where to go from there. Those who managed to hear that one of the Producers got away seemed to think there was still a shred of hope. Many others felt intimidated by Vade's announcement and made giving up one of their options.

Some of the Causes seated about the Delta decided to blame me for not allowing the Radio Tower raid to be carried out. Whatever could be said about the situation was brought into the mesh of speech that soon flooded the area.

My mind wandered, focused on the series of questions Bogen had asked the Fifteen. I recalled how thorough Bogen was with his words. He left no detail out in his attempt to pressure the Fifteen for the truth.

Then I thought about why the Fifteen responded the way they did. They took drastic action to silence the questions we needed the answers to. Lastly, the sound of that woman's voice on the radio repeated in my head:

"Causes! Stay strong! They are hiding something! They have our answers!"

"Causes! Stay strong! They are hiding something…!"

"Causes! Stay strong! They are hiding…"

It clicked, all seeming to be true. "That's it!" I burst out.

"What is it?" Kay wondered.

"It all makes sense! The Fifteen were willing to settle everything peacefully up until Bogen stated demand for the truth, right?"

"Right…" She nodded. Dice and Mika appeared to understand, too.

"So," I continued, "why would the Fifteen suddenly change face if they didn't have anything to hide? What was so important about the answers to those questions?"

"I see what you mean!" Mika replied. "As a matter of fact…" The clever girl paused for a moment then stood, cupping her hands over her mouth. She shouted over the Causes to gather as much attention as possible. "Hey, everybody!"

She got a few of them to look at her. "What the heck are you doing!?" I asked.

She turned back to me with a surprisingly positive grin. "If we're going to think about it, we might as well share our thoughts, right? Nobody seems to be getting anywhere with all this noise."

Dice reached into his pocket and prepared his dice for a roll. "I'm not quite feeling you there, Mika."

I understood. "Well, I think she has a point. It reminds me of something Hatcher once said during the planning stages. 'Even though there are several thousand of us and we're all taking our own path in this, remember that we are still a team'."

"I remember that, too, now that you mention it." He put his dice away.

Kay stood up, joining Mika in drawing attention to us. The two of them working together quickly grabbed the attention of most of the men. Once Dice and I added our efforts in silencing the audience, everyone settled down and waited for what we had to say. However, the others felt that with my name among the most popular, influencing the panicked horde would be the easiest if they let me do the talking.

Many Causes called to me individually, some to support and some to jeer.

I wanted to approach this to get my point across as well as try to calm everyone down. Once I had myself together, I spoke out to the awaiting multitude. "Everyone, suffice it to say, there is no need for me to repeat what has just happened." I took a long beat to make sure I had as much of the audience's attention as possible. "Now, let me ask you all a question. I know there was a lot of chaos coming out of the radio, but how many of you managed to hear that one of the Producers escaped the meeting?"

A few arms went into the air as people turned their heads about to see the results.

I confirmed the outcome and continued. "Yes, one of them escaped, and it is only a matter of time before we hear from that person. We should be aware that the Fifteen have not threatened the Producers' well-being in any way. I'm sure that the Fifteen feel that they have won this. How many of you here feel like the Causes have lost?"

More hands presented themselves. Clearly there were more people who had lost hope than we thought. I actually felt intimidated and almost hesitant to tell these people that the Revolution really was a step in the right direction. Some of the Causes even stood up and began to leave. Regardless of that, I tried to stay focused. There were a lot of people left to reassure.

I took a deep breath and went for it. "Contrary to what Vade said on that broadcast, we are still strong. The results of the meeting are the perfect example as to why we were right to question the Fifteen. We were headed in the right direction, but stumbled on the way. Our advantage has changed because the Fifteen continue to hide the truth from us and the citizenry of Eden."

There was a bit of gabbing among the crowd as I gathered my next thought.

I lightly and nervously shuddered before continuing. "Hatcher once said that we are all a team. Well, I'm standing up here to tell you that what our team has done to Eden is the right thing to do. The Fifteen are holding Eden back from progress and they are hiding what we have the right to know as citizens of Eden!"

Dice leaned in to me and whispered, "This group is looking a little more convinced."

I nodded to Dice as I decided to go for a finishing touch to my speech. "We have the Fifteen up against a wall. They know what we want and have sought desperation to keep it from us. We must press forward and keep the pressure on them!"

A roaring, masculine voice boomed over the audience and echoed off of the buildings surrounding the Delta. "I totally agree with you this time, Brigg!"

The voice had come from my left side. Turning that way, I

saw a slender and elegant young man with lengthy blonde hair rise up from among those who stayed seated. "Who is that guy?" Mika wondered.

"Only one way to find out, right?" I quietly responded.

"Ask him?"

I called out to the youth. "Who are you?"

Upon a first look at the athletic male, one could safely say that he sure liked the color black. Although his trousers and boots were a standard design, his shirt was unlike anything I had ever seen.

The body of the shirt had a low-cut collar and no left sleeve. It was the right sleeve of his shirt that caught my eye the most. It looked like it had been knifed to shreds, being held together only by the shoulder and the wrist. A cloth ring on his middle finger was attached to the wrist of the sleeve by a triangular addition of cloth. Over the bizarre shirt, he wore a sleeveless vest, much like mine except made of black denim.

Cloth elbow coverings and a belt with a decorative buckle finished his outfit.

The youth began maneuvering through the audience to get within a reasonable speaking distance. While making his way over, he introduced himself. "My name is Albion, but everyone calls me…" He had deliberately paused in mid-sentence until he stood face to face with me to finish it. "…Al!"

Though he was a little shorter than me, his all-black clothing and the way he carried himself had me think twice about being overly confrontational. His deep, green eyes glared into mine, telling me that he had something to say.

Slighted, I lightly shoved him to give myself some space. "What brings you to finally show your face?" I asked him.

His attitude was cocky as he whipped his blonde locks and ran his long fingers through them. "Hey, easy! Didn't you just say that we're all a team? Do teammates shove each other?" He brushed his shoulders as if I had gotten them dirty.

I turned his question back at him. "Speaking of teammates, where's Jal?"

"I assume you mean Jalako. She's doing her own thing right now."

Kay charged in. "You had to have come up here to interrupt

Brigg because you have something to contribute, right? If you're going to add to this, then say something."

"Right, right!" he gestured, composing himself. He turned outward and said his part. "As I said a moment ago, I agree with Brigg. We have to keep the pressure on."

Kay distracted me from Al's speech. "Watch out, Brigg. This is the same guy that has been ripping into you all week because of the Radio Tower. I'm not sure if he's being sincere about siding with you."

Mika seconded the motion. "He seems really stuck up and kinda creepy…"

"I wouldn't trust him either," Dice advised. "His tone is a little too facetious for my taste."

I kept my team's advice in the front of my brain and readied myself for anything Al would try to pull on us. My attention shifted back to Al, who was concluding his thoughts. "It's time to show the Fifteen what we're made of. We need to step up our game and show them what real 'rebellion' is!"

I was praying that I misunderstood the context of Al's proposal. "What!?"

Al turned to me while still speaking audibly enough for the Delta. "You heard what those members of the Fifteen said, right? They called our actions a 'rebellion'. Now, correct me if I'm wrong, but aren't 'rebellions' supposed to be a little more…action-oriented?"

Dice filled his question. "Something like that…"

"So as far as I'm concerned…" he resumed, "We haven't been 'rebelling' since the beginning. All we have been doing is merely 'objecting'."

I demanded further explanation. "What are you getting at, Al?"

"My point is that if we want to keep the pressure on the Fifteen, we need to show them less of this diplomatic objecting…" He threw in a long, dramatic pause. "…and take the magnitude of our stand against them to a whole new level!"

With those words, Al seemed to have gained control of the multitude. We could see them nodding, grinning, talking amongst themselves, and rummaging through their bags and items. Once again I began to feel the sting of Al's inherent need to lead the masses. It all seemed to be set in stone once the Causes in the Delta began to applaud Al's speech.

"Wait a minute!" I hollered, reaching for Al's shoulder. "Do you realize what you are saying!?"

Kay scolded him, sharing my thoughts as well. "You're telling Causes to break the Producers' rules again!"

Al lifted his face smugly. He seemed not to care as long as he had followers. "The Producers are no longer in the picture. Therefore, there are no rules now! We'll make the Fifteen talk, even if it means turning Eden upside-down to do it!"

The entire situation surrounding the congregation at the Delta had become much worse than we could have expected. If the Causes began to exhibit violence, there was no telling what the future would hold for us.

I tried one last time to reason with Al. "You forget: there's still one more Producer out there. Hatcher is still out there too."

Al had grown tired of me by that point. He became cross and unleashed passionate fury in a concise, conclusive eruption. "That last Producer doesn't matter! The Gray Police will catch up with him eventually. And do *not* get me started on Hatcher!"

There was substantial approval from the Causes in response to Al's final words on the matter. I watched in heart-stopping despair as Cause after Cause rose from where they sat to follow Al out of the Delta.

I felt my head slightly shaking back and forth. "No…" I said quietly, knowing that protesting Al could escalate the problem. "This is wrong…"

Kay spoke to me softly, trying to relax me. "Brigg, I'm sorry. I don't think there is a way to change this. The circumstances are too extreme."

"See," Dice said, trying to lighten the mood, "she knows you well enough to assume you are planning a way to stop Al."

The truth was that I wished I could. Unfortunately, I felt that all of my luck had been drained back at Naro's Radio Tower. Kay was right. Al had the upper hand over my influence and there was nothing I could do to reverse its impact.

Mika hugged me to try and comfort me, but it was to no avail. As I witnessed each Cause disappearing into the distance behind Al, I could feel the tiny shreds of hope for a peaceful solution slowly fading out of existence.

However, while Al made efforts to convince people to follow his example, some Causes weren't buying into the new trend. Those who refused Al continued to stick to the Producers' rules as best as they could.

Each individual had their own definition of hope for the Revolution's outcome. Whether they sided with the Producer's rules or Al's methods, one fact remained clear: the Fifteen had our answers and it was up to us, the Causes, to get them.

The Producers had been captured.

The Causes were now divided.

The outlook for the Causes and the Revolution was now lost in a fog of conflict.

…And yet, there was still no response from Hatcher.

Episode 5: Separate Paths

The four of us decided to double back into the Fanda Sector for a couple of days after the incident at the Delta.

As it turned out, Bogen's public announcement of the Causes' demands made many of Eden's average citizens a lot more understanding of the role we had given ourselves. In turn, it actually made it easier for a Cause to find a place to spend the night and even easier to find a Contact.

The impact of the meeting prompted an increase in the number of participants in the Revolution. An estimated 3,000 more young people found themselves influenced by the Causes' powerful arguments. The day after the meeting became known as the Day of the Second Walk.

There was a problem with this, though. With our numbers now increased, the Fifteen appointed Gray Police to every residential and business sector in Eden. This meant that six of Eden's Eleven Sectors were being patrolled by Gray Police.

The only fortune in this fact was that since the actual number of Gray Police officers was so limited, they were spread pretty far apart. Therefore, the Causes never saw more than one of them in one place. The only thing they had to be wary of was actually encountering them as they patrolled the streets.

Our time in the Fanda Sector was spent laying low and surveying the situation. Two Contacts teamed up in the same inn we were staying at, making a killing on tips for their services. We managed to stay informed through them.

As we waited for any news, we found no sign of Hatcher, the last missing Producer, or any action by the Fifteen other than the deployment of the Gray Police.

Al & Jal regrouped soon after the Delta incident and quickly took to the forums to turn more Causes to their rebellion. There was no news of any actions perpetrated by them or their followers. However, their time spent in recruitment for their overzealous vision had us worried that that would change very soon. We were thinking Al & Jal were going to plan more events like the Radio Tower siege.

Al & Jal had the advantage now since they would no longer need the forums to organize their plots. Thus, getting a heads up about any of their plans was strictly out of the question.

On a lighter note, Dice couldn't help but notice that both times Albion had been sighted, Jalako was not with him.

He presented two assumptions concerning them: Either Albion had some on and off relationship with her, or Jalako was instructing Albion from the sidelines. Though it would only make Al a messenger and a figurehead, Dice's second guess on the matter made Jalako the person to watch out for.

The 80th day of the Revolution was dawning. But the brilliant summer sun on a warm, breezy morning wasn't going to expel the dark cloud that hung over the heads of the Causes. It was indeed a new day for the Revolution as a whole.

Day 80

I

I greeted the morning with my first smile since Sunday. Hiding ourselves away and analyzing everything hadn't been our idea of fun throughout the day previous. Thus, it was good to see a pleasant morning at the same time we scheduled ourselves to move out.

We decided that with everything going on between the Causes, it was best to get Mika out of the thick of it. We reminded ourselves that Mika was never a Cause to begin with.

With the advent of the Delta incident, Mika had become very afraid of what would happen to her.

The newfound understanding by Eden's citizens would serve to favor our effort to find Mika's father. This opened up a wide range of opportunities to us.

We made our next order of business to find a way to get an image of Mika's picture on the Interactive Network. The circumstances surrounding our goals were finally dismal enough to warrant a key piece of information from Dice.

Previously, Dice had refused to venture back to his home in Binda. What he didn't tell us before was that his father was a painter—an artist. He proposed that for the sake of helping Mika, he would lead us to his home. From there, we would ask his father to lend us his talents to copy Mika's picture to a computer by hand.

By the time Dice was finished explaining all of the minor details, the whole plan seemed like the course we needed to take. We prepared to depart for Binda.

Before we set out, I summoned one of the Contacts and checked the forums one last time. I was hoping to find any new news that we would find useful.

Nothing relevant to our interests turned up in the forums, but I noticed that my private message box had a new message. The message was from, of all people, Blue.

When I announced it aloud, Mika, Kay, and Dice were hovering over my shoulders within seconds. Since Blue's exploits in the hero department were still commonplace, it actually felt like a privilege to get a message from him.

Hey Brigg,

I've been paying attention to what has been going on with you. Looks like you've got your hands full with Al & Jal. I know it's kind of weird getting a message from me out of the nowhere like this, but there are a few things I need to know. I'm just trying to get some info from people who seem to know what's going on. Since the Producers are indisposed right now, I'm going for the next best thing.

First off, I was just wondering, with everything going on with them and all, did you get a chance to find out who Jal is? Back in the Pata Sector, Al helped all of those Causes cross that bridge, but Jal was not with him. I don't even know if he is a she or not. Kinda funny, huh?

Second, you wouldn't happen to know which Producer escaped the meeting, would you? Also, do you know if Black, the Producers' personal Contact, was with them? I'm just looking to be in the know about that so I can spread the word too.

Last but not least, I'm wondering if you are planning to oppose Al & Jal. It seems to be the question on everybody's mind since the meeting. The hot news is about how Al upstaged you at the Delta. The other Causes are waiting for you and your crew to step up to him.

As for me, I'm just going to keep doing what I do best. Now that the Gray Police are all over the place, my job is going to get a lot more fun! Once I find out what I need to, I'll see what I can do to support the remaining Causes in ways beyond what I'm doing now. I want you and your friends to take care of yourselves. Good luck in whatever you choose to do. I'll be rooting for you.

-Blue

I opened a blank message to reply. "Well, it's good to know that some things haven't changed."

Dice had something to say about it though. "Remember, people have had questions about Blue since he first started playing hero. It seems to me that he wants to work alone, but still use others for information. I would be careful of your wording before you decide to type anything."

"Duly noted," I mumbled as I began stroking the keys.

Hello Blue,

It's good to hear from you, even though we never really formally met. We saw you at that bridge, by the way. One of my partners, Kay, was the girl that called out to you while you distracted the Gray Police. I'm glad to see that you're still the same Blue we've heard about; that the recent events haven't changed what you feel is your role in the Revolution.

In answer to your questions, though, I'm afraid I don't have all of the answers. But I will tell you what I do know.

The only things we managed to find out about Jal are that she is a woman and her full name is Jalako. Likewise, Al's full name is Albion, in case he didn't tell you before.

We still haven't found out who the missing Producer is. However, your question about it actually made me remember about Black. Before you asked about her, I had completely forgotten that she was with them.

Lastly, we don't intend to stage any open retaliation to Al & Jal. We've decided that the best thing to do is to continue to set the Producers' example and let the Gray Police handle the rebels that Al rounded up. I have a feeling that Al & Jal will bring themselves down in due time.

We have quite an agenda in front of us. We have a young girl in our group who is searching for her father. Our goals right now involve getting her back to him before she winds up caught on the bad end of the Revolution. So we have our hands full as it is.

We want to know what the Fifteen are hiding just as much as the next person. But for now, we have to focus on this. We'll keep in touch and let you know if we find out anything new. Be careful out there, OK?

   -Brigg

I let everyone read my reply before I sent it out. They approved the content, especially pleased about my use of "we", "us" and other such words that made us a team in writing.

II

We returned to the Delta, arriving around ten o'clock. From here, Dice recommended that we hop on the train via the train stop that cut through the south side of the district. It was only a few blocks south of the landmark, so it was easy to simply walk there and wait.

Even though the events of the past few days were fresh in everybody's minds, people were surprised to see that train service was running as normal. The Fifteen had placed all of their confidence in the Gray Police to bring in Causes one by one from the streets. They apparently felt no need to disrupt the lives of the average citizens.

A lot of Causes were at the station when we arrived. It turned out that we were not the only group who planned to lay low after the meeting. We spent our time waiting for the train making small talk. Many of them asked me the same question Blue did concerning Al & Jal. As such, I gave them the same answer I gave Blue.

Upon boarding the train, the four of us claimed a booth seat.

Dice and I sat on one side as the girls sat on the other, facing toward us. I couldn't help but reminisce about the day I met Mika. I smiled and told her about how once again, I found myself sitting across from her.

Our jog down memory lane led to a discussion between me and Kay. She took the liberty of reminding me that she was still a little uneasy around me because of my temper flares. Other than that, she had finally announced accepting the fact that my intentions with Mika were pure. I was relieved to know that Kay's mistrust of me was slowly withering away. She knew that by letting her feelings go we would all work together much better as a group.

Dice felt a little left out; so he decided to share his thoughts too. He admitted to us that his intentions were to help Mika and he wanted no part in what I could find myself caught up in. Dice felt that I was dangerous to be around since my name was known to too many people. His analysis emphasized that I was receiving as much praise as I was negative attention generated by Al. Since Al was now influencing a sizeable amount of Causes, it was much easier to meet the wrong people at the wrong time.

Hearing Dice's view on things got Mika upset. She began telling us how devastated she'd be if anything happened to us because of her. Mika still felt that if she hadn't been with us, we would not have had to move around so much. To her, it seemed that the more we traveled, the more we were putting ourselves at risk. If she wasn't with us, we could very well have stayed put, moving only when the danger came to us.

We appreciated her concern. However, if we didn't get her back to her father soon, she would also find herself in the thick of our troubles. It was fact that our decision to move on had a long list of risks and rewards, and with the way things were it was easy to focus on the risks. Regardless, that was no reason to change our course since the danger was not certain. I assured Mika that whatever would happen while she was with us, everything was going to be alright.

After discussing the search a little further, I figured it was a good idea to see if we could get any information on the train. It would be a few hours and a number of stops before we reached our destination, so taking the time to ask around seemed harmless enough. I excused myself from the others, taking Mika's picture with me.

While I slowly made my way toward the refreshment car, I

stopped to ask people aboard the train about the man in the picture. The only person who knew anything was trying to direct me back to the Delta. He had seen the same guy that we mistook the other day. That alone made it seem that we needed more than just a hand-drawn picture to get anywhere further in the search.

Time passed, and I soon found myself seated alone in the refreshment car nibbling on complimentary cookies and pondering thoughts I had yet to share with the others.

I really began to feel the burden of my good intentions. Ever since Mika walked into my life, everything had changed. I thought back to those first sixty-two days of the Revolution and how I managed them alone.

I knew that if I had not met Mika, I would still be alone and my name would be lost among the thirteen-thousand others. I had her to thank and yet a part of me was wishing she had never come along.

It was a difficult emotion to fight with, but I knew in my heart that what I was doing was right. It wasn't my fault that my brain was trying to be more realistic about it.

"Is this seat taken?"

The sudden question startled me, snapping me away from my personal time. I turned to look up and saw Kay, standing there with a distraught look on her face. "Hey, what's the matter?" I asked her.

"I've been watching you for the past few minutes. You've been staring at that cookie and haven't moved a muscle. I've never seen you like that." She picked up my bag and placed it on the opposite end of the booth. Keeping her legs in the aisle, she occupied the seat next to me where the bag once sat. "Look, if you want to be alone, tell me now. I don't want to bother you."

"No, you're fine," I sighed. "I tend to get like that when I'm alone. You're not the first person to notice it."

She appeared consoling. "Is there something you want to talk about?"

I didn't look at her. I merely took the cookie I had been staring at and broke it in half. I gave one of the halves to her. "I was just thinking about what we were discussing."

She took a small bite. "And…"

I froze up for a moment. I knew what I wanted to say but I wanted to make sure I didn't say it the wrong way. "…I was just thinking…I'm not sure what I would do if anything were to happen to her."

Kay seemed interested in my choice of words. "You mean Mika? What do you mean by 'what you would do'?"

I didn't really know, so I threw out the best answer I could. "It's about guilt. It was my decisions that brought me to this point and I've dragged her along with me. Originally, I didn't have to go with her and she didn't have to go with me."

Kay stopped me just before I was about to share my true feelings about the whole thing. "Brigg, you're thinking too hard about this. I never realized you could be this uptight."

I shrugged, noticing Kay changed the course of the conversation. "I feel like I'm having so much expected of me now, that's all. For example, everyone is waiting for me to do something about Al & Jal."

"Forget about them! We need to do what is best for us right now."

I continued expressing my position. "I'm still having a lot expected of me. Mika is counting on me to find her father—"

"But no more than how much she's relying on me and Dice. If anything, Dice has taken the burden of the search away from the two of us for a little while."

Kay made an interesting point here. I realized that the only person who was making the search my sole responsibility was me. Now that Dice was directing us, it did seem as though I could relax and go with the flow.

I chortled at the unexpected irony. "Who would have thought that Dice would actually *relieve* people of a hard time?"

"Like he said, he's only doing it for Mika. He probably plans on leaving again once she is safe at home." Kay sighed before stuffing the rest of the cookie in her mouth. She began making audible scarfing noises in an attempt to get me to laugh. It worked without fail. "That's more like it. It seems like everything I say is making you think even more. Mellow out!"

I turned her advice back to her. "…This coming from Miss Uptight herself."

Kay was on top of the conversation as if she almost expected me to say that. "I'm only giving you advice based on the things I've learned over the past few days. You and Mika taught me that I need to calm down and look at things a little more carefully. While I see that you're doing that too, you're analyzing it *too* much. So for both of us, in our own way we both need to chill out and take things one day at a time."

I was moved by her words. This was a side of Kay that I didn't think existed. She showed me that I was being far too analytical about the big picture instead of focusing on the tasks at hand. If I could just stop worrying about other people, it would help all of us get through the day just a little bit easier.

I looked to her and let her know that she was right. "Let's just get over to Dice's house. We'll figure out what's next once we get done there."

She praised me with a pat on the back. "There you go. Now you're getting it."

I exhaled audibly in contentment, feeling like I could finally relax. I'd worry about everything else once we got Mika's picture on the Interactive Network. "You're right. The Revolution, the Fifteen, Al, Jal—they can all wait until after we take care of Mika."

Kay was pleased to hear me declare that. "Good thinking."

I actually felt humbled. It was a much-needed sensation. "Thanks, Kay."

"No problem." She stood and placed my bag back next to me. "I'm gonna go grab some more cookies and take them back to Dice and Mika."

I smiled to her with a thankful expression on my face. "Well, since I don't really need any more thinking time for a while, I guess I'll go back too."

Kay and I walked over to where the cookie trays were displayed and started picking out the biggest ones. My mind was focused on stocking up on anything edible, while Kay appeared to really enjoy that half of cookie I gave her. She didn't waste any time putting the first one she picked up into her mouth.

We stopped for a moment when our hands bumped while reaching for the same treat. Kay suddenly withdrew her hand and used it to take the cookie out of her mouth. We stood silent for a moment. I looked to her, but her face was turned toward the end of the car. "Kay?"

She stayed facing away from me. "Don't get any ideas. I was only trying to help since you looked a little down back there."

"But I..."

"I'm going back. Are you right behind me?"

I was hesitant, not quite sure what this sudden change of face was. "Y-yes."

Kay took a slow step, and then began to walk quickly. I followed at my own pace.

Just before we were about to exit the refreshment car, a voice from another table distracted us. "What just happened?"

Alarmed, we both stopped and turned around. A single group of five male Causes had their eyes transfixed to the windows. I began to make my way toward them, noticing the looks of puzzlement wiped across all of their faces. "Is everything alright?"

All five of them looked to us as the only one of them standing spoke. "We just blew right through the train stop without stopping."

I couldn't believe what I had heard at first. Sure enough, I looked out the window to notice that the train was going at full speed and the station it was supposed to stop at was vanishing in the distance. As I was distracted by that, the five young men left the refreshment car from the other side to alert the other Causes on the train.

Seconds later, a loud clank sounded once from both ends of the car. I felt a jolt in my heart as the sound echoed in my mind.

Kay ran over to the door. "Don't tell me it's locked!" she moaned, pulling on it.

The thought of Mika and Dice being two cars away raced into my mind. My heart pulsed as I desperately shouted with intensity, "For the love of God, please don't tell me that door is locked!"

I saw Kay's arms slump to her sides as she whimpered, "Okay...I won't tell you."

I swiftly walked over to the door and tried to open it myself, dropping all of the cookies that I was carrying. I jerked the handle, pulling and pushing in a futile attempt. "No!" I exclaimed, slamming on the door with my palms. "This can't be happening!"

"What is going on here?"

In answer to our confusion, a voice came from the PA speakers. "Hello, Causes."

A chill ran down my spine as the tone of that voice filled my ears. "I definitely do not like the look or sound of this."

The voice continued. "We have just passed the North Doma station on this non-stop trip to our final destination: the Cora Sector. Your conductor today is Riley and I am your co-conductor, Sydney. Some of you may know me as 'Doctrine'."

My brain felt to have snapped. I didn't know what to think at that time. The only thing I could utter was, "Doctrine!"

"The Cora Sector?" Kay screamed. "Oh my God, we've been captured!"

Still unable to believe what I was hearing, I could only reply by saying, "…By Sydney—Doctrine Sydney. Sydney that…"

Kay grabbed my shirt and shook me. "Snap out of it and pay attention."

Doctrine continued the announcement. "Don't panic, folks. We're going to give you the options to consider during our trip so that when we arrive at Cora, you won't be completely in the dark. For those of you who are *not* Causes aboard this train, we will reimburse you for your time spent with us and take you back to the Delta. You can blame the Causes for this inconvenience."

"This is impossible…" I thought to myself. "How long was Sydney hiding this?"

The air in the car had become cold and heavy. Kay shuddered and shook her head. "I'm scared. What are they going to do to us?"

Sydney announced the options he mentioned. "You will have three options once we arrive. One, we can ship you out to the Labor Fields. Two, we can set you up a private meeting with some of the members of the Fifteen—this option could either work for you or against you. Third, if you really don't like Eden the way it is, we can arrange for you to be sent to the other side of Eden's wall and you can die out in the Great Beyond."

Kay shook and her knees grew weak. She dropped to the floor and began to get hysterical. "What's going on…?"

I was feeling a tad nauseous as well. I slowly sat down next to her, brimming with worry. I gripped her shoulders and rocked her as Sydney concluded his announcement.

"I guess it goes without saying that the Fifteen were prepared to take measures like this. I've been waiting patiently to do my part to put an end to the Revolution. Now that the Producers are out of the picture, it is finally time for our forces to rise up."

"We are the Deserters."

"We are those who lost hope for the Causes' victory. But lastly, and most importantly, we have been offered truth. We are on the path to knowing what you cannot. Let it be known that our side is capable of things that you would not understand."

"The Causes must be stopped and you are the first batch to go. Have a pleasant trip and be sure to get plenty of rest. Good day."

A tear rolled down my face as I placed my forehead on my knee. "Sydney…Doctrine. How could you do this to us?"

"We are so dead," Kay wailed before bursting into tears.

III

There was no calm, only despair and anxiety. Sydney had us fooled the entire time.

I recalled the only moment he let his façade let up. "…*In case there are any regrets.*"

That phrase repeated in my head just the way I remembered Sydney saying it. It made me feel even more foolish for not realizing it from the start.

Now, he was the one calling the shots. He even declared himself as the leader of this new group: the Deserters. I knew that this new revelation would only serve to make the entire Revolution even uglier than it had already become.

Kay and I sat in a booth, facing each other and pondering the options that were given to us over the announcement. She gave me permission to go against our previous conversation and be my usual, analytical self.

In observing the options, the most appealing one was meeting with a Fifteen member. By making the other two options Labor Fields or death, it would take the average person no time at all to decide which was the easiest. We were under the impression that it was made that way for a reason.

Sydney called himself the leader of the Deserters and that we were the "first batch to go". I concluded that locking down the train was a measure taken to actually create the Deserter force—

that Sydney would have no real followers until the train arrived in Cora. It was a clever plan indeed.

Aside from those thoughts, Mika and Dice were my foremost concerns. They were two cars away and we had no chance of reaching them. There was also no guarantee that we would see them upon arrival, either. My heart was heavy at the thought of that young girl ending up as I had feared she would. I felt I had failed her. Now it would only be a matter of time before she was in the clutches of the Fifteen.

There we sat, alone, questioning our fate. Occasionally, Kay would say, "There has to be a way out of this". But the way she was saying it sounded unconvincing, almost saddening. I wanted to feel the same way for real. Every time I raised my head to look around, though, I felt just as helpless as Kay.

After the first thirty minutes, I stood from my seat and began to look around the car for anything that would have been able to help us. Kay watched me as I paced around, looking for an idea to come to me.

Soon she decided to join me. We felt in our hearts that searching the car was going to get us nowhere. We were more or less trying to kill time before our inevitable demise.

The next thing I recall was sitting myself back down and leaning my head against the window. Kay soon gave up and sat next to me. "Where's your crazy idea this time?"

Confused, I rapidly shook my head. "What are you talking about?"

Kay spoke up for the first time since Sydney's announcement. "Come on, you know what I'm talking about. Escaping out of a third story hotel window and deciding to stop a mob of about four-hundred people aren't exactly everyday ideas!"

I knew what she was getting at. She was expecting me to come up with a sudden, brilliant plan like I had done before. It seemed a little farfetched since there wasn't much around us to work with. On top of that, there was nothing in my bag that could have helped us either. Conjuring up an escape was more difficult than Kay made it sound.

That was, of course, until…

I opened my eyes and took a good look out of the window. The landscape of the Doma Sector looked like a blur. But out in the distance, it was much easier to make everything out. That was when I noticed our one chance to escape.

"The river!" I shouted, startling Kay.

"What?"

I instructed her to follow my lead. "Look out the window! See that river in the distance?"

"Yes, yes, I do!" She was getting excited, knowing I had thought of something.

I asked Kay to move so I could stand from the booth. I walked over behind the counter with the cookie trays. "We'll jump into the river!" I excitedly piped out, grabbing the metal stool from behind the counter.

Despite the fact that I presented an option to escape, Kay still found it necessary to protest. "We're going to jump from the train!? Are you insane?"

I climbed onto the stool and examined the fixture around a window, looking for a way to loosen it. "You heard Sydney," I explained. "This train is going non-stop. This is our only chance to get out of here and we're approaching that river fast!"

Kay was still a little hesitant about the idea as she held the stool in place for me. "How high of a jump is that? How deep is the water?"

"Let's pray it's a short jump into deep water." I was soon finding that keeping my balance on the stool was very difficult. Thus, once again bending my mind for the greater good, I picked the stool up and began to swing it into the resilient window.

On cue with the first strike I began to think about Dice and Mika, who were locked two train cars away from us. The thought of Mika in the hands of the Fifteen took me to a sudden stop.

Kay brought my bag to me, snapping me out of the temporary trance. "What about your things? Won't they get ruined?"

I came to my senses and thought a moment, swinging the stool again. "I'll throw them out onto dry land if I can break this window in time."

"You better hurry, we're almost there!" Kay began to fidget as she prepared herself.

Our party being split in half so suddenly was weighing heavy on my heart. Knowing that Dice and Mika were on a one-way trip into the enemy's hands caused a feeling of despair within me. I truly felt having failed Mika in her mission to find her father.

Not realizing my surroundings in my cloud of thought, I zoned out and my swinging slowed. Kay grabbed two of the stool's legs and hollered in my face. "What are you doing? Snap out of it!"

I gasped and slightly jerked at the tone of Kay's voice. "Right…"

We took a side by side position with all four of our hands on all four of the stool's legs. With one wide swing, the window finally shattered.

I quickly grabbed my bag and looked out the window before pitching it out. I watched my belongings soar through the air and land on solid ground near the base of the bridge. I then cleared some more of the glass away to give us a clear space to jump.

We held onto each others' hands, took a deep breath, and ejected ourselves from the train. All the way down, the only thought repeating in my head was, "*Dice, Mika, I'm sorry.*"

My heart was broken.

IV

It was truly a harrowing experience. Dice and Mika were gone and Kay and I were left to wallow in sorrow underneath the railroad bridge. Everything I could have thought of to beat myself up over this was thought. Letting Mika slip out of my hands so easily was not an easy fact to accept.

Kay was in even worse shape since her personal items were long gone. The shock of the sudden turn of events was taking its toll on her as well. Depressed, she sat herself by the edge of the river and wrapped herself in my spare blanket. She was keeping her distance from me since all of our clothes were hanging to dry, leaving us both naked. Most notably, her bandages were also draped across the beams supporting the bridge. It once again made me wonder about her injuries.

This was a good time for me to give the Revolution some thought. The Causes remained the same, loyal to the Producers' rules. Then the rebels came, siding with Al & Jal. Now, Sydney had shown himself again to add a third group to the conflicts. From what Sydney said over the announcement, I could tell that the Deserters were under direct command of the Fifteen. This led me to believe that the Fifteen were no longer pulling punches in their resistance to the Causes.

Kay seemed to have been thinking about the Revolution too. She pulled me from my train of thought and called out to me. "We need to find the missing Producer!"

I knew she was right, but my mood wasn't quite ready to process a positive response. "How do you suppose we do that? I'm fresh out of crazy ideas for today."

She turned back out to face the river, making it difficult to hear her say, "I was just suggesting what we should do next."

I grabbed my damp shirt and wrapped it around my waist. "I'm coming over there so we can talk about this, all right?"

Kay looked back to me briefly before adjusting the blanket to completely cover her. She looked like a dark blue blob with a head by the time I was over next to her. "What's there to talk about?" she asked me.

I sat down, carefully making sure I kept myself appropriately covered. "What we need to do next is figure out a way to get Mika and Dice back."

Just when I thought we were getting along, Kay snapped back at me. "Will you drop it already? Dice and Mika are gone; Sydney has them now. They are trapped and on their own!"

I cringed, knowing she was right. It quickly brought me to frustration. "What good will finding the last Producer do? We've got a desertion and a rebellion and the whole Revolution is being turned into a disaster. So what good does it do to find him, huh?"

She grunted, placing her head on her knees. "I don't know…"

The sounds of the warm summer breeze complemented the sudden silence between us. It was hard to feel anything but hopelessness.

Kay sobbed lightly as she tried to cover her unfinished statement. "…It's just that everything has fallen apart so fast. I can't really think straight about this."

"I know," I regretfully agreed.

Thinking about the missing Producer reminded me of the message I received from Blue, recalling him asking about Black. I put two and two together and realized that if we found the missing Producer, there was a chance that Black would be with him. This way, we would constantly stay in contact with the Causes as a whole.

This was a significant realization. Kay and I were the only ones to escape that train. Therefore, we were the only free Causes who knew what was going on. All of the information concerning Sydney and the Deserters was confined on the train we had escaped. This made me and Kay the only ones who could warn the Causes of the upcoming danger. Finding the missing Producer and Black would assure us the ability to send out a large-scale warning of Sydney's new role in the Revolution.

I was the first to say anything in several minutes. "Kay! You're a genius!"

My curious partner let out a sound like a scoff and a chuckle. "What are you talking about?"

I explained to her how she was right about seeking out the missing Producer. Though, she admitted to not even giving the idea thought before she announced it. Nevertheless, she was glad to share the credit for the idea.

After discussing it, we made our next mission to seek out a Contact and send a private message to each Producer. The purpose of that would be to await a reply. The only Producer to reply would be the one we had to find. Hopefully, that person would help lead us to him.

Of course, our first order of business was to get dry and dressed. The wind helped speed up the process, but it still took several hours. Kay and I spent that time sharing stories of our pasts to each other.

Through long pauses and light tearing, I told her stories about the family I came from and the abuse I incurred as a child. I even took the liberty of finally showing her the scar on the back of my left leg. It didn't take long for Kay to blame my difficult home life for developing my volatile temper flares.

Kay told me about her family as well. Her mother and father were always concerned about her Interactive Study Grade. She, on the other hand, never really cared about what her parents wanted from her. She was always more concerned about doing her own thing; attending to her studies when she was good and ready for them.

Her two younger sisters saw her as their role model though;

and it always displeased her parents that she set such an example for them. On that, her parents focused more on teaching her sisters the "right way of life" while neglecting to be attentive to her beyond typical providing.

When she first saw Mika, she was reminded of her little sisters and how protective she was of them. That is why she found it necessary to jump in between me and Mika the day we met. She told me that she never trusted older men with younger girls. Stories that Kay heard from her parents as well as some she read on the network drove her to be wary of men for the sake of her sisters. I soon saw Kay as a girl who is simply true to her heart as well as her assumptions.

Even though we shared a lot about ourselves until well into the evening, I dared not once to ask Kay about her bandages. I figured if she was still not willing to say anything about them, I would find it best not to ask.

V

When the time finally came that our clothes were dry enough, we took turns getting dressed, having the other look away. Even though we understood each other now, Kay was still being wary of me. Her mental conditioning was strong and her conviction was resolute. She went so far as to tell me to keep fantasies to myself.

I objected to her remarks, denying any such thoughts. I am a man though. Men have thoughts about those kinds of things. The truth was that I was wishing there had been a way to mix Kay's body with Mika's personality. I laughed at myself for even thinking that. My hormones were just going to have to accept Kay's attitude and know that there were probably better women out there anyway.

We chose to follow the river until we found a business area. It was ten o'clock at night by the time we reached civilization again. Another hour passed before we found an inn to rest at.

This particular inn, Riverview, was a cozy, two-story brick building with a nice view that complemented its name. We checked into their last available room, relieved at our luck.

An apparent discontented sigh resonated from Kay at the

sight of a single bed in the quaint room. Stepping toward the bathroom, she grumbled, "I'm getting a shower."

I just shrugged, trying to keep anything I would say from being taken out of context.

The girl had every right to be in such a surly mood all of a sudden. Her bag, along with half of our group, was missing in action. I didn't want to say it to Kay, but I was pretty sure we'd see Dice and Mika again before seeing anything that belonged to her.

The typical male within me was guessing on one last factor that could put a woman in a foul mood. For the sake of my own neck though, I found it best to keep that remark to myself—for a very long time.

As for me, I was trying to keep my head intact, attempting to push aside the thought of Mika falling into Sydney's hands. Upset and exhausted, I tried to take the situation and look on the lighter side.

I found it amusing and ironic that of all the women I could have been stuck with alone, it just had to be Kay. Even though we were a little more civil to each other now, I felt it would only be a matter of time before we were in each others' faces again. To make matters worse, we had two people with one backpack: mine. While I'm well aware that men are supposed to be providers, this was wearing the concept as thin as what resources I had left.

I threw my shirt, socks, and shoes off and claimed the right half of the spacious, double-wide bed. I snuggled underneath the pale red comforter, turned toward the edge of the bed, and shut my eyes, letting the sound of the running shower lull me.

As tired as I was, there was just a bit too much on my mind to go to sleep immediately. I tossed a bit, trying to lay on my back, then my stomach, and then back to the side. Then I tried sprawling out and quickly realized how bad of an idea that was. I rotated again, flopping about as my eyes hung half-open.

I exhaled, aware of how difficult it was to get comfortable under the circumstances.

After a few more minutes, I heard the shower stop. I figured perhaps it was in my best interest to feign being asleep.

No such luck.

Kay stepped out of the bathroom and without hesitation,

ambled over and began to nudge me. "Hey, Brigg!"

My eyes crept open as I continued to play up my tiredness. "What's up?"

She was succinct. "I don't know where you got the idea that I'd share a bed with you, but it isn't going to happen."

My heart became tight and tense. It was too late at night to be putting up with any of her crap. "That's too bad." I smugly mumbled. "Looks like you'll be sleeping on the floor then."

Her attitude stepped in. "Excuse me?"

"No!" I interrupted, sitting up in the bed, "You…excuse me! Who paid for this room again?"

She didn't give an answer, meekly clutching the front of her towel. It looked like getting along didn't last as long as we wanted it to. Except this time, Kay had no leverage for a comeback because she knew I was right.

"That's right!" I continued. "I paid for this room, so I paid to sleep in this bed for the night. The only reason I kept the other half for you is because I figured a comfortable night's rest would do us *both* good. Think about it. How lucky were we to get this bed for the night?"

Kay pushed her hand into the cushy mattress. "Pretty lucky…" She gently lowered herself onto the left half.

"Look," I said, calming down, "I want to share this bed with you just as much as you want to share it with me. I'm willing to ignore that fact though since we both need a decent night's rest. I'm offering you that half of the bed as a courtesy. You can do with it what you want. I'll rest easy tonight knowing that I at least offered." I rolled back over, not wanting to say anything after that besides, "Good night."

Within moments, I felt Kay's movement as she slipped under the covers. "Thank you," she said quietly.

Finding something amiss, I rolled onto my back and turned my head to address her. "Wait a minute. First you're going to tell me you didn't want to share the bed. Now, not only are you climbing in, but you're not wearing any clothes. That towel won't do you any good if it slides off in the middle of the night, will it?"

"Well," she shrugged, "All of my clothes are drying on the line outside of the bathroom window. I don't have my cotton pajamas anymore, remember?"

"Here." I sat up, reached down and took my black shirt from off of the floor. I handed it over to her and turned away so she could put it on.

While Kay changed into my shirt, she asked, "What about pants?"

I mentally rewound back to my last assumption concerning the origins of her disagreeable mood. Considering I only had two pairs of pants, I wasn't about to have one of them...permanently marked as one of hers. With that in mind, I replied, "Just secure that towel around you like a really long skirt or something."

"Territorial about your pants, I see."

"Among other things."

Kay stood and wrapped the towel around her waist. It took her a few moments to get it to where she wanted it. She soon sat back onto the left half of the bed, content with her temporary outfit. "I'm decent now."

The mood in the room began to feel like our time under the railroad bridge. There was that sensitive, tip-toe-ish ambience where one just isn't sure what there is to say next. I decided to keep it neutral and asked her, "Are you comfortable enough?" I hadn't turned back around yet.

She gave a light relaxed laugh. "It's not exactly as comfortable as my cotton pajamas. But this towel is pretty soft and your shirt is very..." she trailed off. "Oh, dear..."

"Very...what?" I rolled over to look at her. On first sight though, my vision was in direct line of Kay's chest. Her breasts were firmly pressed against the inside of my shirt, which appeared to be a pretty tight fit for her. "Whoa!" I mentally exclaimed, turning away.

"It's kinda snug..." Kay mumbled.

That's when I felt it. Unable to purge the glorious mental image of Kay's womanly blessings, I reached down to my own endowment and adjusted it in preparation for further visual bliss. "Are you alright wearing it?" I asked, still turned away.

"Yes, I'll be fine." She hummed as I began to feel her fidget to adjust the shirt. She must have noticed me still facing away from her. "Are you okay over there?"

I stepped up my mental efforts to regain control of my body. I was overcome with a light, warm sensation that could only be defined as a sudden thirst for lust. It soon coursed through my entire being; pumping hot blood to the places necessary for exhibiting such a state of excitement.

Unfortunately, there was no telling how Kay would react if she were to notice my arousal. Thus, I continued to act as casually as I could. "I'm all right. I'm just trying to get comfortable."

Kay, only trying to help, requested the last thing I wanted to do. "Well, for as long as I've known you, you tend to sleep the best on your back. You're usually out like a light in the first few minutes."

I stood my ground and pretended to be relaxed on my side, finding no reason to draw attention to my biological urges. I pulled the covers up further and wrapped myself tight into them. "That's better."

Kay shifted around a little bit more before making herself comfortable. She exhaled with a dreamy sigh. "Good night, Brigg. See you in the morning."

I was in the clear, able to let my mind wander without her knowing. "Good night, Kay. Let's get some good sleep."

The following several minutes were chock-full of thoughts that I'm a little too shy to repeat at the moment. You're better off using your imagination for this part.

As soon as I managed to push my urges and fantasies aside, I went to sleep.

Day 81

I

The events of the previous day had exhausted us more than we thought. The two of us wound up sleeping in until well after the sun had risen.

Actually, I was the first one to awaken. Kay was still out cold. However, I wasn't about to wake her.

Having shifted about in our sleep throughout the night, I ended up on my back and Kay wound up lying on her side with her left arm draped on my bare chest. I took the opportunity to get a good long look at just how tightly my shirt was fitting her, quickly finding myself excited by the sight of her mature, well-developed body and her peaceful, serene disposition.

The whole scenario was a well-deserved treat for my hormonal, teenage self. I was seventeen at the time and most guys my age all had had girlfriends at one point or another. But up until then, I had never been privileged enough to be that close to a mature woman. I decided to make the moment last as long as I could by staying perfectly still, steady, staring and aroused.

Soon enough, Kay twitched; she was waking up. I knew the show was over, so I closed my eyes and pretended to still be asleep. I felt her move around a little bit as she let out that little moan she always would when she woke up in the morning. Her head flopped back down onto her pillow as she whispered to me, a little raspy, "Hey, Brigg…?"

I continued pretending to sleep.

Kay then said something completely unexpected. "For somebody who is asleep, your heart sure is beating awfully fast." She took her arm off of my chest and sat up. "You can stop faking now."

I opened my eyes and innocently replied, "Good morning, Kay…"

She took the blanket and covered herself. Unfortunately, I wasn't fast enough to realize that my obvious indication of excitement was still in plain sight. Kay caught eye of it. "Oh God!" she remarked.

Kay wasted no time in her physical reaction to my…well…physical reaction. The shocked-awake brunette quickly stood up and ran toward the bathroom, pulling all of the covers off of the bed with her. I tried to object by getting her attention, but she seemed like she didn't want to hear it.

Thoroughly embarrassed, I got out of bed and slowly walked over to the bathroom door. I gave it a gentle knock. "Kay?"

No answer.

I tried to reason with her. "Come on, Kay! It's not like you saw me naked or anything! My pants were still on. What's there to be all embarrassed about?"

Kay opened the bathroom door a tiny bit and threw my shirt back at me. She still wasn't talking.

I dared to try a different approach and butter her up with a compliment. "Can I help it if you're so attractive?"

She still said nothing. I could hear rustling through the door. That's when I remembered her mentioning that she hung her clothes out to dry overnight.

Once she was done, Kay burst through the door fully clothed and completely red in the face. She stepped right up to me and stared into my eyes. "I'm giving you one chance to answer this question honestly."

I felt the sincerity of her anger burning me to the core. It made me hesitant to even answer the question in the first place.

"Sure," I peeped, afraid of what she would say next.

She growled in a low and frightening contrast to her usual womanly voice. "How long were you awake before I woke up?"

In all honesty, time had frozen for me while I was checking her out. I really didn't know how long I had indulged myself.

Bravely, I took the best guess and said, "Maybe fifteen minutes. Probably twenty…"

Kay just stared at me. Our eyes were locked as I fearfully awaited her response to my answer. Minutes passed, feeling like an eternity. I desperately wanted to say something else that would defend me.

Kay and I had been butting heads since we met. So naturally, my heart was quivering with the thought of yet another altercation.

Breaking the silence, Kay finally gave a rather unique reply. "You really are sorry," she whispered. "I can see it in your eyes."

Surprised, I lightly nodded. The fear of an upcoming slap in the face was still lingering as Kay continued to examine my expression.

I felt the urge to explain myself. "It's just that…I've never really been that close to a woman before."

Kay's face shifted to that of disbelief. "Are you serious?" The mere idea of it brought a snicker from her lips.

I rolled my eyes and twiddled my fingers nervously. "Yes, I'm actually really shy around…well…you know."

"I wouldn't have guessed seeing as how you're always so open on the forums."

I tried to euphemize my inexperience. "There really isn't much to say about it. I've never had time to specifically focus on girls."

"I don't see why," she remarked. "You seem like the kind of guy that would be a hit with the average lady."

What was that—a compliment? I pulled a mental double-take and suddenly realized that Kay was complimenting me. It caught me completely off-guard.

Slightly confused, I spit out the first thing I could think of the keep the pace of the conversation. "What makes you say that?"

Kay quickly pointed her finger in my face, opened her mouth and froze. Two seconds later, she turned her gaze aside and busted out in laughter.

I found it amusing that a simple question had stopped Kay in her tracks. I smiled wide and pointed back at her. "Well? What makes you say that?"

"It's nothing," she said, composing herself. "Forget it."

I chose to press her in a playful tone. "No. I won't accept your silence!"

"Stop!" she nasally giggled as she ran into the bathroom.

I ran after her. "You're not getting away!" I managed to catch up to her just before she tried to close the door. "Please, tell me! I'll bake you cookies if you tell me!"

The two of us jovially played with each other. Despite how sarcastic and fun we were being, I seriously wanted her to tell me why she felt the way she did about my charm with women. Nobody had ever brought it up before, and I was curious to find out Kay's real view on the matter.

"Come on," I pleaded in jest, pulling the bathroom door, "let me in there so we can talk about this more!"

"Sure thing," Kay complied. However, she chose to be sneaky and completely release the door as I tugged on it.

With a mighty jerk, the doorknob slipped out of my hand. I fell backwards onto the floor, landing on my hip. It hurt, but we were laughing so much that the pain was almost ineffective in slowing the joyous mood.

Kay brought the blankets out of the bathroom and threw them to completely cover me. As I wrestled with the sheets and comforter, she finally decided to answer me.

A swaggering, mellow tone resonated from her lips, making her sound confident and comfortable. "You're handsome and you can be fun to be around. At the same time, you know when to be serious. You never seem to be at a loss for an idea, either. Overall, it seems you can make life more exciting for people around you."

My heart skipped a beat. Hearing Kay say all of that about me created a feeling more grand than a guy like me could imagine. I stammered into my response. "Y-you really think that way?"

Almost immediately, Kay was ready to bring me back into reality by adding her own flavor to her uplifting praise. "That does not mean that you're a hit with me. I only answered so you would bake me cookies!"

Sunk out of my ego trip and amused by her response to

cookies, I threw the covers off of me and slouched as I continued to sit on the floor. "Why did you have to go and say a thing like that? You really had me feeling good about myself there!"

She gave me a lazy smile, whipped her hair once and stared into my eyes. "The only reason I said that is because I'm not an average girl. That and I'd like to see how well you can bake, too!"

I cast the covers in her direction with a laugh. "Don't flatter yourself." I stood up and took a few steps toward her. "I'll be the one to decide if you're average or not."

Kay had caught the covers and was rolling them up in a ball. She pushed them into me as an indication to stay out of her personal space. "Is there any reason I wouldn't be?"

I forcefully snatched the rumpled sheets from her hands and threw them back onto the bed. I smiled to her and continued pacing toward her. "Well, as far as looks go, you're above average." I chose to not stop at just one remark of praise. "You're headstrong, protective and well-intended."

Kay was trying hard not to outwardly react to my compliments. She held back her smile and took a step away from me; turning to the side. "That's very kind of you to say; even after all we've been through."

I reached out with my arm and placed it on her shoulder. It was then that my confidence shot up high. My heart beat fast and my thoughts raced as I tried to find the right words to say to her. That moment appeared to hold still as I began to take full notice of Kay's beauty. Within a moment, my nerves caught up with me.

I wasn't certain what to make of my thoughts. My heart was telling me that having Kay around didn't seem like such a bad thing anymore. And now that that great mood was set, I was asking myself how far I could go with it.

Kay's bandaged left hand came to meet mine. She gave off a brief, contented huff and shyly spoke, "Your hand is really warm."

I chuckled once as my brain appeared to cease functioning under the pressure I was feeling. "Yeah, I get that a lot."

"Your hand is shaking too. It's like you're nervous or something."

I couldn't stand the tension anymore. I took my hand off of her shoulder and placed my finger to her chin; slowly turning her head toward mine. I stared into her glimmering green eyes as her mouth opened ever so slightly with a peep.

With a slow, deep draw of breath, I whispered to her, "Are you nervous too?" Then, I closed my eyes and began to lean into her, prepared to experience my first kiss.

Suddenly, Kay loudly gasped and backed away. Within a split second of her reacting, I felt the palm of her hand swiping clear across my cheek.

Time practically stopped.

I recoiled from the hit and opened my eyes to see that Kay had not moved a muscle after her attack. She was leaned slightly forward with her right arm stretched to her left side. The expression on her face was that of uncomprehending disbelief.

I stared into her widened and frightened eyes, trying to collect myself and my thoughts. It was clear that I had stepped over a boundary. Therefore, I had no right to be cross with her.

Kay's breaths were shallow as she slowly set herself onto the floor. She shuddered in her state of thought, unable to figure out what either of us should say.

Gazing into her eyes, I saw the cries of a conflicted spirit. It was almost as if she wanted me to kiss her, but something within her was holding her back. However, having been the one who got slapped in the face, I wasn't about to assume anything concerning her thoughts on the matter.

I took a shot at relieving the room of the silence that began with the sound of the slap. Being creative, I opted to repeat Kay's exact words from earlier. "You really are sorry," I said with a forgiving whisper. "I can see it in your eyes."

As if what I had said was a cue to do so, Kay's eyes shook before her tears began to well up and trickle down her cheeks.

I finished gathering myself and took a deep breath. Calmly, I said to her, "What do you say we just forget about this? I know you well enough to assume that there was a very good reason you did that."

Kay said nothing. She simply began to cry. She wiped her tears away with the backs of her hands, periodically sobbing.

I took a few paces toward her in an effort to comfort her. I placed my hand on the top of her head, but she quickly swiped it away. "No," she sobbed.

"No?"

She lifted both of her hands with her head still sunk. "Just…"

I waited for her to say something.

Her hands slowly closed into fists and dropped to the floor. "Give me a few minutes alone, okay?"

"Did I…?"

She cut me off. "It's not you, it's me. I need a few minutes to myself."

I nodded, agreeing to give her some space. I decided to step out of the room to give her the time she needed. After entering the hallway, I leaned up against the wall within earshot of the door and listened intently in case Kay decided to comfort herself in an audible fashion.

No such comfort was heard.

I hung my head and shook it slowly. "I shouldn't have done that."

I had the unfortunate feeling that I reset any trust I might have gained from Kay up to that point. However, it was only a gut sensation based on the stinging feeling in my left cheek and the fact that Kay robbed me of my first kiss.

Part of me wished I had caught myself before attempting such a bold move. But the damage had already been done. The only thing I could rely on to heal the impact of my actions was time.

I prayed that Kay would forgive me.

II

Kay seemed to let the incident from that morning slide off of her shoulders. Once regaining herself, she told me that she was understanding of my actions. Kay had a long list of personal reasons that factored into her reaction to my advances.

When I asked Kay about the nature of those reasons, she refused to comment. Based on the sensitivity of the situation, I chose to ignore it and move on.

Although we reached a final say on the matter, it still didn't change that fact that I still had never kissed a girl.

Like many other things in my life, I chose to remain patient. Whether or not it would be Kay's lips didn't matter to me at that point. What mattered was retaining the trust that I had worked so hard to obtain. The first kiss would come to me another day.

Kay and I spent the day staying vigilant for Gray Police and being wary of any new faces among the Causes. With Al & Jal leading rebels and the uncertainty surrounding the Deserters, we were keeping a low profile until contact with the missing Producer would be established.

With our resources limited to only ourselves, it was quite the chore to track down a Contact. It wasn't until around eight o'clock that night that we found one.

The slim, white-clad young woman was sitting on a bench on a bridge. Coincidentally, the river under that bridge was the very one we had jumped into.

Kay and I approached the cute, quiet blonde and established our allegiance to the Causes. We sat next to her on the bench and waited for her to present the laptop to us.

Kay switched seats with the Contact and looked over my shoulder as I prepared to send the private messages to each of the Producers. She called for my attention almost immediately. "You've got two new private messages, you know?"

I ventured some guesses. "One is probably from Blue. The second one is probably Al & Jal harassing me again."

Sure enough, I was right. My inbox presented my first new message from Blue.

What's going on Brigg?

I had no idea you were at that bridge in the Pata Sector that night. That's pretty funny! Anyway, why are you paired up with Kay? Weren't you two always arguing or something?

In response to your answers to my questions though…

Thanks for the insight on Jalako. I knew "Jal" sounded feminine enough.

Also, I'm sure the missing Producer will show up soon. The whole Revolution is probably going to start getting out of hand with Al & Jal planning on going on the attack.

Speaking of which, I see your point about letting the Gray Police handle them.

Thanks for the info. Is there anything else I should know about?

Just give me a shout.

-Blue

Kay found it appropriate to ask, "You think we should tell him about the Deserters?"

"If we can't find the missing Producer, we have to start with *somebody* we can trust."

I typed a lengthy reply explaining what happened to us on the train. I told him everything I knew about Sydney, the Deserters, and the Fifteen's plans for the Causes who were captured on that train.

Kay suggested I add the fact that Dice and Mika were on that train and physical descriptions of them just in case.

I finished by letting him know that Al & Jal were now the least of the Causes' worries now that Sydney had stepped in.

Kay and I re-read the message together then sent it. I let out a disgruntled sigh as I prepared to proceed to my next message. "Let's see what Al has to say about me today."

As soon as my next message appeared on the screen, our jaws fell open and our eyes bugged out wide. "No freaking way!" Kay exclaimed.

The irony was amusing. Having sat down to send private messages to every Producer, I found myself having had a Producer send one to me. Remarkably, my second message was from Bogen himself—the missing Producer.

Dearest Brigg,

I am praying that you are all right. Seriously, I went to a chapel and everything.

I've finally gotten back together with Black. Together, we've been reading up on what has happened since the rest of my team was captured by the Fifteen.

I am furious that Al & Jal have started a true rebellion. That is not what we called the Causes to do and it is going to get us all into serious trouble. We will be lucky if the Fifteen don't instruct the Gray Police to kill us on sight.

Let me get to the point. I've contacted you specifically since you and your partners appear to be some of the very few Causes I can rely on now. I have not made announcement of my escape public yet and I would like to keep it that way for now. That being said, we need to establish a meeting place, regroup, and go from there.

I've escaped the Exta Sector to the south. I'm going to continue southward to Kediel Lake in the Binda Sector. I hope you haven't strayed too far from Fanda and can make it there in a decent amount of time. If you get there before I do, just wait up for me.

Black and I are traveling together now. So as soon as you reply to this message I will be able to see it right away. Be sure to include any updates or anything I may need to know about the state of the Revolution. I hope to hear from you.

This isn't over yet.

Sincerely, Bogen

Kay and I were ecstatic. Bogen's message was the best thing that could have come to us. "I like how he added that this isn't over yet," Kay remarked.

"He doesn't realize how right he is."

I spent the next half an hour pouring out our minds to him, telling him everything I told Blue and more. A lot of it was the message asking what Bogen planned to do about the whole situation. Now that he would be informed of Sydney, I wondered if it would alter whatever Bogen had planned before contacting me.

One thing was for sure, though, whatever he had planned for the long run, he wanted me and my group in on it. Sure, not having Dice and Mika would alarm him. But maybe, just maybe, he would know a way we could get them back.

I suddenly got a brilliant idea. I added to the message instructions for Bogen to contact Blue. I told him that Blue seemed to be a man who was willing to help our side as well. Hopefully, he would give the idea to have Blue join forces with us some good thought.

Our next destination was in front of us—much sooner than we had expected. But we wound up proceeding into it with an empty and guilty air permeating around us.

It was painful to know that my friends and I had been forced into separate paths. All things considered, I couldn't rely on Dice to take care of Mika since his ability to make decisions was hindered by his risky rolling habit. Kay wasn't too keen on the fact that Mika was alone with a man as well. As much as we wanted them back with us, we dreaded knowing that it was unlikely to happen.

Our most important priority now was to meet up with Bogen and prepare to fight back. It was one thing to assume that Al & Jal would bring about their own end, but having Sydney blatantly step forward to bring full opposition to the Causes brought the severity of the danger to a whole new level. I predicted that soon enough, the only people we would be able to trust would be ourselves.

The real fight for the truth had finally begun.

Episode 6: The Paths of Heroes

Our journey to Kediel Lake was a tense and unsettling experience. Throughout the four days it took us to get there, we bore witness to the Revolution's slow dissipation into chaos.

It didn't take long for Al & Jal to create a name for their band of rebels: "Zealots".

With the new name known to all, Al & Jal began orchestrating attacks on landmarks throughout Eden. Their motivation was to see how long the Fifteen would stand for it before giving in.

All the while, Bogen, Blue, and I continued to keep in touch. Although Bogen wanted to stay low for a little while, the news of Sydney and the Deserters prompted him to speak out and issue an alert. Unfortunately for me, Bogen's newfound suspicion of new faces made it more difficult for him to trust Blue.

At this point, mostly every Cause was aware of Sydney and his intentions. The Causes who still supported the Producers had a lot to say about the Zealots and the Deserters. It went so far that Black herself banned "Al & Jal" and "Doctrine" from even accessing the forum. She also demanded that all discussion concerning the Zealots was to go in one single thread and a thread for the Deserters likewise.

All in all, it didn't take long for the once-orderly Revolution to turn into a scene of uncertainty and havoc.

One of the worst parts about the whole situation was how the citizens of Eden were reacting. With a newfound reason for the people to be wary of Causes, it soon became troublesome to find a Contact, let alone a comfortable place to rest. A number of inns stopped serving to Causes altogether since the Zealots clouded the true Causes' good image.

Fortunately for us, Al & Jal failed to realize that Vade and the Gray Police were always a step ahead of their rebellion. Many of the Causes fighting with the Zealots soon found themselves in the captive arms of the Fifteen.

Despite numerous threads demanding that the Zealots stop, they continued to advance their strategies. It soon seemed that nothing was going to change their course and that the true Causes were going to have to act around the carnage that Al & Jal had created.

There was only one point in time that Kay and I were actually able to contribute to the side of the true Causes. Even though our own situation was dire enough, the opportunity presented itself and we took it.

The incident happened on our way to Kediel Lake…

Day 84

I

Kay and I diverted our course from the river when we came across another set of train tracks. This particular section of rail crossed not only the river, but the Doma-Binda border as well.

The decision to waver was based on the previous realization that two people living out of one bag was quite a stretch. We were out of food, low on water, and almost out of Arna.

I began to recall back to the last day I spent alone during the Revolution as I jingled the last twenty-four Arna in my hand. I distinctly remembered having had 182 Arna in coins the morning of the sixty-third day. "So much for 'self-control and knowledge of my priorities'..." I muttered to myself.

Kay exhaled, slightly exhausted. "What are you bellyaching about now?"

I grunted in kind, gripping the coins tight in my fist before pointing to my gut. "Trust me; the only aching from this belly is hunger." I slipped my hand back into my coin purse and freed the coins from my grasp.

Kay sighed again, appearing to relate to me. "Right..."

I brought my bag out in front of me and began to rummage through it, hoping to find any food we might have overlooked.

The first thing I placed my hand on was the series of glass vials provided by Zoe.

I looked to Kay as she stared at my bag from the corner of her eye. "Still thinking about those?" she asked.

"Yeah," I agreed, pulling a vial of red gel from my backpack. "This one especially."

There was a pause just before Kay took the gel from my hand. She pulled the cork from it and quickly smelled the contents. Her face wrinkled into a confused state. "It doesn't smell like anything."

"That's kind of weird…"

Kay was silent for a moment with a thoughtful look on her face. She then replaced the cork and said, "I still don't trust it since it probably came from the Fifteen."

"I wish we could, though," I sighed.

It was at this point that I realized we had run out of things to talk about. We shared enough about ourselves with each other that it wasn't going to be easy to stay away from really personal stuff if it came to talking about something new.

The time came that I finally began to fancy the idea of asking Kay about her bandages. It had always hovered around as the unspoken rule to leave her injuries out of conversations. However, now that the two of us were more of a team than we ever were, it seemed like a good time to bring it up.

Before I got a chance to ask, Kay had something to say. "I have a little confession. It's not a big deal, though."

"What kind of confession?" I curiously replied.

"The other day," she began, "When you showed me your scar and I acted surprised, I really wasn't."

"No?"

She shrugged and chuckled. "Mika told me about it a while back."

I laughed heartily. "Is that so?"

Kay seemed thrown off by the way I responded to her. "You didn't tell her about it in confidence, did you?"

"Of course not," I answered, taking the red gel back from her. "Even if I did, kids her age aren't that good at keeping secrets."

Kay smiled, seeming to be reminded of her little sisters. "I guess you're right."

I saw that as an opening to ask her my original question. "Speaking of secrets, what is the big deal with those bandages of yours?"

Kay immediately stopped and the chipper air that had surrounded us appeared to dissipate in an instant. I stopped and turned, waiting for her to reply.

Her lips were tight as she closed her eyes and hung her head. She then reached her right hand across her waist and gently stroked the dressings on her left wrist.

A shiver clasped my heart as the silence between us grew longer. The only statement that repeated in my head was: "I asked that too soon."

Kay sounded a lone sniffle. She grunted and shook her head hard as if she was trying to shake a bad memory out of it.

I dared to speak. "What's the matter?"

With a jerking sob and a sigh of reluctance, she softly spoke. "I really want to tell you…"

"But…"

Kay did not resume speaking. She simply continued to walk slowly in the direction we had been going.

I remained standing still until Kay was well ahead of me. My eyes stayed on her as the shuddering in my chest began to subside. "I seem to be doing everything too soon with her lately," I mumbled to myself.

I had always felt that there was a lot more to Kay's bandages than most would think. I knew that when the time came to talk about them, there would be a lot of listening for me to do. There was obviously a large-scale explanation surrounding the origins of her pain. Although she was still not ready to discuss it at the time, I was able to take solace in the fact that she said she *wanted* to tell me.

That was the last we spoke of it. I chose to respect her position and save her story for another day—the day she would be ready to open up to me completely.

II

The tracks continued on through a residential area in the southern part of Binda.

This particular area was no different from any other housing area in Eden. Along its wide dirt roads, blocks of white, uniform homes were lined up neatly, five meters from the street and three meters apart from each other. A stone walkway stretched from the front of each house to the road with the property's lawn hugging both sides of it.

Usually in areas such as these, there is one block of properties that are businesses. That was what we were looking for in order to buy what food we could with our remaining Arna. If worse came to worst, we would resort to trading the medicines Zoe gave us in exchange for sustenance.

Once again, the need to keep a watchful eye for Gray Police was present. We had to make our way through to the nearest food store. Unfortunately, being new to this section of town, we were going to have to stop and ask for directions.

Before we resorted to asking, though, we decided to follow a few streets at random and hope to run into a business area. Hopefully, we would be able to buy provisions and get back onto the tracks before being spotted by authorities.

Trying to act casual and remain calm, we made our way through the quiet Binda Sector neighborhood. Kay and I stuck close and watched our sides. We couldn't turn to look behind us for fear of looking suspicious. The way Eden was at the time, it wouldn't take long to run into trouble.

We soon reached an intersection with a small food market on the opposite side of the street. "Thank goodness," I exhaled.

Kay was looking in all directions. "Everything looks clear," she quietly spoke.

I looked both ways before attempting to cross the street. Just as I stepped away, Kay grabbed my backpack and pulled me back.

"What's going on now?" I asked.

Kay had panic in her voice. "Look who's coming out of the store!"

Her tone of voice told me to better hide myself from view of the store's entrance. We still managed to keep the store in view by a simple, discreet peek around the corner.

A young man dressed in black and sporting lengthy blond hair emerged from the corner store with a wide smile across his face. He was stuffing some food into his bag as he turned away from us and continued walking. He did not notice us.

"It's Albion! I'd recognize that shirt anywhere!"

"What is he doing here?" Kay wondered. "Shouldn't he be running around with the Zealots?"

Before I could answer her, we saw Albion stop and turn around. He stood in the street, staring at the front of the store he had just left.

Soon after, two other young men and a youthful girl came out of the store to catch up with Albion.

One of the two males was noticeably taller and more muscular than Albion and the other boy. His need to flaunt his build was apparent in the fact he was not wearing a shirt with his simple blue jeans.

The other male appeared strictly average. All he wore was simple black shorts and a white, sleeveless shirt. He was the first participant in the Revolution I had seen with absolutely nothing unique about his look other than his near-bald haircut.

The girl standing with them was quite petite and sexy. She stood the shortest of the four of them. A large, hooded pink shawl draped over her head and shoulders and appeared to be the only thing covering her chest. Tight, brown pants and brown shoes finished her outfit. It wasn't until she turned to the side that I noticed she had a small pink top on underneath her shawl.

"Check out that crew!" Kay remarked.

We watched as the four of them began to engage in a conversation.

"It's safe to say that they are planning something; perhaps another attack."

Kay seemed a bit confused. "An attack on what? There are no important landmarks around here."

My eyes closed briefly as I gave her quick fact some thought. "You're right," I nodded. "I guess the question now is whether or not we should follow them."

Kay said the first thing that came to mind. "We still need to buy food!"

I was suddenly much more concerned about what Albion was up to. "We can't lose sight of him," I protested.

"You're still just hot about him upstaging you at the Delta."

I admitted to being upset about it. However, paying attention to Albion was just as much about planning payback as it was protecting Eden from his antics.

I decided to shift focus from my sour feelings toward him. "I think that girl who is with them is Jalako."

Kay took a guess. "Maybe. However, Jalako might be with a different gathering of Zealots and this girl is someone else."

"That would make sense," I agreed.

Albion and the three other Zealots began to cross the street coming toward us. To our relief, they were walking in the opposite direction down the street. The pace at which they were walking made it feel like they were up to something.

"We have to follow them," I insisted.

Although she knew I was right about the situation at hand, she chose to playfully groan about our change of course. "F-o-o-d!"

I chuckled as I took her arm. "Come on. Let's go!"

"F-o-o-d," she persisted, slightly more serious. It took her a minute or two, but she eventually cooperated.

III

Kay and I wound up following Albion and his entourage all the way back to the train tracks. Once there, we remained hidden behind a tree as we watched the crew of Zealots walk around the vicinity.

We could hear them talking, but couldn't quite make out any specific words. As they conversed, the Zealots gestured to one another, looking in all sorts of directions and pointing to one thing after another.

"Looks like they're setting the stage for whatever they're planning," Kay observed.

"Would seem so…" I whispered. "But what could they possibly do here?"

The two of us carefully watched over Albion and his team. The average-looking boy had taken one of their bags and was distancing himself from the rest of the group. The girl was discussing something with Albion as the muscular youth rustled through a duffel bag. After a few moments, he produced a length of sturdy wire and a large wrench from the bag.

My eyes went wide at the sight of the items. "Whatever they

are planning, it's about to go down."

"Without a doubt," Kay agreed.

We remained silent for a few moments. I could see Kay turning her face to me out of the corner of my eye. Once her leering met my profile, she said, "I think your line is: 'Not if I have anything to say about it'."

"In most cases you would be right," I mumbled, turning to meet her gaze. "In this case though, it's not that easy. Clearly, it will be four on two if we rush into this head first."

Kay sighed. "There you go with the excessive thinking again!"

"Come on," I defended, "you should know me well enough to see that I don't discount any possibilities."

She smirked with lazy, accusing eyes. "Yeah, you seem to notice the possibility of that bulky guy pounding on your face."

"Since when did the welfare of my face become your concern?' I asked her semi-seriously.

She delivered an equally jocular answer. "About the same time I chose to stick with you through this whole thing. I think it's best to keep you in good health."

I played along. "Not looking to wind up alone again?"

"Pretty much."

I turned back to pay attention to what was happening on the tracks. Unfortunately, the moment I looked out, my eyes met those of Albion's in the distance.

I heard him shout loud in response. "Hold it, everyone!"

The girl asked him, "What's going on, Al? What's wrong?"

His eyes locked on mine, he answered, "We've got company."

Kay heard the announcement of our presence and peeked over my shoulder. "This is bad, right?"

I quivered. "I don't know yet. He's coming over to us alone."

I quickly realized that I had spoken too soon. The girl began to scurry to catch up to Albion, and the bulky male was making his way toward us from another angle.

"Let's run!" Kay advised.

"Too late to run," I muttered, shaking my head in fear.

Albion's confident, masculine voice sounded out as if he was confirming our presence. "Well, well, well. Of all the people to be hiding behind a tree…"

I rolled my eyes and tried to put a tough face on. "I know,

right?"

Albion opted to feel very sure of his influence. "Did you track me down to join the rebellion?"

"Ha!" I huffed. "Get serious."

He shrugged with his arms wide. "Legitimate question, legitimate question…" Albion's casual attitude was making me a little nervous. He, too, seemed a little tense though.

Kay whispered in my ear, briefly distracting me. "Hey Brigg, muscle boy is going back. You can refrain from soiling yourself."

I turned to her quickly, yet slightly relieved to hear it. "Oh, very funny!"

Albion laughed. "I see the two of you are still getting along. Where are the other two?" After asking his question, the other girl came into the conversation.

I chose to keep our party's business out of his ears as I turned to see the truth in Kay's whispered announcement.

As I focused on that, Kay countered with a question of her own. She extended her hand to the girl. "Jalako, I presume?"

The young beauty sighed and stamped her foot, reaching out to shake Kay's hand anyway. "I think I've lost track of how many people have presumed wrong!"

Kay apologized. "It's an easy thing to assume."

"You're telling me!"

Despite the slight tension, Albion introduced us in a calm and mature manner. "This is Memento. If you remember the name and what she did, I'll give you two Arna." Showing he wasn't just talking, he pulled two Arna coins out of his pocket.

Having a pretty good memory on names, I had the answer almost immediately. "I remember hearing a series of three names: Al, Memento and Tricky. The three of you helped Blue at the bridge back in the Pata Sector."

Albion's brow slowly rose as a smile gradually crept across his lips. "I honestly didn't expect you to get that right." He reached his hand out and gave the Arna to me.

Kay pointed to the larger male. "Is that Tricky over there?"

"No," he replied. "Tricky is farther down the tracks."

Even though I knew it was going to open the door to conflict, I said the next thing on my mind. "What is he doing over there?"

Memento interrupted before Albion could answer. "You sure

are nosy, aren't you? It's official Zealot business!"

I chuckled, "That's a new one."

Albion turned the nature of the answer around. "If you're so curious, why don't you come see for yourself?"

I folded my arms as Kay began to gather our things up to move again. "Letting true Causes see what you have planned? What's the deal with this?"

Albion turned back to me. "I just figured that since there are only two of you and four of us, I can safely assume that you can't stop us anyway."

I chose to appear unfazed by his sharp comment. "Confident, are we?"

He laughed, pointing to the muscular young man. "Pibs over there could take you down real fast. If you know what is good for you, I'd recommend you keep your distance and watch the show."

As a testament to having just boasted my good memory; the name stopped me so suddenly, I almost tripped over myself. I spaced out for a moment as the images flashed one by one through my head.

A burly youth blocking a door…

…The doorknob landing at my feet…

…The weathered and panicked expression on the young man's face…

…And posting on the forums to thank him for aiding the Causes out of the Gateway Inn that night.

"Pibs…" I whispered.

"What's with him?" Memento asked, nudging me on the shoulder.

Words accompanied the memories. "*Well, this is probably the end of the Revolution for me.*" My thoughts repeated the phrase a couple of times.

Kay shook me, appearing very concerned. "Brigg, what's wrong?"

A lot of thoughts raced into my mind and a conclusion that I had no time to explain. The next words that came from my mouth served to shock everybody. "Pibs is a Deserter."

Kay responded, almost in a scream. "What did you say?"

Albion was intrigued. "What's this?"

I broke from my near-vegetative state and began an attempt to explain. I turned to Kay, who would understand my opening statement. "Kay, do you remember what Dice said about Zoe?"

She rapidly nodded. "Oh, the girl that gave us the medicine? Yeah, I remember! She was captured back in the Pata Sector."

"Exactly!"

Albion appeared a little frustrated at being out of this loop of information. "What are you talking about? What girl? What medicine?"

I tried to get back on the subject of Pibs. "That isn't important…"

We were interrupted by shouting coming from farther down the tracks. The sudden outburst had the attention of everybody. My first reaction was to run out to the tracks and see what had just happened.

Albion, Memento, and Kay followed closely behind me. My rival was still demanding an explanation. "Are you going to tell me what you're talking about, Brigg?"

Still running off of my assumptions, I replied, "I'll explain later. All you need to know is that Pibs is not on your side."

"I'll believe that when I see it."

"Actually," Memento added, "I was a little uneasy about him from the start."

We stepped back onto the tracks and looked in the direction of Tricky and Pibs. "Oh, you can't be serious!" Albion exclaimed.

Not only did we see Tricky laid out on the ground, but two other figures were standing alongside Pibs. All of the equipment that Tricky was using was flung to the side of the tracks. Within seconds, their eyes met with ours across the fifty meters of track that separated us.

The two men accompanying Pibs stood just as tall as he did and were dressed in broad-shouldered gray cloaks.

Albion seemed as outraged as he was confused. "Who are those people?"

I was civil with my response. "I'll have to explain it to you later. I think getting away from those guys is more important right now."

Kay had something to say about it as well. "I actually think that they are after you, Albion. You're one of the Zealot leaders."

I nodded as I began to take steps away from Pibs and the cloaked men. "That's even more of a reason to believe Pibs is a Deserter. He tipped off somebody and now they are here to take all of us in."

Albion huffed, apparently upset by the fact that he had to team up with us for a little bit. "You better have a good explanation for this. Our plans are ruined now."

"Don't look at me," I defended as I turned to start running. "If I hadn't been here, you would have been on your way to the Fifteen's open arms right now."

Albion countered. "Don't even *think* that makes us a team. As long as you're still clinging to the Producers, we are enemies."

"Same here," Memento added.

No matter what we said to each other from that point, the facts remained the same. The unspoken objective was to escape now and explain later.

Although Pibs and the cloaked men gave chase, it was easy to evade them given the distance between us when we began to escape.

We ran all the way back into the residential area. Once there, we backtracked to the food store to hide for a little while. As we hid, Kay and I began to gather food supplies as we had originally planned.

I felt that the only thing that saved us was the fifty meter head-start. We agreed that if there had been any further hesitation back at the tracks, the outcome of the chase would have been different.

One last passing thought hit me once the coast was clear. Having thought back to my actions at the tracks, I realized that I should not have said anything to Albion and left him to get captured by the cloaked men.

I didn't know what possessed me to actually help Albion at the time. Perhaps it just wasn't in me to see anybody, friend or foe, land in the clutches of the Fifteen.

I rolled with it, though, praying I wouldn't be kicking myself later.

IV

The four of us returned to the river and continued to travel alongside it until dark. Throughout that time, I told everyone where I had met Pibs before.

I recapped the entire story for Albion and Memento while Kay simply waited to hear what had happened after she escaped out the window back at the Gateway Inn. Sure enough, Kay realized that I was more aware of the finer details than she had previously thought me to be.

Albion and Memento were nothing short of impressed with my quick thinking. Of course, Albion found it to be an admirable trait worthy of being a Zealot. He spared no time in mentioning it.

After all was said and done, I took note that the Deserters began being assembled as early as the Ordeal of Pata. We had two subjects, Zoe and Pibs, as solid enough proof that Sydney's numbers were higher than we thought at first.

One last realization was that Sydney lied in his announcement on the train. I recalled him declaring the Causes on that train as being the "first batch to go".

Obviously, the fact that Zoe and Pibs were captured long before that fated train run made me believe that there were still some kinks in Sydney's new act. As with anything else concerning the Deserters or the Fifteen, I felt that some information was being made up or left out simply to confuse and mislead the Causes.

"That's very impressive," Albion complimented, poking at the campfire we had built. "You're the last person I'd expect to be filling me in on information like this. It makes me think that you're looking for a favor back."

"Not really, unless you offer," I replied. "I more or less helped you out of impulse. I said the first thing that came to my mind when I heard the name 'Pibs'."

"I was just as surprised as you were," Kay added from within our two-tarp shelter.

Albion turned his head to her direction, grabbing his long hair to keep it away from the fire. "Regardless of the surprise, Brigg said and did everything he needed to in order to pull all of our butts out of trouble."

"Yeah," Kay agreed, "he tends to do that a lot!"

Albion let out a sigh, one sounding almost desperate. "It's no wonder the true Causes look up to you. You had some balls stepping out there back at the Radio Tower."

I read into his tone. "If you're trying to butter me up to side with you, you're sadly mistaken."

Albion's face suddenly changed to anger. "Don't flatter yourself! You're still stuck on the Producers' rules."

Memento cut in from within the shelter as well. "Shut up, Albion. I know you want him to side with us. Accept the fact that he isn't going to budge. He's going to side with the Producers all the way."

I continued to add to Memento's input. "If what happened today didn't give you the hint, let me spell it out for you. If you keep doing what you're doing, the Gray Police and the Deserters will continue to catch up with you. I'm not sticking around to go down with you. Kay and I have more important things to do on top of keeping morale high among the true Causes."

"I don't care about that!" Albion argued. "All I care about is bringing the truths to light through a different method."

"Oh yeah? Well, for your information, that new 'method' is going to get every Cause and Zealot a one-way ticket to the Labor Fields!"

Memento exited the shelter and continued to speak. "On the contrary, Brigg! In your own words, you stated that the captured Causes have been turning up as Deserters."

Thinking fast, I batted back. "Yes, the captured *Causes*. I'm not sure what they're doing with the *Zealots* that they get their hands on. I see the fields in your future."

"An interesting argument…" Albion nodded, tilting his chin with his right hand.

Kay stepped out of the shelter and over to the campfire, sitting next to me. "That's Brigg for you."

I continued my statement. "Since you declared the Zealots to lead something more like a rebellion, I'm sure that the Fifteen have different plans for your kind."

"Especially with the acts of destruction your party has been carrying out!" Kay added.

"Be that as it may," Albion protested, "the Zealots will stay as is. We'll make the Fifteen talk…"

I cut him off, repeating his words in a ho-hum tone accented with a rolling of my eyes. "…Even if it means turning Eden upside-down to do it." I shifted back to my normal voice. "Yeah, we know!"

"Don't get cocky with me! Just because I stole your thunder back at the Delta doesn't mean you have to mock what worked."

Memento whole-heartedly supported Albion's comment with a loud "Zing!"

Annoyed by his need to rub in his influence yet again, I tried to shift the focus of the conversation. "Speaking of which, what makes you think that your little power trip is going to last much longer?"

"Well," he began explaining, "I'm trying to bring the Zealots together in a way that will not only increase our numbers, but our unpredictability as well. That was the purpose we were trying to achieve back at the tracks this afternoon."

Kay leaned in from her seated position, staring intently into Albion's eyes over the crackling fire. "What exactly were you trying to do there?"

Albion shrugged as Memento excused herself for a moment. "I was experimenting on ways to derail trains. Simply ransacking landmarks and important buildings isn't quite having the effect I was hoping for."

I raised my tone to bring out a sense of ridiculousness to his argument. "It has only been six days since the meeting. Did you honestly expect immediate results?"

"Simply, yes."

"That's absurd!"

He folded his arms in discontent. "A bold claim. Explain!"

I began to scold him. "If you knew anything about the way the Fifteen operate, you would have known better!"

Albion fired back with concentrated sarcasm. "Oh, so you're the big expert on the Fifteen all of a sudden?"

I was now shouting. "I said no such thing! What I meant was that it is impossible to know what the Fifteen are planning. It's safe to say that our enemies are more unpredictable than your Zealots could ever hope to be. The mere fact that Pibs was with you should have told you that the Deserters and the Fifteen are a step ahead of us."

"Then all we have to do is catch up. If we can take their focus away from us and onto repairing the trains…"

I interrupted again, trying to get it through his head that the Zealots were on the wrong path. "They don't call themselves the 'Fifteen' for nothing! *Riley* will take care of the trains while the other *fourteen* track us down!"

Albion gritted his teeth, aggravated, fully aware that what I was saying made sense.

I continued in a calmer tone, leaning my head forward into my hands. "You need to understand. The Fifteen are very meticulous. Everything they do is so carefully planned out, it is as if everything we do is what they expect. It's almost frightening."

"You're intimidated by them?"

A memory from the Radio Tower caught me briefly. The first time I heard the sound of Naro's voice resonated in my head. *"Welcome, Revolutionaries!"* I nodded slightly, "You could say that."

"Same goes for me," Kay chuckled.

Memento returned, having heard our last few statements. "I can only imagine what it was like stepping up face to face with Naro."

I lifted my head with my eyes wide as I threw another stick into the fire. "No, you can't. Trust me, there is no feeling like it."

"Can you describe it at all?" Albion wondered with increasing intrigue.

Suddenly, all eyes were on me as I began to piece together a statement that would satisfy their ears. "It's like…"

"Yes…?"

I gave the best answer I could. "It's like you're talking to somebody who you feel could crush you under their little finger. You just get this gut feeling that anything you say could barrel you into irreversible trouble. The Fifteen have a system where everybody is designated a place in this life, right?"

"Right," Albion mumbled, truly fixed on my words.

"Well," I resumed, "Dealing with Naro that day was like gambling away our place in Eden's structure, running the risk of turning it into an unknown fate. The scariest part was knowing that he had the power to do it."

Kay shuddered dramatically. "That's pretty vivid thinking

there, Brigg."

"So, correct me if I'm wrong…" Albion slowly responded.

"With pleasure."

"Are you saying that the feeling you just described is how we should feel about the Fifteen at all times?" he asked, paying careful attention to his phrasing.

I prodded the fire with a broken branch as I repeated his question softly to myself. It was then I remembered a couple of other things Naro said back at the Radio Tower:

"This…is not going as we had predicted."

"See if you can get a hold of Biktor and ask him why his little friend didn't tell us about this."

After recalling those quotes, my argument seemed to make even more sense. The Fifteen's ability to plan things on a grand scale seemed even more prominent with the recollection of Naro's words.

I sat up and glared into Albion's eyes as I answered him with my greatest sense of conviction. "Yes, we should fear the Fifteen."

Albion suddenly burst into mocking laughter. It startled Memento and Kay as well as brought my attitude toward him down a peg. "That is exactly what the Fifteen want!" Albion declared.

"This I gotta hear!" Kay grinned.

Albion obliged her. "As long as you continue to fear the Fifteen, the true Causes won't be able to get anywhere in relation to the truth. Have you so quickly forgotten that we tried and failed on the diplomatic approach?"

It felt like an insult, but I answered anyway. "I'm aware of that."

Albion stood up and walked over to his bag as he continued to contest my position. "If that is the case, then what could you possibly plan on doing once you approach the Fifteen again?"

Memento added, "…are you going to 'Pretty please' them into submission?"

I took my eyes from Albion and stared into Memento's snide expression. "Of course not! We have to take our time creating our plan. Whatever we decide to do has to be put together with an attention to detail that rivals that of the Fifteen."

"Is this guy serious?" Albion called from the shelter.

"Would seem so," Memento huffed.

Kay stood up to defend me. "You two need to knock it off!" She paused and pointed at me. "If it wasn't for this man's thinking, we would not be sitting here around this fire. That means you would be a lot more ignorant about the facts than you are now."

Kay's interjection was my chance to take advantage of the conversation. "That and you wouldn't have known about Pibs until it was too late!"

Albion returned to the campfire with a bag of nuts. He plucked one out of the bag, tossed it into the air and caught it in his mouth, obviously stalling for a comeback.

Memento sighed to cover her partner's turn to speak. "He's still not getting it, Albion."

He gestured with his hand forward, waiting to swallow. "It's all right, Memento. He is right about that. I'll give him that one."

I smirked, not looking to rub in the temporary victory. "As I was saying…"

"About…?"

"Making a plan…"

Albion grabbed a small handful of his nuts. "Yes, yes. Do go on about that."

To hide our plans to meet with Bogen, I made up something that would tide over their curiosity. "I've been thinking about the Deserters and how they are connected to the Fifteen. It's obvious that the two are working together. I'm figuring that the best way to get to the Fifteen at this point is through the Deserters."

"Interesting…" Kay replied, leaning in toward me.

The fact that Kay even responded was a little unexpected. I went with it, though. "You think so?"

"I think so, too!" Memento agreed.

"You're siding with him?" Kay asked.

"I didn't say that," she corrected. "I'm just saying that it is a useful idea to commit to memory."

I didn't want to reveal that I had just made it up. However, the unexpected support of the concept made it seem plausible.

An important detail was that Memento agreed with me. If one Zealot could agree, then maybe I could get Albion in on the idea.

An intriguing concept popped into my head. Perhaps if I

could convince them to take action toward the Deserters instead of Eden's landmarks, some order could fall back into place. In order to do that, I had to make the Deserters a more appealing target for Albion.

It made sense. Albion was leading the Zealots to go after the Fifteen. Fortunately, I was now in position to divert his course to something a lot less destructive. Now, getting Albion to turn towards the Deserters for answers was my objective.

I continued to add to my proposal. "At this point, I'm willing to focus on this idea from the 'True Cause' perspective…"

Albion cut me off. "It appears that we can finally agree on something, Brigg. Likewise, I'll focus on the Deserters from our Zealot standpoint."

Kay smacked me in the arm and leaned into me further with a hissing whisper. "What are you doing?"

I looked her in the eyes, trying to stare into her the idea of stalling the Zealots with my false vision. "I'm only doing what seems to be the best for both sides."

Kay looked lost. My façade had gone completely over her head. "I don't get it."

I tried to explain it in a way to keep my hidden motive out of the picture. "Right now, it's the Deserters we need to be angering—not the Fifteen. If we can flush the Deserters out, the Fifteen will surely show themselves."

Albion appeared to have jumped to the conclusion prematurely. "Then it's settled!"

I sighed, with relief at my success in changing Albion's point of view.

"However!" he shouted to have all at his attention. "Like I said before, the Zealots will remain as is! I'll just create special units to take care of Deserters. The rest will continue to try to bring the Fifteen out directly."

I exhaled through my nose in obvious frustration.

Albion caught my reaction and jumped on it like a Labor Field prisoner on a side of beef. "Come on, Brigg. Did you honestly think I'd call the Zealots off of Eden's landmarks?"

Annoyed, I grumbled, "Yes."

"A little too sure of himself, he was," Memento commented. "Bold move."

I shrugged, now aggravated, but hiding it. "Can't blame a guy for trying, right?"

Albion laughed again. "Look, I'll admit, what you said had some merit to it, Brigg. I'd recommend you act on your own advice as well."

I groaned, still sullied by my defeat. "Count on it."

Albion walked over and sat next to me. Memento positioned herself next to Kay and put her arm around her. Albion offered me some nuts, but I refused.

"I'll tell you what I'll do for you two," Albion proposed. "Since you've bestowed all of this great information upon us, we're going to play nice tonight. Be warned, though, after we part ways tomorrow, you'd better not cross my path again."

I was a little shocked to hear those words. "What do you mean by that?"

Albion glared into my eyes and raised his finger between our faces. "Again, like I said before: As long as you are clinging to the Producers' ways, we are enemies. Just be grateful I'm showing you this much gratitude."

"I don't think 'gratitude' is quite the word for it," I muttered.

"Me either," Kay sighed.

Memento walked over to the shelter to prepare for sleep as Albion concluded the conversation. "You're tough—I'll grant you that. But you're going to have to try a little harder to steer me off of this path."

Reaching deep down for another approach to use, I opted to harness the violent tendencies I had been trying so hard to suppress. Still in control, though, I slowly gripped the front of his shirt and pulled him gently toward me.

Albion remained relaxed, knowing well that he had the upper hand when it came to exchanges of words. We both knew that resorting to actual violence wouldn't change a single word spoken. We would remain correct in our respective places.

Attempting one last time to drill some doubt into his arrogant skull, I angrily murmured to him through gritted teeth. "I'll tell you for the last time: If you keep this up, I won't have to stop you. The Fifteen are capable enough to do it without me. Your days as a Zealot leader are numbered."

Albion slid his hand up my arm and to my clenched fist. He

wrapped his hand around mine, looked back with a smug grin and said, "Noted."

I released him. "Let's just get some rest. Kay and I have a lot to do tomorrow."

"Like what?" he asked, standing to retire to the shelter.

I grabbed his shoulder as he tried to walk away, turning him back toward me to look him in the eye. "Why would I tell that to somebody who I know is going to be my enemy tomorrow?"

"That's just the thing," he smirked, "You never should. Smart move."

As Albion walked away, Kay stood, kicking some dirt onto the fire to begin putting it out. She came to me, just behind my left shoulder and spoke softly into my ear. "I don't like where this is going. I'm not even sure if we can trust him through the night."

"Same here. The only credit I can give him is that he *sounded* sincere about it."

"What should we do?" she asked, stepping over to my side.

I tilted my head toward her, quieting my voice a little more. "There's always sleeping in shifts."

Kay found something wrong with the necessary suggestion. "You said we both needed rest though."

"I know," I nodded. "I'm sure that you'll be able to sleep easier knowing that I'm keeping an eye on you. Is that right?"

"As long as the same goes for you."

Her response delighted me. She made the whole thing seem like an impromptu trust exercise. "I know *you'll* be paying attention while I'm asleep."

She lightly jabbed me in the back and put a sly, sarcastic tone into her voice. "And I trust that you'll have your eyes on me at all times while I'm asleep, just like you did the other day."

I turned completely to her. "Oh, very funny!" I added sarcasm as well. "True, but funny."

Her mouth flew open and her eyes opened wide. "You are asking for it!"

Albion interrupted by hollering from the shelter. "If you two don't shut up and get in here, you'll find me changing my mind about this really quickly!"

We froze up for a moment as his brief uproar reverberated in my memory. Once again, he sounded sincere about his proposal of a temporary partnership.

I quickly leaned in to Kay as we hurried over to the shelter. "You sleep on the outside of me. I'll pretend to sleep and wake you up in a few hours."

Kay rapidly nodded with a serious expression across her face. It seemed that her inherent inability to trust people was putting a number of thoughts into her mind. She took her time crawling into the shelter, waiting for me to enter first.

We quickly scurried into our sleeping arrangements. Kay was on the far left with me lying next to her. Memento took position to my right and Albion positioned himself on the far right of the shelter.

All of us seemed to be focused on our individual objectives for the next day. Nobody spoke a word, and the only sound that could be heard were the fidgeting and rustling for a comfortable position. It wasn't long before Albion's simple, grating snore sounded throughout the shelter as well.

Memento got close to my ear and whispered, "That's the only thing that bugs me about him—that snore."

I was about to reply when Kay gripped my shoulder and turned me to face her. "You're sleeping between two women tonight. I recommend that your hands stay close to your body as you sleep tonight."

I whispered back to her, a little agitated that she would think I would take some kind of advantage. "This coming from the same person whose arm was draped across my chest the other day…"

I could see her white grin and a shine in her eye as she wittily replied. "True. Except there are two things my chest has that yours doesn't. If I have to tell you what they are, I'll have to smack you!"

"You don't need to tell me *that* twice!"

"Now you're just being a smart-ass."

"Hey, *you're* the one who brought up the subject of boobs!" I had trouble saying that comeback with a straight face.

"I didn't say 'I have boobs, you don't'. I was just saying that it's easy for your hands to wind up—"

I cut her off, giggling, stating quickly and humorously, "…On your boobs."

A plosive laugh burst from Kay's mouth as she tried to

contain herself and finish her statement. "…wind up in an inappro—"

"…On your boobs!"

Our laughter became louder and much less controllable. Kay tried again. "Inappropriate—"

"…Your boobs!" At this point, I had put a flirtatious lilt in my otherwise childish tone.

"Grow up you—!"

"Bo-o-o-o-obs!"

This stiflingly juvenile exchange of laughter and words was harshly torn into by a now-aggravated Albion. His voice burst with equal facetiousness and ire. *"THIS IS THE BEST CONVERSATION EVER! IT'S SO EASY FOR ME TO FALL ASLEEP HEARING THE WORD 'BOOBS' EVERY THREE SECONDS!"*

Knowing that we weren't going to stop laughing any time soon, we excused ourselves from the shelter. We picked up our blankets and returned to the still-burning campfire. "We'll go," I said through a snicker.

"Thank you!" Albion called out.

Kay, still trying to regain her composure, replied to him. "We'll come back when it's no longer—"

"…Boobs."

The back of Kay's arm swung hard and fast into my gut. "Knock it off or you'll be sleeping out here."

"That would be fine with me!" Albion declared.

"Me too," Memento added.

"Fine with us," I breathily responded, still reeling from the blow Kay dealt. I took my irate teammate by the hand and began to lead her back to the campfire.

Kay seemed a little confused about my agreeing to sleep outside. "It's fine?"

I spoke quietly through residual giggling as I distanced the two of us from the shelter. "I wanted him to do that."

Kay hummed disapprovingly. "I don't understand anything you are saying or doing tonight. What are you thinking?"

"Two things," I answered quickly. "First: I'm not going to deal with Albion's snoring. Second: It's better if we shift sleep from a distance to give the other time to wake up if something goes wrong."

"I see," she lightly nodded. "So all of that teasing about boobs was just a way to bother Albion?"

I admitted to her, "At first, no."

"At first…?" She began to stare into my eyes as we sat down by the fire. Kay didn't seem to buy into the idea that I got us kicked out of the shelter on purpose.

I gave up and came clean. "All right, you win. I made it all up! I was just looking to get away with saying 'boobs' numerous times for no reason."

Kay sounded disappointed in me. "That's not like you…"

I hung my head, a little ashamed. The humorous air suddenly died. "Actually, it is."

Kay tersely demanded, "Explain."

I knew myself well enough to offer an immediate explanation. "Immature outbursts like that are just another way I handle high stress. Laughing helps me cope and clear my mind so I can focus."

Kay's eyes narrowed as she appeared to be observing my most recent personal revelation. "Cope? With wh…"

"Do I honestly need to tell you?"

Her eyes led off to the side. Kay knew well that Mika and Dice were on my mind. She said nothing, waiting for me to continue.

"I know this isn't the time to be discussing this, but I just can't shake the sensation that I failed that girl."

She put her right arm around me and gave my shoulder a gentle squeeze. "You didn't fail her, Brigg. She was a victim—a victim of a sneak attack. There was not a single person on that train who could have anticipated what went on."

A cold fear shot throughout my body. I gasped as my being went into a pause. At that moment, my entire conversation with Albion replayed instantly through my mind, causing me to utter on impulse, "That's exactly my point."

"What?"

I slowly lifted my finger to point at the shelter. "It's like I told him: we should fear the Fifteen. We can't anticipate them. You just said so yourself."

Unexpectedly, Kay began to massage my right shoulder, resting her head on my left. Surely, this was a friendly attempt to calm me down. As relaxing as it was though, it was going to take more than that to take my mind off of Mika and Dice.

"Our only hope," I softly resumed, "is getting Bogen's help and putting the true Causes back on track."

Kay's nostrils let out a quick huff. "That's the Brigg I know."

"How's that?" I asked, turning to her with a curl in my lip.

She stopped massaging and sat up. "You used the word 'hope'. You're always looking on the bright side of things."

I rolled my eyes and turned my head away from her. "Strangely enough given the circumstances, right?"

"I guess you could say that."

The conversation seemed to stop there. I turned back to her, having the two of us lock eyes for a few moments.

When my eyes caught focus on Kay's lips, the memory of my attempt to kiss her flashed briefly. I shuddered a bit, then looked to the fire.

Kay was curious about my sudden reaction. "Is something wrong? Anything else you need to say?"

I scowled in the direction of the crackling flames, thinking hard about how to approach her question. It went without saying that the mood around the fire was empty and uncertain. I felt that the next thing I should say should be something to lighten the air and put our minds at ease to prepare for a good night's sleep.

"Anything else you feel you need to get out of your system?" Kay pressed.

I turned to her with a smirk, resorting back to playful, mindless flirting. "I'm debating between 'Thanks' and 'Boobs'…"

Kay turned away with an amused scoff. "You are unbelievea—"

"…Boobs."

She tried to keep from smiling. "It's not funny anymore!"

I continued to joke with her. "Then why are you smiling?"

"Because, I—"

"…Have boobs?"

My childish interruptions had her laughing again. "I'm going to kick your—"

"…Boobs?"

The sheer immaturity of it all brought our spirits back up.

Soon enough, though, as anticipated, the joke got old. I had said "boobs" so many times that the word itself appeared to lose its meaning. I declared that I wouldn't be saying it again for a while.

The two of us decided to stay distant from Albion and Memento. I placed my blanket on the ground a few meters from the fire and set myself down onto it.

Kay gathered a few more large sticks and threw them into the fire. "We'll just let it die from here," she suggested, lying down next to me.

"Do you still want to sleep in shifts?"

She seemed a little more relaxed than before. "It doesn't matter to me. If you want to stay awake, you can."

"Maybe for a little bit…" I sighed, rolling over to face away from her.

"All right then. I'm going to sleep."

"Sweet dreams, Kay."

As Kay slipped into slumber, I found myself lost in thought very quickly, gazing into the dancing flames in front of me.

"Warmth"—it was a strange word to be thinking of at that time.

Again, the memory of my attempt to kiss Kay brought itself to the front of my mind. It was all I could focus on.

I thought of warmth again—the warmth provided by the campfire. The heat, the popping, the flickering, and the bright orange luminescence created a sensation of physical satisfaction from the cool summer night.

I remembered the look on Kay's face when my finger tipped her head up. Just the thought of it made my heart race again.

Warmth, emotional warmth—that was the feeling I desired to experience.

I clutched the front of my shirt as my nerves welled up. I suddenly felt the urge to be bold with Kay again.

Before I knew it, Kay's sleepy breathing was lightly coursing through my ears. She had already fallen asleep.

The breath I had been holding purged itself from my lungs. I shook my head, sensing the unfortunate futility in the idea of trying to get closer to Kay.

I spoke quietly to myself. "Any way you slice it, she's not going to fall for you. Just keep things the way they are."

Thinking into it a little more, I felt that my feelings toward

Kay were not romantic. It was the hormonal surges of typical teenage lust that fueled any inclination I had to try to win her over. It was a difficult realization to wrestle with. Accepting it was even harder.

As the hours of thought dragged on and the fire died out, my carnal tendencies toward Kay appeared to fade away with it.

Perhaps I lost hope.

Maybe I just accepted the facts.

The fear of more than just a slap in the face was something to consider as well.

With those thoughts weighing heavy on my heart, I nudged Kay awake. It was her turn to keep watch.

After she sat up and confirmed her ability to be vigilant, I rolled onto my stomach and quickly went to sleep.

V

That night was the only chance I had to change the course of the Zealots. In a way, I had succeeded. On another view, I failed. What resulted from my attempt was a scenario that only served to slow the advance of the Zealots on Eden's landmarks. That in itself bore the scent of progress.

There was still a lot for both of our factions to focus on though. That fact became apparent over the course of the days that followed our second encounter with Albion.

Amid the commotion that the Revolution was causing, the most dangerous enemy had begun to lurk among us. Sydney's Deserters had finally surfaced.

The big problem about them was that any one Deserter looked like any other Cause. Their only goal was to lure Causes to their capture under the guise of a trusting new face. We took what we learned from the incident with Pibs to warn the Causes of the Deserters' tactics, leaving no detail overlooked.

The news of the arrival of the Deserters was promptly spread across the forums. With it came an awful lot of finger-pointing. The Causes blamed the Zealots and vice versa.

But we knew the truth and spared no time in presenting it to the forum. I posted news of what I knew of the Deserters' origins, citing Pibs and Zoe as prime examples. I let the Causes know that the Fifteen had been creating the Deserter force long before the meeting with the Producers even took place.

The response I received for the news took my popularity and credibility to an all time high. I was praised by both factions for factual proof that neither the Zealots nor the true Causes were to blame for the Revolution's latest obstacle.

The truth was that we were all true Causes at the time the Deserters were being compiled. This left both sides to share the blame equally.

To the amazement of both me and Kay, some of Albion's Zealots actually came back to the side of the true Causes.

It was no time to relax, though. Our mission to meet with Bogen was still our task at hand. After the wave of forum-wide cheers subsided and everyone was back to their business, Kay and I continued on to Kediel Lake as originally planned.

Once we arrived at our destination, we set up a camp with supplies we purchased with most of my remaining Arna. Our shelter wound up being a large, blue plastic tarp slanted from the ground up to a tight length of rope that was tied to two trees. The front and sides were wide open, giving us a view of the lake. When it rained, we would roll the open front down to shield us.

Kediel Lake is isolated from civilization by about three kilometers in all directions. It is surrounded by tall trees and hilly, verdant terrain—perfect for resting for as long as we needed to. Once settled, we awaited the arrival of Bogen, Black and Blue.

Day 87

I

Kay had become accustomed to sleeping next to me. It only bothered her when we would wake up in the morning a little too close to each other. Despite how she really felt about it, she would react a lot more gracefully than the first morning we woke up together.

That particular morning greeted me with a rude awakening. Kay seemed to be rolling around half awake when her elbow became my personal alarm clock.

After profuse apologies, I joked with her that I finally got what I deserved for all the times I was fantasizing about her. She laughed as well, now knowing it was no big deal.

The two of us lazed around in our tiny shelter each waiting for the other to mention breakfast. My stomach was the first to growl, though. The fish that I had been spearing the past couple of days had been just enough to keep us from starving. All of our other food supplies were consumed on the trip to the lake. Luckily, neither of us was going to complain about fish again for breakfast.

I slowly crept from underneath the blanket and quickly noticed how cool the early morning air was. The sun was barely up and there was a misty fog wisped across the surface of the lake. I was only able to imagine how cold that water was going to be once I set foot in it to fish.

There was one little problem though. The spear I made was not up against the tree where I would usually leave it. "Did I leave the spear up against the tree?" I asked Kay.

"I'm pretty sure you did," she replied in a half-awake moan. Kay got up off of the blanket intending to help look for the spear.

Suddenly, the voice of another female spoke, scaring the living daylights out of us. "Oh, you're awake."

We jumped and turned to face the direction of the voice's origin. Leaning up against the tree that supported the left side our shelter's rope was a young lady who appeared to be waiting for us to awaken.

Her odd sense of style caught my eye. "Who are you?" I demandingly inquired.

The girl nudged herself away from the tree with her foot and came toward us. "That all depends on who you are. We can't trust just anybody with the way things are, right? As such, my partner told me not to disclose my name until we find out who you are first."

I was a little frightened. Her clothes reminded me of how Zoe was dressed back in the Delta. Even worse were the similarities between her clothing and that of Albion's.

The girl was sporting a single-strap black top slung over her right shoulder with a black skirt that was up to her thigh on the right side and down to the knee on the left. She had her elbows and knees protected with black cloth covers. A short, white cape with a wide, flat collar draped over her shoulders and comfortable black hiking boots were tightly strapped around her feet. A notable thing about her outfit was that the thumb and index fingers of her black gloves were not there; the first thing I noticed when she pointed at us.

My first guess was that she was Jalako. The second possibility was that she was Black—the Producers' personal Contact. Simply the way she was dressed made both options equally plausible. However, her attitude and secrecy screamed "Jalako" to me.

I couldn't just spit out a name. If this was Jalako, it would be dangerous to let her know we were waiting for Bogen and Black. I even felt that there was no use to saying "the book" either.

I came to a conclusion and asked her a simple question.

"Where is your partner?"

She thought a moment before answering. "He's in the lake, spear fishing." On cue, we heard a light splash from the lake.

Kay kept her eye on the girl as I turned to get a look. The morning fog was enough to shroud the figure standing in the water from identification. I leaned in within whispering distance to Kay. "I'm gonna go see if that's him. Keep an eye on this girl. If she tries anything funny, shout."

I walked slowly over to the edge of the lake to take a good look at the man fishing. Though he was facing the other direction, the two notable differences between Bogen and Albion helped me to identify him; hair length and height. There was no mistaking it—Bogen and Black had arrived during the night.

I left Bogen to concentrate on his fishing and walked back to the girls. I nodded to Kay with a smile before addressing the new female. "It's nice to meet you, Black."

The perky, dark-haired little woman seemed pleased that I knew who she was. "Brigg and Kay, I presume?" she asked.

Kay stepped forward to shake her hand. "You presume correctly!"

Black formally introduced herself. "I am Tana—known as Black—personal Contact of the Producers. I know you've already met Bogen. He told me a lot about you."

A loud, masculine hoot interrupted the introduction. "It sounds like he caught something!" I chortled.

Black laughed as well. "If you know him well enough, you'll see that he always sounds like that."

Hurried splashing footsteps faded into the sound of grass rustling underneath a running man's feet. Bogen emerged from the fog, excited, holding the spear with both hands. His good mood shone in the sound of his voice when he called to us. "I see more than one other person standing over there."

Black called back to him. "Yes, it's Brigg and Kay! It was them the whole time!"

"Excellent." Bogen looked to me and Kay. "Since we found you in the middle of the night, we didn't want to wake you up in case you were somebody else."

I sighed in a way that let Bogen and Black know that I was relieved to be in their presence. "We thought you were Albion and

Jalako for a little bit back there. Looking at the way Black is dressed and all…"

Black chose to defend her choice. "Hey, come on! All of the other Contacts wear mostly white. I'm no ordinary Contact, though, I'm special."

Bogen heartily snickered at her self-praise. "She does have a point there. At least she's wearing *some* white."

"The cape, yes." Black reached over her shoulder and waved her cape about.

There was a pause that was a precursor to change the subject. Bogen lifted the spear up so we could all get a better look at the fish he skewered. The catch had to have been at least fifty centimeters. He sighed with a triumphant air. "This will definitely feed five."

"Five?" I asked, having done the simple math. "Blue is on his . way too, right?"

Bogen regretfully rolled his eyes and inhaled through his teeth. "Actually…" He seemed to be choosing his words very carefully. "Quite a bit has happened on our side since you last contacted us."

I didn't like the sound of it one bit. "What do you mean?"

Black called out to a person we could not see. "We're ready to explain now. You can come out."

Before we saw anyone other than us, Bogen preemptively excused himself. "I'll leave the next part to you three. I'm gonna get to preparing breakfast."

"What's going on?" Kay wondered.

A voice called out from behind our shelter. "A lot. Then again, you would know that better than anyone. Right, Brigg?" The owner of the familiar voice revealed himself to be our missing partner.

"Dice!" Kay gasped in great surprise. "Is that really you?"

He began to methodically lurch around the shelter and slowly pace himself towards us. "No, it's some other guy who just so happens to wear the same exact clothes I do." The sarcasm was genuine in his voice.

She grinned. "Yup, that's definitely him!" Kay was so happy to see him that she actually embraced him. Dice was just as thrown off as I was about her reaction.

While I was also glad to see Dice safe and in once piece, I only had one real question on my mind. Between myself, Kay and Dice, we all knew what that question was.

I could see the weathered look on Dice's face and determined that he had some news that was going to be as difficult to tell me as it would be for me to hear it.

Dice pulled his dice from his pocket. "I've been debating all morning as to how to break the news to you. I know Mika is your number one concern right now."

"Why the dice?" I deeply asked.

In a dark and unfriendly voice, he replied, "I have my own reasons." He jingled the dice in his hands.

Kay backed away from him. Both of us knew that something had happened to him. No doubt he didn't escape the train before it reached Cora. While I felt the need to sympathize for him, what I really wanted to know was what had happened to Mika.

I didn't hesitate any further and asked him straightforwardly. "Where's Mika?"

He huffed. "Sydney has her. It didn't shock me that he chose to keep her since Mika told me that she met Sydney before."

A memory of Sydney on one knee and consoling Mika flashed before me.

Dice gave us a moment to think about what he just said as he spat out his wager for his roll. "Less than ten with two numbers even!" He rolled, letting the dice tumble into the grass. The dice came up three, two and two. He disdainfully winced.

His secretive behavior was getting to me. Here we had a young man who probably knew more than everything we needed to and he was holding it back with whatever game he was trying to play with us. I lost my patience and yelled at him. "Stop rolling those damn dice and just tell us what is going on!"

Black left us to assist Bogen as a stare-down began between Dice, Kay and me.

Dice picked his cubes up off of the ground and kneaded them in his left hand for a few moments. "I said I had my reasons for resorting to this. But if you really want it straight…" he paused to lift his hand up to his face. His dice were placed in the three spaces between his four main fingertips. "…This better come up all threes."

"Not a chance…" I thought to myself.

Dice balled up his fist and flung his dice high into the air. As they ascended, he filled me in on his actions. "I know what to hide from you for your own protection. You fail to realize just how important you are right now." The dice landed one after the other. Before we looked at them, he had something else to say about the dice. "Actually, you should consider yourself lucky. These dice are what kept me on the side of the true Causes."

I couldn't believe my own ears. "Are you serious?" I hollered. "You rolled your dice to decide on your options in Cora?"

He responded with a grunt before further explaining himself. "Well, they wanted to convert me to a Deserter at first. When Sydney saw that Mika and I were friends, he changed his mind and sent me to tell you that he has her." We paused then looked at the dice; three, three and five.

"Knew it…" I thought to myself.

"I know you pretty well," Dice continued as he scooped them up. "You tend to overanalyze things, yet act off the fly. So I have to watch what I tell you or we'll never have a chance of getting Mika back."

I'll admit to having no idea what he was going on about. All I really understood was to trust that whatever Dice would tell me was everything I needed to know…and nothing more.

II

It came as no surprise to me that Sydney recognized Mika. But kidnapping her and setting Dice free to find me was entirely unexpected. What threw me off was that Blue and Bogen had been in contact with Dice and neither of them told me what was going on.

This went back to what Dice was saying about me knowing too many things. If I had known Mika was taken by Sydney sooner, I would have been trying to track down Sydney rather than meet with Bogen as planned. That was why Dice waited to tell me in person as well as be able to tell us all more about what happened in Cora.

According to Dice—when Sydney saw Mika arrive on the train, he immediately began to look for me. He even asked her if

Kay and I were on the train as well.

Not too pleased to see that Kay and I escaped, he decided that in order to find me, he would use Mika as bait and Dice as the lure.

That was where Dice's decisive roll came into play. It was his decision as to how he would present the news to me. His roll was a split decision as to whether he would lure me right into Sydney's hands or stay true to our side and plan Mika's rescue with us.

Fortunately for all of us, luck and fate prepared him to assist us in any way he could.

Dice clearly explained what went on after he was released by Sydney to find me. Since he was afraid of how I would react to the news on Mika, he contacted Bogen only on the assumption that he was the missing Producer.

Bogen set up Blue and Dice to meet.

After Dice told Blue the situation, Blue ran off to trail Sydney and left Dice to deliver the news. Dice then contacted Bogen.

Hearing of that development, Bogen got Dice to meet with him and Black. From there, they traveled to meet with us.

"So that's where Blue is, eh?" Kay asked, nibbling at her fish.

"Yes," Black replied. "We've been doing well on keeping updated with him. He's waiting for the opportunity to kidnap her back for us. On the minus side, Blue says it isn't going to be easy with Sydney and a Gray Police officer around her all day. Fortunately, he says they're treating her well."

"Wow," I nodded. "He must be pretty close to Sydney if he can tell us that."

Black rapidly nodded as her serious tone appeared to deteriorate. "Mmhmm. I just so happened to meet him in person recently—the day before my fifteenth birthday! He is probably the bravest person I've ever met."

"You've met him before?"

Black sweetly sighed with a wide smile on her face. "He's amazing. He's sweet and manly and heroic and smart and—"

"…Apparently admired by you!" Kay interrupted with a laugh.

"Get used to that," Dice warned. "She swoons like that at the mere mention of him."

My brow rose. "He must have done something pretty awesome to get you all giddy like that."

"No!" Bogen promptly shouted.

"Please do not encourage her!" Dice groaned. "I've heard the story once and I do not need to hear it again!"

Kay whispered over to Black, "We'll talk later. I want to know!"

Black giggled and nodded.

After spitting a bone out, I called attention to the situation. "Getting back to the matter, how long do you think it will take Blue to get her?"

Dice filled the question. "Since he says Sydney isn't harming her, there's no sense of urgency. From my side, Sydney told me he didn't care how long it took to find you. He just wanted me to lead you to him."

I inquired further. "I've been meaning to ask why…"

He was succinct and serious. "I think Sydney sees you as a threat to the Deserters. After what happened at the Radio Tower and your recent revelation about the Deserters' origins, everyone seems to think that you're as influential as Blue, Al, or any of the Producers. I'm sure he wasn't going to target you first. With Mika in his hands now, though, it makes going after you more convenient."

Bogen had a question for Dice as well. "Who else is Sydney looking to capture?"

Dice picked the meat off of his section of the fish as he murmured in a dreadful manner. "Most likely you, Bogen. Basically, anybody I listed a moment ago is top priority of Sydney and the Gray Police."

Kay sounded suspicious of the whole thing. She decided to hit Dice with a statement that came from me to her at one point. "You seem to know a lot about what is going on here."

Dice had his defense ready. "I just want you to know that these are all conclusions that I have drawn for myself. Everything I said may not be entirely accurate, but it makes the most sense."

Everyone nodded in agreement to Dice's disclaimer.

Suddenly, I was filled with fear and uncertainty. Sydney had his sights set on me—and Mika was paying the price for it. I knew it would only be a matter of time before Sydney would send me a message saying: "I'm here, come get the girl."

It wouldn't have surprised me at all if anyone were to notice the distress I was experiencing. On one side, Kay and Dice knew more than anyone how I would feel if anything was to happen to Mika. On the other side, Bogen and Black viewed me as just as important as Dice declared. I was once again experiencing the feeling of having far too much expected of me.

My mind drifted when I realized just how much my role in the Revolution had changed within the past several weeks. All of it would never have happened if I had not chosen to help Mika in the first place. It was that lone decision that began the chain of events that had led me to where I was at that time.

Black interrupted my train of thought, ticking away on her laptop's keyboard. "You have a lot of fans out there, Brigg."

"Huh?" I looked up to see that she was accessing the forums. "You mean that there are people talking about me?"

Black clarified her statement. "There are four—no—six topics asking where you, Kay, Dice, and 'the little girl' are. Some of those topics are rumors. I'll get rid of them."

I turned up an open, general question. "Would it be a good idea to let the Causes know what's going on?"

Bogen was thinking strategically. "With Al & Jal still out there with the other Zealots, I don't think it's a good idea to draw attention to ourselves."

It didn't seem quite right to lay low at that time. Nevertheless, we were going to have to trust Bogen's judgment. "Then what do we do from here?" I pressed.

With Bogen's mouth occupied with fish, Black answered for him. "We need to wait until we hear back from Blue. Remember, he's waiting for just the right moment to get Mika back for us. As far as rescuing Mika ourselves is concerned, that is probably the worst idea since Sydney is on the move."

"Blue must really know what he's doing, huh?" Kay was smiling, hoping to get Black to talk more about him.

Bogen caught Kay's intention and answered the question quickly. "Yes, he does!" He then pointed to Kay. "Stop that!"

Black briefly giggled as she turned the screen of her laptop towards us. "Until we hear from him though, here is a map of Eden's train system."

Dice asked her in a manner that emphasized the curiosity of the entire group, "What good is this to us?"

Black pointed to a large train station northeast of our location and began to explain. "We can wait around this area here. Once we hear from Blue, we'll know where we have to travel next, right? Well, if we have to hop a train to reach where he is, it will save us time if we are already near one."

I was impressed by Black's foresight, but skeptical of the idea as a whole. "Considering what happened the *last* time we got on a train, is that really a good idea?"

Black pointed out the six train routes that exited the station she marked. "As you can see, only two of the tracks head out west in the direction of Cora and the other four do not. We just won't get on any trains headed toward Cora. It's that simple."

I breathed in and exhaled deeply, still overwhelmed by the whole thing. "Then, we wait for Blue."

III

We sat quietly for a time as our breakfast slowly disappeared into all of our stomachs. The sound of Black tapping away on her laptop's keyboard was the only noise between the five of us. We were keeping our thoughts to ourselves and taking time to think about the road ahead of us.

I was stiflingly discomforted to know that Sydney was looking to flush me out from amongst the other Causes. It made the future very cloudy and almost intimidating to approach. My heart was tight and my head was in a fog of confusion.

Regardless of the fear, everything seemed to be in order, barring a few minor details. Thankfully, we were certain of our next objective. Also, Blue was taking it upon himself to do the hardest part for us. All in all, we really had nothing to worry about besides being where we needed to be at the right time.

Bogen excused himself and stepped over to the edge of the lake. He seemed to have had thought of a lot within the moments we were staying quiet. "What's with him all of a sudden?" I asked Black.

"Like I said," she replied, "once you know him long enough, you get used to some of the things he does."

I spoke a spurt of optimism. "Think he's coming up with a backup plan?"

Black sighed, "I wouldn't put it past him. He's always thinking."

Dice came forward with an unexpected question. "An admirable trait worthy of the title of Producer, wouldn't you say?"

Our heads turned slowly and locked onto him. None of us had any idea why a question like that came out of Dice's mouth. To my recollection, the difficult youth almost never praised anyone, let alone use the word "admirable" to describe another person.

Black finally answered him. "I'd say so." It figured she'd be the one to answer that since she had not known Dice that long.

After a few minutes to himself, Bogen invited us to join him by the lake's edge. "Hey guys, come over here and check this out."

We all looked to each other with puzzled faces. Unsure of what Bogen had discovered yet intrigued by his hardy, deep tone, we proceeded over to him.

We stood in a side-by-side line a mere meter from the water. Looking far out over the lake and taking in the scenery, I found myself once again reminded of my time spent in the Gova Sector. The sounds of Kediel Lake's lush surrounding greenery rustling in the breeze slowly soothed my shattered nerves.

Bogen drew a deep breath before asking the rest of us, "What do you see here?"

Dice responded with inappropriately timed sarcasm. "Do you want the obvious answer, or is it something else?"

Bogen scratched the tuft of hair on his chin as he resumed speaking. "Look down at the lake and you'll see what I'm talking about."

Our focus shifted to the lake at our feet. Since the fog had parted and the sun was shining, a clear reflection was lightly rippling across the surface of the water. "Do you see it yet?" Bogen asked with a coaxing grin.

"I see us," Kay replied, slightly confused. "What about it?"

"That being said, I'll ask you this…" Bogen presented a deep and serious question to us. "How many of you still think Hatcher is out there somewhere?"

My answer came without hesitation. "I think he is. But I still feel that there's a chance the Fifteen got a hold of him."

"Actually," Dice cut in, "I'm thinking that since the Fifteen didn't mention him, he may be hiding or lost with no Contact."

"For this long?" Kay logically interrupted. "Nobody has heard from him in about two months. How does any Cause go two months without seeing a Contact?"

Bogen called us all to order, leaving Kay's question to linger unanswered. "What I'm getting at by asking about Hatcher is…" he paused to gather his words.

I took the liberty of finishing his statement. "You just wanted to see if we still believed he would show eventually, right?"

"Something like that…" he answered, still in thought.

Always the pessimist, Dice asked, "What good is it to think he's out there?"

"Please hear me out on this," Bogen insisted. "All of the other Producers felt that Hatcher would arrive in time for that meeting. All the while, we maintained the rules and guidelines that we set to keep Eden peaceful while still expressing our protest." His tone of voice changed to that of anticipated inquiry. "Now, do the three of you feel as if you've been holding to those rules pretty well?"

I snickered at the question. "Do you think I would have gone to the Radio Tower if I wasn't planning on adhering to the Producers' rules?"

"I'll admit," Kay began, "I only followed Brigg to the Radio Tower for my own reasons—it just so happened to be for the greater good. As for the rules, I've been doing my best to stick to my own thing while keeping things peaceful."

I mumbled low, unable to help myself. "…And keeping me irritated beyond belief."

Kay turned to me with ire in her eyes. "Did you say something?"

I broke from her gaze and looked to Bogen. "Nothing at all…"

Dice breathily snickered having heard me as he took his dice from his pocket and showed them to Bogen. "I haven't broken any rules yet. I've just been lucky."

Bogen laughed. "Well, as long as you think Hatcher is out there, and you're still willing to stay true to the Producer's rules, I think I'll make you all Honorary Producers."

I quickly got excited. "Really?"

Kay was pleased at his announcement as well. "Honorary

Producers?"

Black shared her opinion. "I was waiting for that. Like I said, you know him long enough…"

"Can you do that?" Dice asked in an appropriately skeptical manner.

Bogen couldn't generate an immediate answer to that. Black, however, had something to say. "It won't be any different than when he chose to start the meeting without Hatcher. Hatcher even said before that each Producer could act on his or her own, that they shouldn't feel the need to hang onto his every word."

"Ironically enough," Bogen laughed, "I completely forgot that he said that."

Black boasted, "Being one of the creators of the forum, you bet I remember more about what's posted than anyone else."

"So," I said, still piecing everyone's words together, "Black is pretty much saying that Bogen can do that."

Dice hung his head, fixing his gaze on the reflection in the lake. "Honorary Producers…" He began to knead the dice in his hand as he repeated the phrase.

Bogen continued his explanation. "Let me level with you. The Causes have to stay together and they need somebody out there to make them aware of that. But I can't do it alone. The capture of the other Producers has demoralized the Causes to a point where Al & Jal…well, you know."

I looked to him, once again taken by the sincerity in his voice.

Bogen exhaled and furrowed his brow. "My point is that Al & Jal have brought the Causes to divide themselves amidst the chaos that the Fifteen and Sydney have created. I feel that we should make it our goal to bring them back together. Once we do that, we can approach the Fifteen from another angle. Another diplomatic meeting is out of the question, of course."

"What angle would that be, then?" Dice asked, looking at him.

Bogen caught Dice's eye, but gave the answer to all of us. "I was hoping that the five of us could figure that out together."

I heard Kay and Black become short of breath. Dice's grip around his black cubes became as intense as the bright expression on his face. I, too, felt the impact of Bogen's heartfelt proposal. The title of "Honorary Producer" sounded thousands of times better than it did at first. Bogen's distinctive way with words was certainly his greatest asset.

I looked Bogen in the eye and nodded. I felt no need to explain myself and simply said, "I'm in."

Kay smiled, reminiscing as she spoke. "I wanted nothing to do with either Brigg or Dice when I first met them. But I guess that doesn't matter now. The Causes and the Revolution have to be put back on the right track. Count me in."

Black took the floor next. "Even though Contacts are not supposed to involve themselves directly in the affairs of the Causes, you guys are going to have a difficult time without me. I'm in too."

We all looked at Dice, who was still thinking it over. He stood and stared into the lake as he shuffled his dice in his hand. "I can't go this alone and there is nobody else who I can trust. At the same time, I'll warn you that I can't be depended on to be totally cooperative. Is that okay?"

Bogen grinned, understanding him. "We'll deal with that if it comes along."

Dice chuckled, catching Bogen's eye again. He brought his dice up to his face, once again holding each one between each of his fingers as if it were a pose that only he could pull off. With a crooked smirk and a gleam in his eye, he announced a wager. "A number between three and eighteen…"

His odds elicited a quick laugh from me. "Oh boy! We don't stand a chance on this one!"

He threw his dice behind him and waited a few moments. Then, without even looking at them, he declared, "I guess I'm in on this then."

Bogen took a deep, relieved breath and thanked us for understanding his position. He was truly grateful of our acceptance to his offer. In summation to our initiation into the Producers, he had one last thing for us to do. "Look down into the lake again and tell me what you see *now*."

As instructed we looked again, this time just a little harder. Kay spoke first in a manner of guessing. "The future?"

Puzzled by her answer, I looked at her. "…Pretty bold words, wouldn't you say?"

"Bold, yes," Bogen declared. "But she is pretty close to the answer I had in mind."

"What's that?"

"We are the hope of Eden," he replied with a whimsical sigh. "The five of us—plus Mika and Blue—are the hope of Eden."

My spirits were lifted to a point where I couldn't help but stare at the reflection on the surface of the lake. Simply hearing the idea that we were the hope of Eden filled me with more confidence than I felt I could handle. I was awash with the sensation that we were unstoppable and the days of the Fifteen's grip would be numbered in no time.

Kediel Lake quickly became a place of pride and vanity as the five of us posed in the reflection on the water. We laughed and joked, trying to create a portrait of what five people who declared themselves as the hope of Eden would look like.

The five of us eventually found an appropriate pose. Bogen, being the tallest, stood in the middle with his left arm around Dice and his right arm around me. Black had her hands on Dice's shoulder, leaning in and kicking one leg up behind her. Lastly, Kay was leaning on my right shoulder with her left elbow; ruffling my hair with her hand.

Black laughed. "Now all we need is some wind to make my cape flap around."

Bogen felt it unnecessary. "This is good enough."

The five of us took a good long look at ourselves before breaking the pose and taking a seat in the grass. Reassured of our purpose to Eden, we returned to planning our next move.

Of the whole list of priorities we could think of, Albion, Jalako, and Sydney had to be taken care of first.

Sydney had Mika and was waiting for me to come and get her. I hoped and prayed that Blue would be able to retrieve her. However, it would have been foolish to not prepare myself in the event that something was to happen to him. I figured since Sydney already resorted to kidnapping, he wouldn't be too hesitant to try other means to lure me out. His band of Deserters served to complicate things as well since it left us without the ability to trust anybody we didn't already know.

None of us were sure what to do about Al & Jal. The Zealots were gradually getting more out of control as each attack took place. They committed themselves to making an example of the Fifteen's refusal to our demands. While the Gray Police were still onto them, resistance against the Zealots only served to anger them further. As a result, Al & Jal were gaining influence at a problematic rate. We had to find another way to slow them down, if not stop them entirely.

IV

The five of us tried to stick to wooded areas and stay out of the view of the public. When we had to cross through developed areas and neighborhoods, we kept our eyes open for any Gray Police. Once again, travel had become a tense and taxing endeavor.

While Kay and Black got to know each other a little better, Dice and I had our attention on Bogen.

Bogen shared with us his opinion that the existing panel of Producers was a lost cause. It upset him greatly that the people with whom he spent so much time planning wound up being captured at the Revolution's most critical moment. He strongly felt that his decision to go on without Hatcher was the worst one he had ever made. Now, seven young people no different than himself were probably suffering because of his haste.

The two of us tried to cheer Bogen up about the whole Hatcher decision. We told him that nobody could have predicted what would happen without Hatcher. To lift his spirits a little, we told him how the Causes in the Delta were reacting to his speech to the Fifteen over the radio. We let him know that every Cause out there felt that going on without Hatcher was the right thing to do at the time. Therefore, Bogen was no guiltier on the decision than anyone else who agreed to it.

Dice had a rather unique angle to look at it from. He stated that we should get used to overwhelming consequences for our actions. Declaring ourselves as the hope of Eden was a broad and bold undertaking. If we were to truly hold ourselves to the title we accepted, we had to be prepared to accept anything that lay ahead for us.

It was a dark and uncomfortable realization; but every word of it was right.

Day 89

I

We were about half a day's walk away from the next train station when the highly anticipated message from Blue finally arrived.

Dear Bogen and Company,

It was quite the task, but I finally managed to get Mika away from Sydney. Don't kill me, but she is injured. She busted her left arm and leg pretty good when she tripped during the escape from the farm house. But she is conscious and in one piece.

If "farm house" caught your attention, I guess you know where we are. I don't know why, but Sydney carted Mika to the Terra Sector.

Yes, the Terra Sector.

I have no idea what his intentions are, but it really pissed me off that I've had to follow him to practically the middle of nowhere!

Mika and I are hiding out in the basement of another farm house. The owner knows we are Causes and is only helping us because Mika is injured. He wants us out of here as soon as she can walk without help.

If you are worried about coming to get her, feel free to know that we're pretty far from where I retrieved Mika. Sydney had her in house

B19. After I retrieved her, I carried her all the way to house D24. That, boys and girls, is a very long walk! My muscles need time to rest as well.

I'm going to see if I can reason with the owner of this house to let us stay until you arrive. Until then, you can easily get here by train since the Cora Sector is in the opposite direction from the Terra Sector. Black is a smart girl. She'll have your way mapped out in no time.

I'll be waiting for you all.

-Blue

Black swooned at Blue's compliment. More importantly, she acted upon it and began to map our course.

Our destination was the Terra Sector, Eden's largest one. Dedicated to production of food and livestock, the Terra Sector is all farmland, stables and widely-spaced houses for the farmers to live in. The houses are addressed in a square grid with each house eight kilometers apart from each other. Aside from the houses, the entire landscape of the Terra Sector is splayed with crop after abundant crop of fruits and vegetables—which sustain the population of Eden.

Even though we would take the train as planned, the Terra Sector would still take a long time to travel to. Since traffic into the Terra Sector was almost non-existent bar supply trains, only two rails actually went into the sector. The rail going through the north border of Terra was for people and farmers to go in and out and the rail from the west sent supplies to and from the farmhouses in the sector. The north rail was our only way in.

Black pulled up two maps from the Interactive Network. The first was of the train system in Eden and the second was a map of the Terra Sector's House Grid. She began to explain the course while pointing the whole thing out.

As it turned out, the only way to access the rail to Terra was to first travel all the way north into the Lucra Sector, where the one rail to Terra began. Once in Terra, we would get off of the train and head to the nearest farm house. According to the grid map, C28 was the closest house to both the train stop and the meeting place.

The trip was going to take us a couple of days. So after ironing out a few more minor details about the course, we continued forward. From that point on, our only concerns were to avoid the Gray Police and keep updated on Al & Jal's antics.

Hopefully, things would not get too out of hand while we ventured to meet with Mika and Blue.

II

We arrived at East Binda Station during the evening's five o'clock hour.

Our vigilance was unsurpassable as we anticipated a Gray Police officer around every corner. Skulking about the station and darting our eyes about appeared suspicious to the few citizens who noticed us. Nobody said anything, though, perhaps because of fear generated by the actions of the Zealots. We were nervous anyway because the scene could change in the blink of an eye.

Soon after we obtained our tickets, we saw that an encounter with Gray Police was close at hand. Bogen was the first to notice them and promptly ordered us to wait.

Two officers were pacing back and forth along the platform for the northbound train, both with their nightsticks at the ready. The one on the right looked younger and more athletic while the one on the left appeared bulky, toned, and more seasoned in his duties.

Minutes passed as we thought of a plan. Surely our unconventional appearance would be a dead giveaway that we were Causes. Knowing that looks would be the key to our discovery was vital to the care we had to take in boarding the train. What complicated things the most was the fact that we were carrying most of our possessions with us, indicating that we were living out of our backpacks as most Causes were.

Dice gave an idea. "We need one of us to go over there and see how they react to anyone getting onto the platform."

"Just one of us?" Kay asked.

Bogen interjected. "I was thinking more like toning down the 'Cause look'."

Kay seemed to be in her argumentative mood, finding fault in every idea at the time. "How can we do that without leaving all of our stuff behind?"

I decided to rub it in to quiet her. "You don't need to worry about that. All of your stuff is already gone!"

Before Kay could react, Bogen continued to push his version of the plan. "That could actually work to our advantage."

Kay didn't like the sound of his tone. "What do you mean by that?"

"Of the five of us," he mumbled, "You—Kay—are the one who looks the least like a Cause right now. You just look like a teenage girl recovering from a twisted wrist and a sprained ankle. We can use your look and Brigg's quickness with words in a combination to test the police's reactions."

"Me!?" I protested. "Why me?"

Bogen pointed at Dice. "Would you trust a guy at first sight dressed like him—or me for that matter? You forget that this robe I wear isn't just for decoration." He shook a little bit, letting his belongings jingle around to demonstrate his point.

I took a good look at Dice and realized that his tall collar and low worn visor were not very friendly-looking traits. Bogen would be noticed as a Cause from a kilometer away and Black's clothing was unique enough to draw any attention.

Bogen began to instruct us as to what to do. "You'll have to empty your pockets into your bag and leave it here with us. Just take your coin purse and your tickets. Once we see how the Gray Police operate here, we'll know how to get past them."

As ordered, I emptied my pockets of all of my small traveling items. While doing that, I found myself jittery beyond belief as I openly asked, "What should we say to them?"

"Just make something up," Bogen shrugged. He then turned to Kay. "Make sure you limp with that ankle. It might drum up some sympathy."

Kay confirmed her role, but issued a warning. "If you see us run, try to keep up."

After many deep breaths, we calmed down and prepared to face the Gray Police.

Kay started off with a very believable limp—noticeable, yet not over-exaggerated.

As we made our way up the platform, I became short of breath and extremely nervous. As a result, I decided to try and interact with Kay rather than engage the police head on. However, without taking the time to think of my words, I blurted out the first thing that came to mind. "Are you sure you're going to be okay, honey?"

She turned her head and shot me a nasty look. "Honey!?"

I gritted my teeth. "Sorry."

Both of the Gray Police officers looked at us as we proceeded toward them. The slender guard nodded to the other then continued to pace and patrol. The other officer called out to us in a deep and intimidating bellow. "Can I help you?"

My mind wandered in anxiety as I tried not to let it show on my face. "Yes, you can." I paused and noticed that there were two trains ready for boarding, one to the left and one to the right. "My girlfriend here and I are headed up to the Lucra Sector to hit up the Gaming Districts. Which of these trains is the northbound one?"

The mustachioed officer pointed to the train on the left while fixing a look at Kay. He pointed at her with his nightstick. "What happened to her?"

"Her?" I was frozen, suddenly stuck for an answer.

Kay slapped me on the back of the head. "This genius here backed into me and sent me down a flight of stairs. This little trip is only a fraction of his apology."

"Good one," I thought to myself.

The officer chuckled in a seemingly reminiscent fashion. "Well, your train is over there." He pointed again. "Have fun."

"Sure thing," I said with a smile.

After the officer turned away from us to regroup with his partner, I told Kay to get on the train. Now I had to figure out a way to get the others past the Gray Police.

When I turned back to the platform entrance, I almost jumped out of my skin at the sight of Dice. He was out in the open and casually making his way toward the northbound train. Before I fully panicked, I calmed upon noticing his collar was down, he was not wearing his visor, and his hair was a little more kempt than usual.

Sure enough, the same burly officer called to Dice. "Can I help you, young man?"

I watched the scene unfold as my heart sank into my stomach.

Dice confidently allowed himself to be approached. "What

can I do for you, sir?"

"Where are you headed?" The vigilant officer had his hand on his holster as he was looking him over. He seemed suspicious of Dice's appearance.

Dice seemed almost like a whole different person as he replied to the man. "I've got my bags packed and I'm ready for some fun over in Lucra."

His words reached out to me. I joined in the conversation while pretending Dice was a stranger. "You're going there, too!?"

He turned to me, having quickly caught onto my act. "You bet! I even have my lucky dice and everything ready to roll." He then pointed to the train. "I take it that's the northbound…"

"It certainly is, sir!" I declared while acting excited. "You can sit with me and my girlfriend. She's got bandages on her wrist and ankle. You can't miss her."

"Sounds good."

The Gray Policemen bought into our act and allowed Dice onto the train with no problem. The last thing I needed was an excuse to regroup with Bogen and Black.

After a quick thought, out came a quick and plausible excuse. "I'll be right back. I'm going to go use the restroom here at the station before the train departs."

The younger officer looked to the clock and said, "Better hurry, then. This train leaves in six minutes."

I nodded as I saw Dice vanish into the northbound train and ran off of the platform.

"I can't believe Dice just did that!" Black exclaimed quietly upon my return.

"Me neither," I huffed, still trying to catch my breath.

Bogen, having heard the officer's declaration of a time limit, was only focused on getting onto that train. "Any way you slice it, in the eyes of those guards, we might as well have 'Cause' written across our foreheads." He looked me in the eye with his point up front. "You're going to have to distract them."

The only expression I could muster was shock. "How do you suppose I do that!?"

Bogen tried to cover the fact that he had made no plan toward his suggestion. "I don't know how you should do it; you're the creative one! The only thing I can think of is to scream 'rebels!'

really loud and hope both of those guys come running."

I took Bogen's blithering into my brain and allowed it to transform his words into a rather interesting blueprint. We would only have one shot, and it required perfect timing and a little bit of luck. All I had to do was await the final boarding call, which would occur two minutes before departure.

We waited, shaking with uncertainty.

When the boarding call came, I put on my best panic face and ran back onto the platform. "Officers! Rebels!"

The two policemen had my undivided attention. "Where!?" the older one asked in an urgent and demanding manner.

"I heard them in the bathroom! They're plotting to derail the eastbound train!"

My false claim caught their ire. "That one is headed for Fanda's Grand Station."

The athletic one inquired hastily, "How many were there?"

I continued to push the act. "It sounded like there were four or five of them. I only heard voices. They left for the eastbound platform just before I ran back here!"

They looked to each other, "Let's go."

The Gray Police left the platform to track down the imaginary rebels. Once they were out of sight, I ran over to retrieve Bogen, Black and the rest of our things.

Bogen beamed with delight as we scurried aboard the train. "That's the kind of genius I will always expect from you! I was smart to trust you."

I felt warm and validated, worthy of the title "Honorary Producer".

We rejoined Kay and Dice and situated ourselves in a semicircle booth. After placing our bags and items in the rack overhead, we flopped into our seats and let the sounds of the train departing lift our anxieties away. "I was on pins and needles that entire time!" I announced in one loud exhalation.

"Nice going, stranger," Dice snickered.

I followed his joke and lazily put my hand out to him. "It's nice to meet you. I'm Dartmouth, but all my friends call me 'Brigg'."

Dice laughed, shaking my hand. "I'm Charles—call me 'Dice'." He began to laugh even harder. "Your girlfriend is very lovely!"

Bogen and Black were amused as well. I tried to contain myself since I figured Kay did not find it funny at first.

She glared at me as she tried to speak with a straight face. "Call me that again and *you'll* be going down that flight of stairs next."

III

Black was seated in the middle of the booth, hammering away on her laptop. Dice and Bogen were intently hovering over her shoulders from both sides. This left Kay and me to enjoy the sun setting in the west.

My attention to the sight was broken as Dice suddenly took his attention away from what Black was doing. "By the way, Brigg, there is something I have been meaning to tell you."

"What's up?" I wondered.

"Remember when we were back at the Delta and I said I would never lie to you?" His question drew everyone's attention to him.

"Yes, I do. All too well, actually."

"Well," he chuckled, "As it turns out, I wound up lying to you by accident during that same conversation."

I sounded a bit ridiculous. "By accident?"

He presented his dice between the fingers of his left hand as usual. Dice intentionally flashed them in a way that had all of the "one" sides facing toward me. "Three is a prime number, right?"

"Yes, we established that back then. What about it?"

He put his dice back into his pocket. "It seems as though the heat of the conversation caused us to both forget that prime numbers are divisible by one *and* itself. That would make *me* the loser of that roll back then."

My right palm struck my forehead as I couldn't believe that something so simple had slipped past me. "Why is it you're telling me this now?"

He reclined and folded his arms. "I just prefer to clear up those rare occasions in which I make a mistake. It's more embarrassing for me, though, since this particular error was associated with math."

"I've never been the best with math either," I openly admitted.

"Which would easily explain why it slipped past you."

I had expected such a comment. But now, I was trying to remember what the erroneous roll was about. I couldn't recall the topic for the life of me. "Why did you make that roll again?"

"Ha!" he burst out. "Like I'd ever tell you that now. You're beat!"

Kay dropped into the discussion with the intention of bringing it to a close. "I think he's got you there, Brigg."

Dice leaned back over Black's shoulder to continue observing her activity. "I recommend you just go on back to enjoying your sunset. I wouldn't want you getting a headache trying to figure it out."

"You're _so_ thoughtful," I sarcastically groaned, turning back toward the window. I decided to drop it, thinking that I would remember it some other time.

Once again, I took focus to the landscape outside of the train and the relaxing sunset that covered it in a whimsical orange glow.

Kay sighed with a feminine lilt in her breath. "It has been a while since we've actually had a chance to enjoy something like this."

"We?" I asked.

Kay shrugged, looking almost like she had said that without thinking. "Well, you know…we've been focusing on all of the commotion lately…"

I recalled several details of the hardships she was referring to. "I see what you mean."

"I've noticed that you've been spending a lot of time thinking lately. You're not doing what I think you're doing are you?"

Assuming what she was accusing me of, I said, "I'm just really worried about Mika."

"Come on, lighten up!" she remarked. "I told you before to stop worrying so much. Blue has her now. She's in good hands."

I exhaled, accepting her position. "I know; you're right." I reached up into one of the front pockets of my bag and pulled out the piece of canvas with the picture of Mika's father on it. "You know…this is the reason why I made finding her my first priority after we got separated." I opened the canvas and looked at it as I tilted it at an angle to which Kay could see as well. "Without this, she won't get anywhere looking for her father."

"Ha." She smirked. "To be honest, I completely forgot that you still had that."

"I noticed it the day we jumped out of the train. It caught me by surprise when I opened up my bag and saw it. My first reaction was how lucky we were to get my bag thrown onto dry land before jumping out. Then I tried to think of how to get it back to Mika; which is why I suggested finding her."

She shook her head and scoffed. "Knowing you, that doesn't surprise me."

I sat back into my seat and locked gazes with her. "What can I say? I'm a man of my word. I told Mika that I would help her find her father and I intended to stick with it."

Kay didn't seem to be in the mood to hear me say that again. She simply flicked her hand in my direction and rolled her eyes as a gesture to close the conversation.

I looked down at the drawing one last time before slipping it into one of my pant pockets. I reclined and slung my head across the back of my seat, fixing my eyes to the ceiling of the car. Everything around me slipped away in a glossy sheet of beige. The thought of the length of our trip took over my body and dragged it into a lazy slump. The only thing my brain could process was rest.

For once in a good long while, I didn't feel like being bothered. It was the first time since the sixty-third day of the Revolution that I reverted to the old mindset of self-concern.

Deep down, though, I hoped that nobody would take my inclinations to ignore them personally. I was simply looking forward to some well-deserved rest.

I emptied my mind and relaxed.

There was one thing I heard that was impossible to let pass. It was the last thing I remembered hearing after shutting my eyes.

It was Kay's voice…

…saying the one thing I had been waiting for her to say since the day I met her:

"I trust you."

Day 90

I

The next time I opened my eyes, it was 1:43 am. It was silent and the only light in the car was coming from dim blue bulbs and the moon. I was alone, the only one awake.

I carefully stood from my seat and looked around the car. The five of us were the only occupants.

I turned to look at the others and could not help but smile. Each of them had claimed their own spot in the car to sleep in. The sight of our team sprawled about like we owned the place brought an unexpected feeling of humor to me. "We are the hope of Eden!" I whispered to myself, withholding audible laughter.

I noticed that Black was using Bogen's robe as a blanket and suddenly got an idea. I took my bag from the overhead rack and took my spare blanket out.

Kay had fallen asleep curved along the semicircle booth. Gently, I placed my blanket over her, watching her shift a little as I did so.

Remembering the last thing she said to me, I whispered to her. "Thanks."

There wasn't a whole lot to do by myself. That's when I realized that the same sensations I experienced in the early days of the Revolution weren't all they were cracked up to be.

I remembered the peaceful, relaxing, and carefree time, the inherent masculine taste for adventure. But none of that seemed to matter anymore. Those concepts didn't have the same effect they did at first.

I caught my reflection in the window and stared at it for a little while as I thought long and hard about how far I had come. Considering everything, I couldn't have asked for anything different to have happened to me. Although there had been a lot of hardship and anxiety, I was glad to have the attention and the company of the few people I could trust. At that moment, I was truly proud to be standing on that train with the mission ahead of me and the people I could call friends.

I amused myself by trying a variety of heroic poses to pass the time. In doing so, I began to think back to Kediel Lake, when Bogen had us examine our reflections. The phrase "Hope of Eden" whisked its way through my mind again. That was when I took a serious look into those three words.

I began to speak to my own reflection. "We are only the hope of Eden because we've chosen a path. It is a path of resistance, defiance. This path bears a million forks and not a single sign. Every move we make and every choice we decide on will have consequences that all of Eden will see and hear. But when the time comes to put it all on the line to free Eden from the Fifteen's grasp, we need to prepare ourselves. When the dust settles and the parties disperse, the truths will be revealed. From those hidden truths, we can start a new era of prosperity and growth. That is how this Revolution must end. This is the path we have chosen."

After saying that, I stopped and continued to lock eyes with myself. Although I felt a little funny having said that only to myself, I felt relieved and reassured that the Causes as a whole were doing the right thing.

Being one of the Producers put me just as in charge of things as Bogen was from the beginning. Therefore, it would only be a matter of time before I would be helping lead the Causes down the right path. With the five of us working together as the new band of Producers, I found a new confidence that things would eventually turn back to our favor.

After one last, hard look at myself, I returned to my seat.

Black's laptop was within reach, so I decided to use it to access the forums for a bit.

First, I checked for any private messages. There was no new word from Blue—or any new messages for that matter.

Next, I looked for any new information concerning the Zealots or the Deserters. The only thing that turned up new was that somebody had allegedly seen Jalako. Within the next few posts though, his claim was dismissed since the user defined Jalako as a "he". It was now common knowledge that Albion referred to Jalako as a woman.

I sighed and began poking around the latest hot topics.

That is when it happened. After all of that time spent boosting my confidence, one glance at the hot topics was all I needed to send my spirits back to the bottom floor. On impulse, I shouted audibly in disbelief, "What is this!?"

Bogen sprang to his feet so fast I could swear he thought Gray Police were on the scene. "What is going on? What happened?"

I couldn't speak. All I could do was stare at the screen, reading the same phrase over and over as if I was trying to believe it wasn't there.

"Did you find something new?" he asked me as the others slowly slogged into consciousness.

I lightly nodded, almost frozen. I lifted my finger and pointed, keeping it there until everybody was over my shoulders to see.

Sure enough, it was all real. Smack in the middle of the hot topics were the eight words that we could have never imagined reading all in the same sentence:

"Bogen and Brigg are traitors to the Causes!"

Making matters worse, the author of the topic was none other than the resident mystery woman herself: Jalako.

"I thought you banned Al & Jal!" I said to Black.

She defended herself. "Yes, I banned the username 'Al & Jal'. They must also have their names separate from each other as well as their combined alias. That was definitely a critical oversight on my part. I'll be sure to ban their names too."

"Please do!"

Bogen opened the topic and began to scan it up and down.

"From the looks of things, the mere fact that Jalako wrote this will draw more attention to it than any other topic."

We read the original post by her. It was a very long and detailed post with very strong arguments to back up her claims.

In short, Jalako stated that since the Producers were captured and Hatcher never showed up, it was the Causes' duty to organize a different method for the Revolution. Albion proposed rebellion after the broadcast of the meeting, and the Causes accepted it. Jalako claimed that from that day forward, the Causes were dead and the rebels—the Zealots—were the new force behind the Revolution.

She went on to sling mud in Bogen's direction. Jalako charged Bogen with plotting to stop the Zealots and bring the Revolution to an end. She announced that he was trying to regain his influence and start the Causes back at square one. This, Jalako argued, would destroy everything the Revolution was and anybody who was captured by the Fifteen would have lost their free will in vain.

A lot of my past posts were marked when Jalako started to take her sights on me. The reason she targeted me in the first place was because Bogen specifically called out my name over the radio at the meeting. She claimed I was in cahoots with Bogen's falsely exaggerated intentions and that I should be ignored or be turned in to the Gray Police.

The rest of her post was her ranting that she didn't know who the rest of "their little friends" were. Regardless, Jalako put it out there for the Causes to be careful of them too. Of course, she was referring to Black, Kay and Dice. Unfortunately for Mika and Blue, they would later be added to her allegations as well.

"Fortunately," Bogen sighed, "there are only fourteen replies to this."

"That could be fourteen replies too many," Black replied with dread in her voice.

Kay added to Black's pessimism. "This topic can spread by word of mouth at this point."

"Everyone, let's just stay calm," Bogen unconvincingly coaxed. "This is something I'm sure Black can easily take care of."

Black's hands quivered anxiously as she took the laptop back from me. "He's right. All I have to do is delete the topic, and then ban Albion and Jalako. It's as simple as that."

We left her to take care of the offending remarks as Dice shared his opinion. "This is obviously a scare tactic. They're trying to generate more uncertainty among the Causes while we are out of the public eye."

His view seemed a bit vague to me. "You mean they're taking advantage of our mission to retrieve Mika?"

"Something like that," he said. "If you think about it, we've been absent from the forums for the past few days. The last thing any of us posted was Bogen reinforcing the Producers' way. Any business we've had on the forums has been private messages."

Black commented. "He's right. We have not been posting publicly. With all of this Mika business going on, we've failed to remember that we have a Revolution going on here. Jalako used that to her advantage."

Hearing Black blame my priorities toward Mika wasn't an easy thing to take in. While what she said was true, I found it hard to find any other way we could have planned our agendas.

Bogen had a solid reply though. "You've got me wrong there, Black. It's Brigg and his crew that are going for the girl. I'm doing this to meet with Blue. There are two separate motives on this trip, yet they go hand in hand."

Black grumbled. "That still doesn't change the fact that both of you have been neglecting to post supportive messages lately."

I flopped back into my seat and grunted. "Looks like we're all perpetrators of oversights today."

A few moments of silence passed before Black made an unfortunate announcement. "Guys, I think we have a problem!"

"What's the matter?" I asked, fearing to hear the worst.

"I can't delete the topic, or *anything* for that matter!"

"Impossible!" Bogen shouted. "You're an administrator. You should be able to!"

"I've looked everywhere," Black wailed in panic. "The option to delete content has disappeared."

"How could that happen?"

"I don't know," she shrugged. "I did manage to ban Albion and Jalako though."

I was relieved. "That's one headache out of the way."

Bogen got a quick idea. "Check the list of administrators!"

"On it!"

After a couple of clicks and keyboard strokes there was a pause. Seconds later, Black exclaimed in a low and frightened voice. "Oh my God!" She covered her mouth with her hands as her eyes grew wide.

"That doesn't sound very good," Kay hesitantly responded.

Bogen was the only one with some semblance of a grin on his face. "I was right, wasn't I? Jalako's name was on there?"

"Worse…"

Bogen's brow hung low. "How…?"

"Like this!" Black shouted, turning the laptop to face us.

To our surprise and horror, three new administrators had appeared on the list: Deserter A, Deserter B and Deserter C.

Bogen seemed to go into a brief panic. "Post a warning, now!" he barked.

Immediately, I knew I was at fault for the apparent forum tampering. Revealing the name "Cause" to the Fifteen was proving to be the most critical mistake I had ever made.

Bogen wasted no time in reminding me of his feelings toward my mishap. "Brigg, you screwed up big-time!"

I exhaled with deep regret in my tone. "Yes, I know."

"What can we do about it?" Kay inquired, hoping to shift the conversation to something productive.

"Since Eliza is able to manipulate the forums, we may have to make another one."

"That would take some time," Black announced. "I don't think we have the luxury of spare time at this point."

"Did you post the warning?"

She quickly nodded. "Yes."

I took a few deep breaths. "That's good. Hopefully, the Causes will act appropriately to this news."

Black suddenly screamed. "No!"

"What now?" Bogen growled in frustration.

"My warning was deleted!"

All of us were silent for a few minutes as we took in what it all meant.

Eliza had the entire Cause forum compromised. Thinking into it, having Eliza control the forum was significantly worse than having it out and out deleted. This was another one of the

Fifteen's methods of breaking down the Causes. Once again, the Deserters were on the front lines.

"This is a nightmare," Black sobbed.

"We are screwed," Kay added. "The Causes won't be able to keep up with the Fifteen if we have a panel of Deserters as administrators."

"Ironic…" Dice interrupted.

I turned to him. "You need to stop doing that, you know?"

"What?" he wondered.

I stepped toward him. "Knock it off with the one-word conversation stoppers! How can you be so casual about this?"

Dice made his point clear. "I was only pointing out the irony in the fact that the forum that brought the Causes together is the same thing that is going to break them up."

Not what I wanted to hear. "Shut up!"

Dice raised an eyebrow, swiftly reaching into his left pocket for his dice. "Your sudden hostility tempts me so." He pulled his dice out in front of his face with one between each finger.

"Dice!" Kay scolded. "Stop it."

Ignoring her, he continued with a wager. "Total will be even!"

The dice rolled to the floor. The total came up as seven: two threes and a one.

"Ooh," Dice grunted, "you're lucky. I really wanted to finish what I had to say. I'm not a cheater, though."

Staying on the main concern, Kay opened up a suggestion. "I'd hate to say it, but we may have to tell the Causes to abandon the existing forum. As long as Eliza has a set of Deserters in on it, it will be impossible to plan a grand-scale move against the Fifteen."

Bogen's robe lifted high behind him as he rapidly turned to address Kay. "That is exactly what they want us to do. Why else would they make it so blatantly obvious that the three new admins are Deserters?"

"Chalk one up for Bogen on that one!" Dice remarked. "I didn't even think of that."

It seemed all too familiar to me. "This is exactly what I warned Albion about. Instead of just wiping the forum, they've created a plan to put us right where they want us."

Kay was onto my reasoning. "It's just like the creation of the

Deserters."

"Correct!" I said. "Consider how long ago I said the name 'Cause' to Naro."

Bogen thought back. "It was about…"

Kay had the answer. "It was three weeks ago…almost."

"Three weeks," I repeated. "It took the Fifteen three weeks to plan on how to use that leaked information against us." I let my words linger in the air for a second before passing my next thought. "I have a strong feeling that the Fifteen know every move we can make from here."

Dice took the floor. "So if we abandon the forums, the Fifteen have us completely divided with no medium for communication. If we make a new forum, the Fifteen follow us. And if we keep using the same forum, the Fifteen will be further ahead of us than we can imagine by knowing every major move the Causes will make as a whole."

It was a heart-wrenching sensation to hear that every one of our immediate options could be stifled by the Fifteen's careful planning. "That pretty much sums it up," I fretfully declared.

"If that's the case," Bogen growled, "then we'll have to go with the least painful option." He called for Black's attention.

She looked to him. "Yes?"

The usually-energetic youth appeared torn. "Start sending private messages to some of the other Causes. Let them know what's going on and tell them to stop accessing the forums. We're going to abandon the forum."

I gasped at the news. "What about Hatcher?"

Bogen was quick with his answer. "If he ever does post on that forum again, I'm sure the Deserters will delete the post just like they did with Black's warning."

"I'm also going to have to tell all of the Contacts out there that they are out of a job," Black regretfully announced.

Dice was still rife with his own comments. "The Causes sure are having a lot of dark days lately."

I ignored Dice and kept to planning our moves. "What are we going to do about Jalako's post?" I asked openly.

"There's nothing we can do about it," Bogen grumbled. "Let's just hope that the Causes see through her arguments."

Dice took the liberty of saying something useful. "It wouldn't hurt to read how the Causes are replying to it."

I gruffly exhaled, agreeing reluctantly to Dice's suggestion. "He's right."

We began to read what few replies had already hit the topic. It was slightly uplifting to see that a couple of Causes still sided with us. However, those who agreed with Jalako dismissed those people as lost and confused about what was best for Eden.

Reading the thread helped us to finally notice the true separation of the Causes. Going through reply after reply was like watching the mighty structure that the Producers built fall apart in our own hands.

"It's safe to say that the forum is a total loss now," Bogen darkly muttered.

"To make matters worse," Dice added, pushing his glasses up the bridge of his nose, "we won't know what this will do to the Causes around Eden until we get Mika back and return to civilization."

"Right," I agreed. "The only people we can trust now are ourselves, each other, Blue and Mika."

Kay gave me a pat on the back for support. "Yeah, let's try to keep our head in the game here. We can't let this bring us down." Kay opened my pants pocket, took Mika's picture out and handed it to me.

It took me several minutes to calm down and get my thoughts back on track. I repeated to myself in slightly audible whispers, "Mika and Blue come first. This is the path."

I stood to my feet and began to pace around the car. I felt that urge to take a few minutes to collect my thoughts. The post from Jalako and the forum takeover were an overwhelming combination to press through. It was going to take a clear head to get any further toward our success against the Fifteen.

At one point, I stood alone on the end of the car opposite the others. I took that moment to greet my reflection one more time. I looked into my own eyes and mustered a confident smirk. Once again, I spoke to myself. "Stay strong, Causes. They have our answers."

I smiled and nodded at how right that sounded. "This is the path we've chosen, and we will see it through to the end."

Episode 7: Death of a Traitor

Traitor. The word passed through my thoughts every minute.

The five of us were deeply distraught by the feeling that there was no end in sight for the Causes' hard times. Every time things seemed to clear up, something else would happen. With the latest move by the Fifteen fresh in our minds, we had no choice but to make the dark decision to abandon the forum.

There was no telling what the future held for us. The only thing we were certain of was our mission to retrieve Mika from the Terra Sector and team up with Blue.

From that point, the only thing that could have made matters worse for our party was to encounter complications during our train switch in Lucra.

Surprisingly enough, there were no Gray Police in sight and the station itself was effortless to navigate. It was the only sigh of relief I could breathe through the turmoil that was taking place otherwise.

We took solace in the fact that we were physically distant from hostile forces on all sides. It gave us the space we needed to decide for ourselves when it was safe to approach the front of the Revolution again. We felt that with Blue on our side and Mika back in our hands, we would find ourselves in a better position to reestablish our influence. Until then, our focus was Mika, Blue, and nobody else. We would worry about Jalako, the Revolution, and the Fifteen later.

We did our best to stay relaxed as we made our approach to the Terra Sector.

Day 91

I

We were on our one-way trip to Terra on the Land's End Rail. The stretch of railroad's name derives from the fact that it is the closest rail to Eden's outer wall. The tracks run as one huge curve and remain an equidistant 25 kilometers from the border of the Zica Sector; and a total of 40 kilometers from Eden's outer wall. This was as close as anybody could get to Zica and still feel safe.

The five of us found ourselves engrossed in a conversation about the borders beyond our reach.

According to our recorded history, when God created Eden, He built a great wall around it. This wall shelled Eden in a perfect circle of protection. Encompassed inside the wall, God granted us safety from the horrible beasts and demons that reside on the other side of it. But God's protection doesn't stop there. That is where the land known as the Zica Sector comes in.

The Zica Sector is the ground that is known as Eden's second defense. If a beast or demon from the Great Beyond were to actually make it into Eden, the spirits of Angels that reside in Zica would fight it off to save Eden. As such, Zica is a treacherous landscape that is also seen as sacred ground.

Anybody who has ever ventured into the Zica Sector has

never returned. It was common knowledge in Eden to stay out of Zica.

Talking about Eden's border with the others was a good way to get my mind off of everything for a while. Soon enough, we found ourselves throwing the conversation in all sorts of directions. It soon became apparent that we were avoiding topic of anything Revolution-related. The long trip soon became grounds to completely forget our worries. We even chose not to check the forum again until we arrived in Terra.

II

We were in a section of Land's End Rail that passed through the Gova Sector. Memories raced back to me of the last day I had spent alone. Gazing upon the natural landscape of forest, fields, ponds, lakes, and rivers had me look back to those days I spent surviving in it. It was inevitable that I remember the day I met Mika and Kay.

I thought of an interesting question, got Kay's attention, and presented it to her. "I was wondering…what were you doing on the same train I was on the day we met?"

She stared at me for a moment as if she would have never expected me to ask that. "The group I was traveling with had abandoned me. So, I chose to just take a ride through the Gova Sector to blow off steam and clear my head. Why do you ask?"

"Just curious, really," I said. "Any ideas as to why they did that?"

She raised an eyebrow and copped an attitude. "Well, if the way we were at each other's throats the day we met was any indication…"

I raised both of my hands. "Say no more, say no more!"

Kay's voice became sarcastic with her upcoming rhetorical response. "Any other questions?"

I answered her anyway. "Not really. I was just remembering how it all started for us back then."

Bogen seemed curious. "You camped out in the Gova Sector, too?"

I answered by going back over the events of that day—the sixty-third day of the Revolution. To keep the conversation positive, I only mentioned Sydney once just to say that I had met him in person.

We all began to share our stories of the Revolution's early days. It was an enlightening conversation that taught us a lot about each other and how we handle situations. My stories weren't nearly as useful since I had spent the first sixty-two days of the Revolution mostly by myself. Any tips on teamwork were better off left to everybody else.

Kay had a lot to say since her original motivation was to help protect the women taking part in the Revolution. Our arguments before the Great Walk only served to fuel her self-acclaimed role as the protector of innocent young ladies across Eden. Her time in the early days of the Revolution was spent keeping a wary eye on the men who accompanied women; making sure they behaved themselves.

Black and Bogen had quite the story too. The two of them practically spent the entire Revolution together. However, there was only one point in time when the two were separate due to a train boarding incident. It was during that mishap that Black met Blue in person. Black was quick to point that out.

Everyone seemed to be very open about their tales except for Dice. Unfortunately, Dice's input made me a little uneasy about what his true motives were. I remembered him mentioning an agenda he had. When I paired that up to the other things he was saying then, it made me skeptical of the amount of loyalty he would show us.

I remembered what he said when he accepted Bogen's offer to be an Honorary Producer: "I can't go this alone and there is nobody else who I can trust. At the same time, I'll warn you that I can't be depended on to be totally cooperative."

It felt like a warning, but I wasn't about to drag everybody's mood down by putting Dice in the hot seat about it. I let it go for the time being and chose not to be surprised if he were to dismiss himself again.

III

After a long and mostly relaxing trip, we finally arrived in the Terra Sector at 8:30 pm. An overly cloudy sky and a vast and open plain greeted us as we stepped off the train. Stations in the Terra Sector were only small, unmanned platforms for entry and exit. Thus, even upon our arrival, the five of us were the only people in sight of each other.

Twilight was fading fast into darkness.

According to Black, our destination, farm house D24, was about thirty-five kilometers west-southwest of the train platform. Unfortunately, that put a very long walk ahead of us. Our chances of reaching D24 before we collapsed from exhaustion seemed very slim.

Kay issued a complaint. "It's a shame that it's so cloudy tonight. We'd have a great view of the stars out in a place like this!"

"I was going to say the same thing!" Black agreed.

I was prompted to look up and observe the overcast sky. Gusts of wind howled past us as clusters of clouds appeared to travel with them. The grasses and plants that surrounded the road rustled about, creating a cacophonic sound that was both soothing and eerie.

Unsettled, the five of us chose to stick close, prepared to run if the need came about.

In the far distance, we spotted a windmill churning. It was a windmill that generated power to the nearest farm house: C28. "I have an idea," Bogen announced.

I was curious. "What's that?"

"We should see what we can do about staying the night in any of the houses we see on the way."

Dice appeared to see the potential in Bogen's suggestion. "That sounds all right. If we can stay, great. If we can't, we press on."

"Exactly."

Suddenly, a bolt of lightning streaked across the sky. Another bolt struck, followed by another.

Dice freaked out and began to run faster than I had ever seen him run. "Yes, C28 sounds like a good enough place to stay."

All of us picked up the pace in an attempt to keep up with him.

Kay found Dice's behavior unlikely and amusing. "Dice is afraid of lightning?"

I smiled with her. "It would seem so."

"He's the last person I'd expect to be afraid of anything," Black added.

"Look," Bogen interrupted, "We can tease him about it later. Let's just see if we can get into that house for now."

"Both parts of that plan sound good to me!" I chuckled, anticipating roasting Dice.

Exhausted from running the rest of the way, we had to pace ourselves up the porch stairs of the quaint little farm house.

The house was built just like any other housing unit in Eden. The only difference was the power being generated by wind rather than sun panels or water turbines. Other than that, it was very plain. It was painted white and had no second floor to it.

"Man," I said, "for belonging to farmers, these houses sure don't look special to me."

"Remember, Brigg," Bogen interjected, "the Fifteen designed the houses we live in. I'm sure there's even a truth behind why every house in Eden is designed the same way."

"Interesting…" I pondered.

"Another thing to remember is that a good number of farmers are also Labor Field prisoners," Dice remarked.

Black wasn't paying attention. The only thing out of her mouth was, "I'm going to contact Blue and tell him that we are here." Once again, she sounded like Blue was the only thing on her mind.

"You do that," Bogen said with a pleased grin. "As for me…" He approached the door, took a deep, dramatic breath and knocked.

Black sat on a chair on the porch as the rest of us watched the door, awaiting an answer. We could hear footsteps coming from the other side of the door. They soon stopped. I held my breath in hopes that we would be welcomed without any trouble.

Bogen took a step back from the door as it began to slowly creak open. The eye of a young girl peeked through to examine us.

At first sight, it was obvious that the girl was surprised to see five strangers at her door. "Can I help you?"

"Uh…" Bogen was a little lost for words. He was obviously expecting somebody much older to answer the door. "One moment…" Bogen pulled us all into a huddle.

Before he could say anything to us, the girl opened the door a little further and poked her head out. "Hey, are you guys rev'lutionaries?"

We all stood still, counting on Bogen to cover the girl's inquiries.

Just as Bogen turned to answer her, she cut him off. "You look like you are."

The little girl opened the door completely and stepped onto the porch in a slow and wary fashion. All the red-headed tyke was wearing was a long, white children's nightgown and a pair of worn, gray slippers.

Bogen exhaled, figuring nothing was going to get past this new face. He answered her honestly. "Yes, we are revolutionaries."

The girl paced around the porch, keeping her eyes fixed on us and her arms to her sides—keeping her distance. "I've heard of the Rev'lutionaries, but never seen any. Are you all lost?" she asked.

Bogen took a few steps toward her and began to speak. But apparently, the young miss was not too quickly inclined to trust us. We failed to notice that she was holding a long knife in her left hand, which she had been keeping close to her side. She brandished it, pointing it at us. "Stay back!"

All of us backed away with our hands raised. Black, thinking quickly, began to pull up evidence of our agenda from her laptop.

Bogen began to explain the situation from our cowering position on the porch.

It took a few moments, but the girl was receptive to our story.

Black stepped forward with her laptop screen loaded with maps and messages from the past several days. "See, this is what brought us here." Black stepped out to the young stranger with the screen facing out. The two girls sat down in the middle of the porch and Black walked her through our story.

Kay was under the impression that getting the young girl to warm up to us was a mission best left to the ladies. She walked over and spoke with her. "What's your name?"

The little one answered without taking her eyes off of the laptop screen. "Amanda."

"Are you alone here, Amanda?"

"Well, my mommy took the carriage to go get food for the house. I'm worried. She's been gone for two days now."

Black went on to ask, "What about your dad?"

"My daddy left a couple of hours ago. He went to his friend's house, house B27. He said I'm in charge until he gets home."

Kay and Black continued to take turns coaxing Amanda into trusting us. Not surprisingly, Amanda was instructed by her father not to invite anybody into the house. With that mentioned, it was a little more difficult to ensure us a comfortable night's rest.

A noticeable amount of time passed and soon, it began to rain. Having heard enough about our situation, Amanda didn't have the heart to leave us out in the storm. She went against her father's instructions and invited us into her home.

IV

We tried to take up as little space as possible as we made ourselves at home in C28. Amanda gave us the living room to use as our base of operations.

The room was modestly furnished with three flower-motif chairs and a big mauve sofa. It remained adequately lit by two strong wall-mounted lamps on both sides of the brick fireplace. The beige carpet was firm, but a little old with a single stain near the side of the table in the center of the room.

Amanda seemed to have taken a liking to Kay and Black. The girls wasted no time stepping into the kitchen to fix a hot meal. All of us understood how deprived we had been of the glory of a home-cooked dinner. Kay and Black adamantly fought their own exhaustion for the sake of everybody's enjoyment.

As for the men, we were busy making sure Blue and Mika were still in position for retrieval. Sure enough, everything was just as we left it. According to Blue, Mika was still having complications walking. But the good news was that the owner of the farm house was being sympathetic. Blue and Mika were trying everything in their power not to wear out their welcome.

We kept our reply to Blue's latest message simple: "See you tomorrow at D24."

Kay called out from the kitchen. "I hope you guys don't mind, but Amanda isn't allowed to cook any of the meat in the house!"

The three of us groaned as our dreams of savoring a slab of beef was washed away by the unmistakable scent of vegetables. Dice was the first to suck it up enough to make a joke about it. "Woman! You best be cookin' me a steak if you know what's good for you!"

I laughed, unable to believe what I had just heard. "He did not just say that…"

Kay fired back in as jocular a tone as Dice delivered. "You best be grateful I'm cookin' at all!"

Bogen seemed to find that exchange very amusing. He patted Dice on the back as his giggling came under control. "I like this guy! He's funny!"

Dice smirked, his eyes focused on the laptop. "Only when I feel like it, trust me." He turned to a serious note. "I'm going to check on…that topic."

"You mean Jalako's senseless drivel," I grunted in spite.

"Yeah, that one."

Slightly frustrated, I stood from the sofa and made my way over to one of the chairs. I sat down and looked out the window. "I don't really want to think about that right now. If there is anything life-threateningly important, let me know."

"Sure thing," Bogen sighed. The two of them went about their business.

I began to go over the next day's itinerary. In doing so, I caught something that none of us had thought of. I felt that it would be totally senseless to have all five of us go to D24. Since Blue was already imposing on another man's house, it was obvious that the last thing the man would want was more company. If anything, I anticipated the man to turn all of us away once we were to arrive.

"Hey guys," I said, "maybe I should go to D24 alone tomorrow."

"Oh no you don't!" Black objected. "I've been waiting for quite a while to see Blue in person again. I'm going to that house whether you like it or not."

Kay had a different approach to my announcement. "Why would you go alone at a time like this?"

I presented to the room the same point I had just thought of. "What is the point of all of us going there when we're just going to come back here and then double back to the train anyway? If it's just me and Blue—"

Black cut me off. "…And me!"

"…And Black, we can take turns carrying Mika back starting from the moment we get there."

Bogen replied next. "If that's the case, then I'll go with Black."

Dice argued Bogen's proposal. "Actually, I'm not sure if Mika would be comfortable with that. Out of all of us, Brigg has known Mika the longest. Although it's not by much, I still have a point, right?"

Bogen didn't seem convinced. "Maybe…" he uttered.

Dice pressed on. "The only time you met Mika was back at the Radio Tower. You didn't stay very long after that. I wouldn't be too sure about what kind of impression that left on her."

"That sounded a lot better, Dice!" Kay remarked from the kitchen.

Bogen was nodding. "That settles that then." He spoke louder. "Black, it's just going to be you and Brigg tomorrow, okay?"

"All right!" she squeaked excitedly.

Kay covered the conversation's conclusion. "The rest of us will stay here and watch over Amanda. Hopefully, her parents aren't in a rush to get home. We're not looking for any trouble, you know?"

The last few details were put into place over our dinner of string beans and herb mashed potatoes. The plan was set up and everything looked good to go. I was going to travel to D24 the next day rain or shine, so Black prepared accordingly to accommodate her laptop.

With a long walk ahead of us, Black and I turned in early on the sofa, resting our heads on the armrests. The others stayed up for a little while longer since they were under no obligation to join us on the trip to D24.

Tomorrow was a big day for all of us as it would complete our team. Combined, the seven of us would get the Causes back on the right track.

Day 92

I

Black and I were up with the sun. A quick glance out the window showed that the cloud cover outdoors was still abundant. The only remnant of the storm from the night before was the glossy sheen that covered the grass. My neck was a little sore, but other than that I was ready to roll.

Mika's location was several kilometers away and would take almost half a day to get to on foot. Since going in a straight line to D24 would take us through fields and crops, a carriage or bicycle was out of the question to use. We felt no harm in our decision to walk other than the discomfort brought on by the gloomy weather.

After everybody was awake, Kay and Amanda cooked everybody scrambled eggs. Amanda also provided me and Black with bananas to prevent cramps on our journey. It was a blessing to have such a fortified breakfast. It wasn't just the good food, though. Having it prepared by caring hands was what made it even more satisfying.

We made our final preparations and bid the others farewell. They wished us the best of luck and a safe return.

Everything was going as planned.

II

The afternoon sky was still filled with clouds as Black and I continued our trek across the Terra Sector's vast and open landscape. Although Black was still brimming with energy at the thought of Blue, my jovial spirits were fueled by thoughts of Mika.

Kay, Dice, and Bogen were on my mind as well. It didn't feel quite right traveling without them even though my decision to do so was voluntary. Sure, I was going to rest for a little while once we reached the other house, but I had every intention of returning to the others by the end of the day. The peaceful image of the three of them resting up was foremost in my thoughts as Black and I idly babbled back and forth to each other about nothing in particular.

The friendly, mindless banter between us was suddenly interrupted just as a windmill became visible in the far distance. A rhythmic galloping sound was closing in on us, accented by the light squeak of a rusty wheel. It wasn't just coming from behind us, though. The noise grew louder and seemed to be coming from several directions at once.

Within moments and without giving us a second to run, three horse-coaches had surrounded us. Just as quickly, two Gray Police officers stepped out of each coach and stood at attention.

Black and I took a back-to-back position and prepared to defend ourselves. "How did Gray Police find us all the way out here?" Black asked me.

"Your guess is a good as mine..." I replied, suddenly growing weak at the knees.

After a pause, I heard a voice all too familiar to me. "You know, Brigg, you look really helpless standing there like that. I figured the big hero you are would be a little more confident here. I'm disappointed."

There was no mistaking it. Even though Blue managed to get Mika away from him, Sydney still stayed in the Terra Sector and waited for me to show up.

Clad in a broad-shouldered gray cloak and sporting a new, near-bald haircut, he emerged from the horse-coach nearest to me. He took slow, methodical steps down the coach stairs and toward me. His posture and garb were an intimidating display that forced me to keep my focus fixed on him.

Unfortunately, while I was focused on Sydney, the Gray Police took advantage of my lack of attention to Black. Her shriek quickly shook my nerves. I turned for a split second to see her being dragged away before turning back to keep my eyes on Sydney.

After Black was restrained and taken into a coach, the action seemed to stop for a brief moment. The Gray Police were eyeing me up as if they were all going to dogpile me the second I moved a muscle. My eyes darted in many directions. Panic and fear slowly crept into my heart, gradually replacing any hope.

The only thing I could think of was to feign accepting defeat and play it by ear from there. I exhaled and stood erect. "If you're going to capture me, save everyone's time by sparing the melodrama and just do it."

"Aww, but melodrama makes important times like this so much more fun." Sydney sounded very confident and sarcastic. He definitely knew what he was doing.

To squelch my curiosity and stall for time, I asked him, "How did you find me all the way out here?"

He groaned, taking a few more steps toward me. "If there was any one thing I knew about you, it was that the girl's safety was your number one priority. Knowing that, I concluded that whoever has her at this point has two things going for them. One: They could not have gotten too far. Two: They must know you pretty well to pull off a move like that."

It surprised me that Sydney didn't know who had Mika. I wasn't about to tell him though.

Sydney continued to speak. "When I saw Mika get off of that train, my heart skipped a beat. I knew for a fact that she was the key to luring you out into the open." He spread his arms wide as if he was presenting the entire Terra Sector to me. "You can't get more out in the open than this, right?"

Though it made sense, I still felt the need to ask him, "That's why you brought her all the way to Terra?"

"Oh, there's more to it than that."

I scoffed, "Obviously…"

Sydney was beginning to take steps around me. "I have to hand it to you, Brigg. Not only did you come here as I planned, but you also brought me the Producers' personal Contact." He laughed deeply. "Are you really the traitor everyone has been saying you are?"

His question was like a punch in the heart. I was so focused on Mika that I had not realized just how serious Black's capture was. Kay, Dice and Bogen were now on their own with no Contact. Without really thinking, I threw up a weak, makeshift defense. "I'm not a traitor! If anything, you are!"

"Wrong!" he shouted back, "Try harder. It won't take much for Jalako to convince the Causes that you 'delivered' her to me. It is indeed an unexpected twist that we can work to our favor."

I was awestruck; soon shifting to anger. "How do you know about that!? Black banned you from the forums!"

His raised his tone, blending fury with a blow to my intelligence. "Uh, hello! Last time I checked I was working with the Fifteen. Do we so quickly forget that Eliza can do *anything* with the Interactive Network?"

My body quivered as the greatness of Sydney's knowledge and power ran through me, chilling me to the bone. It was like all of my efforts toward Revolution were in vain. Sydney appeared to be one step ahead at all times. The only thing I could do at that point was keep him talking. That way, if for some reason I managed to escape capture, I'd leave just a little bit wiser as to how Sydney and the Deserters were operating.

"I know everything," Sydney growled. "And it is because of that that I have sworn myself to the Fifteen to bring an end to the Revolution. The Causes can not succeed."

"What does that have to do with me?" I asked in frustration.

"Simple," he sadistically smirked. "You're a pretty popular guy. Your name is one that the Causes have learned to trust and confide in. Despite Jalako's recent accusations, you still have followers. The true Causes are happy to see that you and Bogen are still out and about. It gives them hope that the Revolution will be a success." His voice then grew with anger. "That is the problem! As long as they have hope, we cannot restore order to Eden!"

I finally understood what he was saying. I quickly decided that I had to take a different approach to the situation. Now my goal was to keep Sydney from tracking down the others. If I could occupy Sydney's time with me, perhaps it would give the others time to realize that something had gone wrong. It was a stretch, but the Causes' only hope was for me to turn myself in to buy more time.

I took a deep breath, unable to believe what I was about to say. "All right then," I exhaled. "Like I said in the beginning, cut the drama and just take me in."

"I'm afraid you've got the wrong idea," Sydney bellowed, shaking his head. He then turned his head up to the Gray Police and gave them all a nod. On that signal, they all piled into the horse-coaches.

Within a few moments of that, the coaches departed. Black was taken away and the Gray Police were gone.

All that was left was me and Sydney, standing merely fifteen meters apart from each other. The sounds of the horses galloping and the faint squeak of the carriage wheel grew softer and softer until the gusts of wind and the light patter of rain in the distance overtook them.

Sydney and I stood alone in silence.

III

I could feel my hands trembling, shaken by the discomforting hostility spewing from Sydney's unwavering posture. "I…"

"You don't understand…" he interrupted me. "That's a line of yours all too familiar to me." In an unexpected move, he kneeled down and sat in the grass. He stretched his legs out and leaned back onto his elbows, looking inappropriately relaxed. "I came here expecting you to not understand my position anyway."

I'm fairly certain the look on my face at the time was that of unparalleled confusion. It felt almost like a mind game to see Sydney go from the sinister Deserter leader he had become back to the Sydney I always knew as Doctrine.

I took a few paces closer to him. He didn't move.

I took a few more steps. Still he didn't budge.

After one more step, I was two arms' lengths apart from him. It was at that point he finally looked up to me and said, "Have you ever wanted something so badly that you'd give up anything for it?"

I backed up three steps. "What are you talking about?"

Without missing a beat, he had his answer. "I'm talking about power."

It intrigued me. "Power, you say? What kind of power?"

"I'm not quite sure how I should explain it," he muttered.

Knowing the mood between us had changed, I slowly sat on the grassy terrain. I wasn't sure what he was getting at, but I was certain it would provide me a few clues as to why he deserted the Causes in the first place.

I stayed silent. It was my way of telling Sydney I would be patient and wait for him to organize his words.

"I've been given an offer," he began explaining. "...An offer by the Fifteen. I was given an assignment to stop the Revolution by breaking the Causes down from the inside out. As you can see, my methods of doing so have been quite effective so far. We're to the point where Deserters could very well outnumber the remaining Causes eventually."

"I gathered that much." I growled, expressing frustration about the Deserters as a whole. "So, what happens when you complete this assignment?"

A sinister grin washed away his previously sullen expression. "I will become a member of the Fifteen. You understand, right?"

My mind went blank at that terrifying thought. It was now apparent that the Fifteen were pulling out all the stops to end the Revolution without revealing the truths the Causes sought. The Fifteen had gone as far as to offer a position of power and control in exchange for the dispatching of the Causes.

Being a commoner, I knew how big of a deal something like that was. Any normal person would drop their life where it was to go off and be in control of all of Eden. Sydney had been given that opportunity, and judging by the expression on his face and the words from his mouth, he wasn't going to let the chance pass him by.

Drizzling rain began as I presented Sydney with a question of my own. "So, why did you send the police away? Why are we here alone?"

Sydney looked to the sky and answered. "I'm not sure if I'm ready for it. Being a member of the Fifteen would require me to do a lot of things that are against my being."

"Like what?"

He spread his arms out again. His face became overshadowed with humane remorse. "Like this—where we are right now and what we are about to do."

"Do?" I was getting annoyed with the cryptic talk. "Can you stop beating around the bush and just tell me what is going…"

Sydney interrupted, shouting at the top of his voice and slamming his fists into the ground, "I was sent by Biktor to kill you, damn it!" He lowered his head and repeated himself in a softer voice. "Brigg…no…Dartmouth, I have to kill you."

On impulse, I quickly began to crawl backwards to distance myself. "Why?"

It appeared that Sydney was having trouble speaking. This was obviously what he meant by giving up anything for power. "I…don't want to."

"Then don't!" I was trying everything in my power to change his mind about his mission.

He raised his head to look at me. "But I have to, don't you see? Once we get rid of the true Causes, we will only have to focus on ridding Eden of the Zealots. The citizens of Eden never saw reason to bring harm to the Causes that followed the Producers' rules. But with the passive Causes out of the picture, we can turn the Gray Police loose to take care of the Zealots as they see fit. This will bring about the end of the Revolution and will open the door to restoring peace and order." He slowly drew his finger to point at me. "You, Dartmouth, are the key—the one who is keeping the Causes united."

I knew that everything he was saying made sense to him. I cared not to bring Bogen into the picture seeing as he could very well be next on Sydney's list. "So, how do you plan on doing this?"

Sydney stood up as I immediately followed to my feet. There we were again, standing about fifteen meters apart. "Don't let my emotional side fool you though," he warned. "I have every intention of ending your life here in this field. The only thing you can count on now is that I'm giving you a fighting chance."

Now I was really bamboozled. "That doesn't make sense! Why would you give me a chance to live?"

He shrugged. "This is where my fate is decided. If I kill you,

I'll be on my way to a greater life. If you kill me, then I won't be around when the carnage sends Eden into total ruin, nor will I live with the guilt of ending more lives after yours." He left space for an ominous pause as he removed his cloak and released it into the wind.

A strong gust caught the cloak and began to send it away. At that moment, the rain had finally picked up. The gentle caress of the raindrops calmed me ever so slightly.

Sydney's clothing was a show of preparedness. His dark blue sleeveless shirt appeared to be padded and his black pants were snug to avoid being grabbed by the leg easily. The scariest sight was how heavy his boots looked. My heart cringed at the thought of being kicked by his monstrous footwear. "One of us leaves here alive. I'll take it either way and accept my destiny!"

"He's not serious!" I thought to myself, wishing I could believe it.

Sydney hunched down for a moment then began to dash straight at me. Before I had another second to think, his clenched fist ran its way clean across my left cheek.

My vision went blurry as I swayed with the impact. "He is serious."

I tried backing away to give myself space, but Sydney was practically sticking to me, waiting to get in another hit through my defensive movement.

With a loud grunt, Sydney landed his next punch hard onto the top of my head. I fell to the ground in a daze.

Knowing my position, the thought of Sydney's boots gave me just the shot of adrenaline I needed. I tucked my arms in and began to quickly roll across the ground. My vision rotated in a sequence of grass, Sydney running at me, and the sky, pouring down rain.

Once I saw Sydney was close enough, I gritted my teeth and made a risky move. I stopped rolling and reached for his legs; managing to wrap my arm around one and pull it out from underneath him.

He stumbled to the ground.

His knee was the first target I could see, so I slammed my right fist into it. Every knuckle in my fist popped as I realized that I had struck a hidden metal plate that was protecting his knee.

Sydney came at me with a left straight, "I told you I was prepared!"

I managed to dodge that punch, grab his wrist and chop at his elbow, which was bare. "Not prepared enough…" I huffed.

Angered, he went for a kick to my chest that fell short. Realizing I was too close to his feet, I scrambled to stand. Sydney got to his feet and continued to press toward me. "This is the kind of fight I expected from you, Dartmouth."

I was still awash with disbelief as the two of us continued to exchange blows. Sydney's relentlessness was certainly a testament to his desire for authority. But the fact that he offered me a chance at survival almost made me feel sorry for him. The passion and entirety of his violent actions communicated much more than his mission and motive. With every exchange, I could feel that the Fifteen had him under their control, and his sense of humanity demanded escape from their grasp.

Sydney was proof that many people were depending on me. He was one of them, counting on me to relieve him of the duties he was assigned to against his will. I knew he didn't want to kill me, but he had to in order to reach his aspirations. It almost seemed as if he was fighting to defeat me purely out of sheer confusion.

We eventually grew fatigued and began to stagger away from each other. I turned my face to the sky to let the torrential rain wash my face of dirt and blood. My hands were sore and the flesh on them had small splits from repeated impacts. I had trouble moving my jaw and breathing, soon finding myself hunched over my stomach and kneeling on the ground.

Sydney appeared to be having problems with his left shoulder. Other than that, all he had was a fat lip and a black eye. He looked me over and began to chuckle sinisterly. "Power is my destiny."

That was the indicator—the last thing I wanted to hear in my condition. Sydney's face grew tense and he began to approach me again. His right fist was tight and ready to put an end to me. The terrifying sight of Sydney's realization put only one sentence in my head. "Oh my God, I am going to die."

Sydney shouted at me in a way that heralded imminent death. "This ends now!"

My brain was scrambling, trying to find a way to get myself

out of this. I didn't want to die in that field. But with only a few split-seconds to react, the soul-sinking vision of Sydney's hand boring into the top of my skull seemed to be becoming reality.

Sydney raised his fist and shouted with intensity. That instant seemed to stand still as I told myself that it was the only chance to save myself.

In a flash of my quickest thinking, I stuck my hand into my mouth to act as a cushion and sprang myself into a standing position right from under Sydney's chin. The top of my head charged into his jaw, slamming his mouth shut and cracking his jawbone.

Sydney howled horribly with his mouth clenched shut. I took the initiative and ran my foot into his stomach. The padding of his shirt cushioned the blow, but he still tumbled into a nearby pat of mud. He was wriggling and squirming from the sudden jolt to his jaw.

I took that moment to look at the huge bite mark I left on my own hand; which was bleeding a little. I caught my breath and prepared to engage him again.

Before I could get too close to him, he was on his feet, covered in mud. He locked eyes with me and spit out two of his teeth in a flow of blood. He smiled and nodded. "You know, Dartmouth," he spoke loud without moving his jaw, "there were regrets…"

Hearing him say that felt like another mind game. I didn't reply as tried to focus and wait for him to make another move.

"All the lies I had to tell you, friend…"

I made an attempt to break his act. "Stop talking and fight me! I don't care about what lies you told me."

Seeming to have had completely ignored me, he continued his tangent. "I knew the whole time. The Pata police left after Biktor came to pick me up. I was the front runner in that operation. Biktor had me give that Jayda to that innkeeper. It was all a setup—a setup that went wrong when I started to grow a conscience again."

His confession rocked me, disturbed me. My focus on the fight shattered at that moment. For that brief second, I forgot that this man was no longer my friend, Doctrine. He was Sydney, the leader of the Deserters and an enemy to the true Causes.

"I'm glad I warned you back at that hotel, Brigg. It gave me one last chance to redeem myself. However, it took way too long for your role in my plan to come to fruition."

"Will you shut up!?" I hollered. "I don't care. You screwed up! All right, I get it!"

Sydney said nothing more. He merely lifted his hand in a gesture that demanded words from my side of the battlefield. I realized that it would be beneficial for me to buy some time. Thus, I threw the motion to speak back to him. "What plan?"

"You were next," he slowly responded. "You were the next person on my list to bring to the Fifteen and convert to our side. I wanted to do it by gaining your trust and bringing you over slowly. That was why I invited you to Roy's that night. You were in the right place at the right time when I set out to find my next target."

I immediately gave him my next question. "What made you change your mind?"

He hung his head, spitting out another mouthful of his own blood. "Deep down, I was still on the side of the Causes. I did what I did for the guarantee of obtaining the knowledge that the Fifteen possess. I was searching for the truth…but I chose the wrong path. Now, I am here, face to face with the man I wanted to call a partner."

Thunder began to rumble as the rain appeared to lighten up for just a moment. I backed away a couple of steps to give myself more space to recuperate. Keeping Sydney talking was a good way to regain some of my energy for the next altercation.

"Now," Sydney continued, "the only chance to end my journey is here and now. Prepare yourself, Dartmouth. You are the last wall that blocks me from my dreams and my destiny. You are not leaving the Terra Sector alive."

It was all laid out on the table now. It was kill or be killed. The energy of my will to live welled up within me, giving me the strength for one final exchange. Sydney rolled his shoulders, wincing as he readied his body for me. Both of us were panting heavily, exhausted and in pain.

To give myself one last push, I quietly gave myself a pep talk. "You have to survive this. For the sake of all of your friends and every true Cause out there, you have to live through this. If that means putting and end to Sydney's life, then so be it. Survive now and worry about the consequences later."

I bared my bleeding fists and planted my feet to the ground. Without a word, Sydney took that as a signal to attack. He stomped confidently into our next clash.

As he drew close to me, he forcefully spit a third tooth and a spray blood into my face. It was a dirty and unexpected move that caused me to flinch as the tooth bounced off of my left eye.

After blinding me, Sydney seized the opportunity and kicked me square across my back. The jarring force of the blow sent me a hop forward and face first into the grass.

I was rolling around on the ground rubbing my eyes and arching my back. I felt a splash as Sydney barely missed stomping on me. My vision was slowly returning with help from the downpour. But the best I could do was roll wildly about until I felt well enough to stand. In the meanwhile, I was taking grazes and nicks from Sydney's boot, which continued to narrowly miss me.

By the next time I could see clearly, I saw the bottom of his foot readied to mash my face between itself and the terrain. I quickly crossed my arms in front of my head to block it, but the force drove my forearm across the bridge of my nose.

The pressure Sydney was applying was beginning to drive the back of my head into the wet dirt. So to get him off of me, I twisted my body toward him and kicked his other foot out from underneath him. He lost his balance and landed on his already injured chin.

That was when I felt my body reach its limit. I knew that if I kept going on like this, I was going to die.

I barely had the energy to lurch to my feet. Once I finally did, the next thing I could think of was to retreat. I was not going to be able to take down Sydney in my condition. So, I began to hobble toward D24 as originally planned.

It took Sydney a few moments to recover from his fall. When he did, I heard him screaming at me as I continued to distance myself from him. "Oh no you don't!"

"Oh yes I do!" I mumbled.

I took one look back to see that Sydney was giving chase, taunting me. "Get back here, you coward!"

I started to escape faster. My head felt light and every time I turned it was like a blur. My body felt tingly and warm as I seemed to lose feeling in my legs. "No..." I thought in a panic. "Not...now..."

I stopped and turned to see Sydney getting closer and closer. But I could no longer run. My body was done; it had had enough.

Gasping for air...

...writhing in pain...

...dripping with blood, sweat and rain...

...seeing Sydney closing in on me...

...and my body collapsing to the ground...

...were the last things I remember before that one final thought:

"I am dead."

Day ??

?

A voice was calling to me; a gentle, feminine voice. "Dartmouth…"

All was dark. I did not possess the strength to respond.

The same soothing voice called again. "Brigg…"

I could feel my face being touched with a cloth. There was a salve on that cloth that caused a stinging sensation. My face twitched as a weak groan sounded from my throat.

"You know," the voice continued, "Sandra will be pleased to know that you are alive."

I heard footsteps as a masculine voice penetrated the soothing silence. "Let's try opening a window." As such, the sound of curtains being swept to the side rattled within the room and the light from the sun beamed through the window.

All of this helped me to realize that somehow, some way, I was still alive. I had survived the battle with Sydney.

I crunched my face before opening my eyes to see the source of the calm, soft voice. Before I could utter even a sound, the young woman giggled. "Remember me? It's me, Zoe—Month of May."

I repeated her name as the man who entered the room came

into view. My eyes grew wide when I first laid eyes on him.

His outfit was an easy window to his identity. It didn't take any more than the denim pants and matching short-sleeve denim jacket to realize that it was Blue.

Surprisingly though, his face bore uncharacteristically dark features. His eyes were narrow and his face seemed to exude a sense of self-righteousness. The back of his hair was in a long, thin ponytail while the rest of his hair remained short. My previous mental image of the man faded away at that moment. By the way he was carrying himself; I had the feeling that my new opinion of him would be far from that of the hero he had made himself out to be.

I was excited to see him nevertheless. I wanted to sit up, but Zoe insisted against it.

Blue spoke to me. "Save your energy!" he recommended. "Sydney did a good job of beating the piss out of you. You've been out for the past several days. We were afraid you weren't going to wake up."

I spoke one word. "Mika…"

"I turned Mika over to Bogen and the others. She is in good hands now."

I tried to sit up again, but Zoe forced me back down. "Don't move!" she ordered, "You might aggravate your injuries."

There was a lot I wanted to say to Blue. So I mustered as few words as I could to relay my message. "Black… caught…"

"Actually," Blue replied, rolling his eyes, "there's something you need to know about that." He paused and looked to me before calling out to the other room. "Tana."

Black's familiar voice called back, "Yes, Dylan?"

I felt as if my breath had been ripped from my lungs. There was no way Blue could have rescued her as well. Something was extremely wrong with this picture. "How?" I asked. "No way! Black and Blue?"

"Yes, you are!" Blue replied with a crooked grin before explaining what was going on. "I've just got to say that you really impress me. I was not expecting you to win that fight. I was really hoping Sydney would live. But since that's not the case, I have to change up my plans a little bit."

My heart grew cold. Blue had set me up to die.

Blue continued, remorselessly casual. "Yeah, I planned the whole thing out and nowhere in that plan did I expect you to survive. Don't get me wrong. I'm not really siding with the Fifteen. I've got my own way of ending the Revolution so everyone can be happy. The Causes will get their truths and the Fifteen will keep their balance. Everything will work out in the end." He shifted to correct himself. "Sure, since Sydney is dead now we have to take a detour on this road to a new era. But that's not going to stop us, right, Tana?"

Black answered reluctantly with guilt in her voice. "Right..."

Blue caught my eye again. "Oh, and don't worry..." He lifted Black's laptop carrier and patted it a couple of times. "...every Cause knows that you killed Sydney."

"You lie!" I challenged. "Black sent a warning to the forums. The Causes have probably abandoned the forum by now."

"Now, now," Blue responded, "let's not be stupid. Take a second to think about where Tana is standing. Then try to tell yourself that she really sent those warnings."

As the truth came to light concerning Black's allegiance, my heart began to race inside of my chest. Blue's guiltless rambling and disturbing news filled me with despair and rage. Against Zoe's advice, I tried to spring up from the bed. Unfortunately, my wrists and ankles were shackled.

"You should consider yourself lucky," Blue euphemized. "You're just strapped to a bed. Sydney was much worse off, having choked to death on two of his teeth." His attitude was unflinching. Blue knew that he had everything right where he wanted it and anything that wasn't would fall into place for him anyway.

Blue laughed and threw my covers off of me. I got a good look at my bruised and battered body before turning a piercing gaze back to him. "Blue—"

He cockily cut me off. "...is going to take good care of his bargaining chip: you. If you thought the Revolution was out of hand before, you haven't seen anything yet! Let's just say that I'll be replacing Sydney until I figure out which party I should get rid of first."

I roared with what grams of strength I had in me. "You're insane! Black, how can you side with him?"

Black tried to justify her actions in a weak and unconvincing explanation. "I…I understand what Blue wants to do. What he says is possible. We can find out what is going on with the Fifteen and still—"

I shouted at the top of my voice, "You betrayed all of us! Do you have…any…?" I stopped as my head started to feel airy.

Blue consoled her in a warm embrace. "It's all right. As long as you feel we can do this together, you have nothing to worry about." It was apparent that Blue was taking advantage of Black's infatuation with him.

"Okay," she said, smiling to him. Blue then kissed her on the forehead and sent her back to the other room.

Blue brought his attention back to me as Zoe put some of my dressings back in place. "I'll have you know that the only reason Bogen and your other friends are still out there is because I don't think it is fair that Mika was never a Cause in the first place. As soon as Mika is back with her father, your friends are due for a visit to the Labor Fields. This whole incident with Sydney makes me antsy about the whole killing thing."

Zoe put the cover back over me and excused herself. "I'll go get your bathing water ready, Dartmouth."

"Take your time; he's not going anywhere." He watched Zoe exit the room before excusing himself with one last tidbit. "We'll be transporting you to Exta in a couple of days. All you have to do is sit back and watch the party. Your role in the Revolution now changes at our decision. You might as well enjoy it, though; Zoe is about to give you a full body sponge bath…you lucky boy you!" He left, chuckling at his own cleverness.

It felt like the end of the Revolution for me. I didn't know how it happened, but I survived being a victim of Sydney's destiny. However, being beaten from head to toe was the least of my problems.

I was a prisoner, unsure of where I was. I had no idea what Blue had in store for me. But from what I could discern, he was a man with his own kind of mission.

Blue was trying to play the Revolution from both sides. It was the only way he could get everybody what they wanted. He was taking a tremendous risk that had the potential to cause either side a great deal of hardship.

It was at that time that I finally realized that a lot had been going on behind me. Becoming such an important face in the events of the Revolution was my greatest accomplishment and the most important addend of my downfall.

It felt like the enemies of the Causes weren't going to stop at just Albion, Jalako, Blue, Black, the Gray Police, and the Fifteen. There had to have been more out there who would go to greater lengths to end the Revolution for either side.

One thing was certain though. Bogen, Kay, Dice, and Mika were in serious danger, especially without Black on their side. The only thing positive that I knew of was Blue's sincerity in announcing Mika's position. It was the only semblance of my dark cloud's silver lining. Also, I was slightly baffled by Blue's compassion for Mika's situation.

As Zoe returned to the room with the bathing supplies, I saw it as my opportunity for some answers. She took the cover back off of me and prepared to wash me down. "You know," she said quietly, "I was wondering why you never used the red gel on your scar."

"Long story…" I groaned.

She scoffed back. "You don't need to give me that. I know that you figured out that Sandra gave me my medical kit. You obviously didn't trust the contents after discovering that."

I tried to justify my mistrust of the red gel. "I hesitated only because my team advised against using the stuff."

Zoe nodded as she sloshed a cushy green sponge in the bucket of soapy water. She gently wiped it across my skin as she broke some news to me. "Blue is going to present you to the Fifteen. I'm not sure what they'll do with you since you helped them out back in Fanda."

I was pessimistic. "I doubt they'll show any compassion…"

She presented a possibility. "They may just ship you out to the Labor Fields once you recover from your injuries. There's a lot they can do with you since the Causes still look up to you."

Her words brought a question to my mind. "What happened with you? How did you end up like this?"

"Well," she grinned, lifting my arm to scrub under it, "as you assumed correctly the last time we met, I _was_ captured back in the Pata Sector. When I was brought before the Fifteen, Sandra chose me and two other girls to be medics for the Causes. She says that her job, as well as ours, is to heal, not to judge."

"So," I wondered, "that would make you a Deserter, right?"

Zoe answered without hesitation. "Yes, it would. The Fifteen have been doing a fantastic job with the captured Causes."

"Is that so?"

She began to sound inappropriately excited about the fact she was a Deserter. "Of course." She then shrugged, taking my point of view into concern. "Sure, Sydney was taken under Biktor's wing and well...you know."

My brow rose. "Makes sense..."

"If you remember the broadcast of the meeting, you may recall Sandra saying something about injuries among the Causes being far too much for her to handle..."

"Yes, I remember that."

"That's why she appointed us to take care of them." She rinsed and wrung the sponge then applied it to my chest. "I was here on standby because Sandra knew of Blue's plan to set you up to battle Sydney. I was sent to care for the survivor: you. Of course, it could have been Sydney as well. It was truly a shame how he had to die like that. Morie was standing by as well to take care of the body of the defeated."

I felt impressed with myself. "I had no idea I messed his teeth up that badly."

Zoe comforted the guilt on my mind with her next statement. "Well, Blue is out there telling everybody that you killed Sydney. I believe that that simply isn't the case. Sydney's death was an accident brought on by injuries you inflicted on him."

I smiled for the first time since I woke up. "That's good to know." I took a deep breath and flinched. Expanding my chest had suddenly caused me a deal of pain.

Zoe comforted me, situating my pillow and coaxing me to speak no further. "Just try to relax until we get you over to the Exta Sector. I have a feeling you're not done with the Revolution just yet."

I heeded her instructions, laid back and shut my eyes, allowing her soothing caresses to wipe my body clean. I tried to calm down and convince myself that I would be able to figure something out once I arrived in Exta. Whatever the Fifteen would offer me or do to me, I knew I would have to keep my eyes open for any chance to turn the tide to my favor.

Until then, I had to suck it up and come to terms with what had transpired.

I was on my own and in the hands of the enemy. So with a sense of dire hopelessness, I shed a tear and quietly apologized to Mika and the others. Considering everything I learned about my teammates in the time I knew them, I smiled knowing that Mika was in the best of care. Bogen, Kay and Dice all had good heads on their shoulders.

I was praying that my friends would not fall victim to the guises and trickery of Blue and the Deserters. It saddened me to know that the danger of the Revolution was now going to be escalated by whatever Blue had planned. Reflecting on what had happened to me, I feared for the lives of anybody taking part in the Revolution.

Fighting tears, I inwardly left Mika to the care of the others and accepted this as my fate. There was nothing I could do for the others now. It was up to them to finish what I had started.

Epilogue

Day 92

IV

Bogen called to me, breaking my train of thought. "Kay! You've been staring out of that window for the past half an hour!"

I lightly jerked at the realization that I was honestly worried about Brigg and Black. With the way things were at the time, we could not afford to lose any people on our side. Black's skill with computers and Brigg's quick, analytical thinking were too important to be lost.

Dice laughed in response to Bogen; being inappropriately cheerful under the circumstances. "Maybe it is just like you said."

Bogen cocked his eye to him. "How do you mean?"

Dice sauntered over to me with his chin high. "Her concern brings to question what was going on while we were separated."

Although nobody in our group bothered me more than he did, I felt no need to feed his intention to heckle me. I mildly dignified his comment. "We managed to reconcile our differences just fine."

Bogen took a rowdy shot at my reply. "…With, or without physical contact?"

The two boys began yukking it up as if they had been waiting for Dartmouth to leave to turn their sights on my time alone with him. Knowing what Bogen was implying made it much less funny to me, though.

I stood strong and calm. "If you count the one time I had to slap him in the face, then it would be with contact."

"Haha, brilliant!" he merrily roared.

If I didn't know any better, I'd have assumed that Dice and Bogen were trying to use jokes and laughter to ease the tension of the wait. I would have felt the need to join in the antics if they had not been at my expense.

Little Amanda approached us from the other room. "What's so funny?"

Since the men appeared to be in a mindset slightly too mature for the young one, I covered her curiosity quickly. "It's nothing you need to worry about…"

Still chuckling, Dice pressed on in a low voice, "…Until you're older, of course."

"That's enough!" I snapped.

Bogen and Dice cut their pleasure short to keep things peaceful. "A bit too far there, Dice."

"Yeah, I know."

The mood in that small farm house had become a true mix of emotions. While we were all nervous about the future of our friends, each of us was expressing our concern in different fashions.

I noticed that part of Dartmouth's personality had rubbed off on me. Now I was the one overanalyzing things and generating hypothetical outcomes. It was comforting in a way, yet a tricky thing to accept.

It seemed that every time I would try to divert my attention, my mind kept reverting back to thoughts of Dartmouth's safety. Soon, I found myself thinking about our time alone.

I sat back in the chair in front of the window and reminisced…

"If you count the one time I had to slap him in the face…"
The one time I had to slap him…
"Are you nervous too…?"

My heart shook as I recalled hearing those words. My right hand clenched as I set it on top of my leg. I sighed loud as I brought that same hand up to meet my forehead. "Why did you say those exact words, Dartmouth?" I muttered, wishing he could hear me.

Suddenly, my view of the Terra Sector's open plain was obstructed by the frightening sight of a horse-coach. It drew the breath from my lungs as I scrambled away from the window.

Bogen saw it as well. "Oh God, we've got company."

The door to the coach opened to reveal two Gray Police officers. Dice spoke up. "This is the part where we hide, right?"

"It all depends…" Bogen replied.

"On what?"

"That depends on if there is anybody else with them." He continued with an observation. "The officers are talking to somebody who is still inside the coach."

We waited and watched. Sure enough, one more figure, a young girl in a black dress, stepped out of the coach after a minute.

I loudly gasped on first sight of the familiar pre-teen. "Oh my God, it's Mika!"

"No way!" Bogen shouted, rushing to get closer to the window.

Dice was thrown as well, but spoke calmly. "What is this all about? And what happened to her clothes?"

"I don't know," I answered, "I think Sydney may have had something to do with it. He probably tried to make her a Deserter, too!"

"Poor kid…" Bogen sadly sighed.

Through the rainfall outside, Mika hurriedly ran to the front door and began to wildly knock on it in a frenzy. "Something is definitely wrong," I growled.

Dice ran to the door. "It looks as if the police are dropping her off here."

"Yeah," I agreed. "The officers just got back into the coach. They're taking off."

Infuriated, Bogen stormed over to the front door with Dice. I followed close behind.

Dice let Mika in. The poor girl was panting heavily with tears rolling down her face. "Guys…help…"

Bogen was not in the mood for any hesitation. "I thought you were injured? What is going on here?"

Mika answered in a panicked wail of several concise facts. "Blue tricked all of us! He teamed up with Sydney. Dartmouth is in trouble. Sydney is going to kill him!"

Mika's news slithered into my ear and shot directly to my heart. A sensation of true fear shook my body as the many angles of the predicament tangled themselves in my brain.

A state of shock spread across all of us as Mika continued filling us in. "Dartmouth is probably fighting off Sydney right now. I don't know where they are. It was all out in the middle of an open field."

Without another second passing, Bogen dashed out the front door. "Let's go! If we head in the direction of D24, we might run into them!"

I wanted to help too. However, I called out the first problem in Bogen's plan. "On foot!?"

Amanda chimed in, knowing this was an emergency. "We have two bicycles on the side of the house. You can use them."

"Thank you," I said. I then turned to Mika to give her a hug and comfort her.

Mika's grip around me was disturbingly soft. Every sniffle and sob from the rattled young girl felt like a pin driving into my chest. "Please, help him," she cried.

I stroked her soaked, blonde hair. "Don't worry, Mika. Everything will be all right."

Deep down, I knew it was a lie. I simply cringed at the thought of Dartmouth not living to see another day.

Without any further delay and despite the pouring rain, Bogen and I hopped on the bicycles and pedaled as fast as we could in the direction of D24. "Dartmouth," I mumbled, "if you die today, I swear I will find you out in the Great Beyond and kick your ass."

Amidst the countless raindrops that were trickling down my face, the fresh warmth of a lone tear streamed along.

With the panic and fear that resided in my heart, I knew that day would be the one that would change my views, my hopes, my feelings…and my life.

Kay will be the next to share her experiences with you in the next installment of the Wanderlust Seasons Saga:

"<u>Autumn of Fates</u>"